Thy Will Be Done

Also Available

The Tudors: It's Good to Be King
Final Shooting Scripts 1–5 of the Showtime Series

The Tudors: The King, the Queen, and the Mistress
A Novelization of Season One of The Tudors

The Tudors: King Takes Queen
A Novelization of Season Two of The Tudors

THE TUDORS

Thy Will Be Done

A NOVELIZATION OF SEASON THREE OF
The Tudors FROM SHOWTIME NETWORKS INC.

CREATED BY MICHAEL HIRST
WRITTEN BY ELIZABETH MASSIE

SSE

SIMON SPOTLIGHT ENTERTAINMENT

NEW YORK   LONDON   TORONTO   SYDNEY

Simon Spotlight Entertainment
A Division of Simon & Schuster, Inc.
1230 Avenue of the Americas
New York, NY 10020

First Simon Spotlight Entertainment trade paperback edition April 2009

SIMON SPOTLIGHT ENTERTAINMENT and colophon
are trademarks of Simon & Schuster, Inc.

For information about special discounts for bulk purchases,
please contact Simon & Schuster Special Sales at
1-866-506-1949 or business@simonandschuster.com.

The Simon & Schuster Speakers Bureau can bring authors to your live event.
For more information or to book an event, contact the Simon & Schuster
Speakers Bureau at 1-866-248-3049 or visit our website at www.simonspeakers.com.

Manufactured in the United States of America

10   9   8   7   6   5   4   3   2   1

Library of Congress Cataloging-in-Publication Data

Massie, Elizabeth.
    The Tudors: thy will be done : a novelization of season three of the Tudors / created by
Michael Hirst ; written by Elizabeth Massie. — 1st ed.
        p. cm.
    1. Henry VIII, King of England, 1491–1547—Fiction. 2. Great Britain—History—
Henry VIII, 1509–1547—Fiction. 3. Great Britain—History—Tudors, 1485–1603—Fiction.
I. Hirst, Michael. II. Tudors (Television program) III. Title. IV. Title: Thy will be done.
    PS3563.A79973T83 2009
    813'.54—dc22   2009004838

ISBN-13: 978-1-4391-0139-1

For Cortney Skinner, with love.

Acknowledgments

Thanks to Michael Hirst for breathing new life and soul into the powerful, passionate, and contemptuous King Henry VIII and into those of his court—Thomas Cromwell, Charles Brandon, Jane Seymour, Thomas and Edward Seymour, Sir Francis Bryan, Robert Aske, Anne of Cleves, and many others. What dire, dangerous, delectable times these were, worthy of the quality Hirst brings to the story.

Thanks also to Cara Bedick of Simon & Schuster for her greatly appreciated help and encouragement, and to Barbara Spilman Lawson for being the best sister in the world.

Chapter One

In all the world there could be no grander estate than Whitehall Palace in London, no more glorious place for worship and ceremony than the Chapel Royal. And, King Henry thought as he proceeded toward the chapel doors with his chamberlain leading the way and scores of courtiers following at a humble, respectful distance, there could be no more powerful, elegant, or revered king than he. God in His great wisdom had seen to it that Henry's enemies had fallen before him and that the love of his life now waited for him.

The betrayers and the liars were gone, removed with the blow of a sword or ax. Gone, their blood washed away, their flesh and bones laid to whatever rest God might grant them, if any. Mark Smeaton, the adulterous musician. Sir Henry Norris, fellow warrior who had become the worst of liars and lechers. William Brereton, lowly groom whose delusions of divine guidance had made him treacherous, yet careless. George Boleyn, onetime confidant turned incestuous animal. Thomas More, the pious traitor.

And then there was Anne. Sensuous, clever Anne. His wife and lover. His lusty, bright, and beautiful foe. Her witchcraft, adultery, and betrayal had been the worst of all. She had lost her head to the swordsman just eleven days prior.

Every one of them had been destroyed, sent to God for His righteous judgment. The matters were done. The fouled air was cleansed from Henry's nostrils, his chambers, and his kingdom.

And today! Today was a day of celebration, not a day of looking back. Today Henry would wed the most beloved of all women. Sweet Jane Seymour. Precious jewel, more beautiful than any creature ever to walk the earth.

Henry tilted his head back even farther, held his arms regally at his sides, kept his strides bold and confident. Even the pain that had plagued his leg since his jousting fall seemed to respect this regal affair, and kept itself at bay. His clothing had been made specially for the wedding, an ermine-trimmed robe over a blue velvet doublet run through with gold stitching and set with so many diamonds it was almost impossible to see the fabric. His leather shoes were fashioned with rubies and emeralds. The heavy jeweled crown upon his head silently proclaimed him to be the King of all England, Lord of the Land, Sovereign Master, and Head of the Church.

The wide doors swung open at Henry's approach, and the chamberlain pounded the gold staff of his office on the floor and exclaimed loudly, "The king!" Even before Henry passed through the doors, he could hear the quick rustle of movement as his subjects stood for his arrival.

The chapel had been prepared for the nuptials. White candles burned atop brass-and-gold floor stands. The air was heavy with the scent of incense, and with expectation. Flowers of May had been fashioned into magnificent sprays that adorned the sills of the stained-glass windows and the altar. The walls that had once borne Anne Boleyn's crest, a heraldic falcon, had been quickly scraped. New, freshly painted crests now took their place: Jane's arms indicating a brightly feathered phoenix rising up from a burning castle, above the motto "Bound to Serve and Obey." Inside the chapel doors, Henry was met by the tall, impressive figure of Bishop Gardiner and eight other bishops in their caped robes and scarlet skullcaps. All bowed in unison.

"Bishop Gardiner," the king said pleasantly.

"Your Majesty," said Gardiner.

"Shall we proceed?"

The bishop bowed again, the solemn man almost smiling to himself, then turned to lead Henry up the aisle toward the altar. Henry gazed straight ahead, not acknowledging those in the pews, but well aware of who they were: Richard Rich, the solicitor-general. Catherine Brandon, the lovely young wife of Henry's friend Charles. Sir Francis Bryan, a man with dark hair and a solid build, who wore a pearl in his ear and a patch over his eye. Other nobles and councilors loyal to the crown. And standing near the back of the chapel, the dark-eyed Thomas Cromwell, Henry's chief adviser. Each bowed silently as the king passed.

Henry reached the altar, which was adorned with a velvet cloth and a great gold cross. And there, to his right, was Jane. Henry's heart swelled.

She wore a gown of white silk trimmed in pearls and satin lace. Her earrings and necklace were of gold and diamonds, and her golden hair was braided through with strands of coral and topped with a pearl coronet. She stood, her eyes downcast modestly, on the arm of her brother Sir Edward Seymour, a tall young man with eyes the same blue as his sister's.

Edward led Jane to Henry's side. She curtsied low.

"Jane," said Henry.

"Your Majesty," said Jane.

Henry held out his hand, and Jane rose. Her eyes caught his for a brief moment, and his soul stirred with passion and utter happiness. They knelt before the altar, and Bishop Gardiner made a broad, sweeping sign of the cross.

"We are come here together, before God and these witnesses," the bishop said, "to join together in holy matrimony this man and this woman. And if there be any among you who can imagine some impediment why they should not be married, let them now speak up—or forever hold their tongue."

Henry slowly turned his head to glance at those in attendance. No one moved or spoke. Their faces were passionless. Though their former queen's blood was not even two weeks dry on the scaffold, his subjects would do nothing but obediently accept the king's new bride.

Pleased, Henry squeezed his betrothed's hand, looked back at the bishop, and smiled.

The walls and the vaulted ceiling of the Great Hall rang with music, laughter, and celebration. Musicians sat in the mezzanine playing lively tunes on flutes, lyres, harps, and tabor drums, the music drawing the dancers about the marble floor in swirling, elegant patterns. Massive brass chandeliers shed merry candlelight upon the revelry.

In the center of the grand room an elevated pavilion filled with the blooms of foxglove, hyacinth, and primroses had been erected for Henry and his new bride. Henry sat on a cushioned throne holding Jane's hand, gazing at her intently, and marveling silently at how her eyes were a more brilliant blue than any flower in England.

Jane noticed her husband studying her, and she blushed. Then she touched the new pendant on her dress. It was made of emeralds and rubies surrounded by gold acanthus leaves.

"Thank you for my gift," she said. "It's so very beautiful."

Henry chuckled with affection. "Sweet Jane. Soon, I trust to thank you for mine." He stretched out his fingers and placed them firmly against her belly. Jane smiled and nodded with understanding.

"Shall we join the dance?"

Jane nodded again and took the king's hand. As they stood from their seats and descended the pavilion steps, the musicians paused in their playing and the dancers stopped to watch and applaud. The crowd parted as Henry escorted Jane to the center of the floor. Then the king tipped his chin, and the music and dancing resumed.

"I don't recognize you, my lady. Are you new at court?"

The red-haired beauty looked up at the man whose hand she had just taken in the dance. He could feel her eyes taking him in: his solid build, the patch over his eye. His coat was the color of cherrywood, his hair a shade darker, and a pearl pierced his left ear.

"Yes, sir," she said as she moved gracefully around her new partner, stepping in the prescribed pattern of the dance, the skirts of her cream-colored gown brushing against his legs. "I am to be a maid for Her Majesty."

"What is your name?"

"Lady Ursula Misseldon."

"Ah. And do you know who I am?"

The young lady arched a brow. "You're Sir Frances Bryan. I have heard about you."

Bryan cocked his head. "What have you heard?"

"That you like to board other men's boats."

Bryan smiled, amused yet not surprised by her comment. He was well aware that his reputation preceded him. As Bryan bowed to Ursula and let go of her hand, he caught the eye of Henry, who was dancing close by. He winked his good eye at the king, and Henry laughed knowingly.

On the other side of the Great Hall, Henry's childhood friend Charles Brandon bowed to his partner, released her, and stepped forward to his next. It was his wife, Catherine. Charles smiled warmly and drew against her for a moment, still keeping time with the music.

"I feel guilty," he whispered in her ear.

Catherine's brows drew together teasingly. "Why?"

"Because I forget sometimes to tell you how beautiful you are and how much I love you."

Catherine put her lips to her husband's hand and kissed it gently. Then she glanced through the sea of elegant bodies to where the king and queen were dancing quite close to each other. "I think she will make him happy."

"With God's help," Brandon said, "I think we shall all be happy now."

Catherine and Brandon spun away from each other, taking other partners, moving on.

Against the north wall of the Great Hall, two men stood observing the festivities. Richard Rich, a man with sandy hair and a trim beard, leaned against the wall, arms crossed and eyes narrowed. Farther down the wall was Thomas Cromwell, equally without humor, his jaw set and his gaze steady. Cromwell was a man in his early forties with dark curly hair, a cleft in his chin, and a permanent furrow above his nose. He carried a silver goblet of wine, which he'd nearly finished drinking. Both men were dressed appropriately for the occasion. Rich wore a dark gray doublet decorated with silver embroidery, and his light brown hair peeked out from beneath a blue hat sporting a peacock's plume. Cromwell wore his black robe and broad black cap with a jeweled pin. The heavy chain draped around his shoulders bore a gold Tudor rose pendant, a symbol of his position and loyalty.

Cromwell let out the breath he'd been holding and spoke to Rich without looking around. "Since both the king's daughters have been declared illegitimate and unfit to rule, we must trust the queen conceives a child quickly, Sir Richard."

Rich nodded, almost imperceptibly. "I still fear that with Anne's death we have lost a great friend and powerful supporter. If the new queen favors the Catholic religion, as she is rumored to do, then our whole Reformation is surely in jeopardy."

"I'm surprised you have such little faith . . . in the king," Cromwell said. He glanced at Rich, then back at the dancers. He took a sip of wine. "All the same, you're right. We must press ahead with the dissolution of those brothels and slaughterhouses: the monasteries."

Pounding hoofbeats echoed through the valley as three black-cloaked men rode hard toward the monastery of Sawley Abbey, sending squirrels, sheep, and children scrambling from the hard-packed road. The squirrels and sheep continued running, but the children stopped and stared as the men passed by, wrapping their arms about themselves then glancing nervously at one another. The air felt chilled in the horses' wake.

The abbey sat in the distant region of Yorkshire in the north of England, in a lush valley surrounded by tall, craggy mountains alive with wiregrass, scrub brush, and bright-eyed birds of prey. Shepherds grazed their small flocks on the lower elevations of these mountains, gleaning from them every bit of green to be had, their animals never quite sated, always restless and wide-eyed.

It was into this land that the Church commissioners rode, at the command of Thomas Cromwell. Dr. John Frankish, a middle-aged man with iron-gray hair and a crooked nose, led the way on his sorrel gelding, across a small meadow and along a narrow riverside road, his body aching from the hours in the saddle but his heart assured and even gleeful about the task at hand.

The sky overhead was as gray as the rocks on the surrounding cliffs, and the air was heavy with impending rain. Gnats whirled about the men and their horses, and Frankish swatted them away. Such tiny creatures were much like the priests and monks of the Catholic Church, worthy of the back of his hand and no more.

The men rounded a curve in the road, dust churning, and there was the abbey in all its stone and stained-glass glory. Monks at the gate scattered, crossing themselves, while others fell to their knees to pray. They knew why the commissioners had come. They knew there was nothing they could do but mourn.

Armed with cloth sacks, the commissioners dismounted, tethered their horses, and flung open the heavy oaken door to the abbey's chapel. It was as Frankish had imagined, full of treasures that only the king of England deserved, not some whorish pope in Italy.

Down came the gold and silver crucifixes from the walls. These were tossed into the sacks along with the silver chalices and Communion goblets. Standing in the pulpit, Frankish carefully jotted down everything the commissioners had collected. More valuables were added: small marble figurines of saints, a jewel-rimmed bowl set into the baptismal font, brass incense burners, the gold candlesticks that had flanked the altar. When the place had been stripped of its portable fineries, Frankish directed the commissioners to destroy everything else. With triumphant smiles, the men proceeded to smash the rood screen with its detailed painting of Christ feeding the multitudes. Next, they moved on to the pulpit and the pews. Books, wooden images, embroidered cloths, and scrolls were tossed into the center of the nave along with the rest.

"Dr. Frankish!" one of the commissioners called. "Here's a fine one!"

Frankish waded through the rubble to a life-size stone statue of the Virgin Mary in a gated alcove. She was draped in capes, cloaks, and coats laden with jewels, which had been presented to her by her humble, adoring worshippers.

A second commissioner looked on, amazed, his eyes traveling up and down the statue. "Pair of jeweled shoes, soiled."

Frankish smoothed his list on the alcove windowsill and jotted down these new items.

"A wool coat sewn with emeralds and rubies," the commissioner said. "Worth a bob or two!"

The Virgin's clothes were removed and put into a sack. Frankish rolled up his paper, sneering. "Well, Lady," he said. "Are you stripped now?"

The men cackled loudly. Then a commissioner placed his chisel against the smooth features of Christ's mother, raised his hammer, and brought it down hard. The nose and cheekbone shattered.

When at last there was nothing recognizable left, Frankish ordered his men to set the place alight. Torches were held to the wood and fabrics, and the abbey went up in a matter of seconds.

Frankish stood in the doorway studying the beauty of his handiwork, until he was certain there would be no saving the place, until his face was stung by the unbearable heat of the flames. Then he and his men returned to their horses, now loaded down with valuables for the king.

Above the abbey, on a forested hillside, a well-dressed man in his forties stood with his arms crossed and his cheeks streaked with tears. A man of intelligence and fairness, he appeared deeply shaken by the sight of the conflagration below. He did not want to watch, but could not look away.

"Mr. Aske!"

Robert Aske glanced back to see an angry young man moving down through the trees to stand beside him. The man was auburn-haired, handsome, with ruddy skin and broad shoulders. Fury had contorted his features.

Aske turned back to gaze at the fiery atrocity below. The flames groped hungrily out through the broken windows and stroked the abbey's roof. "Look what they've done, John," Aske said. He crossed himself and shook his head.

John Constable's eyes were alight with tiny twin reflections of the blaze. "This is all Cromwell's doing! Cromwell and that sect of heretics in London!" Constable spun about and slammed his fist into a tree trunk. He screamed into the heat-shimmering air. "Bastards! You bloody bastards! May you rot in hell!"

Aske put a sympathetic hand on Constable's shoulder. He could detect the torment raging in the man's body. "We all feel the same way, John."

"*Do* you?" Constable turned, his jaw tight. "Do you really, Mr. Aske? Or are you not cosseted by the duke's comfort and care, in that fine office of yours?"

Aske tried to keep his voice even in spite of his anger. "I am the Duke of Northumberland's legal adviser. Would you not expect me to have an office, Mr. Constable? But do you suppose even the duke to be unaffected by this . . . this horrid desecration? He is a proud man, and these are his people."

"I tell you this," Constable swore, "these same people are no longer willing to stand by and watch their faith and everything they care for being stripped away. I heard just yesterday that two of Cromwell's commissioners were attacked in Lincolnshire. And there in Yorkshire a man of the commons stood up in church and said, 'Go we to follow the crosses, for when they are taken from us we can follow them no more!' People think that if this goes on any longer, we shall all be undone forever."

Aske took a breath and looked again at the burning building, now little more than a blackened shell. Black ash drifted on the air like so many martyred butterflies. And now, too late, the first drops of rain fell through the leaves of the trees.

At last Aske said, "What am I supposed to do?"

"The commons here, in Lincolnshire, everywhere, are prepared to fight, to save what they love. But they need captains. They need clever, educated men to lead them."

Aske shook his head. "I'm no leader, John."

Constable held up a hand. "Don't decide now. We'll call a meeting, then decide." He let his gaze return to the ruins below and he shivered. "For the love of God."

Inside her private bedchamber, Jane knelt in prayer on a satin pillow at the feet of Bishop Gardiner. She was tired but still flushed with excitement, love, and anticipation of this, her first night with her beloved husband, King Henry. Her gown was the softest of fabrics, pure white, as was her slender and chaste body. Jane's ladies, who now stood silently along the walls with their hands clasped, had brushed out her hair, sprayed it with lavender water, and woven it with tiny flowers of white and yellow. She still wore the necklace Henry had given her that day; she would leave it for his hand to remove it.

The room was well lit by sconces and tabletop candles. The bed had been prepared with new linens, scattered with rose petals, and blessed by the bishop. Jane's ladies-in-waiting kept a silent vigil, as did the portraits of noblemen and gentle ladies on the paneled walls.

Gardiner raised his hand above Jane's head. "Almighty and everlasting God, give unto us the increase of faith, hope, and charity, and that we may obtain that which Thou doest promise. Make us to love that which Thou dost command, through Jesus Christ our Lord."

"Amen," Jane whispered, crossing herself. Her ladies came forward and helped her on to the great bed. They plumped the pillows behind her and arranged her hair across her left shoulder and down her arm. Once the ladies had backed away, Gardiner stepped close and said quietly, "Madam, if I may, I have a wedding gift for Your Majesty."

Jane nodded, and Gardiner slipped something into her outstretched hand. It was a small, delicate crucifix of silver.

"It belonged to Queen Katherine," Gardiner said.

Jane mouthed, "Thank you," kissed the cross, and quickly slipped it beneath her pillow.

At that moment, the door opened and one of King Henry's young grooms, wearing a black doublet with the red Tudor rose embroidered over his breast, stepped into the queen's bedchamber.

"His Majesty, the king!"

Henry strode into the room, followed by two more grooms, his crown gone now but as regal in his bearing as ever in his red-and-gold silk over-gown. He stood in the center of the room, hands on his hips, head high, gazing at his bride.

"Madam," he said with a slight nod.

"Husband," Jane said.

The grooms drew off the king's overgown, revealing the long white linen shirt beneath. Jane was struck and moved by the raw manliness of Henry's bare chest, visible at the open V of the shirt, and of his bare and muscular legs. One groom drew back the bedcovers for the king.

Henry climbed onto the soft bedding beside Jane. He put his hand over hers, and she felt the reassuring warmth. Then Henry looked out at the grooms, ladies, and clergy, who had moved in unison to the foot of the bed.

"I do not think we need to proceed in public," he said firmly. "Not this time."

With a wave of his hand, the small gathering bowed and withdrew from the room without a word. Jane's maids then stepped forward to pull the curtains closed around the bed, and for the first time, she found herself alone with her love, ready to give him her all. Henry brushed her hair from her shoulder, kissed the pale flesh, and she rolled toward him, her heart cheerful and her body submissive.

When Sir Edward Seymour, Jane's brother, was ushered into the king's Presence Chamber, he wore a look of wary concern that Cromwell savored. There was nothing better than a man who was never quite sure what would come next, for such men were easily controlled. Cromwell watched as Edward strode across the marble floor and dropped to his knees before the dais. Pale morning sunlight filtered through the iron crosswork on the tall windows. Elegant tapestries hung from the walls, depicting the glories of the English landscape and military might, of stag hunts and jousting tournaments, of ladies and noblemen. The chamberlain, a tall elderly man with gray eyes, held his place beside the door, dressed in a black doublet and black trousers, and a broad feathered cap. Select nobles and attendants stood watching from either side of the dais.

Henry leaned forward in his mahogany throne upon the dais, smiled, and nodded. Edward rose and waited to see why he had been summoned.

"Sir Edward," said Cromwell, stationed closest to the dais, on the right. He held up several folded, wax-sealed papers. "As the brother of His Majesty's beloved wife, Jane, it is His Majesty's pleasure to create you Viscount Beauchamp of Hache, in Somerset. And also to appoint you Governor of Jersey and Chancellor of North Wales."

Edward's eyes widened and his jaw dropped ever so slightly. "Your Majesty, I am deeply honored. I assure Your Majesty that I will labor unremittingly in Your Majesty's interests, in the hope of repaying the great trust you have shown in me."

Henry nodded again.

Cromwell stepped up to Edward and gave him the folded papers. "My lord, here are your letters of patent. I congratulate you on your elevation."

Edward bowed. "Mr. Secretary." He took several steps backward and then turned and was shown out by the chamberlain.

Henry rubbed his beard and looked at Cromwell. "We must make plans for the queen's coronation. Ask Mr. Holbein for some ideas."

Cromwell nodded. Hans Holbein was a German artist of incredible skill who had been brought to court to paint portraits at the whim of the king. Holbein had also designed the king's state robes and the stages, pavilions, and murals for the highest of court celebrations. Those he had created for the coronation of Anne Boleyn were long gone, smashed and forgotten, as Henry had commanded. But there was a new queen now, one deserving of the most magnificent decorations possible.

"Your Majesty," said Cromwell, moving on to other matters, "a letter has arrived from the emperor, congratulating you on your marriage. Since he sees no further impediment, he is very anxious to come to a new accommodation with Your Majesty."

"Good," said Henry. "What else?"

Cromwell hesitated. He hated to be the bearer of uncomfortable news, and anything that reminded Henry of his first wife, Katherine, could do nothing but sour the king's mood. "The Lady Mary has also written." Cromwell held the letter out, but Henry waved it away. The smile on his face was gone.

"What does she want?"

"She writes that is it time now to forget the unhappy past. She begs to be taken back into Your Majesty's favor." Cromwell opened the letter and skimmed to the end. He read, "'Humbly beseeching you to remember I am but a woman, and your child.'"

Henry's fingers began to beat a fierce tattoo on the arm of his chair. He stared out the windows. "I will never take her back. Not until she submits herself to me on the matter of her mother's marriage and the supremacy." He pursed his lips, thinking, then looked back at Cromwell. "You will send a delegation to see her. If she truly wants to forget the unhappy past, then she can start by disowning it!"

Cromwell bowed. "Majesty."

Henry dismissed Cromwell with a barely discernible flick of his hand.

Cromwell left the chamber for the crowded anteroom, in which countless courtiers, retainers, and petitioners waited in hopes of an audience with the king. They bowed as Cromwell passed, waving documents and pleading with him to take their concerns to the king. Cromwell ignored them this morning. They could wait another day with their petty complaints. Then he spied Sir Francis Bryan among the mob. Bryan stood in a small windowed alcove watching the commotion.

Cromwell stepped over to Bryan, turned to make sure no one was listening, and said, "Sir Francis, I have some good news."

Bryan's brow lifted curiously over his black eyepatch. "Yes?"

"His Majesty has agreed to your appointment as a gentleman of the Privy Chamber."

Bryan stroked his chin and chuckled lightly. "I'm sure I know who to thank for *that*, Mr. Secretary."

"I may have a small job for you to do. Soon." Cromwell didn't wait for a reply, but tapped Bryan on the shoulder and turned away. Across the wide hallway he noticed that Sir Edward Seymour was now surrounded by a small cluster of courtiers, when before he had been a man alone.

Such is the sign he is a coming man, thought Cromwell. *Such as he will be one to watch, one to manage.*

The morning had been a flurry of activity, noise, and modest gaiety. Her Majesty Queen Jane stood in the center of her private outer chambers dressed in a fur-trimmed violet gown over a lavender kirtle, swearing in her new attendants: sweet and docile young ladies, all of them, vowing to be at Jane's beck and call, to be humble and obedient, to be modest in behavior and speech, and to act cheerfully and gracefully in every assigned chore.

The room had been scoured of all traces of the former queen. While Anne had preferred bolder colors, Jane chose softer, more modest tones. While Anne had desired as much rich furniture as could possibly fit into her chambers, Jane was more comfortable with less opulence. Though Anne had seemed to flaunt a preference for rebellious disarray, Jane could be happy only with order. On one wall hung a portrait of her dear father, John Seymour, who had fought valiantly with Henry against the French, before age took its toll on him. On the wall opposite was her crest, bearing the phoenix, there to remind her of her power and responsibilities.

The queen's chamberlain, a stern-faced matron, called each lady in turn, to be greeted and questioned by Her Majesty.

"Lady Ursula Misseldon," said the chamberlain, announcing the last of the ladies, a pretty redhead in a dark blue gown.

Ursula stepped forward from the cluster of women and curtsied. "Your Majesty."

"Be sworn in," said Jane. "Do your duties honorably and virtuously. Remember we are all bound to serve and obey."

Ursula glanced at the crest, then back at the queen. "Yes, Your Majesty," she said solemnly before moving away.

As the ladies scattered in their assigned directions to do their duties, Jane noticed another young woman near the door. When the young woman saw that the queen had noticed her, she immediately glanced at the floor, her cheeks flushed with embarrassment and confusion.

Jane walked over to the woman and said softly, "Lady Rochford."

Lady Rochford nodded slowly, then looked up again. Jane could see the misery of the last months etched on her face. The accusation and trial of her husband, George Boleyn, brother of Anne. His subsequent beheading. It hurt Jane's soul to see such trouble on such a lovely face.

"I asked to see you," Jane said. "I know things have not gone well for you since . . . since your husband's execution."

Lady Rochford nodded, her lip trembling. "I have been utterly abandoned. I feel I was condemned because of what George did. Even Mr. Cromwell has refused to answer my letters."

Jane smiled sympathetically. "Nothing was your fault. George Boleyn was his own keeper. I want you to come back to court, and I would like to appoint you my principal lady-in-waiting. I hope you will accept the position."

Lady Rochford's brow furrowed, and tears welled in her eyes. "Thank you, Your Majesty."

Jane touched the young woman's hand and found it trembling. She grasped it gently to help the trembling stop. "There now," she said. "Everything is well again. Everything is mended."

* * * *

Castel Gandolfo in eastern central Italy was exquisite in the summertime. The stone manor was surrounded by well-tended gardens punctuated with ponds, fountains, statuary, cobblestoned pathways, topiaries, and lush expanses of flowers bearing every color known to God. Gardeners were busy there every day of the week save Sunday, when they were allowed time off to rest and worship.

A dark-haired man in his mid-thirties, clothed in clerical garb, wandered back and forth along a narrow walkway in the shade of towering cypress trees, his fingers linked behind his back, wondering why he'd been summoned for such a private interview. He was an ordinary man devoted to God and the Church. Surely there was nothing special in his person that warranted the notice of a cardinal.

"Father Reginald Pole?"

Father Pole stopped in his pacing to see a red-robed figure coming up the walkway.

"Yes, Your Eminence." Pole tried a smile, but the cardinal did not smile back. When close enough, he offered the father his hand, and Pole kissed his ring.

"I am Cardinal Von Waldburg," the cardinal announced. "Please, sit."

The men found a nearby marble bench and sat side by side.

"How long have you been at the seminary in Rome, Father Pole?" the cardinal asked.

"Almost a year, Eminence."

"And before that?"

"I studied at Padua and Venice. I left England when it became clear that the king meant to break his obedience to the See of Rome and the Holy Father."

Von Waldburg nodded, then gazed out across the path. "It's true, we have all been shocked by events in England, especially the Holy Father, who has taken the matter personally." The cardinal looked back at Pole. His gaze was hard and steady. "But the death of the whore Anne Boleyn is perhaps providential? His Holiness prays that King Henry will grasp this divine opportunity for reconciliation. Just one gesture of obeisance to the See of Rome, however small, will allow him to lift the threat of excommunication. And then the king can once more enjoy the same authority in his realm as the emperor and King Francis enjoy in theirs, and his people can once more be assured of spiritual comfort."

Pole found himself scooting to the edge of the bench in his enthusiasm to agree. He grasped his knees. "Eminence, believe me, that is something all the faithful in England are praying for. My mother, Lady Salisbury, has written to me expressing her hopes that the new queen is in her heart a true Catholic."

The cardinal looked at Pole, his expression shifting slightly into something unreadable. "Perhaps," he said, "your mother could do more than hope? And perhaps you, yourself, Father Pole, might consider returning to England in order to influence events there." He rested his hand on Pole's shoulder and smiled. "You see, Father," he continued, his voice dropping to a near-whisper. "I know who you really are."

Pole stiffened beneath the cardinal's grip.

Henry slapped his hand on Ambassador Chapuys's shoulder and bellowed good-naturedly, "Excellency!"

Eustace Chapuys, the imperial ambassador, who had been speaking with a nobleman in the corridor outside the king's Presence Chamber amid the shuffling, shifting crowd of petitioners, turned in surprise to find Henry's smiling face.

"Your Majesty," said Chapuys, bowing low. A tall, handsome man with wavy brown hair, a square jaw, and a prominent nose, he was dressed in a long brocade Schaube trimmed in fur. Around his neck was a braided chain set with topaz.

"Come with me," said Henry. "There's someone I want to present you to!"

Chapuys followed the king and His Majesty's attendants along the wide hallway, around and up a long staircase to the section of the castle in which the royal couple had their private chambers. The decided clack of the king's heels echoed off the brick and stone walls as they climbed yet another set of stairs, and then reached the queen's apartments.

Jane was seated on an elegantly carved ebony chair in her outer chamber, embroidering tiny flowers on a lacy nightcap. Two of her ladies-in-waiting sat beside her, likewise engaged in needlework. Henry strode through the door without waiting for the queen's chamberlain to announce him, Chapuys by his side. The ladies looked up in unison. Jane hesitated, then said, "Lady Misseldon, Lady Rochford, a moment." The ladies curtsied, and moved quietly into other rooms off the chamber. Jane put her stitchery aside. She made as if to rise, but then remained seated. It struck Chapuys that she was still becoming used to her position of power.

"Queen Jane," said Henry with a broad gesture of his arm. "Allow me to present His Excellency Eustace Chapuys, ambassador to the emperor Charles V."

Jane extended her hand for the ambassador to kiss. "Excellency."

Chapuys bowed.

"I'll leave you to talk privately," said Henry, and without another word he withdrew from the chamber. Jane looked visibly dismayed at being left alone with Chapuys.

"Your Majesty," said Chapuys. "Allow me to congratulate you on your marriage, and wish you good health and prosperity. Although the device of the lady who preceded you on the throne was 'The Most Happy,' I have no doubt that it is you yourself who will realize that motto."

Jane nodded. "Thank you, Your Excellency."

Chapuys saw his chance to speak openly with the queen, and took it. "I know that the emperor will rejoice to have such a virtuous and amiable queen on the throne, and I must tell you that it would be impossible to overstate the joy and pleasure which every Englishman I have met has expressed to me on hearing of your marriage." Then he leaned in closer, and his voice dropped. "Especially as it is said that you are a peacemaker and are continuously trying to persuade His Majesty to restore his daughter Mary to favor."

Jane drew a sharp yet silent breath. She glanced at the door as if she hoped Henry would come through it and stop this politically dangerous conversation. Yet her husband did not appear, and she returned her gaze to the ambassador. He saw a resolve there that was at once touching and admirable.

"I promise you, Excellency," said the queen, "that I will continue to show favor to Mary, and do my best to deserve the title of peacemaker you have so gallantly given me."

Chapuys pressed: "If you do so, I think you will find, Madam, that without the pain of labor and childbirth, you will gain a treasured daughter, one who may please you even more than your own children by the king."

This was clearly too much. Jane flushed, drew back, and looked again at the door. "I—" she began then stopped. She hesitated, and then said, "I can only say, Excellency, that I will do all I can to bring peace between the king and his eldest daughter."

Chapuys waited, hoping for more, hoping she would offer some plan for easing the rift. Mary's mother, Queen Katherine, had been the noblest and most pious woman Chapuys had ever known. She had died destitute, banished, dethroned, and denied by the man who had promised God and the Holy Catholic Church that she would be his wife, his only wife, as long as he should live. Mary was likewise suffering for Henry's selfish desires, desires that were at that very moment destroying the Church in England.

But Jane would, or could, say no more.

"Ambassador!" Henry called, walking briskly into the chamber.

"Madam," Chapuys said, bowing, and he followed Henry out.

As they strolled back along the corridors to the Presence Chamber, Henry put a confiding hand on Chapuys's arm. "You are the first ambassador she has received. She is not yet used to such audiences. But it's true that she is kind and amiable, and much inclined to peace."

Chapuys glanced at the king but said nothing. It was clear he'd been listening in at the door.

"I swear," said Henry, "for example, that she would strive to prevent my taking part in a foreign war, if only to avoid the fear and pain of separation."

Chapuys frowned slightly, confused. "A foreign war, Your Majesty? Against whom?"

But Henry only smiled. "I was talking hypothetically. Surely you do that sometimes yourself, Excellency?"

And then the king picked up his pace and, trailed by his attendants, moved on ahead up the hallway.

The ride from London had been a pleasant one, down winding lanes that edged the orchards and hunting fields set aside for the king, and then on to the wider countryside. Sir Francis Bryan was in no particular hurry and kept his horse to a slow trot for the majority of the trip. His groom, a young dark-haired man with a ragged ear and bony cheeks, matched the pace of his master, staying a good two lengths behind. The day was damp with an early morning shower, and the air was clean and fragrant.

Bryan and his groom proceeded, along thorny hedgerows, past small cottages belonging to nameless peasant farmers, and across a field filled with curious Kerry cows. Then their destination appeared in the distance.

Hunsdon House was a massive brick fortress sporting tall towers and a wide moat. Built in 1447, it had passed down through private hands until Henry laid claim and converted it into a grand mansion with elegant royal and guest apartments, music chambers, and a gallery filled with exquisite landscapes and portraits. It was out of the goodness of the king's heart, Bryan mused, that the bastard Lady Mary and her attendants were allowed to live at Hunsdon.

Bryan had a message for Mary from her father. It would be the least pleasant aspect of this day. Not that he cared for the young woman's feelings, but it would be a tedious chore, and one he suspected would be met with some resistance.

The little bitch would challenge him, he knew it. But he was ready. And when it was done, he planned on seeking out the nearest tavern and having several tankards of beer and seeing if there might be a willing wench to be had.

Bryan and his groom crossed the bridge over the moat, their reflections fragmented on the surface of the leaf-covered water. Once in the courtyard, Bryan left his horse behind with the groom and boldly walked inside without being announced, his cape thrown back over his shoulders.

Lady Mary and two of her ladies met him in the grand foyer. He was surprised to see how composed and regal the lady looked, her head held high, her manner calm and confident. She had her mother's dark hair and eyes, and around her neck was a small silver crucifix.

"Lady Mary," Bryan said with a bow.

"My lord," said Mary. "I am very glad you have come to see me." She smiled, and it was quite a lovely smile. "I've written a letter congratulating the king on his marriage and begging leave to wait upon Queen Jane, or do Her Grace such service as would please her to command me."

Bryan shook his head to silence her and pulled a letter from the satchel at his side. "I am afraid, Lady Mary, we have not come here to discuss pleasantries. His Majesty urges you to sign this."

Mary looked at the letter, but did not reach for it. "What is it?"

"A list of articles recognizing the king as head of the Church and your mother's marriage as incestuous and unlawful. You must also renounce Rome and acknowledge your own illegitimacy."

Mary's face fell and her eyes grew wide. "But—"

"If you will not sign, I am afraid that Mr. Secretary Cromwell cannot guarantee your safety."

Mary began to tremble ever so slightly. She blinked rapidly and tipped her head back so as not to cry. There followed a long moment of silence between them. Bryan would give her time to think it through. When she spoke, her reply did not surprise him.

"However much I love my father, Your Grace," she said slowly, "and would do anything to please and satisfy him, I still cannot risk my immortal soul for the favor of an earthly king."

Bryan scowled and scoffed. "You are an unfilial daughter! Since you will not submit to your father, he may yet proceed against you for treason!"

Mary's hand went to the crucifix at her neck. "No, he would not. I cannot believe it." She turned away.

Bryan had made the thrust, and now he would draw blood. He walked up to her and leaned in close so he could whisper. "Listen to me. I tell you if you were my daughter I would smash your head against the wall until it was as soft as a boiled apple. Do you understand?"

Mary glanced back at him, still struggling to maintain her poise, though the wet streaks down her cheeks revealed her terror. This was what he wanted. Bryan smiled, stepped back, and bowed.

"Lady Mary," he said, quite cheerfully. And he went out into the sunshine to attend to the rest of his day.

Chapter Two

Though the soot and ash had been rinsed from the air of Yorkshire by English rains, the stink and the bitter taste remained in the noses and on the tongues of the parishioners. In a large timber barn built into a hillside, an assembly had gathered, their faces and souls so full of anger that it appeared it would take only the smallest spark to set off a terrible detonation. Laborers, peasants, villagers, shepherds, wives, and widows—all pressing around one another through the wide doorway and into the broad central aisle along which torches had been secured. Many stood, shoulder to shoulder, while others climbed on to stall sides and doors, and children scrambled for seats upon the straw in the loft.

John Constable and Robert Aske made their way through the throng to the far end of the barn, where they stepped up on hay bales and faced the crowd.

"Friends!" called Constable, raising his hand to silence the mumblings. "We've come here so you can listen and talk to this good man, Mr. Robert Aske. He has always been honest and fair-minded in his dealings with the commons." He paused as Aske nodded slightly, acknowledging the introduction. "Which is all I want to say. Mr. Aske may speak for himself."

Aske gazed at the people assembled before him. He was not comfortable before a crowd, but he knew these people needed wise counsel at such a volatile time. "What is it you ask?" he said.

A grizzled man near the front said, "Mr. Aske, all our feast days are abolished and gone. It should please the king's grace that we might have our holidays back."

The crowd murmured agreement. Another man called out, "We want the abbeys restored and demand that the advance of heresy be halted! We want these new heretic bishops, like Cranmer, to be cast out, and that he and Cromwell be supplanted by men of noble birth."

"Aye!" came the response.

"We hear rumors," shouted an elderly man at the rear of the barn, "that new taxes are to be levied against us, on our cattle, our christenings, on our marriages and our births."

Still another: "Mr. Aske, they've destroyed our abbeys for their greed! And now we hear that they will destroy our parish churches and steal all their treasures, or replace them with tin!"

Aske listened to the shouts, his heart on edge. So much anguish and anger.

A bearded blacksmith, dressed in his sweat- and grime-covered apron, stepped to the front and raised his fist. "Mr. Aske, before any of our lands, goods, or houses be taken from us by the Church commissioners we shall all fight and die! And that is our full answer."

The crowd burst into applause and hoots, and raised the staves and bows they'd brought with them.

Aske held up his hand. "I know you are angry. The destruction of the abbeys is a terrible, criminal thing, since they are greatly beloved by the people. They present by their very presence an exalted ideal to all of us." There were tense nods throughout the assembly. "But this call to arms, to rebellion against the king's grace, is something which on my conscience I cannot agree to."

Wails of rage and confusion erupted. Aske took a reflexive step backward. "Since the king is our body and soul," he said, "then an attack on him is an attack on the commonwealth and upon God!"

But few heard him over their own thunderous voices.

The blacksmith cried, "Did you hear that? The gentry don't care for us!" Then he looked at Aske. "Christ died for the poor. Remember that, Mr. Aske."

The crowd continued their shouts of defiance as Aske turned apologetically to Constable. "I'm very sorry, John."

But Constable's face was set, not with surprise at the outrage of the commoners, but with a challenge for Aske. "Whether you like it or not, Mr. Aske," he said slowly, "the risings are coming. They are surely coming."

The king's dining chamber had been prepared for the royal couple, the table set with great silver bowls and chalices, goblets of crystal, and sprays of fresh flowers and greenery. The king and queen sat near each other, Jane in a gown of forest green and silver, Henry in a broad-shouldered coat of royal blue embroidered with golden threads and pearls. Servants and councilors, including Sir Francis Bryan, Lady Rochford, and Lady Misseldon, stood silently in attendance, hands folded properly, awaiting instruction to serve in whatever fashion necessary.

Henry found the meal of boiled beef, braised tongue, lamb, and breads to be delectable, but his bride even more so. Her cheek was slightly pinked and her eyes bright and innocent. Had he his way, he would toss the attendants out and take his wife at that very moment, on that very table, silver and crystal be damned. But he knew Jane was likewise enjoying the meal, and he wouldn't deny her that. Not now, at least.

"I've been discussing the plans for your coronation with Mr. Holbein," said Henry as he put down his knife and took Jane's hand. "Have you ever heard of the *Bucentaur* of Venice?"

Jane shook her head. "No, Your Majesty."

"It's the ship in which the doge travels out into the lagoon each year to renew his marriage vows with the sea. It's a magnificent thing, decorated with gold and bronze images and statues of lions, Neptunes, angels, and other fantastical sea creatures. And we are going to build a ship just like it, and you will ride in it from Greenwich to the city, where all will be great pageantry and there will be beautiful music."

Jane's eyes widened. "Your Majesty, I don't know what to say."

"You don't have to say anything, sweetheart. It will be the most fabulous coronation that any English queen ever had. *That* I promise you."

As Jane squeezed Henry's hand, Henry glanced up to see Bryan staring openly at Lady Misseldon, and Lady Misseldon doing her best to avoid his gaze. Henry almost laughed openly at the brazen lechery in Bryan's good eye.

A servant brought in new platters of covered trays and set them amid the other serving dishes. The domed lids were removed, revealing sausages, fish, and oysters. Henry nodded his approval, and the servant stepped back.

"Forgive me," said Jane, leaning forward and speaking more quietly. "But I have heard that Your Majesty may still proceed against the Lady Mary. With all my heart, I beg you not to."

Equally quiet, Henry said, "Are you out of your senses?"

Jane appeared cut to her core, and she lowered her eyes.

Henry made sure his voice was soft before he spoke again. "Don't talk of such matters." He paused, then said, "Jane?"

Jane looked up, and Henry smiled. "I have another wedding gift." His voice rose happily, now that he knew Jane had heard him and would obey. "I hope you like it." He clapped his hands, and a councilor opened the door. In walked a groom leading a little black puppy on a leash. Jane rose out of her seat in delight, pressing her hands to her heart. The groom brought the dog to the king, and Henry placed it in his wife's arms. Gentle laughter rippled throughout the room.

And Henry was well pleased.

Thomas Cromwell's office was a large room paneled with dark wood and lined with overflowing bookshelves and stands. There was little space or reason for decoration, as this was a place of important purpose and serious business, where petitions were read, reports and messages received and dispersed, and laws reviewed and prepared for the signature of the king. Scarlet curtains were pushed back to let in the late afternoon sunlight. A wooden screen created a separate niche where Cromwell's scribes sat on tall stools, laboring over documents. Cromwell's own large desk, near the arched window, was buried beneath stacks of papers and books.

Richard Rich was escorted into the office by Cromwell's assistant and stood before Cromwell's desk silently for a moment, watching the adviser examining a peculiar painted box with two peepholes cut into its side.

"What's this?" Rich said at last, catching Cromwell's attention.

"A rood box. The commissioners found it at Boxley Abbey. Take a look."

Rich put the box up to his eyes. Inside, he saw a small image of a saint. *Nothing unusual,* Rich was beginning to think, until suddenly the saint's eyes moved and looked directly into Rich's own. Then the lips began to move as if the saint were talking. Rich pulled away and looked at Cromwell. "How's it done?"

Cromwell turned the box around, revealing, on the back, a small hand-cranked engine made of wires and sticks that operated the image. "They thought the saint's bones were still alive and could work benedictions—if you paid the little money you had to the Church, and to Rome."

Rich shook his head.

"By such false tricks, Sir Richard, have the credulous been deceived for generations, to the discredit of God."

Rich put the box down on Cromwell's desk with a decided, disgusted thud.

Cromwell sat back in his chair. "How do our reforms progress?"

"As you know, my lord, Parliament has now voted for the suppression of all the small monastic houses, and our commissioners are up and about their business in nearly every county in England."

"With much opposition?"

"Not as much as expected."

Cromwell's brow went up triumphantly. "Why should we have expected it? People know very well that these houses should all be condemned for their manifest sin, their vicious, carnal, and abominable living. I was told—it was once an anecdote among many—that when the commissioners went to the London House of the Crossed Friars they found the prior himself in bed with his whore, both stark naked. He offered them bribes to go away."

Both men laughed, and Rich crossed himself mockingly and then crossed his crotch.

"It's true," said Rich, "that ordinary people are so greedy upon these houses, when they are suppressed, that they scavenge in them night and day until nothing is left! They even take the books to use for paper in their houses of easement."

The two men laughed again.

"What about the gains to the king's treasury?" Cromwell asked.

"So far, by my reckoning, we have already doubled the king's income, and taken possession of monastic land worth many millions of pounds."

Cromwell was clearly taken aback. He leaned forward over the pile of papers on his desk. "Millions?"

"Yes, Mr. Secretary."

Cromwell nodded, then paused to flick a hand at the rood box. "We should put that on display, so people can see for themselves the manifest corruption of the Church, and laugh at it."

Rich bowed, turned, and left the office. Cromwell looked into the rood box again, and shook his head at the willing gullibility of men.

Sir Francis Bryan stood in the shadows near the window, night having fallen and taken the color and light from that corner of the room. He watched silently as Lady Ursula Misseldon entered his private palace apartment and glanced about nervously. He held his breath, watching her movements: graceful yet seeming slightly discomfited. The curve of her full breasts was visible at the neckline of her burgundy gown, and her neck was long and graceful. He could imagine the warm flesh of that neck beneath his fingers, could taste the full lips and the youthful nipples on his tongue.

Ursula walked to the hearth, where a healthy fire popped and sizzled. The flames of the mantel-top candles flickered and jumped. Ursula licked her fingers and placed one over a candle flame.

"Lady Misseldon," said Bryan.

Ursula spun about to see him emerge from the darkness. She quickly curtsied. "Sir Francis."

"I hope I didn't alarm you."

"No, sir. You—you wrote me a note that you wanted to see me?"

"Yes, I did." Bryan walked around her slowly, taking in every angle.

"About what?" she said.

"I was wondering if you would like to become my mistress."

Ursula did not gasp or flee, but she did blink in surprise. "Sir, I am already engaged to be married."

"To whom?"

"Sir Robert Tavistock."

Bryan cocked his head. "I haven't heard of him. Can he afford to buy you gifts like this?" He drew a red cloth from behind his back and held it out to her. She hesitated, then took the cloth and unrolled it to reveal an exquisite diamond necklace. The expression that crossed her face gave Bryan hope that the expense wouldn't be in vain. "I didn't think so," he continued. "There aren't many who can. But if it's more important to you to keep your virtue, then keep it—for what it's worth. And I swear I'll never bother you or your conscience ever again."

Ursula's lower lip drew in between her teeth. She frowned slightly, hearth glow bathing her cheeks.

Bryan reached out to take the necklace back, but she put her hand over it and met his gaze. "I—I haven't decided yet," she said, looking him full in the face.

"I cannot sign this. How can I renounce Rome? Or my mother's marriage? After all I have been through? After all of my mother's sufferings?"

Lady Mary dropped the paper and looked at Ambassador Chapuys across the table in the grand Hunsdon House dining chamber. Beyond the windows the world was merry, with willows shimmering in a breeze, wrens calling to one another among the branches, and cattle lowing in distant fields. Yet inside the manor the mood was grim. Mary's ladies stood near the door, their faces tight with anguish. Mary folded her hands as if in prayer and watched Chapuys as if he might, miraculously, be able to lift the burden from her.

But he shook his head sadly. "I understand. But may I suggest that you could sign the document but then make what is called a 'protestation apart'? That is, secretly forswear your submission before witnesses."

Mary recoiled. "Is that not hypocrisy? Surely the emperor is against my signing such a document?"

There was no kind way to relay this. "Lady Mary, I must tell you in all honesty that the emperor is not inclined to interfere any further in this matter. After all, you are not his subject and"—he paused, the words bitter on his tongue—"since the emperor is seeking a new alliance with the king, we would in truth be most reluctant to offend him in any way."

"Then . . . I am on my own?"

Chapuys could not answer, but his silence told the lady what she did not want to know. She stood and paced to the far wall, and then back again, struggling to maintain her composure, head up, shoulders shaking. She stopped and looked at the window and the sunlight beyond. "What if I do not sign it?"

"It is very possible that the king will put you to death."

Mary closed her eyes and did not move for a long time. Chapuys could see the tears cut down her cheek. Then she turned and said, "Very well. I will sign it. Give me the pen."

She went to the table and picked up a pen.

"Do you not want to read it first?"

Mary shook her head. "No. Only I ask you if you can procure papal absolution for what I have done." She dipped the pen into the inkwell and quickly signed her name. Then she thrust the pen at Chapuys and, fighting to keep her voice steady and strong, said, "But so long as I live, I will *never* forgive myself!"

She rushed from the hall, her ladies folding in behind her.

*　*　*　*

"'Here is the real Danae, she would kindle your lust even higher. One touch, one mere touch of her body, and your limbs would melt in fire.'"

Ursula smiled at the seductive lines Bryan was reading from the *Satyricon,* and stretched upon the pillows, her hair spread loosely like the rays of a midnight sun, her naked body lithe across the mattress. She fingered the diamond necklace at her throat as Bryan, straddling a nearby chair, dressed in only a loose white shirt, put down the book from which he was reading and raised his glass of wine toward her.

"The necklace suits you," he said. "I knew it would." He drained the glass, stood from his chair, and pulled his shirt up over his head. Ursula did not look away as he came toward her, ready and able.

Henry scribbled his signature on yet another letter and laid it aside on the table. He twirled the quill in his fingers and looked up at Cromwell for the next matter of business. It was a chilly day for summer, and gray beyond the windows of his private outer chamber.

Cromwell held up a folded sheet of paper. "Your Majesty has received a letter from Lady Bryan, governess to the Lady Elizabeth. Apparently the child has outgrown her clothes, and Lady Bryan asks if Your Majesty will permit her to purchase new ones."

Henry scoffed. "Why should I? I believe she is not even my child. The whole world knows her father was the traitor William Norris, and her mother was a whore." Henry snatched an apple from the brass bowl by the inkwell and took a bite. "What else?"

"There is . . . this." Cromwell placed another document before the king. "The submission of Lady Mary."

Henry paused in mid-chew, then laid the apple aside. He lifted the paper to study the signature, and his glum mood lifted instantly.

"You will make arrangements for myself, and the queen, to meet with her," said Henry. "Not here, and not publicly, but soon."

Cromwell bowed. "Majesty."

Henry leaned back in his chair. "There are rumors of plague in the city. The coronation will have to be postponed."

Cromwell bowed and started to leave, but Henry crooked his finger, drawing his secretary closer. "Mr. Rich showed me the figures. I'm very pleased with you, and will shortly prove it."

Cromwell, so unaccustomed to showing pleasure, couldn't help but smile. Henry enjoyed seeing the man, even if for a moment, let down his guard.

Robert Aske had rescued the defaced marble statue of the Virgin Mary from Sawley Abbey and removed it to his house. It had been covered in ash and debris, but it had not been difficult to find. It was as if the Virgin had expected Aske to look for her and had made herself available. Aske cleaned the statue with soft cloths then hauled it home along the rutted roads in a wagon. It had been given a place of honor in his small study. Aske felt that the Virgin was all the more pious, all the more holy, for the piteous damage she had suffered.

As Aske knelt before the Mother of God to pray, there was a knock on the door.

"Robert?"

He crossed himself and turned on his knees as his wife entered the study.

She looked at her husband for a moment, noting his strange expression. "What is it?" she asked.

"I've made up my mind."

His wife gazed at him for a moment, closed her eyes, and nodded. She understood that her husband had made the dangerous decision to lead the pilgrims in their stand against those who would try to destroy their religion.

Jane sat at her mirror studying the pendant her husband had given her as a wedding present. As she turned it back and forth in her hand, it caught the glow from the hearth fire and seemed to reflect not just green and red but every color of the rainbow.

"Lady Rochford?"

Her lady, who was seated on a small bench nearby, looked up from her evening reading. "Yes, Your Majesty?"

"Take this to Lady Bryan. Tell her to use it to buy clothes for the Lady Elizabeth."

Lady Rochford stood and took the pendant, then curtsied. "Yes, Madam."

Jane touched Lady Rochford's hand. "And we must think of some gift for the Lady Mary. I am looking forward so much to meeting her."

Lady Rochford smiled. "Your Majesty is very kind." She curtsied again and placed the pendant in the small cloth pouch tied at her waist.

Jane looked at her little pet dog, asleep in its basket. It twitched its whiskers contentedly in its dreams. Then she looked again at her lady, who stood awaiting her next command.

"Lady Rochford," said Jane. "It was not your fault that your husband betrayed you. Nor was it Mary's fault or Elizabeth's fault to be born of a king. Women are much put upon in this world. It is my desire, as much as I can, to promote their interests. I must do it quietly, but I will do it all the same. I trust you will help me?"

Lady Rochford's eyes grew soft and humbled, and she nodded.

"Mr. Secretary Cromwell," announced the chamberlain at the open door of the king's Presence Chamber. Henry sat upon his throne on the dais, with Charles Brandon nearby and several of his councilors on either side. Above him hung a broad red-and-white canopy of state. This was a moment of great importance. Courtiers stood at attention on the floor, leaving a wide aisle for the one who was to be honored.

Thomas Cromwell entered the chamber, his hands clasped before him, and approached the throne without a word. Then he dropped to his knees and watched as Henry stepped down, reached for the sword Brandon was holding, and touched Cromwell's shoulders, each in turn.

Then Henry straightened, raised his hand, and proclaimed, "Arise, Sir Thomas Cromwell."

Cromwell stood and lowered his head. Henry handed the sword back to Brandon, and continued, "Also Baron Cromwell of Wimbledon, and from this time forth, Lord Privy Seal."

Cromwell bowed his head even lower. "Majesty," he said softly.

Henry returned to his throne and sat back, satisfied. Cromwell looked up and caught the eye of Brandon, who at that moment seemed so full of silent hatred that he might explode.

Cromwell answered the obvious loathing with a broad smile.

Lady Mary had not slept well, dreading yet desiring the meeting that was scheduled for the late morning. She got up early to dress herself, then spent several hours in Hunsdon's small chapel, praying for guidance, for forgiveness. When the entourage arrived, she placed herself in the center of the foyer, head up, eyes set forward, ready for whatever was to happen.

Queen Jane entered first, followed by several of her ladies. The woman was quite beautiful and looked to be a gentle soul, though Mary knew well that looks could be deceiving. Then the king entered the hall, attended by his grooms. At the sight of him, Mary's breath caught in her throat. It had been more than a year since she had seen her father. He appeared taller than before, stronger, and . . . kinder?

Jane stepped forward and handed a small velvet box to Mary.

Slowly, Mary opened the box and gasped. She touched the diamond ring inside, and then looked up at the queen with an expression of surprise and gratitude. "Your Majesty," she whispered. "You are too kind."

Jane smiled as Lady Mary took her hand and kissed it. "Mary," she said, "gifts such as these are easy, compared with gifts of the heart. It gives me more pleasure than I can say that you will be reconciled with your father."

Henry stepped forward, smiled, and offered his hand to his daughter. "Mary." His voice was deep yet soft.

Mary kissed his hand. "Your Majesty."

Henry led his daughter to a quiet corner, and she felt him slip something into the pocket of her skirt. "Here is a cheque for one thousand crowns," he said. "But if there is anything else you need, you need only ask."

Mary felt a stinging in her throat and she swallowed against it. "Thank you, Your Majesty."

Henry tipped his head to look her in the eye. "Father," he corrected.

"Yes. F-father. Father." Tears stung her eyes and anguish pierced her heart. He was being so generous, yet what he had commanded her to do to earn his generosity had been so dreadful!

Henry reached out and touched Mary's shoulders, and she began to weep in earnest.

"My lord," said John Frankish, standing before Cromwell's desk with two of his commissioners as servants hurried about, taking messages to and from the secretary. "We have come here in haste to tell you that a great part of the north, as well as parts of Lincolnshire, have risen in sudden rebellion against His Majesty! There are musters of the commons everywhere, and beacons of rebellion burning all night across the hills."

Cromwell laid down his quill and glanced at Richard Rich, who stood by the sideboard, arms crossed and brow furrowed.

"Just four days ago," Frankish went on, "while we were collecting taxes at Hexham, we were set upon by an angry mob. They captured a commissioner called Nicholas Bellow, pulled him down from his horse, and beat him to death with their staves."

A black-bearded commissioner nodded anxiously. "Among the mob, my lords, we saw some armed priests urging on these rebellious knaves with cries of 'Kill them! Kill them!' Then we heard that another man, William Leach, who was known to be in your service, Mr. Cromwell, had been hanged from a tree!"

"What do these rebels say they want?"

"So far as I can tell," said Frankish, "they want to keep their holy days. They want the monasteries restored, their churches unmolested, and no more taxes!"

"I heard it declared that if they prospered with their journey," said the bearded commissioner, "they intended to kill the Lord Cromwell, four or five bishops, and you, Chancellor Rich, as 'devisers of taking Church goods and pulling down churches.'"

Rich blew out an angry breath. "Why do the local gentry not intervene and suppress these traitorous assemblies?"

Frankish shook his head. "They try. But then the mobs come back even greater. Some say that not hundreds but *thousands* have risen."

Cromwell said nothing, though his mind raced in circles. *How dare these piggish mobs threaten to kill my men! How dare they threaten me!*

He clenched his teeth. *And how do I tell the king?*

Standing from his desk, he gave a sharp jerk of his head to send the other men out. It was time to face His Majesty.

"Why didn't you know?" demanded Henry, who paced across the floor of his private outer chamber, his jaw set. "You are supposed to know everything that goes on! You told me there was little opposition. On the contrary, you said most people were glad to see these places dissolved. You were wrong. You didn't know anything!" Henry jammed his fist angrily against the air, then spun about and approached Cromwell. His face was red, his expression tight. Cromwell awaited the king's next words of chastisement, but instead Henry raised his hand and struck Cromwell soundly across the head.

Cromwell took a sharp breath as a stinging pain raced along his skull.

"Knave!" snarled Henry. He gestured to the table in the center of the room. "Sit down. Write this."

Cromwell sat immediately, pulled a sheet of paper from a stack, dipped a quill into the inkwell, and waited for the king's dictation.

"We take it as great unkindness," said Henry, beginning to pace again, "that our common and inferior subjects rise against us without any ground. As to the taking away of the goods of the parish church, it was *never* intended."

Cromwell scribbled quickly, his face expressionless.

"Yet," said Henry, pausing at the window, "even if it had been, true subjects would not have treated us, their prince, with such violence, but would have humbly petitioned him for their purpose . . ."

Cromwell dipped the pen again, and continued to write.

"I command you rebels to disperse and sin no more. Above all, remember your duty of allegiance, and that you are bound to obey us, your king, both by God's commandments and by the law of nature."

The hillside timber barn in Yorkshire had been transformed from a benign structure holding hay and cattle into a fortress for a most serious matter. Benches and tables had taken the place of tools and barrows, and a large banner had been painted and strung up above the altar. It showed the figure of the suffering Christ with his five bleeding wounds.

At a table at the back of the barn, Robert Aske sat with John Constable, Sir Ralph Ellerker, and four other captains, preparing to swear in a long line of recruits. Aske no longer wrangled in his heart as to the right course of action. He was where he belonged, doing what he knew God and his people wanted him to do. In this he found both a sense of duty and righteous anger.

A young man with a wine-stain birthmark on his face approached the table, a bow and quiver slung across his back.

"What's your name, lad?" Aske asked.

"Charlie, sir. Charlie Raw, shepherd." He grinned, revealing a mouth void of teeth.

"Do you know what we're about, Charlie?"

"Yes, Captain Aske."

"We're not rebels. We're pilgrims, and we have a pilgrimage to go on. If you want to join us, then you shall swear to be true to Almighty God, to Christ's Catholic Church, to our sovereign lord the king, and to the commons of this realm, so help you God and halidom and by this book."

Constable held out a volume of the Gospels, and Charlie put his hand on it confidently. "I do swear!" He crossed himself.

"You will also wear this badge," said Aske. He held out a small round cloth patch with a crude portrait of Jesus embroidered into it. "It shows the Five Wounds of Christ, to prove that the commons will fight in Christ's cause." He pointed to the badge he himself had sewn on the breast of his doublet, and those the other captains wore.

"Yes, Captain," said Charlie with a wide, toothless grin.

"God bless you, Charlie."

And with a deep, enthusiastic bow, Charlie turned about and left the barn, passing the scores who still stood in line awaiting their turn to join the cause.

On their return from Hunsdon, the king and queen supped in the queen's private outer chamber. Jane had prepared herself with special care, hoping to calm the king's mind of all the troubles that were clearly stirring there. She wore a pale blue dress, sapphire earrings and rings, and a cream-colored French hood over her hair. She complimented each dish that was brought to the table by the black-coated grooms—boiled fish, eggs, slabs of pork, soups, and crusty breads. She tried small talk, but though Henry would nod and smile, he continued to jab at his meal with his knife, often forgetting to put the food in his mouth.

Jane changed the topic of conversation. "Mary was so sweet and affectionate. She was everything I hoped she would be."

Henry said nothing, then broke off a piece of bread and sopped it in the blood pudding. He absently took a bite.

"It seems to me no wonder that she is so marvelously beloved for her virtue and her goodness in the hearts of people."

Henry frowned and took another bite.

Jane persisted, "Your Majesty must invite her to court to show her off."

Henry glanced at the row of ladies near the table, waiting for any orders Jane might give. Jane noticed his gaze linger on Ursula Misseldon.

"Your Majesty," said Jane, reaching for Henry's arm. "Why will you not speak to me?"

"Because I am disappointed."

Jane was taken aback. Was it something she had said, or done? "Why?"

At last Henry glanced at her. "I am disappointed because you are not yet with child." Then he looked away and said, "That's all."

Cromwell held up his hand as Richard Rich entered the office and stepped to the secretary's desk. His head ached from thought and with the issues he found himself having to correct. The candle on the desk had burned low; it would soon be in need of replacing.

"You must excuse me," he said to Rich without looking up. "I am writing to the gentry and justices in Yorkshire, reminding them of their duty to suppress these traitors, and the penalties for not doing so."

Rich huffed audibly. "Is there any case for suspending the work of the Church commissioners until the rebels are dealt with?"

"No." Cromwell glanced up. "There is no better way to beat the king's authority into the heads of the rude people of the north than to show them the king intends to continue with the reformation and correction in religion, whatever they say and whatever they do."

Rich nodded, though to Cromwell it seemed a reluctant concession.

There was a commotion at the door, and it blew open. Servants in the office drew back as Frankish pushed past them, panting, and slammed his hands on the top of Cromwell's desk, forgetting in his panic to bow. "My lord! The rebels have taken Lincoln. They have destroyed the bishop's palace, and their rebel flags fly over the city gates."

Cromwell's heart began to pound heavily.

Frankish's eyes grew even wider. "And more of them are now marching on York!"

"York?" exclaimed Rich. "May God help us now!"

Henry turned as Charles Brandon entered his private outer chamber to the announcement, "His Grace the Duke of Suffolk." Brandon had been summoned to come immediately. He'd heard rumblings from the other councilors at court of the trouble in the north, and realized Henry was preparing to act.

"Charles," said Henry as Brandon removed his wide-brimmed cap and bowed. Then the king turned away to the brass armillary sphere on the stand beneath the window. He placed his hands on it as if he could hold the whole of the universe.

Brandon waited silently. At last Henry spoke again.

"These events provoke unwarranted memories," he said. "When I was five years old my blessed mother hurried me across London and into the Tower. There was a rebellion against my father. The Cornish rebels were actually approaching the city walls, and inside the city there was a panic." Henry looked back at Brandon. "For six days my mother and I were kept in the Great Keep. We heard no news about the royal army or my father. My mother tried to be calm, but she was terrified, and so was I. I was sure we were both going to die."

Brandon nodded sympathetically.

Moving to the table, Henry picked up a scroll bearing the royal seal. He handed it to Brandon. Brandon could see fear in the king's eyes; he knew men were often not far removed from the boys they once were.

"I am appointing you commander of the royal forces. You will ride north as soon as possible. You will find ordnance and guns waiting for you at Hungerford—but don't tarry there."

"No, Your Majesty. I will do all Your Majesty commands, and more."

Henry's eyes darkened dangerously. "These rebels are false traitors full of wretched and devilish intents. They must be punished for the detestable and unnatural sins of rebellion against their sovereign. Just as my father punished those Cornishmen!"

Brandon galloped home to his own manor, a good hour's ride west from London, and sent word for his wife, Catherine, to meet him right away at the stables. She found him there, his grooms fitting him with his armor. Brandon saw the worry in her eyes when she stepped into the shadows of the hay-littered aisle.

"Charles!" she called as she watched a groom tighten her husband's breastplate. "What is it?"

"His Majesty has charged me with leading his army against the northern rebels."

Catherine put her hand to her heart and leaned against the door of a stall, causing the horse within it to nicker as if expecting a treat. Brandon waved his hand, dismissing the grooms for a moment. Then he took his wife gently by the shoulders.

"You aren't to worry." He moved closer to her and ran his hands through her hair. She frowned but did not pull away. "I shall have at my back enough men and arms to subdue them easily. I have His Majesty's promise."

Catherine closed her eyes. Brandon could see her cheeks pulsing as though she were trying not to cry. "I hope to God he keeps it," she whispered.

Brandon ran his fingers down her cheek. "There is another reason, sweetheart, why I am so happy to accept this charge. Cromwell is being blamed for everything and the rebels are demanding his head. With God's help, I may well be able to deliver it!"

Henry stood in his bedchamber panting against the excruciating pain in his leg. The wound had reopened, tormenting him even as the rebels in the north had decided to torment him. Anger and agony boiled inside him. He wanted the pain gone, the rebels dead. He was the king of England! He and he alone was in charge of his body, his life, his subjects, his kingdom!

Throwing his walking stick aside and dropping to the bed, he reached beneath his jerkin, fumbled with the ties on the linen braes he wore against his skin, and pulled them down. He hissed at the sight. The ulcer on his thigh had burst open, and blood and pus streamed down his leg beneath the binding.

"The lord privy seal," announced a groom at the king's bedchamber door.

With sweaty hands, Henry drew his braes up and walked as evenly as he could to his outer chamber. Cromwell bowed, then waited for the king's command.

"I have dispatched Suffolk with a royal army. If need be I shall send after it a second army, to destroy these rebels!"

"Yes, Majesty."

"Unless they agree to disperse and send one hundred of their ringleaders to the Duke of Suffolk with halters around their necks, then he has our permission to burn, spoil, and destroy all their goods and make a fearful example of them to all our subjects."

"Yes, Your Majesty."

Henry came close to Cromwell, so close he could smell the other man's sour fear beneath his calm exterior. "If they do not submit, Mr. Cromwell, then I promise the utter destruction of them, their wives, and their children. Do you understand? I will destroy all of them!"

Cromwell nodded.

"And you, too, Mr. Cromwell!"

At this, Henry saw the anxiety in Cromwell's eyes. That was good. Let him worry, let him suffer, too. Henry hobbled back into his bedchamber and slammed the door, leaving Cromwell alone.

Pilgrims, staves in their hands and ecstasy on their faces, reined their mounts to a halt along the wide, green expanse of a Yorkshire moor. John Constable and Robert Aske, riding in the lead, turned their horses to face the men. Aske's heart swelled with joy and divine purpose. These men—these noble commons—had vowed to fight to save their holy churches and way of life. Surely God was smiling on them at that moment.

Constable raised his hand. "All commons stick together! Now is the time to arise, or else never! Forward to York! Forward in pain of death! Forward now, or never!"

The men stood in their stirrups, shouting and waving their hands in the air. Aske took it all in, savoring the glory and the hope, and knew they would certainly be victorious. And as if offered more proof, he turned to gaze down from the moor to a winding road below, where thousands of pilgrims from other farms, hamlets, and counties, armed with staves and bows, proceeded in confidence, in determination. Some rode, some walked, but none faltered. Above their heads fluttered banners proudly displaying the Five Wounds of Christ.

It seemed there was no end to the army of faith.

Praise God! thought Aske. *Praise Him for the victory that is surely ours!*

"Your Majesty," Lord Darcy's letter read. "We are in great danger and see no means of resisting these rebels. Pontefract Castle's well is dry, its bridge in disrepair, its walls and ramparts much out of frame. There is not one gun here ready to shoot. The Archbishop of York himself has come here to seek shelter, with other nobles and gentry. But without speedy succor, I fear we are all lost. But I remain your humble and obedient servant, Darcy."

Henry crushed his fist around the news from Yorkshire. He stared at the paper, his hand so tight and hot he thought the letter might burst into flames.

Cromwell snatched up a stack of papers that needed the king's attention and left his office for the castle's main corridor, where courtiers and nobles took quick glances at his face and knew best to get out of the way. Richard Rich, who had been talking with one of the ladies beneath a narrow window, spied Cromwell and hurried to catch up with him.

"What is the news?" he asked.

Cromwell raised a hand. "This matter hangs like a fever—one day good, another bad. Promised a pardon, and with the threat of an advancing royal army, the rebels in Lincoln have dispersed and gone home."

"And in Yorkshire?"

Cromwell grabbed Rich's arm and took him aside into a small alcove. He spoke quietly, pointedly. "In Yorkshire and the north we are facing the most dangerous insurrection that has ever been seen. The rebels entered York three days ago and celebrated Mass in the cathedral. Some say they now intend to march south!"

He paused a moment, watching the news sink in, watching Rich's expression change from concern to genuine fear. The men left the alcove and continued walking, picking up their pace.

They passed between the ax-bearing guards in their red uniforms and entered the king's private chambers, where they were immediately met with a howl of extreme pain. Cromwell and Rich exchanged anxious glances, and Cromwell stepped aside slightly to peer through the open door of the king's bedchamber.

Henry sat at the edge of his bed, his damaged leg propped up on a cushioned stool, the bandages removed. The king's face was slick with sweat and his fingers were entangled in the bedcovers as a surgeon dug about in the raw, red wound with iron pincers. Several other physicians stood watching, along with Sir Francis Bryan. Beside the bed, a groom held a tankard with both hands. The stench of putrid flesh was thick in the air.

At last the surgeon extracted something from the leg, dropped it into a silver dish, and stepped aside to show it to the other doctors.

"What is it?" Henry demanded. "What have you found?"

"A splinter of bone, Your Majesty," said the head surgeon.

Henry snarled. "I don't understand. You told me before it was just an ulcer. You told me it was easily cured!" Then he nodded at the groom, who gave him a long drink from the tankard. Strong spirits and drugs, Cromwell guessed, to help counter the pain.

"Majesty," began the surgeon apologetically, "when men reach a certain age . . ."

"God's blood, physician!" Henry shouted. "You don't know what it is, do you? Do you?"

The head surgeon bowed low. "Your Majesty must not be alarmed. We shall apply a poultice to draw any more splinters to the surface. Then we shall look to other remedies to heal, permanently, Your Majesty's wound."

Henry stared at the man, his eyes red and suspicious. "You treat me like a fool. Nearly everyone here treats me like a fool!"

The surgeons shuffled nervously in place.

"Majesty," said the head surgeon, his face gone instantly pale.

"You're quacks! Charlatans! I will find my own remedies!"

With fumbling hands, the head surgeon reached out with a pair of tongs for the steaming poultice that another doctor had heated on the hearth. This cloth, spread with a scalding mash of oats and oil of bay, was laid directly on the king's festering wound. Henry threw his head back and howled in agony.

Out in the king's chambers, Rich flinched at the pitiable wail. Cromwell grabbed him by the arm and drew him close. "I am putting you in charge of the defenses here in London," he said. "We shall need to organize new levies. Send word to every lord and gentleman to be ready with his power. Take the weapons, harness, and ordnance you need from the Tower. Buy more if you need to, from the merchants in the city."

Rich took a step back. "Then it's true! We *are* in trouble!"

Before Cromwell could reply, Francis Bryan stepped out of the king's bedchamber and nodded. "Mr. Cromwell, His Majesty will receive you now."

The king had been propped up in his bed against pillows, his leg newly dressed and tied with a white cloth. Sweat cut swaths down his cheeks and neck to the open collar of his shirt. The shirt itself clung to his damp flesh. Cromwell and Rich bowed and waited for Henry to address them.

"Lord Darcy has sent me a letter," said the king. Cromwell could hear the fury and pain in his voice, melded into one powerful, frightening emotion. "He says he is in danger from the rebels and sees no means of resistance." Henry snorted and his eyes narrowed. "And yet he occupies a castle! A great stronghold. Does he not mean to stand firm against these traitors?"

"Your Majesty," said Cromwell, "I'm told that the rebels have already entered the town of Pontefract with overwhelming numbers."

Henry pointed his finger at Cromwell. "Mr. Cromwell, Pontefract is the gateway to the south. It has great strategic value. You will write at once to Lord Darcy informing him that I expect him to hold the castle. At all costs!"

"Yes, Your Majesty."

"And what of our royal army?" Henry continued, sitting up straighter, leaning toward the secretary. "What progress are they making to crush this rebellion? Where is His Grace the Duke of Suffolk? And Shrewsbury? I ordered him, too! What in God's name are they doing?"

Cromwell had no answer.

Chapter Three

Charles Brandon, Duke of Suffolk, caught sight of the small party of dignitaries ahead at the side of the road. Through the morning haze and dust, he recognized the mayor of London in his black coat, cap, and chains of office. With the mayor were several other officials, all gazing in Brandon's direction, hands shading their eyes.

Brandon and his entourage were dressed in armor, prepared for battle. Some carried Tudor pendants and others flags bearing royal heraldic designs. Brandon, upon his sorrel mare, took the lead. He waved his arm in the air, indicating to the captains behind him that they join him to greet the waiting party. They broke from the others and spurred their horses ahead quickly. Dust rose in the air like a swarm of insects.

"My Lord Mayor!" Brandon said.

"Your Grace," replied the mayor with a bow.

Brandon glanced around at the fields on either side of the road and frowned. "My lord, I was promised artillery when I arrived here. But I don't see any guns."

The mayor stroked his chin, touched the chain at his neck, and answered, "Your Grace, we have guns, but we have been unable to find enough horses or drays to transport them."

Brandon heeled his horse, riding up so close to the mayor he forced him to take a step backward. "Perhaps you don't understand! I am about the king's most urgent business. If you cannot commandeer some horses for His Majesty's use, then how can you call yourself mayor of London?"

The mayor looked at his fellows for help. They stood silent. "Your Grace!" he said. "I . . . I did not want to produce panic by forcing people to part with their horses and drays."

"Idiot!" Brandon roared. "I charge you personally to find enough horses within two days to bring the guns on after our army, or God help me I will hold you to account. With any luck, Mr. Mayor, I will afterward get the chance to see you disemboweled at Tyburn!"

The mayor stared at Brandon in horror. Brandon gave the man one last stern look, and then urged his horse onward up the road, with his men following.

Lord Darcy of Yorkshire stood atop the battlements of Pontefract Castle staring down at the rebel delegation as it galloped up the hillside toward the fortress, the fluttering flag with the Five Wounds of Christ held high. Darcy was an old man, with arthritic hands and a bad hip, who had served under King Henry's father. The past years of his life had been peaceful, with his servants, children, and grandchildren tending to him. But now that peace was being torn apart by the cries and demands of criminal peasants.

Robert Lee, the Archbishop of York, stood beside Darcy, along with several other wealthy gentlemen who had fled to the safety of the castle. "My God, Lord Darcy," Lee said, crossing himself anxiously. "What a sight is there! Arrant rebels against the king's majesty, brazenly bearing their badges of shame!"

Darcy nodded. "Indeed so, Your Grace. I never thought in all my long days to see such a sight."

"What are you going to do?" asked Lee. "Fire on them?"

Darcy shook his head bitterly. "You know very well I have almost no useful guns."

"You could resist them all the same, and close your gates. After all, those are the king's orders."

"As to that," said Darcy, "I think it better to talk to them first, as fellow Englishmen and fellow Christians."

Lee looked unconvinced, but he said no more.

They gathered at a table in the Great Hall, an enormous, cold room with cracking, uneven stone floor tiles and fading tapestries and banners as old as the castle itself secured to the damp walls. Darcy, Lee, and several select nobles sat at a cloth-covered table, ready to meet with their adversaries. Once the men were settled, Darcy nodded, and his servant opened the door. Aske, Constable, and six of their captains and pilgrims entered the room, removed their caps, and bowed respectfully.

"My Lord Darcy, Your Grace, gentlemen," said Aske. "We come here in peace, and not as rebels but as pilgrims, who seek no profit for ourselves or hurt to any other private persons."

Darcy folded his hands on the table. They pained him but he did not let it show. "So what is it you *do* seek, Mr. Aske?"

"My lord, we have entered upon our Pilgrimage of Grace for the common good, for the love we bear to God's faith, our holy Church, and the maintenance of it, for the preservation of our sovereign king and the expulsion of villain's blood and evil councilors. We mean to petition the king's highness to stop the destruction of our monasteries and abbeys."

"Master Aske," said Lee, raising a hand. "You claim to be loyal to the king, but your very actions defy and deny the king's supremacy."

Aske took a step forward. "Lord Archbishop, there is no man now alive in England more loyal to the king than I am. And I trust in time to prove it. Our quarrel lies not with him, but only with those close to him."

"It's very well for you to sound so high and mighty," said Constable, "but you and your kind are also to blame for not advising the king honestly about the spread of heresy and abuse throughout his kingdom. For what are Cromwell and Cranmer if not heretics and manifest abusers of the commonwealth?"

Aske gave Constable a look that urged him to watch his words. Then he said, "As a man of God, Your Grace, we would expect you to mediate on our behalf, rather than repeat false and malicious rumors."

Darcy considered this. "Mr. Aske, I do not question your sincerity. But you must know that as the king's representative I have the means here to hinder you and do some injury to your cause."

"Lord Darcy, I told you we mean no displeasure to any private person. All these pilgrims have sworn an oath not to slay or murder out of envy, but to put away fear for the commonwealth and march with the cross of Christ and their heart's faith before them." And then Aske's face darkened, mirroring the rage in Constable's. "But we will fight and die if you try and stop us."

Archbishop Lee stood aghast as hordes of smiling pilgrims—rebels— streamed through the open gates of Pontefract Castle and into the graveled courtyard. Darcy and his servants and soldiers walked among them, shaking hands and welcoming the unwashed mob warmly.

Lee could stand it no longer. He strode to Darcy and whispered angrily in the old man's ear. "For the love of God, Darcy!"

But Darcy only turned, smiled, and replied, "Yes, Your Grace. For the love of God!"

A mild wind blew from the west, stirring the cypress and fig trees and drawing out the fragrance of the late summer flowers in the Renaissance Garden of Castel Gandolfo. Hummingbirds and honeybees darted in and out among the lavender, sunflowers, and valerian, while the more timid crickets called from the depths of the hedges.

A sharp voice pierced the garden's calm, sending a pair of startled doves into the air. "It seems we were wrong to suppose that the king of England would realize his mistakes and the dangers to his soul!"

Father Reginald Pole nodded solemnly and widened his stride to match that of Cardinal Von Waldburg as they strolled along a garden path. A good ten yards behind, a silent servant kept pace.

"Instead," Von Waldburg declared, "he continues to encourage those bloodsuckers, gangsters, emissaries of Satan, Cromwell and Cranmer, to vandalize and defile the houses of God and steal their treasures. All for his own use and pleasure!" The man let out a disgusted grunt, then stopped and gazed up at the castle on the knoll above them. "And yet, even in the darkness there is light. I mean, this great uprising of the faithful. This . . . Pilgrimage of Grace."

"I've heard of it, too," said Pole. "How the pilgrims march beneath the banner of Christ."

The cardinal stopped and looked at Pole. His face was pinked with the sun and his passion. "The Holy Father asks you to write a pamphlet in English denouncing the king and his advisers as heretics."

Pole bowed. "Of course! I will start work on it straightaway."

As Pole bowed again, prepared to leave, Von Waldburg held up his hand. "Father Pole, His Holiness needs more from you than just your signature. With my encouragement, he has decided to appoint you an official legate. You will travel to France and to the Low Countries and meet with representatives of the king and the emperor."

Pole frowned, confused. "Eminence?"

"You will persuade them to provide monies, arms, and mercenaries to support this most holy crusade in England."

After a moment, Pole closed his eyes, lowered his head, and said, "If that is what His Holiness asks me to do, then of course I will do it, like an obedient son to a father."

Von Waldburg motioned to the servant, who came up to them carrying a red bundle, which he handed to the cardinal. Pole watched uncertainly.

"In order to enhance our prestige abroad," said Von Waldburg, "for after all you might have to talk to kings and princes, His Holiness has agreed to make you a cardinal. Here is your birretta."

"I can't accept it!"

"Why not?"

"I'm not worthy!"

Von Waldburg's brow arched. "I see you prefer your own judgment to that of the Pope, your Holy Father. No doubt you suppose that makes you seem humble. But actually it is the sin of pride, Father Pole."

Pole nodded slowly and took the hat. Von Waldburg embraced him. "Eminence," he said.

Henry leaned heavily into his walking stick as he left the Presence Chamber, his steps uneven. With each swing of his leg, agony flared up through his spine and back down to his knee. His face was taut and grim, and beads of sweat had gathered along his forehead and at his temples. How could he focus on matters of state when his own body was betraying him? Yet how could he not force himself to deal with the dire matters at hand? The leg infuriated him, but the rebels infuriated him even more.

Sir Francis Bryan and Cromwell followed at his sides, waiting for a direct question or command. Courtiers bowed and muttered, "Your Majesty," as the king passed. The three men took the corridors around and up to the king's private chambers.

"Darcy and York have betrayed me," said Henry, his words seething through a set jaw. "We shall see what end they come to. And why have neither Shrewsbury nor Suffolk attacked yet? All I hear are their complaints and excuses! You know what I think? I think they have grown afraid of their own shadows!"

Henry flashed a furious glance at Cromwell, then at Bryan, and limped on, the sweat on his palm making it hard for him to grasp his stick. "I have a mind to go north myself. I will lead the army and teach those ingrates and rebels a fearful lesson in slaughter!"

They approached the open door to the king's outer private chamber. The guards to either side nodded silently and respectfully as the king and his advisers passed through. The door was closed behind them with a solid thump.

Only then did Bryan speak. "I wish, Your Majesty," he said, "that you would not consider doing so."

Henry spun about. "Why? Do you suppose I am too feeble?"

"No. I mean that Your Majesty's life is far too precious to be put at risk against such a common rabble. Of course if you chose to go, you would be like a lion among wolves."

Henry spat at this. "Sir Francis, I don't require you to flatter me."

"No, Your Majesty!"

Henry walked to the nearest chair, which was cushioned and tasseled and bore an intricate carving of England's lion and unicorn. He placed his hand on the chair's arm then looked back at Cromwell. "Send a plain message to the duke. Ask him why he refuses to obey my commands and if he is a coward."

Cromwell bowed. "Majesty."

Bryan and Cromwell turned to leave. Henry eased himself into the chair and lifted his leg up on the stool before it. He grimaced with the pain in his thigh. Damn it that a king should have a body as unreliable as that of a peasant. "And Mr. Cromwell!" he shouted.

"Majesty?"

"If things go badly, I know well enough who is to blame."

Cromwell said nothing, bowed again, and left. Henry motioned for Bryan to wait.

"Can I get Your Majesty anything for your pain?" Bryan asked.

Henry nodded. "Yes. I believe you can." There was only one thing that might take his mind off his agony.

Bryan watched the king, waiting to see what that might be.

Logs burned in the huge fireplace of Pontefract's Great Hall, bathing one end of the room in warmth and casting bright sparks out into the air as the damp bits of wood caught fire. The table had been dragged closer to the hearth, where all who had gathered could more easily see the maps and reports spread out before them. Aske, Constable, Darcy, and the captains of the pilgrims leaned upon the table, pondering what was before them and what was to be done.

Constable jabbed his finger at a spot on the map. "Shrewsbury's forces are here," he said. He moved his finger. "And Suffolk's are here, not far from Newark. It seems likely that they had originally planned to hold a line here, on the River Trent, to block our advance south. But Shrewsbury's move has separated the armies and spoiled the plan."

"How strong are they?" asked Darcy.

Constable straightened, his face reflecting the flickering glow of the fire. "We think that Shrewsbury has about six thousand men, Suffolk a lot less. They also lack cannons and horses."

Aske nodded. "And how many are we?"

"By my reckoning," said Constable, "somewhere over thirty thousand. And more joining every day. All well disciplined. We have kept large forces here at Doncaster, at Jervaulx Abbey, and we are presently laying siege to the Earl of Cumberland's castle at Skipton. North of the River Don we have almost complete control of the country."

Aske smiled, and the others, their confidence solidified, smiled with him.

"Let them come to us!" said Constable. "With God on our side, Mr. Aske, we shall prevail."

The evening was pleasant and quiet, with only the soft voices of the ladies as they chatted over their sewing and the occasional whines of Jane's little dog as he lay on his cushion at Jane's feet, seeming to chase rabbits in his dreams. Jane was pleased with the order and civility she had orchestrated as queen. No more chaos like that when Anne Boleyn held the title. No more wild parties and dances in the private chambers. Jane had her strict standards, and they were obeyed. Voices were to be restrained and the music kept gentle. She had even determined how many pearls a lady could have sewn on her dress or in her coif. There was no need for those around her to be brash and ungodly in word, action, or dress.

Lady Rochford entered the chamber and curtsied.

Jane paused with her needle. "Lady Rochford?"

"The king is still confined to his chambers by his physicians' orders, but sends you his regrets and hopes you are well."

Jane shook her head sadly. Her poor husband, suffering so with his leg, and now troubled by the uprising of the commons. "I worry for him so much," she said. "Especially at such a time."

"Your Majesty is right to do so," said Lady Rochford, her pretty face clouding with dark passion. "These rebels are nothing but villains. They are totally alienated from true religion. Instead of believing in God and the Gospel, as we do, they want to take us back to the dark days of ignorance and superstition. And by force!" She paused and lowered her voice in respect of the queen's rules. "I hope to God they will soon be overcome."

Jane nodded. "Yes," she said. Then, instinctively and with a pang of guilt, she touched the cross around her neck, which had belonged to Katherine of Aragon, Henry's first and most pious Catholic wife. "Lady Rochford, there is something I wish for you to arrange for me. I'm sure it will give the king a great deal of pleasure."

Lady Rochford curtsied again, and waited for her instructions.

"Ah," said Ursula Misseldon as she carefully unwrapped the soiled bandage from the king's thigh. "Poor you, Your Majesty."

The king lay upon his bed propped against pillows, dressed in only a long white shirt. He'd drawn up the shirt to expose the wound. His grooms had been sent away, and it was just the two of them, with bedside candles bathing the floor and counterpane in a warm, golden glow.

Henry watched as the red-haired lady, sent by Sir Francis, sat on the edge of the mattress, tenderly slid the bloodied bandage from beneath his leg, and dropped it into a pan beside the bed, taking care not to jostle him as she worked. As she began to unroll a clean bandage, Henry nodded at the small glass vial on the bedside table. "Pour the ointment over it first," he said.

Ursula lifted the bottle, removed the stopper, and sniffed the contents. "I smell sorrel. And . . . linseed?"

Henry nodded, pleased with her curiosity. "Meadow plant, crushed pearls, herb of grace, other things. I concocted it myself. I don't trust my physicians."

Ursula poured the fragrant liquid onto the clean cloth and laid it on the king's wound. He winced sharply and pulled his leg away.

"Hold still!" she said, her brow furrowing.

Henry glared at the woman, but then his face softened. He liked the fire and the confidence he saw in her eyes. He placed his leg back down and allowed the lady to wrap the bandage securely about his thigh.

"You're very brave, Lady Misseldon," he said as she tied off the bandage. "Braver, I think, than my captains."

Ursula smiled at the king, leaving her hand resting on his thigh, tantalizingly close to his naked groin.

"And much more beautiful."

"There," she said. "It's done. I trust Your Majesty is more comfortable."

Henry felt a hot, erotic charge travel from her fingers along his nerves and to his center, where his organ rose stiff, ready, and demanding. Reaching out, he cupped Ursula's face in one hand and pulled the pins from her red hair with the other. As the hair tumbled down over her shoulders, the lady's confident gaze grew into a willing one in the candlelight.

Charles Brandon leaned over the table in the farmhouse's small front room, reading the dispatches that had just arrived, sorting them, making notes, his veins abuzz and his head pounding with urgency. Through the window he heard the practice shots of the soldiers in the meadow beside the house, and the shouted commands of their superiors. It was a stiflingly hot day, and flies had found the table to be a shady place to congregate. Yet again, Brandon hissed and waved them off. Lesser officers stood about the room talking in low voices.

A soldier ducked under the low threshold and into the parlor. Brandon looked up.

"Your Grace," the soldier announced. "The Earl of Shrewsbury is here."

Brandon nodded as the earl entered the room. "My lord."

"Your Grace." Shrewsbury was a man in his late thirties, of medium stature, with broad shoulders and thinning hair.

Brandon dismissed the other officers so he and Shrewsbury could speak alone. Once the door had been closed, Brandon sat on the edge of the table and gestured at the papers strewn across its surface. "We meet at a desperate moment," he said. "Not only are the rebels overwhelmingly strong against us, but even those men I have got I cannot altogether trust. Many of them, I swear, think the rebels' quarrels to be good and godly."

Shrewsbury grunted softly. "Still, the king has urged us to attack as soon as possible."

"His Majesty would not do so if he saw our plight with his own eyes. I have almost no horsemen, and most of those I have are rather the flower of the north. It is not possible, your lordship, to give battle knowing defeat to be a certainty."

Shrewsbury glanced out the window at the soldiers drilling with their sergeant. They were competent, certainly, but so few in number. "Do you have some other plan?"

"I intend to parlay with them. If your lordship agrees." Shrewsbury glanced back sharply, but Brandon held up his hand so he could finish. "My lord, our first duty is to stop them escaping and marching south. If they are talking, then they are not marching! At least we buy some time."

"Then," said Shrewsbury, the twist in his lip showing he was not entirely convinced, "*you* must tell the king."

Members of the king's Privy Council had gathered in the Council Chamber to hear the latest missive from the Duke of Suffolk. Henry leaned back in his chair, staring at Cromwell as he scanned the message that had just arrived from the field. Francis Bryan, Edward Seymour, Richard Rich, and the other councilors were silent around the table, watching their monarch on one end and the bearer of hard news on the other.

At last Cromwell looked up from the paper. "His Grace informs Your Majesty he has no choice in the matter but to treat with them . . ."

Henry narrowed his eyes, and Cromwell hesitated. Then he continued. "In doing so, he hopes to bring the gentry and nobles to treachery, that for their own sakes and their own interests they will disown the commons, if promised a pardon, as in fact what happened in Lincolnshire."

Henry shook his head. "They are not to be pardoned, Mr. Cromwell. Not the leaders. Never the leaders." Several councilors nodded in quiet agreement. Others looked doubtful, but held their tongues. "But," Henry continued, "what terms does my Lord Suffolk intend to offer the commons to make them go home?"

"His Grace does not go into details," said Cromwell. "But to allay Your Majesty's fears, he writes, in his own hand, 'I beseech Your Majesty to take good part whatever promises I shall make to these rebels, for surely I will never keep any of them.'"

This is what Henry liked to hear. He chuckled and tipped back his head. Brandon was the right man for the task after all, a true Machiavellian.

Queen Jane waited in the Presence Chamber for an audience with her husband. She stood in the center of the room near the dais of the thrones, where wide pools of patterned sunlight from the tall windows bathed her golden hair and the rubies on her red kirtle and hood. Jane's ladies gathered quietly and attentively about the marble columns by the door. Other servants waited for orders along the walls beneath the massive ornamental tapestries. Jane's dog trotted in and out among them all, tail wagging, sniffing shoes and hems.

The sight of Jane's sweet face lifted Henry's spirits as much as the plan of action put forward in Brandon's letter. His leg ached, but not so much as earlier in the day. The evening would be a fine one, he would make sure of it.

"Madam," he said with a broad smile, walking to his wife as his courtiers and attendants remained near the door.

"Your Majesty," replied Jane, curtsying, her light yellow gown rustling and the jeweled pendant on the bodice of her kirtle sparkling. "It makes me happy to see you so much improved."

Henry took her hand and kissed it tenderly. "I have a good physician." He was well aware that one of Jane's ladies in attendance was Ursula Misseldon, but in that moment, he loved Jane only and loved her wholly. "But I intend that we shall visit the shrine of Sir Thomas Becket and give thanks."

"I've arranged something else which I hope, with all my heart, will please you." She nodded in the direction of the doorway. The courtiers stepped back, and there was Lady Mary, looking regal in a deep blue gown of satin with wide light blue sleeves. A small coronet of gold and topaz was nestled in her dark brown hair. She approached the king, with Lady Rochford following behind. Henry heard the soft murmurs of approval from those about the room.

Henry said nothing, waiting to hear how his once-arrogant child would appeal to him. And he was pleased when, after curtsying, she dropped to her knees. She gazed at the tiles of the floor and said, "I ask Your Majesty for your blessing."

His heart swelled. At last his daughter acknowledged his complete power and authority. He took Mary's hand, raised her to her feet, and kissed her cheek. "My own darling daughter," he said. Then he stretched out his hand and said, "May I present you to Her Majesty Queen Jane?"

Jane stepped forward and embraced the girl fondly and warmly.

Henry spun about abruptly and pointed his finger menacingly at his councilors. "Some of you, I remember, were desirous that I should put this jewel to death!"

The room went instantly silent, and the councilors blinked with embarrassment. Several looked as if they felt they should speak, though it was clear their tongues were frozen in their mouths. Courtiers glanced at one another nervously.

But then Jane smiled and put her arm around Mary. "It would have been a great pity, to lose the chief jewel of England!"

Henry laughed, and those in the room joined in, quite relieved. Yet Henry saw Mary falter beside him, and then with a soft groan she collapsed to the floor.

Mary's ladies and several courtiers rushed forward, and Jane stooped to pat the girl's pallid cheeks. Her skin was damp and cool, and her eyes were closed. Jane glanced up at Henry, who knelt to help.

Jane pushed the girl's crown from her head and stroked her hair. "Are you all right? Lady Mary?"

Mary stirred, moaning again, and opened her eyes. She glanced at Henry, then back at Jane. Slowly she nodded.

"Are you sure?"

Mary nodded again. Jane and Henry took her arms and lifted her. Jane took the small crown and placed it back on the young woman's head. Mary straightened herself, regained her composure, and turned to offer a trembling smile to those who had come to her aid.

Taking his daughter's hand, Henry drew Mary apart from the others and spoke quietly. "I want you to be of good cheer, Mary. Because I swear to you that nothing now will go against you."

Mary said, "Yes, Your Majesty," and she managed a smile, though Henry saw little joy in it.

Jane joined them, her face still showing worry for the girl. "Are you happy?" she asked, taking the girl's hands.

"Yes, Your Majesty," said Mary.

"His Majesty has agreed to give you lodgings at Hampton Court and others at Greenwich Palace. I've seen them, and they are very beautiful!"

"I am very grateful to Your Majesties."

Henry left the women and joined Sir Francis Bryan beside the windows. Francis's arms were crossed, and he wore a smirk on his face. The king and the noble watched as Jane escorted Lady Mary about the chamber, introducing her to courtiers, who bowed low and made to impress the king's child. Mary moved in such a way that Henry was suddenly and uncomfortably reminded of Katherine and her insufferable dignity.

Henry leaned against the wall, stretched his leg to ease it a bit, and said, "Everyone says my daughter is totally pure, that she doesn't know any foul or unclean speech. Do you believe that? Do you suppose anyone could be that innocent?"

Bryan glanced curiously at the king.

"Go," said Henry. "Find out."

Bryan made his way through the crowd and stood until he caught Mary's attention. She left Jane and walked over to him, her expression doubtful.

"Lady Mary," said Bryan as he bent forward in a lingering bow. "I wanted to apologize for my behavior. I hope you can find it in your heart to forgive me."

"I will try, Sir Francis. Jesus asks us to forgive everyone."

Bryan stood straight and smiled. "If you like dancing, Lady Mary, there is a new game you might enjoy at court."

Mary's brow went up. "What is it?"

"It's called cunnilingus. It's an old country practice."

"How do you play it?"

"Well, you . . ." Then Bryan's shoulders began to shake, and he bit his lip to keep from laughing aloud.

"I think you're making fun of me, Sir Francis," she said, her voice suddenly cooled. She turned and stalked away.

Bryan chuckled out loud once, then moved to Lady Misseldon and tried to squeeze her hand. But she pulled it away and said, "No! *Noli me tangere*. You can't touch me. For Caesar's I am!"

The sound of approaching hoofbeats reached the men atop the narrow bridge, and they turned to look up the road. In the broad field of ripened hay behind the bridge stood a muster of hundreds of Christian pilgrims, shoulder to shoulder, holding their banners and crosses aloft. The sight they created in the sunlight was impressive in its strength and holy defiance. Surely, Lord Darcy thought, the king's men would see this and know the truth, the devotion, and the power of the God behind the uprising.

Darcy, Robert Aske, John Constable, and Captain Sir Ralph Ellerker caught first sight of glittering armor through the autumn-bright trees. Darcy placed his arthritic hands on the bridge railing and offered a quick and silent prayer.

Guide us with Your almighty hand, our God.

The king's men appeared on the road's straightaway and trotted their horses to the foot of the bridge, where they reined them in and then sat studying the vast army in the field. Then Charles Brandon, head of the king's soldiers, dismounted and strolled onto the bridge.

"Alas, you unhappy men," said Brandon, his face set and as cold and hard as his armor. "What fancy, what folly has led and seduced you to make this most shameful rebellion against our most noble and righteous king and sovereign?"

Darcy and Aske exchanged quick glances.

Brandon scowled. "Are you not ashamed? How can you do this, not only giving offense to our natural sovereign lord but also giving you occasion to fight with us that have loved you more than any other part of the realm, and have always taken you for best friends?"

"Your Grace," said Aske, "we mean no offense to the king. But we have a petition which we desire humbly to submit to him, for the restoration of many things which have gone amiss in this realm."

Constable took a step forward, his eyes bright with the challenge. "We demand the restoration of our abbeys and our ancient liberties!"

Ellerker, a thick-barreled man with a pale beard and scarred nose, nodded. "And for a new Parliament to be summoned to address all the people's sincere grievances."

Brandon shook his head. Then he looked at the faces of the adversaries, each in turn. "I can decide nothing here," he said. "But I propose a truce, during which time two of our captains can take your petition and present it to His Majesty. The truce to be maintained until they return. My Lord Darcy, may we talk a moment?"

Constable gave Darcy a sharp look of warning, but Aske nodded his agreement. Brandon led Darcy to the far side of the bridge, away from the others. Darcy could feel hundreds of pairs of eyes watching them from the field.

"Well, Your Grace?" asked Darcy.

"My Lord Darcy," said Brandon. "You more than anyone here have cause to be grateful to the king for his bounty, for the trust he reposes in you and would like to repose in you still. And yet here I find you con-sorting with rebels and traitors."

Darcy held up his hand. It hurt mightily, but he did not let the pain show on his face. "Your Grace, I would rather have my head struck from my body than ever defile my coat of arms. For it will never be said that Old Tom had one traitor's tooth in his head. For my part I have been and always will be true to the king our sovereign lord, as I was to his father before him, and I defy him that says the contrary. For I have always said one God, one faith, and one king."

"If you are as true and loyal as you say, then you can prove it by giving up your captain, Mr. Aske, into our hands."

Darcy's heart clenched in anger and dismay. He glared at Brandon. "Sir, that I cannot and will not do. For a man who promises to be true to someone then deserts him may *truly* be called a traitor! For what is a man but his promise?"

"Your Majesty!" the chamberlain announced with a pounding of his staff. "Sir Ralph Ellerker and Mr. John Constable."

Ellerker and Constable entered the Great Hall of Whitehall Palace side by side, and Constable immediately felt the harsh collective stares of the nobles, courtiers, and aristocrats who had gathered to witness the spectacle of the rebels come to court. Dressed in the richest of clothing and jewelry, they stood close about, haughty chins raised and eyes set and cold, giving the two men only the smallest of space to approach the throne of King Henry. Constable sensed agitation in Ellerker: the man was breathing rapidly, and his gaze flitted about as if he thought he might drown.

Constable uttered a silent prayer for strength for himself and his com-panion.

The king was seated, dressed in white satin and fur, with a crown of gold and rings of rubies. Above his throne was draped an awning of gold cloth. Henry's face was impassive, his back erect, his eyes seeming not to blink. To his right stood his closest advisers: Cromwell, Edward Seymour, Richard Rich, and Lord Shrewsbury.

Constable and Ellerker knelt on the floor before the king. There was a long silence.

"Gentlemen," Henry said at last. Constable and Ellerker looked up, but the king did not give them permission to rise. "I ask you this: What king has kept his subjects so long in wealth and peace? So ministered justice equally to high and low, and so defended you from all outward enemies?"

Constable hesitated. Should he answer? But the look on the king's face told him he was not allowed to respond.

The king rose and stepped down to the kneeling men. "I have read your . . . submission. Your first pretense is that you seek to maintain the faith. But I tell you that nothing is more contrary to God's commandment than rebellion. Rising like madmen against your prince, leaving lands untilled and corn unsown is not the behavior of the proper commonwealth you claim to be!"

"Your Majesty, I . . ." began Constable.

"Hush!" commanded Cromwell. "You are before the king's majesty!"

Constable stared at Cromwell. Here, in this black-robed man, was his archenemy. Here was the root of the evil that had flowed from London to poison the whole country.

Henry stepped around the men, circling them like a matador circling the wounded bull. "You make false claims about our intentions toward the Church. We have done nothing but what the clergy of York and Canterbury agreed was in accordance with God's holy word."

The king leaned over to Constable's ear and cried, "God's *holy word*, gentlemen!" The shout rang through Constable's head, but he did not flinch. Henry stood up straight again. "So how can the simple people then say the contrary? What madness and presumption is it for them to claim the knowledge of God's law? When they are ignorant and less knowledgeable and should rather know their duty?"

The king returned to his throne and settled himself. Still, he did not give permission for the petitioners to stand. "You have seen before, in Lincolnshire and elsewhere, how temperate and forgiving is our inclination. Though rebellion is against God's will, I declare my intention through the pity and compassion of our princely heart to pardon all of you who have transgressed, on condition that you will now lay down your arms. His Grace the Duke of Suffolk will come north again to Yorkshire to moderate with you and make peace and see you disbanded." With that, he waved his hand, and the audience was ended.

Jane kissed the king's hand as he rolled from on top of her, his seed spent and his body drenched in the wash of vigorous lovemaking. She drew her knees up along the crumpled bedcovers, savoring the heat and the intimate pulses that lingered between her legs. Perhaps this was the night she would conceive a son for her lord. Perhaps at this moment God was fashioning a boy in her womb.

Henry sighed contentedly.

"I thank you and Your Majesty for your great mercy today," said Jane. "I think you are the kindest of rulers, and I wish with all my heart the world knew it."

Henry's face turned on his pillow and he looked at his queen. "Sweetheart, the world chooses what it wants to know."

"But you can change its mind."

Henry rolled toward her and kissed his wife on the lips, a kiss that was moist and gentle. "How?"

"I beg you to restore and keep the abbeys. Think what . . ."

Henry's face clouded. "Jane . . . Jane . . ."

But she felt compelled to finish her request. "Think what the world will make of it? That you listened to your people and to your heart . . ."

"Jane." Henry's voice was stern now, though it remained even and quiet. "I've told you before not to meddle with my affairs. Don't you remember what happened to the late queen?"

Jane's arms flushed cold. "Yes . . ."

Henry smiled. "I love you more than her. More even than Katherine."

Jane held her breath, waiting to see what he would say next.

Henry kissed Jane's forehead. "Don't spoil it." With that he rolled over and said no more.

Constable listened to the song of a lone mockingbird beyond the window of the small, sparsely furnished chamber he and Ellerker were given at the palace. Evening had come, and with it a strong autumn wind from the east that threatened rain. However the weather might be, though, the two would stay no longer than morning. They would return north at daybreak to meet with Aske and Darcy, to tell them what the king had said. The mockingbird's melody, so often a sweet and peaceful lullaby, sounded more like a shrill call of caution on this night.

Ellerker and Constable placed their clothing in their respective trunks, packing for their long journey. Neither had anything to say to the other.

The door opened suddenly, and Brandon walked in. Both men stood straight immediately, surprised by the unannounced visit.

"Your Grace?" said Ellerker.

Brandon shut the door behind him.

"Your Grace should know," said Constable, "that our army of pilgrims will not disperse just for promise of a pardon. Our pilgrimage is not over."

Brandon nodded. "I do know. And I have told the king. That is why he has given me permission to negotiate with you further in good faith."

Ellerker put down the shirt he was holding. "On the basis of our petition?"

Brandon nodded. "Yes."

Ellerker smiled and shook his head in relief.

But Constable was not convinced. "Does Your Grace have some token of this 'good faith'?"

"Don't you trust my word?"

"Not for me," said Constable. "For our captain, Mr. Aske. He's a lawyer."

Brandon paused and then drew a letter from his shirt. It bore the royal seal. "Here is a promise, in His Majesty's own hand, to deal with you fairly, openly, and reasonably, as his loving subjects."

Ellerker took the sealed letter and bowed low. "We are grateful and bound to His Majesty."

Constable was silent. The mockingbird sang again.

The evening was late, and the candles on Cromwell's desk had burned down low. Most courtiers and servants were long gone to bed, and the halls beyond the office were silent except for the footsteps of the guards. But the king's secretary could not sleep. He dared not rest while the king's ax hung over his head. He would rather die of exhaustion than beneath the blade of Henry's headsman.

Cromwell finished writing his letter, folded it carefully, and dropped hot wax on the crease. He pressed the royal seal into the wax then motioned to one of his servants, who stood waiting by the door.

"This is for the Lancashire herald," he said. "See it is dispatched."

The servant bowed, took the letter, and left.

The servant did not leave the palace. Looking back and forth to make sure there was no one to pay him any mind, he slipped along the dark corridors to his own small chamber on the lower floor of the castle's north end. Other servants had been dismissed to their rooms and their slumber, but this servant had more to do before he could dispatch the letter and then claim a few hours of sleep himself.

Closing the door quietly, he wedged his chair up against it, then sat at the tiny desk beside his bed. He lit a candle, and as it flared brightly, he heated a knife in its flame. Then he slid the hot metal through the wax seal and opened Cromwell's letter. He read the first few lines, then smoothed out a new piece of paper, lifted his quill, dipped it in the well, and began the laborious chore of copying the letter.

Nearly an hour passed, and the servant removed the chair from his door, put the folded copy into the pouch at his waist, and moved with great care and stealth to the chamber where Constable and Ellerker were spending their last night at court. He leaned in close to the door and spoke urgently and softly.

"Mr. Constable! Mr. Constable!"

He heard a grunting and rustling from within and he waited, his cheek pressed to the wood. Then: "What is it? What do you want? Who are you?"

"I am a faithful man, Mr. Constable. God speed you!" With that, he pushed the letter beneath the door and slipped off into the darkness.

The day was bitterly cold, with winds that lashed bare flesh and stole the breath. It was with great relief that, at long last, Constable spied Pontefract Castle in the distance. He clucked to his horse, and the animal, as anxious as her rider to be out of the wind, picked up her pace from canter to gallop. Ellerker, several strides behind, urged his mount forward as well. Side by side they took the frost-covered hill, reached the summit, and passed through the gate.

Guards of the castle, wrapped in heavy coats, cheered Ellerker and Constable's arrival and gathered around closely to hear their message. But Constable only nodded, tossed the reins to a soldier, and entered the castle, with Ellerker a few steps behind.

Pilgrims and captains greeted them in the great hall with handshakes and vigorous slaps on their backs. Darcy and Aske hurried from the hearthside table to welcome them back. Aske drew Constable and Ellerker into a warm embrace.

"John, Ralph!" said Aske, his eyes wet with gratitude. He seemed to have aged since they'd last seen him, the furrows on his face deeper, his hair fringed with more gray. "We've waited and prayed for your safe return. Thank God! Thank God!"

Smiling and rubbing his hands to work out the cold, Ellerker said, "The king in his mercy has offered us a general pardon!"

Aske whirled his hand about, directing the men and the captains to the table. Once seated, Aske motioned for a servant to bring out tankards of hot cider for all. They raised their cups to one another in salute, then drank.

Then Ellerker wiped his mouth with his hand and said, "The king is also sending the Duke of Suffolk to negotiate and treat with us, without preconditions and on the basis of our demands."

"Is it true?" Aske's eyes widened, and he looked at Constable for confirmation. But Constable said nothing and took another drink.

"I am satisfied," said Ellerker, "as to the king's good faith and mercy. And here's the proof of it." He drew out the letter the king had given them. Aske took it and read it, then handed it off to Darcy.

"We are to meet again. Here," said Ellerker.

As Darcy perused the missive and then showed it to the other captains, Aske gave Constable a hard look. "You have not said anything yet, John. Is it because you do not agree with Sir Ralph?"

Constable ran his finger along the lip of his tankard. "No, I cannot agree."

Aske and Darcy frowned.

"How should I agree when I think that devil Cromwell has such a hold over the king that I account these promises to be absolutely worthless!"

"You don't think we should meet with them?" asked Darcy.

"No, I don't. We should expose their lies. Call a general muster, take over all of the north, and only *then* condescend to a meeting."

The captains murmured among themselves uncertainly.

Aske glanced at Ellerker then at Constable. "Why are you so sure that their word is not to be trusted?"

"Because of this!" Constable pulled out the letter that had been slipped under his door, which he'd carried from London in the satchel at his waist. He slammed it on the table so hard, the tankards rattled.

"What is it?" said Aske.

"A copy of a letter from Cromwell to the Yorkshire gentry. I'll read some to you! 'There is hope they may disperse peacefully, but if these rebels continue with their illegal assemblies and their defiance, then their rebellion will be crushed so forcibly that their example shall be fearful to all subjects, so long as the world does endure!'"

Constable felt a thorn of rage in his throat, cutting his words, his heart. He took a breath and lowered his voice. "As long as the world does endure," he repeated.

"But the truth is they cannot crush us," said Aske. "And that is why the duke is forced to negotiate."

"This sure sign of their deviousness does not impress you, then?"

"I say we do not stop our vigilance. But prepare for our meeting. Clarify our position. Strengthen our arguments and have our church leaders endorse them." Aske leaned on his elbows and gave Constable a solemn smile. "Why should we fear, John, when we are about God's work?"

Constable looked at the captains all around the table, at their hopeful, confident, pious faces. Then he said, "I know we are. I only hope to God that none of us, nor our grandchildren, live to regret this moment."

Chapter Four

"Charles, I wanted to wish you every success for your journey and conference with the rebels," said Henry. He sat at the table in his outer private chamber dressed in a leather jerkin and gold shirt with wide slashed sleeves. One booted foot was extended casually. A low fire crackled in the fireplace, and a servant was busy stacking wood to keep the blaze going.

Brandon bowed. "I am grateful to Your Majesty."

"You know," said Henry, looking at his friend, an expression of magnanimity on his face, "we desire more than anything else a peaceful remedy. You have our permission to prolong the truce for as long as necessary. You may also affirm our general pardon to the rebels."

Brandon nodded.

Then Henry smiled darkly. "Except for their leaders. I will never forgive their leaders. I want them brought to you still, with halters around their necks."

Brandon considered this for a moment. Then he spoke carefully. "Your Majesty knows the rebels no doubt unjustly blame Master Cromwell for many of their actions. Repeatedly they ask for his removal and punishment. What should I tell them?"

Henry snatched up an oddly shaped yellow fruit from a basket on the table. He took a deep bite of it and winked at Brandon. Wiping juice from the corners of his mouth, he said, "You know what this is, Charles? Fruit from the New World. New things come in. Everything changes.

I have a great appetite for novelty." He took another bite and grinned. "Tell them what you like!"

It was clear to Brandon that efforts had been made to ensure that the meeting between him and the leaders of the rebels—or the pilgrims, as they preferred to be called—was a historic, significant moment. The great hall of Pontefract Castle had been dressed in tapestries and colorful flags, and the table was draped with a white cloth embroidered in gold. Fresh beeswax candles burned in stands against the wall and in brass holders at the center of the table. It was too late in the year for flowers, so velvet ribbons of blue, red, and white—England's colors—and sprigs of berry-bearing holly had been gathered into arrangements along the walls and on the mantel. Seated at the table, Brandon was dressed in half-armor and flanked by Shrewsbury and attending nobles of his choice, all wearing their robes of office.

Opposite Brandon were the pilgrims' captains: Aske, Darcy, Constable, and Ellerker. They sat proud and erect, yet Brandon could see in their faces that they were war-weary and hopeful for a resolution. Except for Constable. His young face was shaded and troubled. Behind the captains stood other, lower-ranked pilgrims, invited to witness the meeting. Rugged men all in their plain tunics and pilgrims' badges. They stood somberly, arms at their sides.

"Gentlemen," said Brandon, putting his hand atop a piece of paper before him. "I've read this, your new petition. Among other articles, you ask for the setting up of a special convocation or parliament to debate without fear or His Majesty's displeasure questions of royal supremacy, heresy, and the maintenance of faith. I can tell you now that the king has graciously conceded to your request. A special parliament will be summoned, to be held not far away at Westminster, but here in York, to debate and decide on all these questions."

A murmur of pleasant surprise ran through the assembly of pilgrims.

"Your Grace," said Constable, raising a hand to interrupt. He was not smiling. "We have asked for the heresies of Luther, Wycliffe, and Tyndale to be annulled and destroyed. We have asked that the heretics, bishops, and temporal be punished. That Cromwell, Audley, Sir Richard Rich be punished as subverters of the good laws of this realm and maintainers of false sects."

"That is not for me to decide, whatever my true feelings," said Brandon calmly. "Such questions are exactly what the special parliament will be constituted to decide."

Aske leaned on his elbow. "Is it true that this parliament can also debate the question of papal obedience, touching the cure of souls, and the legitimacy of the Lady Mary?"

"Yes, Mr. Aske. I guarantee all these great matters can be laid before the Parliament without fear or favor."

"And the king is still willing to offer a general pardon?" asked Darcy.

"Yes," said Brandon. "I say that without hesitation. The more His Majesty understands the causes of this uprising, and the loyalty of the pilgrims to his person and rule, the more is he persuaded to show clemency."

The captains of the pilgrims glanced at one another.

"There is one other great matter," said Aske. "Your Grace knows that we demand the suppressed abbeys should stand, or be restored. This is our sticking point."

Brandon nodded. "What I can say about that is that all further destruction of the abbeys will cease, until Parliament meets. It will decide if and when to restore the others."

Aske sat back, pondering this, and then glanced at his fellows. Most showed signs of general approval, while others were clearly delighted with the meeting's outcome. Constable's face, however, was unreadable. Then Aske looked at Brandon again. "Your Grace will appreciate that I must put these peace terms before a muster of the commons—before the people—for their approval."

Brandon inclined his head. "Certainly."

The sight stirred Aske's heart greatly, and he found himself holding his breath before he could speak. Spread out before him across the wide sloping hillside was a gathering of hundreds of pilgrims who had come to hear the proclamation. They still wore their badges upon the breasts, still clutched their arms and held aloft the banners of the Five Wounds of Christ, which snapped in the cold wind. The men's upturned faces were beautiful to their leader: stoic and proud, strong and fearless, etched with scars, pockmarks, and reverent determination.

To Aske's right stood Darcy and Constable. To his left, a herald with a scroll. Overhead, the sun winked in and out from behind winter-white clouds.

"My friends," said Aske in a voice loud enough for all who had congregated outside Pontefract's walls to hear. "We thank God and the king's majesty for the peaceful success of our pilgrimage. Which is why I ask every one of you now, after you have heard the king's herald, to disperse and lay down your arms. It's almost Christmas. Go home and celebrate the birth of our Lord Jesus Christ with your wives and families, firm in the knowledge that our faith is saved."

Aske nodded to the herald, who unrolled the paper and held it out to read. "'His gracious Majesty King Henry VIII hereby pardons by royal command all those subjects who have transgressed and risen in unlawful rebellion. In his great mercy they shall not be punished or oppressed so long as they do now agree willingly to end their rebellion and disband their unlawful armies. So help you God.'"

"Those who are agreed," Aske called, "say, 'Aye.'"

A collective reverberating shout erupted across the field. "Aye!" Relieved of their duties, the pilgrims then dropped their staves, cheered, and embraced one another. Then, in unison, they saluted Aske, who felt his spirit rise in thanksgiving.

The day was nearly over. There was one last important matter to attend to before the cause of Christ's pilgrims in England was finished. The captains of the uprising gathered in the great hall ready to accept the king's terms. Brandon stood before the assembly, head high, waiting. Alone and with great dignity, Aske approached Brandon and knelt before him.

"Our faithful people have accepted the king's pardon," he said, "and have gone home."

Brandon gestured for Aske to rise and clasped his hand. Both men exchanged a nod and smile. Then Aske turned to the others. "My friends and brothers, I humbly ask that you no longer call me your captain."

Darcy stepped up to Aske. "We are agreed. From now on we will all wear no badge or sign but the badge of our sovereign lord." With that, he tore the cloth badge from his chest and held it high for all to see. The others in the hall followed suit, holding up the ragged emblems like candles that had been blown out after a long night.

Near the back of the congregation stood Constable, arms crossed, mouth turned down. Aske nodded toward him, encouraging him to come forward. Constable hesitated, then crossed himself, reluctantly removed his badge, and held it out.

Ursula Misseldon gazed straight ahead, her eyes fixed on a portrait of a pompous-looking hook-nosed man in a dark robe and broad cap. She had no idea who he was, and she didn't particularly care. Some noble from years back, maybe a hundred or more years, destined to hang for eternity on the paneled wall of the king's bedchamber. The man stared to the side, his tiny eyes looking more ratlike than human, his lips thin and white. The thought that this old man might have loved seeing a beautiful, naked woman lying on a bed just feet from where he hung on the wall made her giggle softly.

"Hold," came the instruction, and Ursula went still again.

She was stretched out on top of the covers of the king's massive bed, one hand placed beneath her cheek, the other draped casually across her chest, beneath her breasts. Her hair had been arranged so that it flowed in shiny cascades along her shoulders; her nipples were hardened in the chill of the air.

On a stool a few feet from the bed, the artist Hans Holbein sat at his easel, a piece of charcoal in his hand. His gaze flicked back and forth between the nude and his composition, a portrait Henry had commissioned of his mistress. Ursula had no idea how long it would take; she would be patient. It was the king's command.

There was a strange rustling noise on the other side of the curtains that had been hung between the door and the bed to prevent unwanted intrusions and curious onlookers. Ursula turned her head toward the sound.

"Keep still!" Holbein said sharply. But he'd heard the sound, too, and he cocked his head, listening.

Suddenly, the edge of the cloth flipped up and a young man's face appeared; it was twisted in confusion and anger. His eyes were red-rimmed as if he were drunk.

"Oh, my God!" he wailed. "It's true! I didn't believe it!"

Holbein leapt to his feet, nearly knocking over the easel. Ursula snatched the edge of a blanket and drew it up to her shoulders.

Holbein advanced on the young man, his fist raised. "Get out!"

"No!" said the young man, pushing through the cloth and swaying unsteadily. "She's my . . . she's . . ."

"This is the king's business!" said Holbein. "You have no cause being here. Get out! Get out now!"

But the young man dodged Holbein's fists and lurched toward the bed. "Ursula! Ursula, my own love!" Ursula stared at him, unable to speak.

Holbein snarled and jumped at the man again, colliding with him and throwing him backward against the shelving along the wall. Several shelves broke and fell upon the man's head, along with glassware, brass bowls, and candlesticks.

"I warned you!" said Holbein.

The man lay still beneath the debris. Ursula crawled to the edge of the bed. "Is . . . is he alive?"

Grabbing the young man by the front of his coat, Holbein hauled him up and toward the curtain. "Yes, but I . . ." Then he stopped and shook his head furiously. "Get dressed! And lock the door."

Holbein took the man out.

* * * *

Henry turned from the window of his outer chamber, surprised to see the artist Holbein approach him and drop to his knees as if the weight of the world had fallen upon him. The painter was slightly disheveled, his graying hair standing out in places, his face flushed, the chain around his neck knocked to the side.

"Master Holbein?"

Holbein began to shake. "Your Majesty," he said. "I must beg Your Majesty's pardon."

"My pardon? For what?"

"I have committed an assault, within the verge of the court."

"As assault? You?" A small smile formed on Henry's lips. "But you're an artist!"

Holbein could not return the smile. "I was painting the portrait of Lady Misseldon that Your Majesty commissioned, when a gentleman interrupted us."

"What did you do?"

"I . . . I threw the gentleman into some shelves."

Henry began to laugh. He shook his head and came closer to Holbein. He put his hand on the artist's shoulder. "You did the right thing, and I pardon you very freely, Mr. Holbein. I would have done the same."

Holbein nodded, then slowly stood to face the king.

"Just finish the portrait," said Henry, leaning close to Holbein's ear. "I can't wait."

Holbein's fear seemed assuaged. He bowed deeply. "Thank you, Your Majesty."

As Holbein left the chamber, Sir Francis Bryan entered, accompanied by the defeated young man, who bore cuts on his forehead and a swelling beneath his eye.

"Sir Robert Tavistock, Your Majesty," said Bryan.

Tavistock bowed at the waist, and when he looked up, Henry could see anger and trepidation working across his face.

"Sir Robert," said the king mildly. "You look out of sorts."

"Majesty, I have a great complaint to make against Master Holbein. I am engaged to a young woman, but found him painting her . . . naked!"

Henry tried not to laugh. "Naked?"

"Yes, Your Majesty! On a bed. Like some . . . like some concubine. I demand that Your Majesty punish Mr. Holbein severely, for his lewdness and his immorality and his violence against me."

Suddenly the little man was no longer charming in his indignation, but a yapping little dog baring his teeth. Henry advanced on him, so close their noses almost touched.

"You have not to do with Holbein, but with me! I tell you frankly, if I had seven peasants I could make seven lords. But out of seven peasants I could never make *one* Holbein!"

Tavistock flinched and stepped back.

"Now," said Henry through his teeth. "Tell me truthfully. Do you still want me to punish Mr. Holbein?"

Tavistock bowed again and kept his head down. "No, Your Majesty. I ask Your Majesty's pardon. I am Your Majesty's humble and obedient servant and have no complaint to make against Mr. Holbein."

With a curt jerk of the chin, Henry sent the wounded young man out of his sight.

Robert Aske's manor in Yorkshire was built of gray stone and set in a vale surrounded by fields of cattle and sheep. Small outbuildings built of the same stone ringed the main house. The ground was covered with a thin layer of snow that had fallen the night before, and frost iced the windows.

Inside, Aske had gathered his family in the parlor, the curtains pushed back to let in the gray of the winter afternoon. Aske's wife sat beside her husband, her fingers clasped at her waist, her mouth drawn down in worry. His son and daughter, both handsome young adults, stood next to their mother's chair.

Aske opened the letter he held, working apart the wax royal seal that kept it closed. Then he unfolded the paper slowly, nervously.

"The royal seal!" his wife whispered. "What does it say, Robert?"

Aske scanned the first few lines silently, then let out an audible sigh.

"Father!" his son urged.

Aske read aloud: "'My trusty and well-beloved Aske. I am informed that notwithstanding your offenses committed against us in the late rebellion attempted in those parts, you are now at heart repentant. And since you are determined to be a faithful subject, we have conceived a great desire to speak with you . . .'"

Aske's daughter gasped in relief, and took her brother's hand.

Aske continued to read: "'. . . to speak with you and to hear from your mouth the whole circumstance and beginning of that matter.'" He looked up from the letter and into the eyes of his wife. She was smiling broadly, and she reached out to touch his arm. "The king wants to talk with *me*. Can you believe it?"

His family encircled him and embraced him joyfully.

He took the letter to Pontefract Castle the following evening, to share it with Constable, Darcy, and Ellerker. They'd gathered in a small chamber on the north side of the castle. Darcy was seated in a large chair near the fire, his hands wrapped in heavy cloth to ease his arthritis. Ellerker sat beside him on a cushioned hassock, leaning forward on his knees. Constable stood with his arms crossed by the fireplace.

Aske reached the final passage: "'I therefore order you, as our true and faithful subject, as we now repute you, to come to court for Christmastide. You are not to let anyone know, but you will use such plainness and frankness in all things we shall demand of you, that we may have cause to reward you further.'" Aske nodded, as much to himself as to the others, then looked up. "There is a credence attached that I shall safe come and safe go from court, returning before the twelfth day of Christmas."

Constable grunted. "You must make sure that he means to honor the promises Lord Suffolk made on his behalf."

"Is it not obvious that the king has taken this matter to his heart?" said Aske. "This is a letter in his own hand."

"You are still too trusting. I would not go there on my own."

"But there is a promise of safe return."

"Promises can be broken."

Ellerker sat back on the hassock. "Mr. Constable, the promises of a king are worth a great deal more than the promises of ordinary folk."

Constable pursed his lips, then picked up the poker and jammed it about in the coals, stirring up a great red flare.

"Here's what we shall do," said Darcy. "I will arrange to lay post horses all the way between here and London. So that if, God forbid, Mr. Aske, you were imprisoned or otherwise badly treated, I would hear about it straightaway and raise the people again for your defense."

Ellerker and Aske nodded. Constable removed the poker, studied its glowing tip, then reluctantly nodded as well.

The Feast of Candlemass was an elegant celebration representing the purification of the Virgin Mary and the entry of Christ, the Light of the World, into the Temple of Jerusalem. The ceremony was one of the most cherished at Whitehall Palace, at once solemn and reverent and lavish, attended by the royal couple and a congregation of nobles and courtiers, many of whom wore white in honor of the Virgin Mother. Gold and white cloths had been draped along the pews, and countless candles had been lit in the windows, on the altar, and on tall stands in the nave. The light bathed the Chapel Royal with a dazzling, ethereal glow.

From his place on a raised rear seat in the chapel, Richard Rich watched the pomp with a bitter taste in his mouth. He could see the king and queen, in their private pew near the altar, watching reverently as the procession of candle bearers walked up the aisle behind a priest holding a statue of the Christ Child high for all to see. The choir in the loft sang, *"Adorna, thalamum tum, Sion."*

Rich felt someone slip into the seat beside him. He glanced over to find Cromwell in his black robe and gold chain, his heavy brows shadowing his eyes.

"How in God's name, Mr. Cromwell," asked Rich, "are we supposed to banish idolatry, superstition, and empty rituals from all our churches when they are still practiced here at court?"

The look Cromwell gave him chilled and silenced him immediately. Rich followed Cromwell's gaze down to the congregation. It was clear he was searching for someone. Suddenly Rich saw Cromwell draw up, his eyes narrowing much like those of a snake preparing to strike. The prey he'd spotted was Robert Aske.

Aske was overwhelmed by the beauty, glory, and mystery of the Candlemass. It was grander than any he'd attended at home in Yorkshire, glorious, befitting Christ and His Mother—if anything fashioned by human hands could be so called. Standing at the wall near the royal pew with Edward Seymour, the queen's brother and Chancellor of North Wales, he found his attention going back and forth between the ceremony and the king at the far end of the pew. At last, he turned to Seymour and asked quietly, "When shall I meet His Majesty, my lord?"

"Very soon," said Edward. "His Majesty is most eager to talk to you, Mr. Aske. In the meantime, he encourages you to write a lengthy declaration of everything you did during the rebellion, and the reasons for it."

This was to be expected, Aske supposed. The king wanted to understand what had happened among his people to cause such an uproar. Aske looked back again toward the altar and crossed himself. Then his gaze returned to the king's pew and he caught the eye of the queen. She smiled at him, and nodded.

The palace was well decorated for the merry season of Christmas, the chambers, corridors, and Great Hall strung with wreaths of holly and pine boughs and ribbons of red, green, and purple. Exotic fruits filled silver bowls, and an ensemble of musicians had been commanded to entertain at the many banquets and parties. The mood inside and outside Whitehall was cheerful and light, with the maids more likely to giggle, the groundsmen and stable hands—normally quite humorless—more likely to smile. Even the petitioners who came to seek audience with the king spoke more kindly to one another in the hallways rather than engage in their usual mindless bickering.

Henry and Jane sat on their thrones in the Presence Chamber dressed in new clothing sewn for the evening, in deep burgundy and red velvet, fox and ermine fur, and wore crowns with glistening gemstones. They laughed, chatted, and held hands as a quartet composed of fiddle, tabor drum, lute, and pipe played lively tunes commissioned by the king. Attending the royal couple were Cromwell, Rich, Brandon, and Bryan, as well as Jane's ladies-in-waiting and Henry's grooms.

Lady Mary entered the chamber, her head up, her heart pounding. She had been invited to join her father this evening, and of course she would obey, regardless of the feelings of discomfort she felt among many of the others, especially Sir Francis Bryan. The court was raucous and loud, and often looked at her as if they found her more a curiosity than a woman. With Mary was an old friend, whom she had invited to court—with the queen's permission.

"Majesty," Mary said as she approached her father's throne and curt-sied.

"Sweetheart," said the king.

"May I present someone to you?"

Henry smiled openly. "As you like."

Mary turned and nodded, and an older woman stepped forward. She was dressed modestly in a dark gray kirtle and black gown, and her gray hair was pinned up and back beneath a white hood. Her earrings were simple single pearls. "The Countess of Salisbury was my old governess," said Mary.

"I know. I know the lady very well."

Lady Salisbury moved forward another few steps and then dropped into a deep curtsy before the king and queen.

"Lady Margaret," said Henry.

"Your Majesty," said Lady Salisbury.

"You are welcome at court. I know how rarely you quit your fine house."

"It's true I prefer to live a life based on piety and traditional ways, Your Majesty," said Lady Salisbury.

Henry nodded. "You are an example to every courtier here. And how is your son, Reginald Pole? Is he still studying in Italy?"

"Yes, Your Majesty. He is now at Padua University, and has more reason than most to be grateful to Your Majesty, since until very recently you continued to pay his fees."

"I took an interest in him. He showed great promise as a scholar. As well as being my cousin. Still, when he refused my offer to make him the youngest-ever bishop of Winchester, I remember I had to thump him!" Henry laughed, and those within hearing laughed, too.

Lady Salisbury appeared chagrined. "Your Majesty must believe it was not ingratitude on Reginald's part. He was in tears after leaving Your Majesty's presence. But the truth is, my son is too much of a scholar and private person ever to desire public office or notoriety."

"Then, after all," said Henry with a nod, "I forgive him."

Lady Salisbury curtsied again. "Majesty."

Mary cast a quick glance at Jane, who smiled and nodded. Henry saw this and said, "What is that? Are you ladies conspiring something?"

Jane squeezed her husband's hand gently. "We—Mary and I—would like to present someone else to Your Majesty, at this Christmastide."

Henry rubbed his chin. "Very well."

Jane nodded toward the door, and Lady Bryan entered, accompanied by a beautiful red-haired child dressed in a gown as green as a summer forest and wearing a miniature coronet of gold. Her head was held high and her gait was as cultured as that of any proper lady.

"Your Majesty," said Lady Bryan as she and the child reached the dais. "This is—"

Henry stepped down from his throne. "My daughter Elizabeth. You need not tell me." He gestured to the girl. "Come here, child."

The guests in the chamber had ceased their conversations and were focused intently on the little girl, who was now nearly four years old. Elizabeth moved to the king, curtsied, and said, *"Votre Majeste. Ça va?"*

Mary could see that Henry was enchanted. He looked around the room to make sure all had witnessed his clever, beautiful child.

"*Ça va bien, ma petite. Vien ici!*"

Henry picked the girl up in his arms and spun her about. "*Je suis en famille maintenant!*"

Mary looked at Jane, and Jane nodded. The king was happy at this moment. He was with his family. The courtiers burst into applause.

As Henry put the child down, Edward Seymour approached him and bowed. "Your Majesty," he said, "Mr. Robert Aske."

"Mr. Aske," said Henry. Before Aske could bow, Henry strode forward and held out his hand. Aske kissed it, and then dropped to his knees.

"Majesty," said Aske. His voice was raspy with emotion.

"Come," said Henry, raising the man with a smile. "Come with me."

"I am very glad to see you, Mr. Aske," said the king as he ushered his visitor into his private outer chamber and motioned him toward a chair. Hesitantly, Aske sat, and the king followed suit, casually leaning back and crossing his feet. Grooms closed the door and stood beside it, awaiting orders. "For a long time I believe I was badly misinformed about the causes of the disturbances in the north parts of our kingdom. Having now read your full and frank explanation, and listened to the advice of my councilors, I am persuaded of the justice of your cause. I esteem the commonwealth of the realm and the love of my subjects, Mr. Aske, far more than any other riches."

Aske's heart was moved, overjoyed by the king's kindness and openness toward a subject that had caused such anger and torment. It gave him the courage and confidence to speak his mind. "I am truly humbled by Your Majesty's words. And ask, in all humility, if your sacred Majesty intends to fulfill those pledges made in Your Majesty's name by His Grace the Duke of Suffolk?"

Henry thrummed the arm of his chair. "In every part," he said. "The general and liberal pardon agreed to will be extended to all our northern subjects. There will be free election to a Parliament, to be held at York, where members and churchmen, without our displeasure, shall and may speak and show their learning and their free minds. And where all things reasonable shall be restored, for the good stay and ordering of our faith, and of all spiritual causes."

Aske bowed his head. *Thank God for this,* he thought. *Thank God for King Henry.*

Henry leaned forward, smiling. "Furthermore, Mr. Aske, after my Lord Suffolk has come down to you with the great seal to proclaim all this, then—to show the great love we bear our northern subjects—we ourselves shall come to York. And there my queen shall be crowned."

Aske met the king's eyes. He trusted what he saw there, and knew his trip had been well worth the gamble. Darcy and Constable would at last have their fears allayed. "Your Majesty is truly gracious. I swear to you that you will find no more loving and loyal people in the whole of your realm than those in Yorkshire."

The king stood then, came to Aske's chair, and leaned in. "One more thing," he whispered. "You have written against some of my advisers, protesting at their lack of noble blood."

Aske's own blood went cold at that moment. He blinked, then looked down and away from the king. "Your Majesty," he began, "I . . ."

"No," said Henry. "I agree with you. But don't say anything." Then he stood straight and gestured to Aske to join him. "Now I have a gift for you." He nodded at a groom, who stepped forward with a crimson satin cloak. Aske looked at the cloak and then at the king. He bowed deeply. "Majesty," he said, dumbfounded.

Henry signaled, and the groom draped the cloak over Aske's shoulders. As Aske ran his hands over the cool, rich material, Henry said, "It suits you well. Happy Christmas, Mr. Aske."

The light of the moon through Aske's chamber window was like the eye of God, unblinking, constant, sometimes so close he felt he could reach out and touch it; at other times, invisible behind a veil of clouds. The moonglow silvered the bare floor, the bed, the desk, and Aske's hands, which were folded in fervent prayer.

"*Pater Noster, qui es in caelis, sanctificetur nomen tuum. Adveniat regnum tuum. Fiat voluntas tua, sicut in caelo et in terra.*"

A powerful gust of wind slammed against the window, banging the glass as if God were knocking. Aske smiled and continued to recite the Lord's Prayer.

"*Panem nostrum quotidianum da nobis hodie, et dimitte nobis debita nostra sicut et nos dimittimus debitoribus nostris.*"

The door creaked open, and Aske spun about on his knees to see a dark figure silhouetted against the wall. He gasped.

"Mr. Aske?"

"My lady!"

Lady Mary stepped forward into the wash of moonlight on the floor. She wore a long dark cloak and hood over a black dress set with diamond buttons.

"I am sorry to disturb your prayers."

"Not at all, since you are always part of them." Aske stood, and Mary offered him her hand, which he took and gently kissed.

"I only came to wish you well, Mr. Aske, for I know you are here upon God's work. I trust the king's majesty will grant you and your people all their desires."

Aske nodded. "I have every hope now." He looked at the young woman, and his soul was stirred with a great and tender love. "And I hope that one day you will succeed as queen of England, for the better maintaining of our faith."

Mary's smile faded and she looked away, toward the window.

"Lady," said Aske. "You must know how beloved you are to the people. As was your mother before you, God rest her."

Mary looked back at Aske, then took a small diamond button from her dress. She pressed it into his hand. "Remember me by this. God bless and keep you, Master Aske." Without another word, she was gone.

* * * *

The eye of the moon watched through yet another window of Whitehall Palace, staring coolly in at Sir Francis Bryan as he flipped a young woman over on his bed, held her down, and gazed at her naked body. She gazed back, first at his face and then at the organ between his legs, which was more than ready to do its duty. The young woman's long dark hair was tangled with sweat, and her lips were moist and taunting. She smiled, and Bryan pressed his mouth against hers, hard, kissing the smile away. Then he drove himself into her, and then again and again, as the young woman clutched at the bedcovers and moaned.

When they were spent, Bryan rolled away and took a drink from his wineglass, beside the bed. He lay back down again and ran his fingertips over her nipples as if seeing them for the first time.

The woman looked at him with equal curiosity, then pulled up his eye patch, revealing a shriveled dead orb within the socket. Unaffected, she put the patch back.

"That was quite entertaining," she said finally, drawing her hands up beneath her head and winding a strand of hair around her thumb. "But you don't even know who I am, do you?"

Bryan's hand cupped the fullness of her breast and squeezed it just enough to make her wince. "Of course I do. You're Edward Seymour's wife."

She smiled coolly. "If he ever discovered us, he would probably kill you."

"Really?" Bryan smirked. "He always seems so nice. Cold, perhaps, but pleasant enough."

"Oh," she said. "That's a mistake they all make."

The River Thames had frozen over in the season's brutal grip, and London's roads were covered in grit-tainted snow, yet the mood outside the front gate of Whitehall Palace was warm. A large, happy crowd was gathered to watch King Henry and his queen Jane take leave to ride to the great cathedral across the city. The bells had begun to chime, echoing across the river and over spires, chimneys, and rooftops.

Grooms held the royal couple's prancing horses as Edward Seymour escorted his sister through the throng.

"God save the queen!" shouted the crowd. "God keep Your Majesty!" "God bless our queen!"

Jane walked close on her brother's arm, smiling and nodding at the well-wishers, then she whispered to Edward. "How is Father? They told me he had fallen ill."

Edward patted her hand upon his arm. "I was going to tell you at a better time. Father is dead."

Jane stopped and turned to him, stunned. "Dead! But when . . . why?"

Edward squeezed her arm again, and this time it was painful. He turned her to face forward and began walking again. "Keep smiling!" he hissed. Then his voice softened, but only a little. "A week ago."

"A week?"

"Yes, a week!" The exasperation in his voice cut Jane's heart. Tears welled in her eyes, but she blinked them away. She couldn't let her subjects see her distress. "I arranged the funeral. Everything was done to honor him."

"But you didn't tell me," Jane said. "I should have been there."

"I wish it could be otherwise, but it can't now. Your place is here. You have to understand. Later you can visit his mausoleum." Then he raised his hand. "Ah, here we are!"

Jane's bay mare was draped in a red cloth, with a gold-studded breast-piece. Edward helped his sister mount the horse and then stepped back as she gathered the reins and watched for the arrival of her husband.

Edward felt a hand on his arm. He turned to find his wife, Anne Stanhope, who had just stepped out of the cheering multitude.

"I presume you told her about her father?" she asked. "Is she all right?"

"Of course," said Edward sternly. "She's the queen!"

Henry came out through the crowd smiling broadly as the throng broke into fresh cheers of "God save the king!" and "God bless His Majesty!"

Collecting his mount's reins from the groom, he swung up into the saddle, settled his feet in the stirrups, and then gazed upon his people. He scanned the faces—the Seymours, Sir Francis Bryan—and then spotted the face he was seeking, that of Robert Aske. When he spoke, the king raised his voice and placed his hand to his chest.

"Gentlemen, noblemen, and worshipful men of this country, I swear, by the faith that I bear to God and St. George, that I have not only forgiven and pardoned all my subjects of the north by writing under seal, but also freely in my heart. It is my order that those men should now wear the Cross of St. George who have thankfully accepted my free pardon and mean to be as loyal as they were before the insurrection." Henry smiled directly at Aske, who inclined his head.

"And the queen and I wish you all a very happy and prosperous New Year."

Giving the queen a nod, Henry wheeled his horse about, and the royal couple trotted off to the road and then across the bridge as their mounted entourage followed close behind.

"I tell you frankly," said Aske, leaning forward and lifting his hand to make his point. "The king is a good and gracious lord who has granted us, as far as he may, all our desires and petitions." He looked at his friends and former captains as they sat together in a small chamber in Pontefract Castle that was furnished only with chairs and a sideboard with tankards of wine, and breads. A fire roared on the hearth. The harsh weather did not play fair with the old palace; frost had collected inside the windows and along the stone walls of the room, creating tiny crystalline tendrils that seemed to grow and move like living things. Cold drafts circled the room, playing with the flames on the candles and chilling the napes of the men's necks above their collar ruffs.

Lord Darcy, Ellerker, Constable, and several other captains had gathered to hear Aske's report. Aske had thought his words would be received with open, welcoming hearts, and he was dismayed to see the doubt in his friends' faces.

"It's true," said Aske as one of the captains snorted with derision. "I heard it from his own mouth that he intends to hold a free and fair Parliament at York and have the queen crowned there."

Constable, dressed in a plain brown doublet and black boots, stomped a foot and shook his head. "Promises, Mr. Aske! Just more promises!"

"No!" said Aske. "Not just promises! Lord Suffolk is sworn to come here to bring both great authority, the king's seal, and, as he told me, many comfortable answers."

Constable stood and stalked to the window, where he pressed his hands to the sill and stared out at the sleet blowing their way.

Darcy let out a heavy sigh. "I have to tell you, Mr. Aske," he said, "though it grieves me to do so, that since you have been away, there have been many rumors and a widespread mistrust of the king and his council."

"Aye," said one of the captains closest to the fireplace. "The northern lads are up and mustering again at Carlisle, and this time won't be betrayed."

Aske found himself without words for a moment. He looked at Constable at the window, and Constable stared back.

"Tell them to believe me, John," he said desperately. "Tell them to wait for the coming of Lord Suffolk. For another rising now risks *everything*!"

Constable's young, rugged face was set with the clear and terrible conviction that treachery was at hand. "Robert, there was a time when nothing was more sure than the promise of a prince. But now we think these promises nothing but a policy to blind the people. And when we rise again, we will trust no promises."

Aske stood and walked to the door and back, then leaned one arm on the mantel. He felt the hostility in the room, from his very companions and brothers in God's cause. "I cannot believe this. I *cannot*! If you will not trust the king, then at least trust *me*. Have I not guided you so far? Have I not secured a pardon for us all?"

Darcy rubbed his gnarled hands. The captains frowned.

Constable said, "Did you secure the king's absolute promise to restore our monasteries?"

"His Grace promised me that all these matters would be freely discussed and decided in Parliament. I trust him. He offered as much as true and good men could desire of their sovereign."

"But you have no proof," said Constable.

Aske had no reply to this.

Two of the captains stood, and Constable joined them at the door.

"Where are you going?" said Aske. "I beg you, plead with you, for the love of God, not to put this agreement in jeopardy by rash actions and false judgments!"

Ellerker, who had been silent until that moment, said, "Their minds were already made up, Mr. Aske. Even before you came back."

Constable flung his cape around his shoulders and tied it at the neck. "There is no agreement. Only base and empty promises. The king will be moved by actions and not words. We must do now what we should have done before." He and the captains stalked from the room.

Aske looked into the hearth, then down at Darcy's sad, rheumy eyes, which offered back twin reflections of Aske's own face: dark, troubled, uncertain.

The portrait was exquisite. Ursula Misseldon in the hands of Hans Holbein was as beautiful as Ursula Misseldon by the hand of God. Henry stood in his bedchamber gazing at the portrait on the wall near his bed, remembering the texture of the Lady Misseldon's skin, the taste of her mouth and her breasts, the warmth of her flowing locks, and the coarser hair that hid her private treasures. He took a deep breath and left the bedchamber.

Brandon and Cromwell stood waiting in the outer chamber. Both bowed low before the king.

"You," said Henry, pointing at Brandon, "will go north at once."

"Yes, Your Majesty."

"In order to establish due obedience, you will administer an oath to the notable leaders and gentlemen of Yorkshire and Lancashire. They will acknowledge that they made other oaths contrary to their allegiance, and to the great offense of God. They must utterly renounce them, and swear to be our true and faithful subjects."

He thought of the painting of Lady Misseldon, her curves and her sensual charms. Tonight he would call for her. Tonight she would ease his mind and body for a while.

"They must specially commit themselves to obey and even to spend their blood maintaining *all* our laws and assisting the Church commissioners in their duties," he said, continuing his orders to Brandon. "If they will not take the oath, then there will be no clemency. You will apprehend such persons, where it is not dangerous to yourself, and they will be judged by law to suffer execution."

Brandon's expression changed from attentive to uneasy. "What are Your Majesty's instructions regarding the setting up of a Parliament at York?"

Henry rubbed his chin, considering this. Then he said, "You may say there is . . . an unnecessary delay. But let them understand first there is no pardon without submission."

Brandon glanced at the silent Cromwell, then back at the king. Henry could see him struggling with his conscience and felt a growing rage. Let the duke struggle; this was a matter not of conscience but of royal supremacy.

"Majesty, I . . ." Brandon began. "I gave them my word, upon my honor!"

Henry spoke evenly without raising his voice, but even then he could feel Brandon's tension as if the words were screamed in his face. "Let me remind Your Grace that *rebellion* is a heinous sin which cries out to God for punishment. It is the sin of sins, for where there is no right order there is only abuse, carnal liberty, enormity, and Babylonian disorder. These wretched men have threatened the whole realm with uproar, just as they have threatened *me*. And they must pay for it!"

Cromwell lifted his chin. "I agree with Your Majesty. If I might advise Your Majesty . . ."

"No," said Henry, snapping up his hand for silence. "No, you may not." He stared at Cromwell coldly, and Cromwell met his gaze with no sign of emotion. "Your birth, Mr. Cromwell, makes you unfit to meddle with the affairs of kings."

With that, the king waved his hand, and the men were dismissed.

Chapter Five

The forest near Carlisle was cold and damp, a heavy sleet having fallen just several hours earlier and the heavy clouds overhead showing no sign of breaking. Locating dry tinder and wood was a chore, but the men at camp were well experienced in the art of surviving and were able to find the spark within the wood regardless of how wet it was. Smoky campfires burned in scattered spots amid the crude but sturdy timber shelters the soldiers had built. Men stood about the fires warming their hands, talking, and adjusting the spits on which they roasted rabbits and squirrels. Dogs from neighboring farms had wandered in, attracted by the aromas and the men, and were sent away with well-aimed kicks.

Constable rode into camp flanked by six pilgrims. He dismounted and tethered his horse alongside the others on a line that stretched from one tree trunk to another.

"Charlie!" Constable called as he recognized a painfully thin young man with a wine-stained face. He clapped Charlie on the shoulder.

"Captain Constable!" said Charlie, his wide, toothless grin flashing.

"How are we? In good spirits?"

"Aye!" said Charlie. "The lads are up for it."

Constable nodded. "Good. Good. And the rest of them are joining us tomorrow. We'll walk into Carlisle and take the castle as soon as you can fart!"

Charlie erupted with laughter, and waved the captain over to share the warmth of the nearest fire.

Evening fell, and with it another burst of icy rain that came and went within twenty minutes. The hottest fires had been saved; the others rekindled. The men sat upon blankets draped over downed trunks, their coats drawn tightly around them, chewing bits of rabbit off the end of sharpened sticks and drinking ale. Constable looked across the sea of faces in the bobbing firelight, thinking how great God was to bring together such noble and fearless souls. What an honor it was to lead them against the great royal heretic and his soldiers of the Devil.

There was a rustling in the trees behind them, louder than what would be made by a rabbit or a fox. Constable held up a hand. "Hush," he said. A man muttered something, and Constable said, "Hush!"

They sat and listened, their eyes trained well past the fires and into the shadowy cloak of night, where the trees blended together and lost their shapes in a solid sheet of black.

Then, from the darkness, came a muffled shout.

"What's that?" said the captain seated across the fire from Constable. He stood and walked softly to the edge of the camp, tipping his head back and forth to listen, to see. Constable watched, holding his breath.

Then the captain stiffened and stumbled back. He crashed to the ground with his hands to his neck, an arrow through his throat.

"Jesus!" Constable cried, and leapt to his feet, grabbing his sword, bow, and quiver. In that same moment, every other man in camp was up, snatching weapons from the ground, shouting, cursing, and racing for the trees.

The bedraggled pilgrim stumbled into the great hall of Pontefract Castle, his age-worn face gashed and bleeding, his legs threatening to give out from under him. He breathed in great gulps as if he were drowning, and grabbed the edge of the table around which Aske, Darcy, and Ellerker had gathered for a late-night meal.

Ellerker immediately poured a tankard of wine and thrust it into the pilgrim's hand, but he just held it, his hand trembling madly, the wine splashing about the lip of the cup.

"What in God's name has happened?" Aske demanded.

The pilgrim put the tankard on the table. "We were starting to gather, Mr. Aske, near Carlisle, ready and eager to assault the castle." He took a shuddering breath. "But then Sir Christopher Dacre and Lord Suffolk came out of the castle with their men and they broke their spears on us and afterward made a bloody chase and captured scores! And I . . . I saw my two boys slain! And . . . and sirs, we are broken!" With that, the man collapsed into violent sobs.

Aske came around the table and put his arm on the man's back.

"What of Mr. Constable?" asked Darcy.

It took a moment before the pilgrim was able to speak. "Captured," he said. "Wounded. Slashed about!" Then he shook his head and closed his eyes. "But not cold and under the mud, like my poor, sweet boys!"

Cromwell stood from his desk and snatched up the report he'd just been handed. It was the best news he'd read in a long time. He felt a rush of sweet air and the taste of triumph on his tongue.

"We've got them now!" he said to his curious servants as he headed for the door. "They broke their pledges. We shall impose martial law on the whole of the north!"

With that, he was gone.

The tribunal was held in a barn in Carlisle, a high-ceilinged timber structure emptied of its wagons, tack, and tools so that those so appointed by the king could efficiently and hastily question and judge the captured rebels. At a table made of several planks set atop barrels, Brandon and Shrewsbury sat with their hands folded, a scribe at their side, taking statements and pronouncing their decisions. Chaff drifted down from the loft in a golden spray, and scissor-tailed swallows argued in the rafters.

Such a sad lot, Brandon thought, watching the rebels standing in a line that reached out of and beyond the barn. Pushed forward by stern-faced soldiers, they looked beaten-down and defeated, the light of passion burned out in many of their eyes. A few still carried an air of defiance about them, but when brought before the lords and given their fates, most kept that defiance in check.

Brandon spoke to Shrewsbury, and then looked up to see Constable being shoved toward the table by two burly soldiers, who did not let go of his arms.

"John Constable?" said Brandon.

Constable held his young head high. One eye was blackened, and blood was encrusted along one ear. "Aye."

Shrewsbury raised a furious finger. "Say, 'Your Grace'!"

Constable did not repeat the words.

"Do you deny that you acted as a leader and captain of this rebellion?" asked Brandon.

Constable glared at Brandon, his teeth set and his breathing heavy. "No," he said at last. "And I'm proud of it!"

Brandon knew the words he was to speak next, and he did so with regret. "You are to be taken to London and examined further as to your actions and motives."

Constable snarled. "You mean tortured?"

Brandon didn't reply. He jerked his head in the direction of the side door, and Constable was turned by the soldiers to be led away. Suddenly, he broke free of their grasp and lunged forward over the table and leaned into Brandon's face. Brandon sat back quickly.

"You promised us a parliament!" said Constable. "But you lied! You betrayed us! You never meant to honor any of it. Did you? Did you, Your Grace?"

Brandon said nothing, only watched as the soldiers grabbed Constable and wrestled him away.

Shrewsbury took a sheet of paper from the scribe and put it down before Brandon. "Here are the names of those who refuse to renounce their actions and sign the oath."

Brandon glanced at the list. "How many?"

"Seventy-four."

Brandon nodded, and signed the paper.

Horse-drawn carts rumbled across the rocky ground toward the grove of trees, flanked by mounted royal soldiers and followed by weeping women and children. Pilgrims stood in the carts, thumping back and forth against the railings, their hands bound tightly behind them. They looked out at their families with grim expressions of anguish, anger, betrayal, and terrified resignation. Every few moments a wife would rush forward and cry out, "My poor husband, no!" but a soldier would spin about on his horse and threaten her with a whip, and the woman would fall back and her voice would rejoin the eerie chorus of wailings, creaking wheels, and cawing crows.

The carts were guided beneath the low-hanging branches of several large oaks, where ropes with nooses had been tossed and tied. Soldiers climbed onto the sides of the carts and placed a noose over each pilgrim's head. Some of the condemned closed their eyes and uttered silent prayers. Others stared straight at Brandon, who kept back a distance on his horse, watching the proceedings.

Brandon waited until all the nooses were secure and the soldiers had remounted their horses. Women grabbed their children and fell to the ground. Others tore out their hair and ran in helpless circles. Then Brandon nodded. The carts were driven forward. Pilgrims slid off the open back and were left to dance in the air at the end of their ropes.

The screams of the families grew louder. Brandon made the sign of the cross and forced himself to watch until all the twitching bodies had gone still.

"It was all well done, Your Grace," said Shrewsbury over the sounds of soldiers' laughter and belching, and the tune of a pipe. The soldiers had requisitioned a farmhouse for the night, forcing the owners to flee to a neighbor's home, and were celebrating their crushing of the rebellion and the execution of the holdouts. One soldier leapt from his bench beside the fire, straightened up his neck, clasped his hands behind his back, and began to convulse violently. "I dance for the priests!" he laughed. "I dance for the abbeys and the saints and all the wretched shit beloved by the Catholic Church!"

Brandon leaned his elbow on the table and took a drink of his ale. He turned away from the cheerful recounting of the hangings.

Standing near the window, Shrewsbury walked over and dropped down on the bench beside Brandon. He tapped the duke on the arm and raised his brow. It was clear he was well past drunk, and his words slurred happily. "You know," he said, "that His Majesty has ordered us to arrest Lord Darcy, Sir Ralph Ellerker, and Robert Aske. They are to be charged on suspicion of treason, but must not know it."

Brandon looked sharply at Shrewsbury. He knew that the dismay showed in his face, but he didn't care. He upended his mug, downed the rest of the ale, and called for more. Tonight, drunk was the best option.

Holland was trapped beneath the cold cloak of March, with sheens of ice skimming ponds and puddles, glistening on the still-barren tree branches and the tips of windmills, and stiffening the sails of seagoing vessels. Vast fields of spring bulbs pressed up from below the soil, seeming hesitant to burst forth yet forced on by the command of a higher power.

Reginald Pole waited beside a closed door in the front room of a small, tidy Dutch house, trying not to pace about, his hands clutched prayerfully before him. He wore the red robe and cap of a cardinal of the Catholic Church, but was still growing accustomed to their weight and feel.

At last the chamber door opened and six gray-bearded men in plain black garb welcomed him into the room. They were dark-haired and olive-skinned, decidedly Iberian in appearance. The youngest of the six—a handsome man with black curly hair and large, dark eyes— stepped forward, bowed, and kissed Pole's hand.

"Cardinal Pole," the man said. "My name is Diego Hurtado de Mendoza, and these gentlemen are all advisers to His Imperial Majesty, King Charles V."

The other men bowed respectfully.

"Shall we be seated?" Mendoza gestured toward a long, thin table along which chairs had been set. Pole nodded, and the men quietly gathered around the table.

"Sirs," said Pole, fumbling to extract from his robes a letter bearing papal seals. "I carry this letter of legatine authority from His Holiness Pope Paul." He handed the letter to Mendoza, feeling his own hand trembling slightly and trying not to let it show. Once Mendoza had the paper, Pole folded his hands tightly on the table.

Mendoza passed the letter to another man and nodded for him to open it. The man looked it over and passed it to the others.

"We were aware, Eminence," said Mendoza, "that you were on your way here. But, forgive me, we remain a little unsure as to the exact nature of your mission."

"His Eminence Cardinal Von Waldburg told me it was safer not to talk publicly or openly about it before meeting your honors."

Mendoza smiled appreciatively, and nodded for Pole to continue.

"But I am sure you are already aware of the risings which have taken place across England against the king, that heretic Cromwell, and all his sect."

"We have received some information, certainly. And naturally we are intrigued."

Pole leaned forward, his nervousness melting in the heat of his passion for the matter at hand. "These popular risings are the greatest chance we may ever have to restore the true religion to England. But the faithful people of my country need support. Each of us, Señor Mendoza, in our own way must encourage the risings to continue and to grow in strength."

"Even if that means the overthrow of the king, himself, not just his wicked council?"

"Yes. We can imagine such an outcome without fear, because there is another close to the throne with a legitimate claim and a true faith. The Lady Mary." He noted the expressions of approval around the table. "And if not her, there is still another Catholic with a legitimate claim.

A scion of the Plantagenets, who ruled before the Tudors, and would gladly rule after them."

The men glanced at one another and then at Pole, clearly eager to hear more.

"Of whom do you speak, Your Eminence?"

Pole took a breath. "I speak of myself, Señor Mendoza."

"Your Grace must surely know," said Lord Darcy, his aged voice tremulous and his pale eyes blinking rapidly, "that Mr. Aske, Sir Ralph, and I were firmly, emphatically, and openly against this new rising. We believed, and believe still, in the promises and sureties and good graces of the king's majesty."

Brandon stood before the men in the small chamber of Pontefract Castle, having just brought news that had both startled and distressed them. His feet were planted apart firmly, his hand on the hilt of his sword, his face unmoved.

Aske lifted an open hand in appeal. "It is also true that nothing can be done or imagined here against the king's majesty but that I can henceforth and in future give you and the council good warning of it."

Brandon nodded, but said, "I am assured of your loyalty to His Majesty. Nevertheless, the king requires you to come south with me, to explain these recent events, which seem so contrary to his expressed hopes."

Darcy looked at the others. He saw in their faces the same doubts that now cut into his own soul. "Your Grace can see with your own eyes that I am old and sick and unfit to travel."

Aske took a step forward. "Allow me to speak openly to Your Grace. Although I love and trust the king absolutely, and know he would always judge me justly and mercifully, I cannot say the same for some of his councilors. I would rather fear to fall into their hands, my lord."

"Allow me to reassure you," said Brandon. "I will write letters to both the king and to the council in all your favors, which I will show to you before we leave."

Darcy rubbed an aching hand across his lips. The Duke of Suffolk's words were encouraging, but Darcy could sense no truth behind them. His heart shuddered. "Then," he said, "we must go?"

"Yes," said Brandon. "It is the king's command."

Darcy closed his eyes and lowered his head. "Then God have mercy on us!"

The following day broke with a red sun and dark clouds rolling in from the southwest. A crowd gathered outside the castle walls to watch the three men leave for London under the escort of Brandon, his groom, and several royal horsemen.

Lord Darcy sat upon the horse that had been assigned him, a bony-backed chestnut with impatient hooves. It did not care to stand in place, but shifted back and forth, snorting and staring downhill toward the road. Darcy's shoulders were already aching, and his hands, clenched around the reins, felt as if they were full of thistle thorns.

Aske's family had gathered to watch him leave. He drew his wife close and breathed in her sweet and loving scent.

"God bless and keep you, my own dear husband," she whispered.

God, bless and keep my family, Aske prayed silently, his face nestled a moment in his wife's soft hair. For though he trusted the king's good graces, he knew that should some of the king's men have their way, he would be disposed of, and cruelly so. *Keep them, and keep me. Amen.*

Then Aske held his wife at arm's length and smiled gently. "And you, my darlings. But I shall be all right, for I trust in the honesty of His Grace. He showed me the letter he has written to the council on our behalf, and it was good. He said he stood surely for us, and I doubt any harm will come to us. After all, what could be gained by it, when the north must now be appeased and quieted?"

Aske then gathered his son and daughter in his arms. "There now, daughter. Don't weep. You're a Yorkshire lass, and Yorkshire lasses have iron in their souls! Just like your good mother."

Brandon gestured curtly to Aske. It was time to leave. Aske mounted his horse, settled himself in the saddle, and said, "You will see me again soon. I promise." His wife nodded, and his daughter dabbed at her tears.

"Gentlemen," said Brandon. "Are you ready?"

Darcy drew his reins up short, and his horse snorted. "As much as I can be, Your Grace. I trust my horse is slow and kind."

And with a wave of Brandon's hand, the men were off for London.

One of Jane's ladies eased another log onto the fire, bringing on a brief yet bright shower of sparks that went black in the cool air. The queen's outer chamber was quiet, the evening having come and the time for visitors and duties past. While Jane and several ladies sat and sewed, others took care of the final business of the day: bringing in water for the bedchamber, trimming candlewicks, folding the day's soiled linens and replacing them with clean.

Lady Rochford sat closest to the queen, her nimble fingers creating delicate leaf patterns out of silver thread on the kirtle in her lap. Jane was embroidering satin sleeves for a new gown.

After a moment, Jane said, "I wish the Lady Mary would live at court. I miss her very much."

Lady Rochford nodded, her fingers still working the needle. "Yes. And the Lady Elizabeth, too. Is she not the sweetest, brightest, cleverest child?"

Jane smiled. "It is so strange and wonderful that they should love each other so much."

"It has not been easy for either of them. And for all my troubles, I am glad I never had theirs."

Lady Misseldon, who had made the bed in the queen's bedroom, emerged and crossed the outer chamber, linens in her arms. When she was gone through the far door, Lady Rochford glanced at the queen, laced her needle through her stitching, and put the fabric down. "Madam," she said, "I did not know whether to tell you, but the king has taken Lady Misseldon as a mistress."

The queen continued to sew. The fire popped and crackled, and a lady across the room sneezed softly. "He must do as he will. It is *we*, Lady Rochford, who must always honor and obey." Then Jane looked directly at her lady. "Do not be troubled for me. In any case, I have a great reason to be happy." And she smiled.

The following day Henry dined with Jane in her chamber. He arrived in good humor, looking healthy and handsome in a scarlet doublet embroidered with black threads and countless tiny pearls. She noticed him walking more evenly in his tall leather boots, as if his thigh were paining him less. Her heart rose in love and joy as he kissed her hand and sat beside her at the table.

The dinner was served by honored courtiers and witnessed by select nobles, an elegant spread of boiled and seasoned meats, baked fish, breads, fruits, and puddings. Jane refused offers of pastries and duck, preferring a special delicacy that a servant spooned into her bowl.

Henry looked at his wife curiously. "I see you are eating quail's eggs again, sweetheart. Did you not eat them yesterday?"

"Yes, Your Majesty. I . . . I have developed quite a fondness for them."

Henry shifted in his chair, one brow up, his hand reaching out for his wife's. "A *special* fondness?"

"Why, indeed." Jane lowered her eyes modestly. "For some reason I desire quail's eggs above everything else. Even in the night, I find I must send out for some." Then she looked back at her husband and saw the understanding in his eyes.

Henry gestured to those in the chamber with them. "Leave us!"

All bowed and withdrew without comment.

When they were alone, Henry stood and walked to his wife's side. He knelt beside her and touched her cheek lovingly.

"Sweetheart, I think you are with child."

Jane smiled. "I am." And she saw the joyous tears that welled in Henry's eyes. "Oh my love, my love." She reached out, touched his tears, and then kissed her wet fingertips.

*   *   *   *

They dragged him along the dismal passages in the lowest bowels of the Tower, random torches set in the craggy stone walls casting dull, tainted light along the way. Shadows created by the flames were long and distorted. Distorted, too, were the cries within the sealed chambers of the dungeon, where men deemed the worst of criminals were left to rot in the cold and their own terror. The air was thick with the odors of decay, sweat, and torment.

Constable was bound with heavy chains, with two guards at each arm. His hair and beard were dirty and matted, his body was covered in bruises, cuts, and sores, and he had been stripped down to a filthy white tunic and linen braes. He tried to keep his bare feet under him, but the guards' strides were longer than his own and his legs could not match their pace.

He did not know what they had planned for him, though his mind raced ahead madly, trying to know, not wanting to know. His heart beat like a mallet in his chest, threatening to break through bone and flesh.

Ahead was an open doorway with a low threshold. An intense light glowed within. Constable could hear the roar of flames being stoked. He instantly, instinctively leaned backward against the guards, against his chains.

Dear God have mercy! Christ have mercy!

The guards growled and yanked his arms, nearly drawing them out of their sockets, and threw him through the doorway.

Edward Seymour stood in the shadows beside the great furnace, his arms crossed. More guards stood to the other side of the furnace. The door to the furnace was open, revealing a fire too hot and intense to look at directly. The floor, irregular walls, and ceiling of the room were bathed with orange-red tongues of light.

Constable righted himself with effort and stood, sweat coursing down his face, chest, and legs. His breathing came in ragged terrified gasps.

"John Constable," said Edward, stepping from the shadows and coming close to the prisoner. "You are a principal, unredeemed villain and a traitor against the king's majesty. Nothing can save you."

Constable's knees tried to give way, and he struggled to keep them still. He lifted his ravaged face to the ceiling and began to pray in a loud, tremulous voice. "O Lord, forgive them!"

Seymour slammed his hand over Constable's mouth to shut off the prayer, but Constable tipped his head back farther, frantically searching the blackness overhead, watching for the hand of God to come for him, to save him, to protect His servant.

"Forgive them, Lord," he cried, "for they know not what they do!"

Seymour shoved Constable hard and he stumbled backward. "Damn you to hell!" he shouted. "Guards, do it! Do it!"

Guards seized Constable and hauled him across the floor to a wooden table. They threw him down across it, one slamming his head to the rough surface; another dropped the whole of his weight across Constable's back to keep him still. A pair of hands grabbed Constable's braes and pulled them down and off his ankles. His mind and heart reeled, unable to stop what was to come, unable to imagine what was to come.

Oh sweet Father dear God my savior help me!

From the corner of his eye he could see Edward remove a white-hot poker from the furnace and hand it to a guard. *No! NO!*

"Father!" Constable cried to God. "Father!"

The guard brought the poker to the bench. The others spread Constable's legs and held them apart.

"Father!"

The guard forced the poker deep into Constable's rectum.

Constable bit through the flesh of his cheeks and screamed.

Immediately after arriving at Whitehall Palace, Brandon led Aske through the court at a brisk pace, saying nothing, leaving the other man to wrangle with all the possibilities as to what was to come next, few of which were good. His heart began to beat hard against his ribs and his breath came shallow and quick.

"Your Grace," he said as he matched pace with the Duke of Suffolk, looking back and forth at the curious courtiers in the hallways. "I am concerned for Lord Darcy. I think the journey from Yorkshire almost broke him. Where might he have been taken?"

Brandon spoke without looking around. "His lordship is taken care of." They continued on, to the west end of the palace, where Sir Francis Bryan stood waiting for them at a door that led out to another court-yard.

"Here is Sir Francis Bryan," said Brandon with a nod. "I commend you to his care."

"Mr. Aske," said Bryan.

Aske bowed dutifully. "Sir Francis. May I ask where I am to be lodged?"

"I have orders to commit you to the Tower."

Aske's heart froze. He swallowed against a sudden lump in his throat. "But . . ." He looked at Brandon, whose expression confirmed the fears he had tried to dismiss on the long journey south.

"It is for your own safety," said Bryan. "You will be lodged comfortably enough. Mr. Cromwell desires to ask you a few questions."

Cromwell? God help me.

Aske gestured to Brandon, pleading, "I trust Your Grace will—"

But Brandon raised his hand to stop him. "I swear I have done my best for you, Mr. Aske."

Aske looked from Bryan to Brandon, seeing no hope in their craggy faces, no comfort.

"The Duke of Suffolk, my lord," said the servant.

Cromwell glanced up from his desk to find Brandon standing just inside the doorway of his office, his eyes narrowed, his hands tight fists at his sides. Cromwell felt hatred pouring off the man like steam off a hard-ridden horse. He savored the moment.

"You asked to see me," said Brandon.

"Yes, Your Grace." He gestured for Brandon to have a seat near the desk. Brandon did, not taking his eyes off the king's secretary.

Cromwell silently considered the duke with a cold stare.

"Well!" Brandon said. "Explain yourself! What do you want?"

"I have some reports."

"You always have reports!"

Cromwell nodded, pursed his lips, and touched a stack of papers on his desk. "But these are very interesting. They are reports from the assizes at Carlisle, when you sat in judgment upon the rebels who threatened to overthrow the king's majesty."

Brandon scowled. "Everything was done legally and properly. Seventy-four rebels were judged and hanged."

"There's the problem. At one point, all agree that there were at least forty thousand rebels armed and in the field. And yet Your Grace found only seventy-four guilty."

"I hanged those who were the leaders and the most guilty of inciting the rest to rebellion. If you had actually been there to hear the evidence . . ."

Cromwell stood from his desk, his hands clasped behind him, and paced to the window and back. "I must be honest with you, Your Grace. You have been accused of too great a leniency toward the rebels, toward recalcitrant monks and other upholders of the old religion. It is disputed whether your heart and soul are truly engaged in this struggle against these traitorous villains. Or whether, in your heart, you are still a papist." He stopped close to Brandon, a brow raised in question.

Brandon shoved his chair back and jumped to his feet. "Who accuses me?"

"His Majesty." Cromwell enjoyed the taste of that answer on his tongue. "Consequently, His Majesty demands that you now return to the north, and carry out proper and efficient reprisals against these rebels and traitors. You are to make a terrible example of them, and teach those parts the virtues of loyalty."

Brandon stared, stunned into momentary silence.

Cromwell went back behind his desk and lifted a handful of the reports toward Brandon. "Seventy-four is an inadequate number," he said.

* * * *

Lord Darcy struggled to his feet as Cromwell stepped through the door of his Tower cell and stood glancing around the room and its modest furnishings. It was as Cromwell had instructed. Only the barest of comforts for the noble: a bed and blanket, a chair, a desk with several candles, a washbasin, a chamber pot.

"My Lord Cromwell," said Darcy. His voice was weak, his body trembling from the effects of the trip and, Cromwell hoped, great fear and awe.

"Lord Darcy," said Cromwell. He did not motion for the old man to sit. *Let him stand.* He pulled a paper from the satchel at his hip and unfolded it. "Here is a letter of yours. On the nineteenth of January you wrote to reassure the mayor and commons of Pontefract. You wrote that 'I shall keep a clean true heart to God and the king and will ever more further and be a true petitioner for the commonwealth's good.' You signed it 'Yours faithfully, T. Darcy.'"

Darcy nodded. "I remember it. But I am not sure what is wrong with it?"

"I've just told you," said Cromwell. "You wrote it on the nineteenth of January. That is *after* the king declared his pardon, and the rebellion had ended."

"But I understood that the king had also agreed to a free Parliament, where his subjects could still show their griefs and complaints. My letter was only meant . . ."

Cromwell stepped forward, causing Darcy to go silent. "I'll tell you what it meant, my lord. It meant that even after the king's gracious pardon, you had not changed your traitor's heart and opinions. You continued to seek the annulment of laws made for the commonwealth, and you still wished to depose the king."

"Since you ask me for the truth," said Aske, "I will answer that, in all parts of the realm, men's hearts were most hurt by the suppression of the abbeys. Because they thought, perhaps with reason, that this was the first fruit of the destruction of their whole religion in England."

Cromwell nodded. He glanced at the scribe seated at the desk in Aske's dark Tower cell, writing in the light of the single candle allowed the common. This room was even grimmer than Darcy's. The bed had a shallow mattress of straw and a threadbare blanket. The desk had a wobbly leg. The window was high and narrow, facing a jutting exterior wall and letting in very little daylight. "Can you not agree that it was rather the spreading of false rumors—for example that the parish churches were going to be pulled down—which actually caused the rebellion?"

"No," said Aske. "The rumors came later. It was the fact that the monasteries were being suppressed and burnt."

"Tell me why they were so important to you?"

"Because the abbeys in the north gave alms to poor men and laudably served God. They were one of the beauties of this realm to all men and strangers alike. They took care of their tenants, servants, and local communities in every sort of way, from maintaining bridges and sea walls to seeing that girls and boys were brought up in virtue. And when they stood, people not only had worldly refreshment in their bodies, but they also had a spiritual refuge."

Cromwell nodded. "So you begrudged the suppression, and the king's supremacy?"

Aske sighed silently, looked out his small window, then back at Cromwell. He nodded, then smiled ruefully. "After such confessions, what forgiveness?"

Cromwell gestured for the scribe to collect his pen and paper. "You may be surprised to learn, Mr. Aske, that for some good reasons, I am determined to save you." Then he left the cell, feeling the eyes of the rebel leader upon his back.

Catherine Brandon peered into her husband's study and silently watched him for a moment. He sat in a chair staring intently into the fire on the hearth. It was beyond her what had him so troubled. And it hurt her heart.

She stepped into the room and knelt beside him. "You have been here for two days. But still you don't talk to me. Even though you are unhappy."

Brandon would not look at her. "How do you know?"

"You wake in the night. You say things."

"What do I say?"

Catherine put her hand over his, but he made no move to reach for her. "Unburden your heart," she said.

Brandon looked at her then, and she was stunned at the agony she saw in his face. "If I do, believe me, *everything* will change," he said.

It was then she knew that it was not that he'd taken a mistress. It was much more serious. She braced herself for what was to come. "You must still tell me."

Brandon picked up a goblet from the table beside his chair and downed the contents. "I am commanded to return north, to carry out retribution. I must execute more rebels. Only this time without trial or proper process."

Catherine blinked. "Many?"

"Yes, many. Many. Hundreds. Thousands. I must kill men, women, and children, or lose the love of my king."

Catherine sat back, still holding her husband's hand, a cold dread coursing through her veins. "Women and *children*?"

"I have no choice."

"Of course you have a choice! What if they were your own children?"

Brandon shook his head. "I would still have to do it."

Catherine jumped to her feet, letting go of her husband's hand and staring at him as if he were someone she did not know, a man with his conscience bled dry, his heart crushed beneath the boot of the king. She fled, crying, from the room.

Aske stood from his sagging bed when he heard the key in the door's massive lock. *What now, my God? What have they planned now?*

The constable of the Tower stepped in and announced, "His Majesty the king."

Aske fell to his knees as the king crossed the dirty threshold, and he held the position, not knowing whether to look up or keep his eyes on the floor.

"Mr. Aske." The king's voice was pleasant and friendly. Aske glanced up to see Henry gesturing for him to rise. Then the king motioned for Aske to sit on the bed. Henry turned Aske's chair around and placed it so close to the bed that when he sat, his knees almost touched Aske's.

"Mr. Cromwell has reported your words to me," said the king. "I wanted to speak to you about the abbeys and religious houses you care so much about. You have so much affection for the monks, but I can prove to you how far they are from good, religious men. They claim to live in willful poverty, chastity, and obedience. Yet they amass possessions and put themselves outside the law! They are richer than princes, but without our responsibilities. What is *willful poverty*, anyway? And as for their *obedience*! God help us!"

Henry laughed and put a friendly arm across Aske's shoulder. Aske did not move. His gaze flicked uncomfortably from the king's face to the wall.

"How can they be obedient when they disoblige their sovereign lord to whom by God's commandment they ought in all things to obey?" the king continued, clearly enjoying himself. "Instead of thinking of them as good men who have forsaken the world, as they claim, we should think of them instead as sturdy and idle vagabonds!"

Henry sat back. "I like you, Mr. Aske. You may be misguided in certain matters, but your mistakes are honest. I know that, at heart, you are among the most loyal of men."

"I love and respect Your Majesty above all things," said Aske softly, urgently. "I would never seek to offend you."

Henry smiled again, and nodded.

"Majesty," said Francis Bryan as he entered the king's outer private chamber. "The boatman from Calais is here!"

"Let's see," said Henry, waving the man in. The king shoved aside papers from the central table to make room for the heavy crate the man was carrying. The boatman slid the crate on to the table and then bowed deeply.

"Majesty!"

Henry nodded for the man to get on with it. The boatman put a key in the lock, pulled open the latch, and lifted the lid. Inside was a thick nest of straw.

"Careful," said Henry. "They're fragile. Here, now, let me." He pushed the boatman aside and gently felt under the straw. His fingers quickly found what they sought: small, delicate oval objects. He collected two and drew them up out of the straw, holding them as if they were diamonds. Grinning, he motioned Sir Francis to come take a closer look. "Quail's eggs, Sir Francis! Quail's eggs, to feed a queen!"

The rain had been constant for two days, darkening the sky outside Lord Darcy's Tower cell, making his room all the more dank and desolate. Yet as Darcy sat on his bed he focused on the sound of the rain and not on the darkness. He turned his mind to the steady pouring of water from the heavens, and thought of the Lord's good mercy, how, no matter how filthy the body or how lowly the circumstances in which the body found itself, it poured from above to wash the soul clean.

As he pondered this in his heart, his eyes nearly closed, he heard the lock jangle and the door scrape open. He turned to see Cromwell walk in. There was no scribe with him, no papers for him to sign.

Darcy struggled to his feet. "Sir Thomas," he said.

"Lord Darcy," said Cromwell. "Please be seated." He motioned for him to sit. Darcy eased himself back down on the bed.

Cromwell stared at the old man. Then he said, "I've talked about your case with His Majesty. The king thinks it no little shame that noblemen like you and Sir Ralph Ellerker should have suffered such a villain as Aske, a common peddler of law, to sign letters sent to the Duke of Suffolk as if he were your ruler! What on earth brought him, a man lacking in both wit and experience, into this unfitting estimation among you?"

Darcy couldn't help but smile a little. Cromwell had everything planned out, and nothing would deter him from accomplishing his goal and having his way. Not reason. Not truth. Not God.

"Forgive me," said Darcy. "But only someone who does not know Robert Aske could venture such a question. Mr. Aske may indeed be, as you say, a peddler of law, but he is as far from common as it is possible for a man to be. Indeed, I should say, with God as my witness, that he is a very great man."

Cromwell's face drew up and his eyes flashed. "No! He is a vile villain, and the chief cause and provoker of these insurrections!"

Darcy shook his head, feeling something akin to sympathy for the rich and powerful royal secretary. He had no doubt that though the man was first on this earth, he would be last in the hereafter. "Mr. Cromwell, it is not Mr. Aske but you who are the very original and chief cause of all this rebellion and mischief. And though you could probably find some way of having all the noblemen's heads in the realm struck off if you wanted, I trust there might be one left who could still strike off yours."

In his own words Darcy heard his inevitable end, but it did not surprise him, and it no longer frightened him.

His horse was ready, his resolve steady. His goal was his duty, and his duty was to obey the king. Before setting off, Brandon adjusted the stirrups on his saddle then checked to make sure the horse's hooves were clean of stones. The groom held the reins as Brandon ran his hand under the girth to test the saddle's snugness, then gave the horse a firm pat on the flank.

"Father!"

Brandon turned to see his young son, Edward, standing alongside Catherine on the walkway outside the door of their home, watching his preparations. Brandon moved toward them, but Catherine drew the boy close, as if protecting him. Brandon's heart was cut through, but he said nothing. Instead, he stopped and looked at them, wishing his wife could understand.

Edward pulled away from his mother and stepped close to his father, holding out his hand. "Father," he said again.

"Son."

"I know you will do your duty by the king's majesty, and to the further glory of our illustrious house."

"Thank you," said Brandon. He took his boy's hand and shook it. Then he moved toward Catherine.

"I don't ask for your blessing," he said, "but please don't send me away with your curse."

"You are a man of honor," she said slowly and evenly. "I pray to God I shall never have cause to curse or disoblige you. But I beg you—show mercy. Especially to the innocent."

Brandon nodded, but could not look at her directly. He knew he lied with his nod.

Catherine took his hand and held it tightly. He felt the heat of her love, her fear, her passion and conviction. "Always remember that those who have the power to hurt, but don't do so, will rightly inherit Heaven's graces."

Brandon inclined his head and kissed his wife, but he still could not look her in the eye.

Her eyes closed, Jane knelt beside the tub of hot water wearing only her soft linen undergown. She held a pitcher of water in her hand. The front of her gown was damp and clinging to her breasts, revealing the soft white skin beneath, the dark nipples.

Henry stood in the doorway, unseen by his wife, watching her wash her hair. He savored her beauty, her purity and graciousness, her sensuous air and the lovely, rounded bulge of her belly.

She leaned farther over the tub and emptied the pitcher over her head. The water poured down along her hair, her cheeks, her neck, like liquid silk. He wanted to touch the silk, but didn't want to break the spell of watching.

Then Jane saw him, and smiled at him through the warm mist rising from the tub. Henry felt his heart swell. Surely, he thought, never had a king so loved a queen as he loved his Jane.

Aske had been brought into another chamber higher in the Tower, where he was placed before a small panel of judges dressed in black robes and black caps, who stared at him as if he were less than the cockroaches who shared the cells with the prisoners.

Richard Rich, the head judge, folded his hands on the table before him. "Mr. Robert Aske."

"Yes, Your Honor," said Aske.

"You have been accused of conspiring to deprive the king of his title of head of the Church, of seeking to compel him to hold a Parliament, and finally, of levying war against him, all after His Majesty's gracious pardon was granted."

Aske said nothing. His chest was tight, and his stomach in pain from the poor food he'd been given in the Tower and from the certainty that he was doomed. He looked out the tiny window at the patch of pale blue sky beyond. *This is my end, Father*, he prayed. *My fate is sealed. Have mercy on my soul! Give my dear ones strength!*

Rich looked at the other judges, then back at Aske. "On all these counts we find you guilty as charged. You are to be returned to York— where you enjoyed your most frantic triumph—and there hanged in chains as a punishment for your grievous sins against His Majesty's Highness and against this realm."

It was spoken, and it would be done. Aske nodded his head.

Thy will be done, O Lord.

Amen.

CHAPTER SIX

The model of the ship was extraordinary, made of polished walnut and cherrywood, showing in minute detail the features that Henry had desired on his new vessel. He lifted it from the table, turned it about, gazing into the tiny cabins and at the delicate curved canopy and tall, fragile masts. The craftsmanship was superb. *Perhaps,* he thought, *I should reward the designer with something: a title or a coat of jewels.*

Turning back to the business at hand, Henry glanced at Cromwell. "Has Suffolk been dispatched to the north?"

"Yes, Your Majesty."

"What did you say to him?"

"I urged him, as a true knight to his sovereign lord, and a man of war, not to spare but to slay plenty of these false rebels. I said there was no need for courtesy when shedding the blood of traitors."

"And?"

"The emperor will shortly be sending an envoy here with authority to discuss with Your Majesty possible candidates for the hand of Lady Mary."

Henry nodded, then looked back at the model. He could imagine the actual ship on the Thames, bedecked in flowers, flags, and banners. "Tell me," he said. "What do you think of this? It's the *Bucintoro,* the doge's galley. When it's built, the queen will ride in it to her coronation."

"Then it will indeed be a memorable occasion."

"Of course it will have to wait until after my son is born."

Cromwell nodded. Then Henry noticed the paper in his hands. "What's that?"

Cromwell shook his head slightly and the side of his mouth drew up. "This is a pamphlet, widely distributed. Its author is Reginald Pole, of Your Majesty's acquaintance, who has lately been made a cardinal by the Bishop of Rome."

Henry put the ship down on the table. "A *cardinal*? What does the paper say?"

"It . . . it condemns Your Majesty in the vilest terms."

"As what?"

"As a heretic and an adulterer."

Henry grabbed the pamphlet out of Cromwell's hand and ripped it apart. He flung the pieces up in the air and they scattered like snow. "So much for gratitude!"

"Unfortunately," said Cromwell, "there is more. My creatures tell me that the same Cardinal Pole is now in France, and was given a private audience with King Francis, as *papal legate*. He is apparently trying to persuade the French, and others, to help rekindle the rebellions against Your Majesty."

There was a long, heavy silence in the chamber. Henry heard voices in the corridors and ravens arguing in the trees beyond the window. He walked back to the table, leaned on his hands, and gazed at the model of the *Bucintoro*. He touched the smooth polished wood of its bow and smiled. "Every year, the doge sails out in his ship, into the lagoon, to renew his vows of marriage to the sea. To be married to the sea! What prince would not aspire to have such an elemental mistress?"

The punishments had begun. Brandon's soldiers crossed the northern countryside with arrow, sword, and dagger, slaughtering those suspected of being rebels and those who communed with them. Spring fields, newly sown with potatoes, beans, wheat, and cabbages, were trampled beneath the hooves of royal mounts and watered with the blood of the farmers and tinkers and blacksmiths and their families. Vultures fed on the remains.

In a small village, Brandon watched as his men herded the citizens from the rocky hillside vegetable plots they were planting and into an impenetrable corral made up of horses and foot soldiers. Most of the villagers rounded up were men, but there were some women among them, and children, in bare feet. The mothers clutched their children and cried. Several of the men rushed the cordon of horses, but were beaten down with the cold blades of broadswords. Children dropped to the ground and covered their heads, as if flesh and bone could protect them from His Majesty's army, His Majesty's orders.

Brandon rode close to the encircled villagers and called out over the din. "You are traitorous, all of you! You were bound, by law and by nature, to obey the king's majesty, and yet you followed the traitor Aske and rose in unholy rebellion against him. You are—"

Out of the corner of his eye, Brandon caught sight of a young man, no more than a boy, so close in age to his own son, standing in the crowd. His young face was covered in dirt, sweat, and blood from a vicious gash in his forehead. He looked directly at Brandon with an expression of both terror and hope. Terror of what Brandon would demand of the soldiers. Hope that somehow it would not come to pass.

Brandon took a sharp breath, blinked hard to regain his composure, then turned away from the boy and focused his gaze on a distant tree. "It is my purpose here to set a fearful example to subjects who would disobey His gracious and sacred Majesty, who after all in his mercy offered you all a pardon, whereupon you continued with your willful disobedience and your traitorous hearts. For these reasons, His Majesty will not forgive you. And neither will God."

With that, he signaled to his men, who began to move forward, closing the circle even more tightly and driving the commons into one another. They then lifted their swords and brought them down. Again. And again.

Brandon wheeled his horse around and rode away from the pleas, the screams, and the curses of the butchered.

The air was cool, but it did not dry his sweat. The sun in the white sky was hot, but it could not warm the ice in his veins. He rode on, the hooves of his mount thundering beneath him, his hands in a death grip on the reins. To where he was riding, he wasn't certain, until he saw the copse of trees ahead, and the swaying, severed cords tied to the branches. It was here that the first of the rebels had been hanged, their necks broken, their breath crushed out of them—and all at Brandon's word.

God has brought me to this place! God has steered my horse by His hand, that I might know what abominations I have done!

He slid from his horse and landed on his knees beneath the ropes. He scooped up a handful of dirt and stared at it. Was that blood there, still? Blood of martyrs to the cause of God's true Church? Brandon wailed, then struggled to his feet. He paced about beneath the trees, holding the earth to his chest, praying aloud, "Our Father who art in heaven, hallowed be Thy name. Thy kingdom come, Thy will be done on earth as it is in Heaven." He flung the dirt aside and buried his face in his hands. "Forgive me, Lord, Thy poor servant His trespasses against Your flock. O Lord! Batter my heart and let me bleed! Crush and annihilate me and deliver me from evil. Forever and ever, amen, Lord. Amen! Amen! Amen!"

Darcy was dead. Soldiers had placed his head upon a spike outside the Tower for all to see, for all to consider, to make clear to those who gazed upon the ghastly sight that His Majesty held supreme authority and sovereignty, and he would not be challenged, questioned, or mocked.

Yet a small smile remained upon the lips of the executed lord, the smile he had found in his last days of life. It was a curious thing, suggesting a sense of peace and understanding that even the headsman could not destroy. Suggesting a power beyond that of an earthly ruler, a worldly kingdom.

"Sir Ralph," said Richard Rich, "you are accused of taking part in the late insurrection that so wretchedly, unkindly, and unnaturally offended the king's majesty and his whole realm."

Ralph Ellerker stood before the judges in the dark chamber of the Tower. The only illumination came from the candles on the desk behind which the judges sat and from the pale daylight pooling through the narrow windows on the room's northern side. Rich, head judge in charge of Ellerker's fate, studied the prisoner for a moment. Time in the Tower had stripped him of his health and crushed his rebellious spirit, until all that was left was a dirty man with sweat-clotted hair, a tangled beard, and eyes that flitted back and forth as if waiting for the next blow.

"However," Rich continued, "we have taken account of your deposition to the court, that you only joined the rebels out of fear for your own life and the lives of your dependents. We also note your subsequent vows of contrition."

Ellerker blinked as if struggling to understand what Rich was telling him.

"We ask you to sign this," said Rich. He pushed a document to the edge of the desk, but Ellerker only stared.

At last the man said, "What is it?"

"An oath. You swear that you are heartily sorry that you have offended the king's highness in this rebellion. You promise never again to make unlawful assembly and also promise to inform against anyone else who does."

Ellerker stepped close to the desk, staring at the paper as if unable to believe what was being offered him.

"From henceforth," said Rich, "you shall be a true and faithful subject unto the king our sovereign lord Henry VIII, King of England and of France and on earth Supreme Head of the Church of England. So help you God." Rich held out the pen. Ellerker took it in his trembling hand.

"In return," said Rich, "His Majesty will grant you mercy."

Ellerker held the pen for a moment, his eyes pinched together at the corners, and tears coursing down his cheeks. He bent and signed the paper.

*   *   *   *

The deeds were done. Brandon's tally was complete, and the example had been laid before the rebellious traitors of the north.

Brandon and his soldiers turned their horses homeward and rode slowly along a tree-lined road. Early evening shadows crawled across the hard-packed ground in front of them, and unseen owls began their lonely evening calls. Overhead, dangling from the tree limbs, were the last of the guilty commons, their hands bound, their necks bent at odd angles, their faces twisted and frozen in their final moments of agony and fear.

Brandon paused to look at the body of a young man whose eyes were still open, gazing heavenward. Flies had found the orbs and crawled across them, probing with their tiny legs and mouths. This boy, like the other at the village, resembled Brandon's son. How many sons were dead now? How many sons hanged and butchered and trampled did it take to please a king? Would these thousands satisfy him, or would he find need for more blood to be shed? Was his taste for death insatiable?

Digging his heels into his horse's sides, Brandon took off at a gallop, his men shouting to one another and to their own mounts to pick up the pace and follow him.

Henry walked back and forth across his private outer chamber. His dark blue cape flapped about his shoulders each time he turned on his heel. Sir Francis Bryan stood still watching, waiting for his orders.

"Reginald Pole has shown us his true heart," said Henry, his mouth stretched into a frightful grimace. "I want you to go to Paris to protest to the king, on our behalf, for the solemn and pompous reception granted him. Especially since King Francis had already warned me of his 'traitorous purposes'!"

Bryan nodded. "Majesty."

"Ask Francis to deliver the traitor into your hands or face the consequences, and our perpetual enmity!"

Bryan nodded again. Then he drew a breath and said, "What if the king refuses?"

Henry stopped in his pacing, the grimace on his face becoming a cold smile. "Were you not a spy once, Sir Francis?"

"I was, Your Majesty. Indeed. As well as a breaker of codes."

"Then perhaps you could revisit some of your old skills. I would be very glad to have Pole trussed up and taken to Calais. Rather alive than dead."

Bryan bowed, and returned the king's smile.

The queen entered the Great Hall on the arm of her brother and followed by her ladies, and was met with warm and enthusiastic applause by the members of the court. Jane nodded in return, then took her place on a cushioned throne beneath an awning of gold cloth. She folded her hands in her lap over her swollen belly and looked out upon the dancing and merriment. Musicians piped a lively tune that matched the happy beat of Jane's heart. It felt as though the child himself were dancing about inside her in joy and expectation, keeping rhythm with the drum and flute. Henry, she hoped, would join her shortly.

Then she paused and gazed at a far corner of the hall, where Cromwell was speaking to several richly dressed courtiers. The secretary had a furtive air about him as each man bowed in turn and passed something to him, which he quickly slipped into a pocket of his black robe.

"Edward," said Jane, calling for her brother, who was standing nearby with his wife. Edward quickly came to her side. "What is the lord privy seal doing?"

Edward's gaze followed Jane's in time to see a last man offer something into Cromwell's hand, to see Cromwell smile slightly and tuck that something away.

"I imagine those nobles want to buy the leases of some of the suppressed abbeys."

Jane frowned. "So what are they giving Mr. Cromwell?"

Edward rubbed his chin. "Bribes. Mr. Cromwell is already a rich man. Some say the richest in the kingdom."

Jane gasped and looked at Edward sharply. "Does the king know of this practice?"

"He asks no questions, as long as the crown receives its ten percent share."

"Is it not terrible that sacred buildings should be used like this for profit?"

It sounded to Jane as if Edward chuckled, ever so quietly. "If you say so," he replied.

"Then have *you* . . . ?"

Edward took his sister's hand and smiled. "You must understand how clever it is. By allowing all these new men to buy a stake in the kingdom, Cromwell makes sure of their loyalty to the king and to himself."

Sir Francis Bryan followed Anne Stanhope from the Great Hall when the festivities were over. She was heading back to her apartments alone, without her husband, Edward, who remained behind to chat with several other nobles. Bryan caught up with Anne in the corridor and took her by the arm. She spun about and drew a sharp breath as Bryan pulled her into a small closet off the hallway. He shoved the door shut with his boot, pushed the lady against the wall, and began to kiss her face and neck.

"Stop it!" said Anne.

"I have to go away."

"So?"

Bryan paused in his kissing long enough to shove a hand down the front of her bodice to fondle one perfect, round breast. "So I can't go until I've had you."

Anne squirmed against his touch, but Bryan would have none of her resistance. He shoved his body against her even harder and pinched her nipple. The lady sucked air and moaned in anger and delight.

"This is madness!" she said.

"I like madness!"

"It's too dangerous. For God's sake, someone will come in. And what, tell me, what if I conceived your child?"

"And if you do? Lots of women lie about the fathers of their children! What does it matter to you?"

Bryan pulled his hand from Anne's bodice and drew up her skirts. "Admit it, lady, this is your game, too."

Anne shook her head in resignation. "Just do it!"

Aske's cell in York was darker even than his cell in the Tower of London. Yet it was quieter. He no longer heard the screams and cries of the tortured, only occasional muffled footsteps passing by; the scrabbling of mice in the straw that was his bed; the clinking of the chains on his arms, at his waist, around his ankles; and his own drum-loud heartbeats, pounding at his temples. He had been thrown there several days earlier and knew he would never step out again, except to face his death.

The door to the cell grated open and a curate, wearing a black gown and gold cross, entered. Aske could barely see the man's features for the dark.

"Mr. Aske," said the curate. "My name is Richard Curwen. I am an ordained priest and I have come to hear your confession."

Aske swallowed with difficulty. His throat was raw and dry. He stared at the shadowed figure, uncertain if he could trust the man. But what could it matter now? He said, "I confess, Mr. Curwen, that I have sinned in many ways, and will tomorrow make amends with my death. And tomorrow I shall say what I have to say, to show my courage and spare my family, but to you here now, in the privacy of the confession, as God is our only witness, I confess my fear and my hurt."

Curwen stepped closer. Aske could see his face now in the faint ambient torchlight leaking into the cell through the small gaps around and beneath the door, and it was a kind and compassionate one.

"May I speak honestly to you, Mr. Curwen? Promise you will not betray my trust?"

"Never, Mr. Aske." And then, slowly, Curwen reached into his robe and drew out the cloth badge with the design of the Five Wounds of Christ. He kissed it devoutly.

Aske nodded, feeling a rush of love for this dear man. Then he said,

"Tomorrow I must beg the forgiveness not only of our gracious Majesty but also of Cromwell and the other heretics. It sticks in my craw. Cromwell openly said that all us northerners were traitors, and it offended me so much. And then, many times, he promised me a pardon for my life for confessing the truth!" Aske lifted his chained hands to his face and rubbed his eye. Then he shook his head adamantly. "Cromwell is the Devil's messenger, Mr. Curwen. And yet I must beg his pardon or he will hurt my family, and that I will not allow! Bad enough that my wife and children will see me hanged and left to rot in these chains." He suddenly struggled against the chains, shaking and tugging them as if with this one last effort he might be freed. But the chains held, as they always had.

"Mr. Aske," said Curwen. "Is there anything I can get you, for solace?"

"There can be no solace. I will weep awhile, here, in private, and thereafter give myself into God's hands and into His loving mercy."

Curwen closed his eyes for a brief moment, then made a sign of the cross above Aske.

"Wait!" said Aske. "There is one thing. Sewn into my collar." He angled his head as best he could. "There."

Feeling along the hem of Aske's collar, Curwen found a lump, picked the threads free, and removed a small diamond. Seeing it again gave Aske a brief moment of relief, imagining his family and the provisions this would offer them when he was gone. "I was given that by Lady Mary. As you love our cause, Mr. Curwen, please hand it on to my wife. For it will ease her burden."

Curwen nodded and put the diamond in his pocket. Then he put his hands on the prisoner's shoulders. "Shall we pray together, Mr. Aske?"

"Yes. But only in the old way. The way to which I have gladly given my life."

Curwen knelt beside Aske, clasped his hands, and began to pray in Latin.

"Pater noster, qui es in caelis, sanctificetur nomen tuum. Adveniat regnum tuum . . ."

The curate stayed with Aske throughout the night, praying and sitting silently, until the door was opened and he was required to leave. Dawn had begun to creep up on the land, and the gallows had been built in the field outside the castle so that all the citizens of York could come and see the fate of the leader of the rebellion. But Aske knew of these things—the daylight, the gallows—only because of the conversations held outside his cell door. The cell itself was no lighter or warmer for the coming of the day. Mice continued to prowl, and Aske continued to sit in the darkness.

At last he was brought up and out, and the daylight was nearly blinding, causing him to squint. Guards pushed him forward through a muttering crowd, and then he heard the voices of his wife and children. He looked over to see their faces, which were twisted in torment.

"My poor husband!" cried his wife. "Why? Why do they do this to you?"

Aske could not put his arms around his family; the chains held them close to his sides. But he made himself smile and speak calm words from a heart ravaged with grief. "Wife, I promised I would see you soon, and here I am! At a station of the cross, on my way to a better place, where for now you cannot follow."

The guards jerked him forward, but Aske's wife fell on him and wrapped her arms about his chained body. "My darling! Oh my heart!"

"Pray for me," said Aske as the guards pushed her back and away. "That's all. Remember me always in your prayers. I deserved this."

His wife stared at him, shocked. "No. *No!* You do not deserve it! You are a good man, Robert Aske!"

The steps to the gallows were steep and difficult to climb in chains, but the guards gave Aske no assistance. He struggled upward, one step at a time, his shackles cutting into his ankles, his wrists. But this was the order of the king, to further his humiliation and pain. The crowd that had gathered below was silent, some with their hands clasped in prayer, others just staring. Aske's wife, daughter, and son were let through to the front, where they stood gazing upward and weeping.

When Aske reached the platform, a guard slipped a noose about his neck and adjusted the knot under the side of his chin. Then he was pushed to the edge.

Aske took in the silent sentinel below, their precious and pious faces, those who would not understand the apologies he was going to make, would not know that it was for the lives of his precious family that he would utter lies. "I ask you to pray for me, for I have grievously offended God, the king, and the world. God I have offended by breaking his commandments in many ways. I have greatly offended the king's majesty by breaking his laws, to which every true subject is bound. By the commandment of God." He looked out at the hillside past the castle, at the sun rising up above the trees, brilliant, unmoved, callous to the sufferings below, single-minded in its intent.

"And the world I have offended since," Aske said, still staring at the sun. "For my sins, so many have lost their lives, lands, and goods. I ask forgiveness of"—he stopped, steeled his soul, and looked back at the crowd—"of His Majesty, also my Lord Privy Seal, my Lord Chancellor, and . . . and of all the world." With that he looked down at his family, who at that moment didn't seem to care to whom he begged forgiveness but were consumed with the horrific spectacle to come. They lifted their arms up and out as if they might catch him and save him.

Then he saw Brandon to the left of the gallows, apart from the others, his eyes tight and his jaw set. The man had come all this way, yet again, to witness the execution.

"And to my lord of Suffolk," Aske said finally, "whose trespasses against me I also forgive with a free heart."

With that, and with no help from the guards, Aske stepped out and over the edge of the platform. The world rushed up and around him, with screams and cries on the air, and then it shattered and went black.

"Your Majesty," said Ambassador Chapuys, with a deep bow. He was dressed in an amber brocade doublet with wide sleeves and a heavy chain of gold and emeralds. His full head of hair had been combed back, revealing his broad and furrowed forehead. He held his bow until Henry directed him to rise and join him and the queen at the table in Henry's private chamber.

Chapuys sat and bowed his head at Jane, who held her head high, smiled, and said nothing.

"Well?" Henry asked impatiently.

"The emperor sends you his love. And he has charged me with the grave responsibility of negotiating with Your Majesty a suitable marriage for your daughter, the Lady Mary."

Henry saw Jane's smile widen. He was pleased that she was pleased that this was at last moving forward.

"Who does the king propose?" Henry asked.

"His Highness Don Luis, the heir to the throne of Portugal and the brother of the emperor's wife, Isabella."

"What kind of man is this Don Luis?"

Chapuys leaned over the table and folded his hands, his face most serious. "He is in every way a paragon. A man of great integrity and virtue. A man who has fought military campaigns and won. A man with a profound knowledge of the world."

Henry nodded. "My daughter has no experience of the world. She is an ingénue, an innocent. She is a very spiritual person. How will Don Luis treat her?"

"Ah," said the ambassador. "He will treat her like a nun."

Jane put her hand over her mouth to suppress a laugh, and Henry grinned and scratched his neck. "In which case, alas," he said, "they may find it difficult to produce children."

After being dismissed by the royal couple, Chapuys rode with his servants northeast from London, along the deer-hunting fields of King Henry, to Hunsdon, to speak to Lady Mary. He found her waiting in a parlor, standing at the window dressed in a gown of dark green and a French hood of gold. She took his hand as he bowed, and they moved to sit next to each other in chairs by the fireplace.

Chapuys was surprised to see Mary looking a bit more cheerful than he'd seen her before. He suspected that the prospect of marriage had brightened her otherwise drab life.

"The emperor has suggested a splendid offer for your hand," he said. "His Highness Don Luis is twenty-four years old, from a very rich and distinguished family."

Mary nodded and cocked her head to the side. Her smile was charming, and quite coquettish. "Go on," she said.

"I have been told he is a great favorite at the imperial court."

"With . . . women?"

Chapuys chuckled. "With everyone! Because he is so honorable and gallant and good-natured."

Mary hesitated, pursed her lips, then asked, "Is he good looking?"

"Yes. I have seen him myself. He is tall, with very dark hair, but piercing blue eyes."

Mary drew back in her chair and her face flushed. She twisted the ring on her finger, then quickly folded her hands to regain her composure.

"I am sure your mother, God rest her soul, would have approved," said Chapuys. "And everyone at court is talking about you! They say the queen has persuaded His Majesty to reinstate you to succession."

Mary's smile faded slightly, and she stood and walked to a small table at the wall, on which were several icons of saints, a burning candle, and a silver crucifix. She touched the heads of the saints, then gazed down at Christ on the cross. "Poor Robert Aske," she said. "I was told his body is still hanging trimmed in chains, for all to see."

Chapuys nodded, and crossed himself.

"I should not be thinking of my own happiness."

Chapuys stood, walked to Mary, and spoke gently but certainly. "Sweet Madam, you have *every* right to think of it."

But as Mary turned from the table, he saw that she was not convinced.

*   *   *   *

Brandon was in his bedchamber, on his knees before a small altar, his hands clasped in prayer. The words, though silent on his lips, were a fierce and furious incantation in his mind.

Our Father, who art in heaven. Hallowed be Thy name.

He heard movement near him, and he turned to see his wife standing above him. She looked at him with pleading eyes, then knelt, crossed herself, and folded her hands.

Forgive us our trespasses . . .

Catherine closed her eyes.

Lead us not into temptation, but deliver us from evil.

Brandon said, "I am reconciled with God."

Catherine opened her eyes and looked at her husband. He said it again, his voice raw with emotion and conviction. "I am reconciled. I have done nothing against my conscience."

His wife's eyes were sad. She sighed.

But Brandon pressed it. "To serve the king *is* to serve God."

Catherine nodded vaguely, crossed herself, and then lowered her head again in prayer. Then she whispered, "I am with child."

The gardens at Whitehall in the late spring were filled with every flower known to the kingdom, in full bloom, bobbing in the breezes and scenting the air with heady perfumes. The afternoon was sweet and warm, with a near-white sky and strands of clouds as soft as baby's hair.

King Henry and Edward Seymour strolled the West Garden, moving slowly around the pond, through the hedge gates, pausing to look at the marble statues of nobles from times long past. Servants followed at a distance, silent shadows in black tunics and embroidered Tudor roses.

At last, Henry spoke. "In a while the queen will reach her full term. I want you to organize the celebrations for the birth of my son."

"I would be honored," said Edward with a bow.

Henry stopped in front of Edward and turned to face him. "I want them to be truly spectacular, with *Te Deum*s and bonfires throughout the kingdom, and free wine for everyone!"

Both men laughed, then Henry leaned in closer. "And a tournament! I had planned a tournament to celebrate the birth of a prince by my former wife. But of course it had to be canceled."

Edward smiled broadly. "This time Your Majesty will have no need to cancel it."

Henry nodded, patted Edward vigorously on the shoulder, then began walking again.

"May I ask Your Majesty's opinion on another matter?"

Henry stopped, tilted his head.

"In the recent rebellion, which thank God and Your Majesty is now suppressed, and the worst rascals properly put to death, great cause was made by some against the lord privy seal, who in some quarters was blamed for it. Frankly, we thought him in danger, whilst trusting he was not so."

Henry considered this, reaching out to break a small branch from a nearby sapling. He rolled the stick in his hands and said, "It was the rebels who demanded Mr. Cromwell's head. Therefore, my lord, by doing so, they saved it!"

They laughed again, and Henry tossed the stick into the pond, where it drifted and spun in the wind.

Sir Francis Bryan slid from his horse and tossed the reins to a waiting groom outside the inn. He turned to watch as Tom Seymour swung his leg over the back of his own horse, pushed free from the stirrups, and landed on the ground. The groom took up these reins, too, and guided the horses around toward the lane leading to the stable. Both beasts were foamy with the ride; they had been many hours on the road. But now the two men had reached their destination, a tavern nestled in the vast wilds of the French countryside.

A young maid with pink cheeks showed the men their room at the top of the winding stone stairs. Bryan opened the door and was startled to find a bloated gentleman in lace and black velvet sitting at a table sipping wine. The man stood and lifted his goblet in greeting. A servant waited by the sideboard to pour more glasses.

"Ah!" the man bellowed happily. "Sir Francis Bryan? Allow me to present myself. I am Count Talleyrand. His Majesty King François has sent me to meet you."

Bryan bowed, not pleased with having his privacy invaded from the outset, but realizing he had a task to accomplish, and here it began. "Count," he said. "Allow me to present my companion, Mr. Thomas Seymour, the brother of the queen of England."

"Monsieur," said Talleyrand. He motioned to the servant, who poured two more goblets and brought them to the Englishmen.

Bryan and Thomas took several long drinks, then Bryan said, "So if the king has sent you, you know why we have come to France?"

"*Oui.* I know."

"And that we expect your government, under its treaty obligations, to apprehend the rebel Reginald Pole and deliver him into our custody."

Talleyrand took another sip and put his goblet down. He touched his belly as if he would belch, and gestured for the men to have a seat. When they did not, he lowered himself into his chair and crossed his legs. "Unfortunately," he said, with a thick French accent, "His Majesty had already granted this Reynold Pole a safe passage, so it would have been dishonorable for the king to hand the man over. Nevertheless, he promised your king by letter that he would expel Pole within ten days. And so he did."

"Then where is Pole now?"

Talleyrand shrugged and took another sip. "All I know," he said, "is that he was allowed to travel to Caserta, under the emperor's jurisdiction."

Bryan glanced at Tom, then moved closer to Talleyrand, put his hand on the back of the man's chair, and leaned down. He spoke evenly and slowly. "It seems to me that your manner of proceeding has been very strange. I fear it may easily lose your master the friendship of mine." The two men held each other's gaze, then Bryan, satisfied the other understood him, stood up straight. "Now I'm hungry. Good evening, Count."

Talleyrand stood, drained his goblet, and bowed. "Good evening, Sir

Francis. Monsieur. *Et bonne vacance!*" He waddled to the door, followed by his servant. As he left, the maid entered with a wooden tray bearing pastries and a boiled chicken. She curtsied and said softly, *"Messieurs, votre repas, s'il vous plaît."*

She stepped to the sideboard and began to arrange the foods on pewter plates. Thomas eyed the maid more than he did the food.

Bryan said quietly, "Tom, the conquest of a French spy is really no conquest at all."

Tom sighed. "What a pity."

Done with her chore, the maid curtsied again and went out. Bryan and Thomas drew chairs to the table.

"So," said Thomas as he picked up a large bun and tore it in half, "where is Caserta? Forgive my ignorance."

"In Italy. North of Naples. Nice old town." Bryan pulled a leg off the chicken and took a bite. In between chews he said, "I tell you this, Tom. If we find Pole, I'll not truss him up. I'm going to kill him with my own hands!" Then he grinned and wiped the grease from his mouth with his shirtsleeve.

The king called the bishops together to meet with him in his private chambers. They came with haste, dressed in their heavy robes and capes, skullcaps and rings, with stern faces etched by years of piety and holy devotion, and for a few, perhaps from the sacrifice of chastity. Henry had words for them, and they would hear him and obey.

Among the clergy were Bishops Gardiner and Tunstall, who stood at the front of the gathering, heads up at the pious angle that seemed peculiar to men of God.

Henry paced before the bishops, studying them for a moment, then he stopped and said, "Your Graces, as Head of the Church, I am vexed by your continuing inability to agree on fundamental issues of doctrine and practice. I listen to your sermons and sometimes find them full of evangelical excesses which have never been agreed to and have no place in the Church of England."

Some of the bishops blanched visibly, even as a small smile drew across Gardiner's lips.

"Your Graces," the king continued. "I want unity and agreement established throughout our Church. I desire diversity of opinion to be ended and uniformity imposed. I therefore command you to establish a commission among yourselves to settle these matters and determine the basic articles of our faith."

The bishops glanced at one another and then bowed, robes rustling. Gardiner held his bow longest. "Majesty," he said.

Henry noticed a shuffling by the door at the back of the chamber. A young groom had entered and stood glancing nervously between the bishops and the king. Henry waved him forward with a sharp flick of his hand. The holy men parted to let the groom through, and the young man stooped low before the king. His eyes and Adam's apple were bobbing.

"It's Her Majesty," the groom said. "She—"

But Henry did not give him time to finish his announcement. He shoved his way past the bishops and raced for the door.

My dearest Jane! Dear God, no!

He took the corridor that led from his bedchamber to hers, followed by the groom. His heart thundered and the backs of his hands had gone cold. With every quick step he prayed that God would preserve his family. Bursting into Jane's chamber, he rushed to her bedside as the queen's ladies dropped into instant and startled curtsies.

"What is it?" he asked. "Sweetheart, what is it?"

Jane was sitting up in bed smiling. She took his hand and placed it on her swollen stomach, and then put her own on top of his. Henry frowned, waiting. And he felt it. Beneath the fabric of Jane's gown and the taut flesh of her belly there was a strong, sudden movement.

"Can you feel it?" Jane asked. "Can you feel it move? It's kicking!"

Henry put both hands on his wife's belly and gazed in wonder and awe as the child within her tossed and turned, demanding, Henry supposed, a more comfortable position. Just as would any prince!

"Yes! I feel it. He must be so strong!" He lowered his cheek to Jane's stomach and squeezed her hand. Tears of ecstasy burned his eyes. "Edward! My son!"

"A crown I catch the next one!" laughed Brandon as he and his son, Edward, stood fishing on the riverbank. The October morning was exquisite and seemed heaven sent—the sun was kind and warm, the breezes were mild, and the insects that tended to swarm at the river's edge had decided to leave the fishermen in peace.

The river ran through Charles Brandon's estate, a wide flow that meandered over the fields and through the forests like a lazy snake. Brandon and Edward had ridden for a while, seeking out the best place for fish, and their instinct had been correct. On the grass by the river were several lines of the fat, glistening fish they had drawn from the water.

"We shall see!" Edward laughed and flicked his pole, hurling the line and hook out into the river's depths, where the water rushed fast and cold. Brandon ruffled his son's hair and then cast his own line into the river.

It was then that he saw the man standing on the narrow island in the center of the river. The man held motionless, shadowed by the brush and a small copse of trees. Brandon saw no boat. How could the man have made it to the island safely? He shaded his eyes from the bright sunlight to have a better look, and then he gasped and dropped his rod into the water.

"Father?" Edward asked, frowning. "What is it?"

The man on the island was a rebel. One of Aske's pilgrims. He was dressed in a plain tunic covered in soot and blood. Stitched on the tunic's breast was the badge of the Five Wounds of Christ. Around his neck was a raw and red wound. The man's gaze was steady, accusing.

Brandon's heart began to pound like that of a trapped animal. "Can't you see him?"

"See who, Father?"

"Over there! On the island! Can't you see him? Look!"

Edward looked, and shook his head.

"Tell me you can see him! That man! He's there!"

"Please, Father." Brandon heard the fear in his son's voice, and this frightened him all the more.

"You can see him, can't you? For God's sake, do you see him?"

"No! I don't see anyone. There's no one there!"

Brandon stared at his son, and then looked back at the island. The man was gone. There was nothing on the island but the brush, the trees, and a handful of blackbirds that had alit on the stones to peck about for dead crayfish and bits of bugs.

Slowly, Brandon picked up his rod, and then walked toward his son. But Edward shrank back slightly, fear lingering on his face.

Brandon's spirit sank.

Jane shifted in the chair in her outer chamber and waited until the ache in her back had eased. The pain had come off and on throughout the morning, though never severe or enough to make mention of as yet. Her ladies were seated around her, intent on their sewing, and one read aloud from the Bible. Some mended gowns, others stitched infant clothes, coverlets, and quilts. Each of these bore in some fashion the queen's coat of arms, the rising phoenix.

Lady Rochford put down her sewing, approached the queen, and curtsied.

"Yes, Lady Rochford?"

"Your Majesty," said the lady. "Lady Lisle has written to me asking if Your Majesty might find a place in your household for one of her two daughters. I told her I would mention it to you."

Jane tucked her needle into the infant's cap she was sewing and swept a strand of hair back from her face. She was beginning to perspire, and she could feel a flush on her face and arms. "Have you warned Lady Lisle that life at court is full of pride, envy, indignation, mocking, scorn, and derision?"

Lady Rochford looked pained and surprised. But Jane smiled to show she was teasing, if only a little. "If you have, then she may send her daughters to see me so that I may choose one. Remember, they must bring two changes of clothes, one of satin and one of damask."

"Madam." As Lady Rochford stepped away, Jane felt another pain, this time in her lower abdomen. She put down the infant's cap and pushed herself to her feet. "Lady Misseldon?"

Ursula stood immediately. "Yes, Your Majesty?"

"Help me unlace my gown. It seems to grow tighter by the hour."

"Yes, Madam."

Ursula quickly began unlacing the front of Jane's gown, allowing it to expand to the full extent of its velvet fabric. As she did so, Jane whispered, "If anything should happen to me, be a comfort to His Majesty."

Ursula looked at Jane, her lips parted as if she wanted to protest, but then she only nodded.

Jane took several steps, pressing her hands to her back and trying to straighten up against yet another spasm of pain. But then she stopped, bent over, and clutched her belly.

"Madam!" said Lady Rochford.

Jane shook her head and smiled at her ladies. "Don't be alarmed. But I think my time has come. Lady Mary?"

Mary, who had been closest to the window, embroidering a small silk blanket, hurried over. "Madam?"

Jane spoke softly. "You must promise and swear you will stay here with me now and not forsake me."

Mary nodded anxiously. "I do promise."

"Then all shall be well. Now, go," she said, "and fetch the midwives!"

Henry looked up from the table where he stood, leaning over missives and reports about the state of the treasury, the subdued behaviors of the subjects in the north, the goings-on with the bishops, the building of the ship for Jane's coronation—all things that weighed on him constantly. But one great issue outweighed them all at the moment. How long would it be? When would God bring his son into the world? He thought of it as he lay down to sleep and as he rose in the morning. When would he have his son?

The guards at the door let a groom through to the chamber, and he immediately bowed. Henry saw the look of barely contained joy in the groom's eyes.

"Well?" Henry demanded. "Is it time?"

"Yes, Your Majesty."

Henry pushed away from the table with the heels of his hands and motioned urgently to his servants. "Send my physician to watch over her!"

"Yes, Your Majesty," replied one servant, and he scurried from the room.

To another, Henry ordered, "Fetch my Lord Beauchamp. And Bishop Gardiner. And send the royal heralds into the city with the news! And tell Cromwell . . . tell Cromwell that whole worlds hang in the balance!"

Jane's labor went through the day and into the night. She felt time slipping away from her in the current of pain that rode her body. The contractions came like pounding waves upon a shore, relentless, unending, stealing her breath and causing her to draw up her legs and clutch the bedcovers in a futile attempt to ease the agony. How long had it been? She could not tell. Why wasn't the baby coming? She could not know. She was aware of the midwives, her ladies, and the king's physician milling around her room, watching her, touching her, helpless to do any more than they had done. Lady Mary knelt beside Jane's bed, praying.

As a contraction eased and Jane was able to speak, she reached for Mary's folded hands. "Lady Mary."

Mary looked up, her eyes rimmed red. "Yes, Madam."

Jane whispered for her to bring her the silver crucifix from the jeweled box on the sideboard. Quickly, Mary obeyed, making sure no one else was paying attention. She retrieved the crucifix, brought it to the queen, and slipped it into her hand. Jane kissed it reverently.

Through parched lips she said, "This belonged to your mother."

Mary nodded. "I believe with all my heart she is here and will help you."

Jane nodded, and then another surge of pain coursed through her body. She closed her hand tightly around the crucifix.

The evening was excruciatingly long. Henry had tried to sleep, but to no avail, and so he left his bed for the outer chamber, where Edward Seymour sat at the hearth rolling an empty tankard around in his hands. Henry lifted the wine carafe and slammed it back down, then paced to the wall and back.

"Lord Beauchamp, we have to do something!" Henry snarled. "But what can we do?"

Edward put the tankard down. "Tomorrow there will be a solemn procession through the city, all to pray for the queen, if she is still in labor with child."

Henry stopped his pacing and drew his hands into trembling fists. "If she is still in labor, then God help us! I think to lose both of them!"

He sat with Edward until the sun sent its first pink rays through the chamber windows, and then he donned his cloak and, followed by his servants, went to the Chapel Royal. There, ordering the servants to stay outside, he went in alone and approached the altar.

Dropping to his knees on the floor, he raised his hands toward the cross above him. He prayed with every fiber of his heart and soul, tears and sweat mingling on his cheeks.

"Almighty and everlasting God! Mercifully look upon our infirmities, and in all our dangers and necessities, stretch forth Thy right hand and defend us. Through Christ our Lord!" He held still, waiting to feel the spirit of God come upon him and comfort him, but the chapel remained silent.

Henry squeezed his eyes shut and waited. Surely God would not ignore the prayer of a king!

But God did not speak.

After a time, Henry stood, wiped his face, and left the chapel to return to his private chambers. The court was hushed as he strolled along the corridors, with courtiers bowing silently and then speaking in whispers as he passed. Perhaps, he thought as he reached his private chambers, it would be over now. Perhaps there was good news waiting for him.

Yet the only one waiting for him was Edward Seymour, who had nothing to say. It was all Henry could do to keep from shattering every piece of glassware in the room. They seemed to want breaking in that awful moment, sitting upon shelves and tables, catching the daylight from the windows and fireplace and scattering it into tiny fragments.

Henry dropped into a high-backed chair, rubbed his face until it was raw, and then shut his eyes in hopes of sleep. But it would not come. He got up to pace again, running his fingers through his hair, clenching and unclenching his fists.

After a while he sent Edward out for word, and when he returned, his expression was more solemn than before.

"What?" Henry asked.

"Your Majesty, I have talked to the physicians. In their opinion there is not a great deal of time left. The baby is likely to die unless they cut open the queen's belly to release it, in which case, it is almost certain that she herself will die."

Henry drew a loud and furious breath. This could not possibly be true.

"Your Majesty will have to decide soon between the life of the mother and of the child."

Day gave way to early evening. Jane lay on a sweat-soaked mattress, her head back, her jaws clenched so she would not scream. Lady Mary wiped the queen's brow with a wet cloth as the midwives wrung their hands and stood helplessly at the foot of the bed.

"Please, my lady," said Mary. "Don't give up. For the love of Jesus, don't give up."

Jane heard the words but could not respond. It was all she could do to be in that torturous moment, remembering to breathe, to breathe, to breathe. And then to push with all her might, though it seemed hopeless, futile. She was aware of activity in the room. She had caught a glimpse of the king's physician opening a cloth bundle on a small table he'd moved to the center of the room. There was a low mumbling as the physician said something to a midwife. She saw a flash and then another. Knives? The physician was putting knives out on the table. Jane's weary mind wondered, *Why knives?* but another contraction caught her, and the pain drove all thoughts from her mind.

Edward Seymour had come to keep vigil in his sister's outer chamber, on command of the king. Night arrived, and with it no change in the queen's condition, no child born. It infuriated and terrified Edward that he, a strong man of noble birth and position, was powerless to alter this course of events.

He listened at the door then moved quickly away, wanting to hear what was going on in the bedchamber but afraid of what that might be. He knew the physician was ready to act on the king's command, to perform Caesarean surgery on Jane to save the infant. But he knew that would mean the death of the queen. Either choice was hellish. To lose the prince? To lose his sister and his own blood connection to the throne?

The candles on the tabletops and in the sconces flickered as he strode back and forth across the floor. He stopped for a moment to look at the newly made infant garments upon a table, the handiwork of Jane and her ladies in joyous preparation for the arrival of the child.

If he arrived at all.

He returned to the door, hesitated, then put his ear to the wood. He heard the sharp cry of a newborn baby. He jumped back as if he'd been stung. The child was born. And the queen . . . ?

The door was flung open and Lady Rochford came out holding a kerchief to her face, weeping for joy. Over her shoulder he could see a midwife holding the infant in her arms, while other midwives swarmed around the bed, bringing water and clean linens to bathe the queen. Everyone was smiling and whispering happily.

Jane and her baby were alive. Jane and her son.

He raced through court, bumping into several slow-moving courtiers and knocking down an old petitioner in the middle of the corridor. He found two messengers and sent them for Cromwell and Gardiner. The news was a royal proclamation and it would be done properly.

The men met outside the king's rooms, nodded to the guards, and the doors were opened. They stepped inside to find King Henry seated near the window as if he had not moved for hours, his gaze fixed at something outside, his face drawn with exhaustion and worry. He turned as they came close to the chair and bowed.

Edward spoke. "Her Majesty is delivered . . . of a healthy son."

Henry gripped the sides of his chair as if he thought he might collapse. "A son?" he said, his voice raspy with exhaustion. "I have a son?"

Edward grinned, and the other men bowed in relief. "Yes, Your Majesty. You have a son!"

Henry stared at his subjects for a long moment and then turned to look out the window. He was smiling. "And a future king!"

The days that followed were ones of celebration, in Whitehall Palace and across the city of London. The king ordered fireworks set out along the Thames each evening, launched from every field within the proper as well as on the outlying farms. The citizens were enthusiastic in their compliance. There was a new prince! On the eve of the third day, the cannons of the Tower were set off, exploding joyously and thunderously, alerting all who still might not have heard that God had blessed the union of King Henry and his queen with a son.

The fourth morning dawned with a warm late autumn sun and a whirl of activity and excitement. Nobles and aristocrats gathered in the Chapel Royal for the christening of the prince. Garlands and sprays of autumn flowers—scarlets and ambers and golds—filled the chapel, and pure white beeswax candles representing the purity and goodness of the new infant burned on the altar, in the tall stands, and at the windows.

In the loft, the choir sang a joyful hymn of praise. *"Te Deum lauda-*

mus, te Dominum confitemur. Te aeternum Patrem omnis terra veneratur.
Tibi omnes Angeli; tibi Caeli et universae Potestates! Sanctus, Sanctus,
Sanctus!"

The baptismal procession entered the Chapel Royal, led by King
Henry, Bishop Gardiner, and his fellow bishops in their dark purple
robes. Following the king were his councilors, noblemen, and ambassadors, dressed in their finest capes and cloaks of satin and damask.
Behind the ambassadors came Edward Seymour, carrying the young
princess Elizabeth in his arms, who in turn held the infant Edward's
richly embroidered white christening robe.

The prince followed, carried on a pillow by Catherine Brandon,
flanked on either side by Thomas Cromwell and Charles Brandon. Four
lords held the poles that supported a canopy of cloth over the heads of
the baby and those tending him.

Henry and the bishops reached the altar. The king turned to watch
the procession, and Gardiner held his hands up in silent blessing.

When the infant arrived, Gardiner gathered his naked body gently
from the pillow, then, with his finger, anointed the baby's chest and
forehead with oil. "In the name of the Father, Son, and Holy Ghost I do
baptize thee Edward. May God bless and keep you all the days of your
life, and give you abundantly His grace, through Jesus Christ our Lord.
Amen."

Little Elizabeth, grinning shyly, held out the baptismal robe to the
bishop, who gently dressed the baby. Then the garter king of arms, standing erect in his red-and-gold embroidered tunic and black cap, cried out,
"God, of His Almighty and infinite grace, give and grant good life and
long to the right high, right excellent, and noble Prince Edward, Duke of
Cornwall and earl of Chester, most dear and entirely beloved son of our
most dread and gracious lord, King Henry VIII!"

With that the choir in the loft sang, "Hallelujah! Hallelujah!"

When the ceremony in the chapel was done, an entourage brought
the tiny prince to his mother's bedchamber, accompanied by black-and-
red-coated trumpeters, who stood to either side of the door to herald his

arrival. Only a few entered the chamber—Edward Seymour and Charles Brandon, Lady Rochford and Lady Misseldon, and Lady Mary, who carried the child.

Jane had been clothed in a mantle of crimson velvet trimmed in ermine, and her hair had been brushed and laced with flowers. Henry sat at her side in a chair of estate, a crown of gold on his head, holding her hand. Jane smiled weakly upon seeing her baby.

Mary took the child to the bedside and held him out so Jane, too weak to hold the infant herself, could lean forward and kiss his brow. "Bless you, sweet child," the queen whispered.

Then Mary turned and curtsied as Henry rose from his chair. She placed the baby in his father's arms, curtsied again, and stepped back.

The king stood for a long moment, his head high, his eyes surreally bright. To those around him, gazing upon the king, the most powerful who had ever sat upon the throne of England, Henry had never appeared as tall, as glorious, as commanding as in that moment. He kissed his child, and then began to cry. The tears came unabashed and unashamed. When he spoke, his voice wavered with emotion.

"Edward, Edward my son, I bless you in the name of God, the Virgin Mary, and Saint George."

Those in attendance dropped to their knees, greatly moved.

The evening was late, and a wind had picked up outside, shaking the windows and throwing clouds in a mad spin across the face of the moon. Lady Mary and little Elizabeth lay side by side in a great bed in Mary's bedchamber, dressed in plain white satin nightshirts, staring out at the moon. A single candle sat on a bedside table, its flame dipping and dancing.

"He's a sweet prince," said Elizabeth, turning to look at Mary.

"Yes, he is." Mary rolled over and put her arm around the little girl.

"And he is our brother."

Mary nodded. "The king has waited a long time for a son."

"But," said Elizabeth with a pout, "he still loves us."

"A boy is more important."

Elizabeth crinkled her nose and frowned. "I don't think so!"

Mary sighed and held the little girl closer.

The last days and nights had been long and difficult, but a new morning had dawned. Henry had a son. The world was set right and all was well.

Henry strolled the royal gardens alone, weary but ecstatic, thinking of the future. He would teach his son to ride, to shoot an arrow, to play and write music. When he was older, the boy would learn to joust, though Henry prayed nothing evil would befall him as had befallen his father, leaving him with a leg that was in almost constant pain.

"A son!" he shouted, then listened as the words echoed happily off a far brick wall draped in ivy.

The air was cool and the sun warm, sparkling off the water in the lily pond. Henry looked at his reflection and wondered how much Edward would favor his father.

There was a sudden shift in the air, causing Henry to glance up at the sky. Dark gray clouds rolled in at a frantic pace, churning like angry waves on the sea, covering the face of the sun. Though there was no wind, the leaves on a single tree across the pond began to shake as if blown by a supernatural breath.

Henry's heart was filled with foreboding. This was a sign from God, or from some dreadful hellish demon. Something was terribly wrong.

Jane!

When he reached the queen's private chambers, he found not joyful servants tending mother and child, but weeping ladies and mournful physicians. No one spoke above a whisper. Jane lay upon her bed unconscious, her face slumped to the side. The room smelled of infirmity. Henry grabbed a physician's arm hard enough for the man to wince. "What's wrong with her?"

"Your Majesty," the physician said, "the queen's health has rapidly deteriorated. Yesterday evening she had a loosening of the bowels, and we were sure we could save her. But during the night her fever grew worse again. We have tried everything we know. But . . . her Majesty continues to weaken."

Henry stared in disbelief from those who should have been able to heal her, to his wife, so small, so frail, upon the bed. "I know what it is!" he shouted. "It's child-bed fever. I know, because my mother died of it!" He flung out his arms. "Get out! All of you!" The ladies, physicians, and servants bowed and left the room.

Henry approached the bed, his soul welling in apprehension, his heart overcome with love. He slumped beside Jane and took her hand. "Don't go now, just because you have done everything you promised. Please don't go now. You are all the goodness in the world. You are the milk of human kindness." He stifled a sob. "Sweet Jane! Without you there is only desert, a howling wilderness. Please, God, don't go. Don't leave me! I could not bear it!"

He put his face next to hers on the pillow and wept hot, bitter tears.

Queen Jane was laid out in the Chapel Royal, her body placed tenderly upon a satin bier, dressed in gold and adorned with a jeweled crown and diamond rings. White lilies were laid across her chest. Jane's ladies stood about the bier holding candles, and Lady Mary knelt upon a pillow beside it praying silently.

Slowly Henry approached the bier, with Cromwell, Brandon, Edward Seymour, and Bishop Gardiner following closely. Then they stopped, allowing the king to walk alone to his wife. Jane's ladies stepped back, and Mary rose from her prayers, bowed, and moved away.

He stood gazing upon his great love, his tender, precious, and darling wife, who had given him her greatest gift and then had left him for God's kingdom. Was not Henry's kingdom enough for her? Or had God chosen to taunt Henry's heart now that He had given him a son?

The Lord giveth and the Lord taketh away.

Henry stared at his wife, speechless. And the whole chapel waited in silence.

CHAPTER SEVEN

A slouching fellow in a filthy hooded cape pushed a wide handcart filled with manure and straw down the center of a narrow, muddy London street, scaring off the feral cats and crows that were drinking from the puddles. A middle-aged gentleman with short white hair and a haughty face came along from the other direction and found himself unable to pass by the cart. His face screwed up and he put his hand on the sword at his side.

"Get out of the way, fellow!" he demanded.

The hooded man cocked his head. "Sorry, sir. Were you trying to pass?"

The gentleman snorted. "Of course I'm trying to pass. I'm going to court. Quickly now!"

Other men and women crowded around, grumbling and shaking their heads at the interference, some squeezing past.

"If I knows anything, sir," said the man with the cart, "you's Mr. Robert Packington, member of Parliament. Friend of the lord privy seal. Ain't that right, sir?"

Packington tossed his head and his cape. "Yes on all counts. But I thank you again to move aside!"

"Ain't *you* in a hurry."

"I am!"

"No need. This is the end of hurrying." With that, the hooded man pulled a pistol from the straw, aimed, and shot Packington in the face. And as women screamed and men cried out, the assassin dropped the gun and ran back the way he'd come, disappearing around a corner at the end of the road.

Cromwell signed the paper, laid the quill aside, and placed the document atop the tall stack on his desk. He cleared his throat and looked at his secretary, Risley, who was sorting yet more papers.

"So. Have they caught the villain?"

"No, my lord," said Risley. "He ran off into Cheapside. The sergeant at arms has men swarming all over the area."

Cromwell nodded. "Pray God they catch him. I'm sure Mr. Packington was in every way an innocent victim."

"Then why was he killed?"

"I assume to send a message to me. I am not short of enemies, Mr. Risley. For there is nothing more difficult to carry out, or more doubtful of success, or more dangerous to handle, than to initiate a new order of things."

"Then you think Bishop Gardiner could be behind this? Or my Lord Suffolk?"

Cromwell raised a brow. "I don't want or need to speculate. All I will say is that there are dark forces at work, inside and outside court. They must be defeated. But we must be careful not to act until we are completely sure of who they are and what they want. In the meanwhile," he reached across the desk for the paper Risley was holding, "we must set to work to find a new bride for His Majesty. It's true he has an heir, but one is scarcely sufficient. To be safe, he must produce another." He rubbed the bridge of his nose and skimmed the report.

"How is the king?" asked Risley.

"He's shut himself away. They say for grief, that he is all broken. And he will have none attend him, but only one."

"Who is that?"

Cromwell glanced up but didn't reply.

*   *   *   *

The windows were draped in black cloth, holding back the day, throwing the king's private chambers into the shadows of an endless night. Henry himself was dressed in a doublet of black brocade and black trousers. He had not changed in two days, in spite of the frantic confusion this caused for his grooms, whom he banished for the most part to the corridor outside his rooms. His mind and mood were dark, in a deep mourning that would not release its brutal hooks.

Henry sat at his desk, a single candle burning, and sketched wild architectural fantasies of minarets, towers, tall castles and pointed spires. Born of some strange dream, these rough, childlike drawings he felt compelled to create were fantasy upon fantasy, an unreal world apart from everything he knew, everything solid, everything tangible. He rubbed his neck and called out, "Hey!"

A raspy, ancient voice came from the darkness. "Majesty."

"Well? What do you think?"

There was a shuffling movement and an old man came from the shadows and toward the desk. He was twisted and bent, with rheumy eyes.

"I don't think!" said the old man. "Are you mad? Thinking is dangerous! But I'll *wink*!" He hitched one watery eye, and Henry laughed.

"Idiot!" said the king.

"What?" said the old man. "What about you? Think about it. You find the perfect wife. She's sweet, pliable. She even has good tits! On top of that she gives you a son, like you always wanted." He spat. "And then you let her die! Jesus Christ a-mercy! And you think I'm the idiot? And she's not the only one. Poor abandoned Katherine . . ."

"Careful," said Henry.

"And that other one, whose name escapes me, as her head escaped her. All lost! All lost!"

Henry snarled and threw some of the sketches at the old man, who skipped back a step. "Go to hell!"

"What?" asked the old man, looking around. "Go there? I thought I'd already arrived! For surely, gracious lord, this *is* hell!" Then the old man grinned and began a slow, shuffling dance to cheer up the king, singing, "And the rain, it rains . . ."

The queen's private chambers were quiet and somber, devoid of laughter or cheerfulness, with black cloth draping the windows and tables. The ladies in waiting were dressed in black gowns, their headdresses black and white to symbolize that their mistress had died in childbirth. Some sat sewing, heads bent in sorrow, while others moved about as if uncertain as to what they should do.

Lady Bryan entered and felt her heart sink at the sight. Such a dear queen gone too soon. The ladies curtsied to her, and in turn, Lady Bryan curtsied to Lady Mary.

"Lady Mary," she said, "how is the prince?"

"He has just sucked from Mother Jack, his wet nurse, and is sleeping. Over here, come."

Lady Mary showed Lady Bryan into the queen's bedchamber, which, like the outer room, was shrouded in black. Yet the child's gilded crib, set beside the royal bed, was a hopeful sight within this place of sorrow. Lady Mary folded her hands and gazed down at the baby, whose tiny hands clenched and unclenched in his sleep.

"Poor lamb," she said. "Never to know his own mother."

"He *will* know," said Mary. "Through me and others who knew her gentle kindness. We shall keep her memory so green that he will think it always spring, and she still so young and fair, when he first hears talk of her."

Lady Bryan smiled briefly, then drew up and spoke in all seriousness. "My Lady's household is to be dissolved. The king himself seems very grieved by her death. But he has commanded that no effort is to be spared to protect this precious jewel, his only son. A new household will be established for him at Hampton Court. And I am to head it, responsible altogether for his nurture and education."

"I can think of no one who could be trusted more, Lady Bryan."

"Perhaps someday soon," said Lady Bryan, "you may, God willing, have a child of your own. I heard some rumor of a Spanish prince?"

Mary was clearly uncomfortable with the subject, and she shrugged slightly and raised a brow. "Yes, but there is nothing definite. And in the meantime I shall return to Hunsdon and live quietly in the country like an English gentlewoman. Except that I shall take the Lady Elizabeth with me."

Lady Bryan smiled again, and this time it held. "Then, knowing that young lady, you shall have no quiet at all!"

"I don't mind," said Mary. "She, and this innocent child here, are, excepting for the king, my only family. I shall love them all."

Lady Bryan curtsied and turned to leave the bedchamber.

"Oh," said Mary. "I had forgotten. How is your son, Sir Francis? Is he not gone abroad for the king?"

"He has, my lady. But alas, I have no news of him." Then she curtsied once more, feeling a tug at her heart, and was gone.

The door to the tiny hotel room slammed open, startling Sir Francis Bryan and Tom Seymour, who sat atop a lumpy bed playing cards with three pretty painted whores. An official of the emperor, dressed in a red-and-gold coat, stepped in with an armed guard. Bryan glimpsed two other guards standing outside in the hallway, unable to enter the cramped chamber, but staring in with cold expressions that matched that of their compatriot.

"Sir Francis!" bellowed the official. "I came specially to welcome you to Caserta. We were just told of your arrival."

Bryan tossed down his cards. "Thank you."

The official shook a finger at the whores. "Leave!" The girls, grinning sheepishly, scooped from the mattress the coins they had won and pushed past the official and his guard. The sound of their laughter trailed down the corridor. Bryan bent to gather the rest of the cards from the bed, and in doing so made a subtle motion with his finger to Tom, who got up and moved to stand by the door.

"May I see your letters of passage?" the official asked.

Bryan stood and took several documents from the leather satchel on the bedside table. The official examined them as Bryan reached inside his tunic and pulled out several other documents.

"These are letters of introduction to the prince of Naples," said Bryan, holding these out for the official. As the official reached for them, Bryan jerked them back. "Don't you trust me?" he asked, his eyes narrowed and his voice lowered.

The official grunted angrily. "I need to see those letters."

"And I need to see Cardinal Pole."

The official blinked, and the guard took a step forward. "Do you really suppose you can threaten me, Sir Francis?" the official asked with a cold smile.

But suddenly Tom Seymour slammed the door in the faces of the guards in the hall and barred it, then drove his body against the one in the chamber, knocking him to the floor. At the same time, Bryan drew a knife from his tunic, jumped behind the man, and drew the blade up to his throat.

The official's eyes went huge, and the guard on the floor did not move, for fear his master would be butchered.

"You're sheltering a traitor," said Sir Francis, his voice matter-of-fact. "I want to know where he is. You're going to tell me. Or God help me, I'll kill you. And I have the immunity to do it."

The official stammered, and Francis pulled the knife tighter against the soft flesh, drawing a line of blood and causing the man to groan. "So, is he here?"

The official said nothing. The blade tightened again.

"Is he here?"

The official managed to nod slightly, and Bryan almost chuckled in the man's ear. How easy to get what one wanted when one had a few skills and a bit of experience.

The fantastical drawings hung on lines that crisscrossed the king's dark outer chamber. Each sketch was a revision of the one before it, with the last showing an exotic fairytale castle with impossibly delicate towers, arches, and balconies, peaked roofs and turrets, surrounded by stone and glass walls upon a high cliff.

The old man shuffled along the lines, straining through the shadows to see the sketches. Henry, still at his desk, said, "It's called Nonsuch Palace."

"Why?" said the old man. "Because it doesn't exist? Ha!"

"No, because there is no such place like it."

"But it doesn't exist."

"I'll build it."

"Then you will have built an imaginary palace. And you will need imaginary people to fill it."

"Are there lots of those?"

"I think so. For you are one and I another. And the whole court is imaginary. And all of this is a dream."

Henry rubbed his eyes, and still the old man remained. "It's all I have," he said.

"Then dream on." And the old man walked away and was swallowed up by the emptiness.

Cardinal Pole stood in the center of his tavern bedchamber undressing for the evening in the light of several candles on the mantel. His robes had been hung on a wall peg and smoothed out carefully and reverently by his own hands. His servant, a grumpy man with a boil under one eye, stood silently as Pole removed his papal ring and skullcap and handed them to him. Now, in just his long white shirt, the cardinal looked like any other man: humble, vulnerable. The servant kept these thoughts to himself. The cardinal was nervous aplenty as it was.

"Good night," the servant said with a bow. As he turned for the door, Pole said, "Wait. Wait!" The servant looked back as Pole glanced around the chamber as if expecting to find someone hiding in the corners.

"Eminence?"

"No," said Pole, raising one hand and shaking his head. "I've grown . . . afraid of my own shadow." He smiled and then, from the bedside table, picked up a heavy lead disk strung upon a ribbon. On one side of the disk were the images of Peter and Paul and the inscription *Sanctus Petrus Sanctus Paulus*. On the reverse was the name Pope Paul.

"Do you know what this is?" asked Pole. "The papal seal. The Holy Father blessed it himself. I feel safe with it."

The servant nodded.

"Will you sleep outside the door?"

The servant nodded again.

"Good night, then."

"Good night, Eminence."

The servant left the room, closing the door behind him. He sat down on the clump of straw he'd placed at the top of the stairs, pushing it about with his foot to make a more comfortable pallet. Grumbling, he spat on his hands, wiped his face, and then hunkered down.

The moment he closed his eyes he felt something sharp on his chest. He opened them again, his mouth wide in terror. Above him were two men, one kneeling over him with a knife to his heart. The other wore an eye patch, a sword, and an expression of pure hatred.

The man with the knife pressed it a bit harder, and as the servant drew in a sharp breath, he put a finger to his lips. "Don't move," he whispered.

The man with the eye patch kicked open the door to the cardinal's chamber. The servant craned his eyes through the opening to see the man draw the sword and stab it over and over again through the bed-covers and into the cardinal's body. "Traitor!" he cried.

God help him!

Then the man ripped back the covers to find only several pillows that had been placed beneath them to simulate the shape of a body. The man cursed and slammed his sword into the wall.

The man with the knife jumped up and joined the other. He peered out the window and turned to his murderous companion. "He got away!"

The servant stared through the door and shook in terrified relief as feathers swirled about in the chamber and landed on the empty bed.

*   *   *   *

Charles Brandon entered the house, removed his cape, and tossed it on the back of a chair. Then he strolled into the dining chamber to find Catherine standing by the window and gazing out upon the northern field, her brow knit. One hand held the sill, the other her belly, which was showing the roundness of her condition.

"Sweetheart?"

She didn't look around. Brandon went to her and put his hand beside hers to feel the warm, smooth bulge.

"Is it well with you?"

She turned to him and shook her head. "No," she said. "For sometimes I think I do not want this child in my belly."

Brandon's heart caught in his chest. "Oh, my love! Why do you say so?"

"For it will always be haunted by the ghosts of other children. Murdered children. Unwanted, unloved for the bloody memories it provides." She stared hard at him, her lips quivering. "Better it was gone before it was born!"

She pulled away from him and left him alone.

Henry slid the card to the center of the deck: a heart. He squinted through the darkness to watch his fool, who sat across from him with his own hand of cards. They had been playing for a long time, throughout the day or throughout the night? Henry did not know how long and did not care. The Fool was good at the game, offering only quips and jokes, never documents or missives or news of the outside world. The sketches of the castle remained on their lines, crossing the room in the shadows like so many spider's webs.

"I have other ideas for the palace," said Henry as the Fool considered his cards. "I'll construct beautiful gardens full of groves and hidden delves and paths. There will be a grove of Diana, showing the goddess in her bath. Statues everywhere. Fountains spouting water—one round, the other like a pyramid—while marble birds pour forth water out of their bills." He sniffed. "What do you say, Fool?"

"I like it all. I like everything about it," said the Fool. He was a tiny man dressed in a red-and-blue-striped doublet and a belled cap. His face was as pale as moonlight. "Except the groves. I don't like the groves. Or fountains. Or the marble birds. Or the paths. Everything else I like."

Henry shook his head. "You don't understand. The French king has a palace at Chambord which is the envy of the world. Nonsuch will trump it a hundred, no, a thousand times!"

"Then, in time," said the Fool, "like everything else it will dissolve away. Like the ruins of ancient Rome, like the Colossus of Rhodes! All things tend to their ruin, even great houses, and the fools who build them. And so, in a little space, there will indeed be Nonsuch Palace, for it will all be gone. A vacancy, a green thought in a green shade."

"And yet people will say there was once a great palace there! A palace beyond compare, beyond beauty. And King Henry built it! And so it will still exist!"

The Fool nodded. His bells jingled. "True, true. The only things that exist are in people's heads. And you never found a head so fine but you could make it fly!"

Henry snorted angrily and leaned forward, his eyes hooded. "Your turn."

The Fool turned up a card. It was the fool.

"Don't play the fool!" said Henry.

"Why not?"

"You'll lose the game."

"Indeed," said the Fool with a grin. "But hey, I should much rather lose the game than lose my head!" He laughed aloud.

Henry cuffed him over the head. "Fool!"

Risley was seated to Cromwell's left, taking dictation, when a servant announced the arrival of Richard Rich.

"Ah, Richie," said Cromwell, waving a hand to both welcome the chancellor and dismiss his scribe. "Come in."

Risley bowed and retreated behind the lattice scrim as Rich stepped up to Cromwell's desk to hear whatever news Cromwell had for him.

"There's something new I want to discuss with you," said Cromwell. "You know, of course, that His Majesty has seen fit to start remodeling most of his palaces, including the enlargement of Hampton Court."

"My lord, I have already released funds for the project. And also for the construction of St. James's Palace, and several other works His Majesty has proposed."

Cromwell nodded, then picked up several papers. His jaw tightened. "Well, here is one more." He passed the papers to Rich, who studied them with an expression of growing concern. On them were the king's sketches of his imaginary castle and all its near-impossible embellishments.

Rich frowned, shook his head, and looked at Cromwell, aghast. He lowered his voice. "But . . . this is fantasy work."

"It may well be, but the king intends to have it built. It will be called Nonsuch, being without equal. Its park alone will cover a thousand acres."

Rich looked from the papers to Cromwell. "It will cost a fortune!"

"As a result of the dissolution of the monasteries, His Majesty has gained a large fortune."

"Yes!" Rich declared loudly, then his voice went soft again to keep this from any ears but Cromwell's. "But did you ever suppose it would be squandered on fantasies?"

Cromwell said nothing as Rich tried to regain his composure.

"What a great charge it is to the king to complete his buildings in so many places at once," Rich began again. "How proud and false all the workmen are. Believe me, if the king could hold back for just a year on these projects, how profitable it would be to him. Can you not talk to him?"

"Richie," said Cromwell, "what the king wills, the king must have. He is not to be argued with or crossed. He is still mourning the death of his wife. And he will talk to no one but Will Somers."

Rich's mouth dropped open and his eyes went wide. "Will Somers? His fool? He talks to no one but his *fool*?"

"It's not the first time. In extremis, always."

"But for how long?"

"I don't know. But I wish he would come out, for without him we are all gone to hell."

The man was young, yellow-haired, and dead. Cromwell stood over the body staring at the bloody hole in the young man's chest, then shook his head and drew a sheet over the corpse. The sergeant at arms stood by, silent, having summoned the lord privy seal to witness this terrible scene in a small corridor off the castle's main thoroughfare.

"Who is he?" asked Cromwell.

"Sir Gawen Carew. One of Lord Seymour's retainers."

"Why was he killed?"

"It may have been for a gambling debt, my lord."

Cromwell looked at the man sharply. "*May* have been, Sergeant?"

"We're investigating, my lord."

"You don't have the killer?"

"No, my lord. Although it seems possible it is one of my Lord Sussex's retainers."

Cromwell turned directly on the sergeant and pointed a finger. "It's illegal to carry arms in the court when the king is in residence! The penalties are severe."

"Yes, my lord."

Cromwell glowered. This had happened in the middle of the day, when someone should have seen or witnessed something! Another murder to solve, another cold reminder that he, himself, could well be a target soon. "What about my friend Mr. Packington? Have you not found *his* killer?"

"No, my lord."

"No?" Cromwell stepped close to the sergeant and narrowed his eyes. "It occurs to me that as the man appointed to keep order at court, you are singularly failing in your duties. I trust now you will apprehend the villains and prevent any further violence. Otherwise you will pay the price for your failures."

He walked away from the sergeant, hearing a soft rustling as the man bowed to empty air.

The sunny corridor in Hampton Court was a flurry of activity, with maids and servants scrubbing the floors and walls with buckets of water and an acrid soap that stung the nose and the eyes. Sir Francis Bryan tucked his letter of authority into his coat as he walked beside his mother along the hallway, shifting back and forth to avoid stepping in an errant puddle or tripping over a kneeling servant.

"What's this?" Bryan asked, nodding at their industry.

Lady Bryan smiled at her son. "The king has given orders personally for all the rooms and chambers and passages around the prince's apartments to be scrubbed with soap three times daily. No member of the household can speak to persons suspected of having been in contact with the plague, nor are we permitted to travel to London at all in the summer months without permission."

They reached a spiral stone staircase, and Bryan nodded to let his mother pass first. More maids were washing the walls along the stairs, pausing to curtsy as the couple moved up and past them. "The prince also has his own kitchen, where all his food is prepared, now that he is weaned from Mother Jack. Everything he might touch has to be washed, and everything he might eat, tasted for poison."

At the top of the stairs was a closed door beside which four armed guards stood alert, erect, watching.

"His personal chamberlain supervises the prince's meals," said Lady Bryan, "as well as his robes and daily bath."

Bryan smiled. "He must be the cleanest baby in England."

Lady Bryan's face grew instantly serious. "He is the most precious baby in England."

A guard opened the door and stepped back to let mother and son enter the child's private bedchamber.

The room was small and clean, with a portrait of the king and of Queen Jane on the wall above the mantel. Several chests lined one wall, and against another was a table covered in white linen and topped with gold candlesticks and a cross. The cradle sat in the center of the room, covered in a canopy to keep harsh sunlight off the infant.

Bryan stepped close and looked down at the sleeping baby. What fine facial features, much like his mother's, Bryan thought. And what thick dark hair and strong arms, much like his father's.

Then Bryan heard someone enter the room and he turned about to see Edward Seymour. Seymour glanced from Lady Bryan to her son, his face set and unreadable.

"My lord!" said Lady Bryan, curtsying low.

"Thank you, Lady Bryan," said Edward, indicating she was to leave. When she was gone, Edward took a step closer to Bryan and said, "Why have you come here?"

Bryan put his fists on his hips and tipped his head back. "His Majesty is anxious to assure himself of his son's well-being."

Edward shook his head slowly, dangerously. "He has no need to be concerned. The protection of the prince is also my first priority, since he is also of *my* blood." He took another step closer. "I thank you, Sir Francis, in the future to leave my nephew alone. And my wife, too. Do I make myself clear?"

The king and the Fool, drunk on wine and lack of sleep, sat on the floor of the king's dark chamber. The furniture was pushed back to give them room. Time had no meaning to either.

Henry took a sip from his goblet, then took another, then held his cup out, licked his lips, and nodded. "Now, Fool! Here's something else to do. We have to decide which articles of faith and which commandments are best . . . for our new Church, for our people. So they shall walk in good ways. So . . . thou shalt not . . . what?"

The Fool rubbed his nose. "Play the fool?"

Henry grinned. "Covet your neighbor's wife!"

"Unless she is very pretty!"

"Or," said Henry, putting the goblet down but sideways, causing it to spill its contents and roll away. "Or his manservant, maidservant, ox, ass!"

"Or your neighbor's wife's ass!" said the Fool.

Henry laughed. "Don't be facetious." He fumbled for the goblet, pulled it to his mouth, and upended it to get any remaining wine. "Did you know, Fool, that in Exodus there are six hundred thirteen commandments?"

"Thou shall not suffer a witch to live!"

"Three times you shall keep a feast unto me in the year."

"Thou shalt never vex a stranger!"

Henry scooted about and put his arm around the Fool. "Whosoever lies with a beast shall surely be put to death."

The Fool raised his cup as if in a toast. "Sheep shaggers! Pigeon fanciers!"

"Thou shalt not venerate the vicar of Rome."

"Or lick his arse!"

They rocked back and forth, clutching their guts. Then Henry pushed the Fool away. "For thine is the kingdom!"

"The power and the glory!"

"Amen!"

"That's the doxology."

Henry laughed, then crawled to the nearest table and scrabbled for the flagon of wine atop it. It tipped and he caught it, then drank straight from it. "Doxology?" he said. "It's the dog's bloody bollocks!" Then he put the flagon on the floor, buried his face in his hands, and began to weep. "I miss her. I miss her, Will."

"I know," said the Fool. "But this, too, shall pass." He crept closer and put his arm around the king's shoulder. "Why go on dwelling in darkness? You know that the land of the wounded king is only a parched wasteland thirsting for rain and Your Majesty's grace!"

Henry wiped his eyes and stared at the Fool.

The sergeant at arms had just sat down in the Whitehall Palace guardroom to stretch out a leg cramp brought on by the damp night air when a yeoman burst into the room. "Sir! There's a fight. You'd best come quick!"

The sergeant snatched up his sword, held it aloft, and followed out and down the torchlit corridor. He heard shouts up ahead and the sound of metal striking metal. Rounding a corner, they found the scene of the clash: several groups of men battling one another in the shadows and flickering torchlight. It was nearly impossible to see their faces, to know who they were, but as they darted forward and back, in and out of the darkness, slashing at each other with brutal rage, he saw that the groups wore different colors: yellow, red, blue. The retainers for different nobles, filled with hatred toward one another, hatred unto death.

"Whoever you are!" the sergeant shouted, raising his sword for all to see. "Hold! In the name of the king. Put up your swords, for it's treason!"

Still, the men continued their battle, snorting and roaring like bulls.

"Hold!" the sergeant repeated. "Give up your swords, sirs! I say, on pain of death, give them up!"

The fighters paused and turned toward the sergeant and yeoman. Some of them were smiling coldly; others just stared.

The yeoman stepped forward and gestured. "You heard the sergeant. Give me your swords!"

"Very well, you bastard," said the retainer closest to the yeoman. "Here it is!" He slashed his sword across the yeoman's arm, driving the blade deep, causing the yeoman to scream and drop his weapon. Then a great cry erupted from the retainers, and several of them turned upon the sergeant as others cheered encouragement.

As the yeoman wailed upon the floor, his arm nearly severed, the sergeant fell into the fight, shouting and driving his sword up, across, down, but finding himself unable to move forward as the men jumped in to have at him one at a time. They moved him farther and farther back, against a wall. Sweat poured down his face and arms; his teeth were set on each other and his lips curled back in a snarl. He saw that some of the men had stopped their own battling to watch this scene, some shouting, others laughing.

A sword whistled down and across his leg, drawing a long line of blood through his trousers. He slashed out, striking at one attacker as yet another sword came down upon his thigh, sinking into the flesh. In the corner of his eye he saw new arrivals on the scene, about thirty men dressed in gray—Thomas Cromwell's retainers, their swords and knives raised. The men fell back into brawls, some using fists now, others weapons, some kicking and shoving. The battles seemed less vicious suddenly, as if the blood being drawn from the sergeant was enough for them.

God help me!

The sergeant parried, knocking swords away in rapid succession. He felt the cold stone of the wall pressing his spine and he smelled the fetid breaths of his enemies. His legs coursed with red hot agony, yet still they held him up. "Halt!" he cried, though he knew his commands were futile. They were a pack of dogs now, coming in for the kill.

He struck another blow and another, both deflected by the others' swords. But then he flicked his blade upward and caught one man in the throat. The retainer stumbled backward, gurgling, dying. Those with him paused and stared as if surprised, but then they turned against the sergeant with renewed fervor, growling and shouting, and he could no longer keep them at bay. A sword was driven into his arm, then another through his bowels, and then his chest. He staggered back into the wall, slid down it, and was dead before he hit the floor.

Cromwell heard them arguing even before he reached the wide arched doorway to the palace's Great Hall. How much like children they sounded, snide and petty, shouting each other down, well out of earshot of the one who could make them behave, make them bow and be silent, make them act like the nobles they claimed to be.

"The prince, my nephew, is in my custody," he heard Edward Seymour bellow, "and *no one* will be allowed to see him without my permission!"

The next voice was Charles Brandon's. "He's the king's son! The property of the state. He is not *your* property, my lord!"

With his gray-jacketed retainers behind him, Cromwell appeared in the doorway, and the chamberlain banged his staff soundly upon the floor.

"The lord privy seal!"

Cromwell stepped inside, followed by his servants, and immediately noticed the retainers of a number of nobles lining the walls, dressed in their lords' colors, swords and knives at their sides, should they be needed. The nobles, gathered for the most part in the center of the hall, turned at Cromwell's entrance. Though the noise died down a bit, some men continued to grumble. Richard Rich was among them, but he appeared to be apart from the rancor, and disturbed by it.

"My lords!" Cromwell spoke loudly and clearly. "Your Grace! I beg you all, can we not come to order?"

Lord Hussey, an aging gentleman with red hair and a crooked nose, said, "By what right, and by whose command, Mr. Secretary, do you summon the king's council?"

"My Lord Hussey," said Cromwell, "you ought to know that the king is incommunicado . . . "

There were shouts of anger and frustration. Lord Oxford, thin and balding, shook a fist. "Then you *have* no authority. Or only a usurped one, to put yourself above all others!"

Sir Francis Bryan huffed and crossed his arms. The Earl of Surrey nodded.

Cromwell inclined his head slightly to show he'd heard the complaint, but watched them with a steady eye so they would not see him as weak. It took effort to keep any emotion out of his voice. "As lord privy seal, I think I have the right and responsibility, in loco parentis, of summoning your lordships to council."

There was a fresh uproar, with the men shaking their heads and their fists.

"Gentlemen!" Cromwell continued. "Surely you understand that there must be a meeting of the council? In the king's absence there has been so much malevolence at court! So much violence, including now the death of the sergeant at arms!"

Brandon stepped toward Cromwell, his hooded eyes cold. "I have heard that your own servants were much involved in the violence, Mr. Secretary. Some say they may even have provoked it."

In that moment, the room went silent. All the bickering had ceased, and all eyes and ears were trained on Cromwell. Cromwell could feel the hatred rising up beneath the silence, stinking like the pus in a boil. He chose his words carefully. "If that could be proved, then I should rightly forfeit your lordships' trust. But I assure Your Grace it is not true, and others here should look to their *own* consciences."

"What do you mean by that?"

"I mean that there are some who desire disorder with all their hearts, thinking to use it, at the end, to their own advantage."

Brandon stepped even closer, so that his nose almost touched Cromwell's. "Mr. Cromwell," he said slowly, "you presume too far above your very base and low degree. Until the king is well you will not summon me anymore to anything. Not even to a dog fight!"

Signaling his retainers, Brandon stalked out. The other nobles followed suit, each with their armed servants close at hand. Cromwell watched them leave, then went out himself. His retainers kept pace.

In the corridor, Richard Rich caught up with him and spoke urgently. "For God's sake, have you any news of the king?"

Cromwell kept up his pace. "Yes! I know what he's doing in there!" Then he whispered, "He's rewriting the Lord's Prayer and the Ten Commandments."

Rich caught Cromwell's arm, causing him to stop walking. His mouth hung open. "What?"

"Exactly!" said Cromwell, then pulled free from Rich's grasp and continued on to his office.

Edward Seymour's dining room was well suited to a noble, brother of the former queen of England, and uncle to the future king. The table was English walnut with matching chairs set with green damask cushions.

The windows, which looked out over trellised gardens and ponds, were treated with heavy velvet drapes. The fireplace was wide, deep, and alive with an afternoon blaze. Above the mantel and along the three other walls hung portraits of the Seymour family, one Edward especially liked of himself done by Master Holbein.

Servants moved in and out of the room bringing in new dishes and removing those that had been emptied. Edward and his wife, Anne, dined in silence, he at the head of the table, she to his right. After a few minutes he gestured for all of the servants to leave.

Alone with Anne, he said, "How are the prawns?"

Anne raised a brow and tilted her head. She was quite beautiful. It was easy to see why other men would desire her. She held up one of the large shrimps and said, "Delicious." Then she took a bite.

Edward picked up his knife. "I've warned Sir Francis Bryan to stay away from you."

Anne glanced at him then dropped the translucent prawn tail in her bowl. "Why?"

"He's dangerous."

"Not to you, surely. Not with the boy."

Edward shook his head. "The king listens to him. That makes him dangerous. I shall have to destroy him."

"A pity," said Anne, cocking her head. "He makes me laugh."

"I'm sure he makes a lot of women laugh."

Anne put her elbows on the table and wove her fingers under her chin. "You think that a very small thing, don't you, Edward?"

"I think there are more important things, yes."

"No doubt you're right." Anne sat back in her chair. "But as long as you think that, please don't expect me to be faithful to you. Now"—she smiled sweetly—"may I have some more prawns?"

"Wakey-wakey!"

Cromwell felt something thump the side of his bed, and his eyes flashed open. Faint morning sunlight trickled through his bedchamber window and onto the floor and across the edge of the bed, where the king's fool, in his belled hat, sat cheerfully grinning at him.

"His Majesty would like to see you!" said the Fool. Then he shook his hat to make it jingle. "At once!" Then he hopped up, bowed, and skipped out.

Cromwell called for his dresser, and within the hour was groomed, sprayed, and on his way along the passages and up the stairs to the king's private chambers. A cold stone of apprehension sat in his gut, for he had not seen the king in days, and as reports were, he could not think of what His Majesty might want so early in the morning.

The armed guards opened the door to the outer chamber, and Cromwell went inside. He was immediately struck by the oppressive heat and odor in the room. The windows were covered in black cloth, as were the tables and portraits and chairs. But it was the condition of the king himself that caused Cromwell's heart to sink.

He was greatly altered by his suffering: his clothing wrinkled and dirty, his face sunken at the cheeks. The king's eyes were dark and suspicious. He appeared to have aged years in a short time.

It was all Cromwell could do to hide his shock. He bowed low.

"Master Cromwell," said Henry, moving to a chair and dropping onto the seat. "How goes the world?"

"Majesty. The king of France has written to congratulate Your Majesty on the birth of your son."

Henry strummed the arm of the chair. "Tell Francis that divine providence has mingled my joy with the bitterness of death, of her who brought me this happiness. And what of Nonsuch?"

"Building work on the palace has already begun, and the foundations are laid."

"There are other foundations to be laid." Henry crossed his feet. "Ghostly foundations. Spiritual foundations. I want to see Bishop Gardiner. I need to talk to him."

"Of course, Majesty."

"How is my son?"

"Everything has been done to protect the prince, in strict accordance with Your Majesty's instructions."

Henry nodded, and looked toward the shrouded window. "I love that boy! If any harm should come to him . . ." He sat for a long moment, his eyes moving back and forth, as if watching something Cromwell could not see.

"Majesty," Cromwell began. "I wonder if—"

"You wonder?" Henry whipped around and leaned forward, daring Cromwell to go on.

"I . . . I wonder if Your Majesty should now frame your mind to a new marriage? After all . . ." He steeled himself to speak the words. "After all, however much you may seek to protect the prince, still, death may take him."

Henry got to his feet and took several steps toward Cromwell, rage darkening his face all the more. But then he stopped and tipped his head, the anger fading. "I may well frame my mind. Why not? Do you have some candidates in mind?"

"I took the liberty of instructing our ambassadors in France and the Low Countries to begin inquiries."

"And?"

"The French have proposed two possible consorts for Your Majesty: Margaret, the king's daughter; and Marie, daughter of the duc de Guise. Our ambassador in France sings the latter's praises, although it seems she is half-promised to the king of Scotland."

Henry said nothing. He looked back toward the black-curtained window as if he'd heard not a word. Cromwell's heart sank.

"Majesty?"

The king turned and gazed at him with haunted eyes.

He approached Jane's tomb alone, with longing and trepidation, desiring to be near his beloved wife and fearing that he would once again have his heart cleaved in two with fresh memories of her body, her touch, her tenderness. The chapel room in which the tomb was placed was dark, lit by lanterns. Flowers lay on the tomb and were scattered on the floor around it, though many of them were now brown and wilted. Henry knelt at the tomb and brought his hands together prayerfully.

"My darling," he whispered. "One day I shall lie down beside you again, I promise, and we shall sleep together for eternity. Oh sweetheart." He wiped tears from his cheeks. "Oh sweetheart."

Bowing his head and closing his eyes, he saw her again: beautiful, leaning over her bath, washing her long, golden hair, the water pouring around her as if bathing her in preparation for a journey. She turned her face and smiled at him with pure and perfect love. And in that moment he knew she was freeing him, releasing him to the duties of this world. And as much as sorrow would hold him there, he knew it was time to return.

CHAPTER EIGHT

Still wearing the black of mourning, but in fresh new velvet and brocade garments sewn in the last week by his tailors, Henry walked the paths along the ponds of the royal gardens, taking in the sun and morning air. Around the statuary and trees and under the vine-covered arbors he strolled with Sir Francis Bryan and Lady Ursula Misseldon. The queen's little dog bounded along happily, reined in every few moments by Lady Misseldon, who had him on a leash. Ursula's mother followed at a discreet distance.

"Jane's household is now broken up," said Henry, catching his hands behind his back. "Where will you go, Lady Misseldon?"

"To live with my mother."

"What about the gentleman you were engaged to?"

"Robert Tavistock? I think he is not so interested in me."

Bryan turned to the lady. "He's a fool, then."

"You are kind to think so, Sir Francis."

Henry continued walking, gazing above the trees at the palace roofs. "Is he so foolish that he will turn down a peerage, and the gift of one of the dissolved abbeys—if he agrees to marry you?" He looked at her then, expecting to see surprise and gratitude. But instead, she looked sad.

"Majesty," she said. "I would think less of him if he needed to accept gifts in order to love me. Your Majesty is more than generous and gracious, but I am settled in my plan to go home and see what becomes of me."

"In my state," said Henry, "you could not have said anything more admirable. You may leave with our love and blessing." Then he leaned in close to her ear and whispered, "One more night."

Ursula looked at him without a word, though her eyes revealed her willingness to obey his command. She curtsied and, with the little dog, walked away to join her mother. Henry and Bryan moved on down the pathway.

"The traitor Pole escaped you!" said Henry after a long silence.

"Yes! We had other agents looking for him. But he was smuggled back to Italy. No doubt he's sitting on the pope's lap even now."

Henry snorted. "His betrayal hurts me. Pity is that the folly of one brain-sick Pole, or to say better, one witless fool, should be the ruin of so great a family." He stopped, snatched a black stone from the path. "Though I cannot touch him, I swear I will make him eat his heart." Then he hurled the stone into the pond, where it broke the surface and scattered the sunlight like fragments of glass.

The same sunlight reflected off the river on the Hunsdon estate, along which Lady Mary and Ambassador Chapuys strolled in the chilly morning air. She wore a modest gray gown trimmed in pearls, and a cape of wolves' fur. Chapuys's cloak was of heavy black brocade.

"How is the king?" Mary asked.

"He has just lately emerged from his seclusion. It is said that although he is little disposed to it, the council is urging him to take the extreme step of marrying again." Chapuys watched the lady for her reaction, but it was mild, with just a small sigh.

Then she said, "I . . . I do not suppose you have heard any more about Don Luis and my own marriage?"

He spoke softly, knowing that the issue was sensitive and the lady naïve and vulnerable in this arena of life. "As to that, I am afraid I have no news for you, whether good or bad. It seems perhaps the issue is in abeyance, at least for the time being."

Mary looked at the ground. "Perhaps it is my fate never to marry."

"No, gentle lady. I am sure the king will make up his mind to arrange a most brilliant marriage for you. If not to Don Luis, then to someone even more eligible."

"I thought you said Don Luis was incomparable?"

This caught him. "Madam, I did not mean—"

But Lady Mary smiled at him. "No, you meant well. You always mean well." She stopped to watch a deer in the distance bounding across the field above the river, followed by two fawns. "I hear the king has developed a passion for houses."

"Indeed. I confess he is very greedy to have the funds from the sale of the monasteries, so he can spend them on buying more houses or enlarging those he already possesses." Then he paused. "Forgive me. I meant to speak no ill of the king. But the fate of the abbeys and monasteries still touches me."

Mary put her hand to her heart as if wounded. "Do you not think it still touches me? One day, perhaps, if God wills it, I will have the power to restore them."

"Then, my lady, you would rightly inherit heaven's grace."

She touched his arm gratefully, then continued her walk, moving along the path that wound even closer to the river's edge.

"There is in any case," he said, keeping pace with the lady, "one great estate which His Majesty cannot get his hands on, though he would if he could."

"Whose estate is that?"

"Your mother's. Since he swore before every court in Christendom that he was never legally or properly married to her, then how can he now make legal claim to it as her widower?"

Lady Mary laughed lightly. "I suppose that annoys him!"

They found a smooth, dry boulder beside the water, and Mary carefully climbed onto it, smoothed her skirts, and sat. She folded her hands in her lap and looked out over the rushing waters. "I still dream of my mother," she said. "I wish I had seen her before she died."

"And yet you had another mother. Did not Lady Salisbury look after you with gentle care?"

"She did, and I shall always be grateful."

"Then watch after her," Chapuys said. Mary glanced over at the sudden change in his voice. "They say the king is violently angry against her son, Cardinal Pole. It means Lady Salisbury and her whole family are in the greatest danger."

Henry gestured for Cardinal Bishop to have a seat at the table in his private outer chamber. The cardinal bowed, then pulled out a chair and eased himself down. He clasped his bony hands on the tabletop and waited for the king to speak. The room was bright again, the black drapes having been removed and put away, replaced by curtains of red, and the walls and floors having been swept and scrubbed.

"My Lord Bishop," said Henry, standing over the bishop, his arms crossed. "You and your committee were asked to examine and determine the doctrine of the Church of England. But it seems you have been unable to agree on anything."

"Your Majesty," said Gardiner, his gray brows knitted. "Unfortunately, there continue to be some fundamental theological differences between members of the committee."

Henry nodded, then put his hand atop a stack of papers beside him. "I am aware of that. But I am grown very impatient, and will not tolerate any more divisions." He shoved a single sheet toward the bishop. "I have formulated six fundamental doctrinal questions. The answers to these questions will form the basis of our faith."

Picking up the paper, Gardiner looked at the scrawled notes. Then he regarded the king with an expression of uncertainty. "Of course, as Your Majesty wishes. I shall go at once to Canterbury and consult with the archbishop."

Henry tilted his head. "My lord, save yourself the journey. I think we understand each other very well. Let's leave Archbishop Cranmer to cultivate his own garden. There's really no need to bother him. Don't you agree?"

He knew Gardiner would be in approval even before the older man smiled.

Cardinal Pole had found a competent adversary for his occasional games of chess, a pastime that both sharpened his mind and gave it temporary respite from a greatly troubled world. Pole and Cardinal Von Waldburg sat hovering over the board at a small table in Pole's sparsely furnished whitewashed cell, studying each other's moves and planning their next.

As he pondered the positions of the pieces, Von Waldburg said, "The Holy Father mentioned you in his prayers today. He thanked God for your safe deliverance." He moved his knight.

"I was sure I was going to die."

Von Waldburg chuckled silently. "Death is not ready for you yet."

Pole countered with his bishop, causing Von Waldburg to purse his lips.

"God has something else in mind," Von Waldburg continued, keeping his eye on the game. "How else to explain the miracle of your survival? Ah!" He moved his bishop into a threatening position.

Pole countered again. Then, with effort, brought up the subject that had been weighing heavily on his heart. "My brother, Lord Montague, has written me a letter."

"Show me."

Pole removed a letter from the pocket of his robe and handed it to his senior. Von Waldburg unfolded the paper and read aloud.

"'I send you God's blessing and mine, though my trust to have comfort in you has turned to sorrow. Alas that I, for your folly, should receive from my sovereign lord such a message as I have lately done, and to see you in his indignation. It made my poor heart so lament. It is incredible to me that by reason of a brief sent to you by the bishop of Rome, you should be resident with him this winter. If you keep that way, then farewell all my hope. And God save your mother and all your family.'"

"What should I do?"

Von Waldburg held the letter over the flame of the candle beside the chessboard and it caught fire immediately. Pole reached out to snatch the letter away, but then pulled his hand back and looked at Von Waldburg for an explanation.

"Do you not understand?" the elder cardinal asked. "That letter was not written by your brother, but dictated to him by Cromwell, the messenger of Satan!" He tossed the burning letter to the stone floor, where it flared, burned, and then was reduced to cinders. "Never let the Devil beguile you, either with his threats or his promises. The price of your soul is eternal vigilance, for as the peasants say, if you once let down your guard, the Devil will slip like a serpent into your mouth and forever afterward he will speak for you."

The night had grown late, with wind rattling the windows of the king's bedchamber. A single taper burned in its silver base on the bedside table, casting a glow across the crumpled counterpane, the pillows, and the king. He waited, naked beneath the covers, gazing in the direction of the door. She would come. One last time, she would come.

He watched the patterns the shadows of his hands made upon the bed, thick at first, like the massive claws of some predatory bird, then, when turned, becoming the vague, ethereal appendances of an angel.

The door creaked open. Henry stared into the darkness, listening to the soft footsteps upon the floor. And then Ursula was there, in a white linen nightgown, the top buttons unfastened, her red hair combed down and around her shoulders. She paused, smiled at him, and stepped forward, placing her hand on a post at the foot of the bed.

"Stay there!" Henry said. He crawled out from the covers to the end of the bed and gazed at her. Then he raised his hand and began to recite words of the holy sacrament of the altar.

"Deus qui nobis sub Sacramento mirabili, passionis tuae memoriam reliquisti . . ."

She fell into him and he into her, and he tore her gown apart and away as she moaned in ecstasy.

* * * *

A great table had been set in the Presence Chamber, and the ten bishops invited by the king stood solemnly around it. They were dressed formally, in black robes with red trim, with red skullcaps sitting snugly on their mostly balding heads. Gardiner was among them, as was Bishop Tunstall, but Archbishop Cranmer was not present. He had not been invited or told about the meeting, as was the pleasure of the king. Cromwell, Rich, and Brand were also in attendance, to represent the laity.

All waited in silence, hands folded, until the king entered the room. They bowed in unison, and the king took his place at the table's head. He nodded for the men to sit and for Gardiner to begin.

"Your Majesty," Gardiner said, lifting a leather-bound volume for all to see. "Here are the six articles of faith upon which Your Majesty's Church of England is to be built and sustained."

Henry raised his hand. "Read them."

Gardiner opened the cover. "The first article concerns the truth of the transubstantiation of God. By the consecration of the bread and wine at holy Mass there takes place a change of the whole substance of the bread into the substance of the body of Christ our Lord and of the whole substance of the wine into the substance of His blood. To deny the blood and body of Christ is not only to deny Christ Himself, like Thomas, but to betray Him to death as a second Judas. The penalty for denying this is death by burning, even after recantation."

Henry nodded approvingly. "Continue."

Tunstall took up the book. "The second article concerns the withholding of the cup from the laity during communion. For if we offer them the blood of Christ they would lose all their reverence for the holy sacraments, and the power of the blood would be washed away."

Henry listened, but his thoughts drifted back to his bedchamber the night before: Ursula's torn white gown tossed aside like the cocoon of a newly hatched butterfly, her pale arms and belly, her soft hair.

"The third article," said Gardiner, "prescribes the continued validity of the vows of celibacy for all priests and nuns."

Ursula's body consecrated by Henry's touch, hot and willing for his hands to worship her. Her eyes wide with rapturous passion, her lips as red and wet as roses covered in dew. *Gloria Patri, et Filio, et Spiritui Sancto* . . .

"For does not St. Paul say, 'He that is without a wife is solicitous for the things that belong to the Lord, how he may please God. But he that is with a wife, is solicitous for the things of the world, how he may please his wife.' Those priests already married must forthwith desert their wives, or face the penalty of death."

Her body, covered in sweat as sweet as wine, her breasts as delicious as delicate cakes. Rolling her onto the floor and tasting every inch as she whined with desire. *Gloria Patri, et Filio, et Spiritui Sancto* . . .

Tunstall read, "The fourth article concerns the observation of the vows of chastity. A priest makes a vow of chastity, and the violation of that vow must always be a sin against religion."

Ursula, spreading wide her legs to receive his offering of flesh and blood, body and soul, tossing her hair and arching her back to accept him, her fingers clawing at his shoulders, her mouth parted, panting. *Et nunc, et semper, et in sæcula sæculorum* . . .

"The fifth article herby decided confirms the continuation and practice of private masses, whereby good Christian people do receive both godly and goodly consolations and benefits for their souls."

Henry shoving her arms down, pinning them against the floor, thrusting his fingers into her first, and then his manhood. His very soul consumed with the power and the glory of the explosion. The flame of the bedside candle leaping in joy. *Amen, Amen!*

"The sixth article confirms the importance of confession. You pig-heads of Augsburg hear your own voices screeching over those of the Church fathers, but hear our Venerable Bede: *Confitemini alterntrum peccata vestra*. Confess your sins to one another."

Henry shifted in his chair and rubbed his face casually, ridding it of the line of sweat that had appeared. His mind threw Ursula back into the past, leaving only his pounding heart, which no one could see. He looked across the table at Cromwell to see if his secretary had any visible reaction to the articles. Cromwell's face was set in stone.

"Those who dispute against these six articles of our faith," said Gardiner, "must now be considered heretics, like those Sacramentalists, Anabaptists, and extreme Lutherans who now roam this land. The penalties for transgression will be death by hanging, drawing and quartering, as well as forfeiture of estates and goods. And any person who tries to flee England in the face of these new articles will be considered to be guilty of treason and suffer accordingly the awful fate of traitors."

Gardiner stood, bowed, and handed the volume over to his king.

"Thank you, my Lord Bishop," said Henry. A scribe handed him a quill, and he signed his name, then poured wax upon it and pressed his seal into it.

Brandon nodded around the table. "Your Eminences are to be congratulated for your hard work and manifest wisdom. Here are six articles we may all adhere to with a clear conscience."

"There is one final amendment," said Henry. "From henceforth the Lord's Prayer is altered to include the doxology 'For thine is the kingdom, the power and the glory. Amen.'" Then he pressed his hands to the table and stood. "My lords, Eminences, Your Grace. Now these matters are determined, let us prosecute with diligence those who stubbornly stand against us."

The bishops, Brandon, and the king had departed, leaving Cromwell and Rich alone in the Presence Chamber. Cromwell stared at the doorway through which his hopes of a reformed church and an assurance of personal power had just vanished. Late-afternoon shadows of stands, tables, and chairs lay long across the floor. In the midst of them was his own shadow, making him appear as some stretched and distorted creature.

"Those aren't six articles," he said at last to Rich. "They are a whip with six strings!"

Rich shook his head in stunned agreement and disbelief. "Cranmer will have to send his wife and son back to Germany, or be burned."

Cromwell glared at Rich. "It's not just that, Mr. Rich! Private masses! Confession! The body and the blood of Christ! Don't you understand? He's rolled back the reforms. These are Catholic measures! It is the end of our Reformation!"

"But why?"

"Because," said Cromwell, "in his heart he has always been a true Catholic, excepting this one thing, that he would have neither Pope nor Luther nor any other man ever set above him!"

Lady Salisbury smiled as her son Henry, Lord Montague, and her twelve-year-old grandson laughed about their morning in the fields surrounding Warblington Castle: chasing a stag that had led them knee-deep into muck and then stood atop a hillside gazing down as if very pleased with its handiwork. Lord Montague, a round and muscular man with large feet, had become stuck tightly in the mire, and his son had to pull him out with a branch, leaving one boot.

The dining table was spread with the evening meal, featuring venison, boiled eggs, apples, tripe sausages, and a platter of breads. The room was large but plainly decorated, with few ornaments or family portraits. A gold crucifix sat upon the mantel. Lady Salisbury did not approve of shows of wealth or vanity, and would have none of it in her home. Even her clothing bore only a smattering of the jewels she could have afforded had she so chosen. Her gray hair was pinned up beneath a simple lace coif.

Lord Montague said, "Perhaps we should go out into the fields again tomorrow, if there is no rain, and try to fetch the boot again."

The boy said, "I fear it's already a nest for snakes or mice!" He giggled.

Suddenly Lady Salisbury held up her hand. She'd heard an unfamiliar noise, a rumbling deep inside the manor house, and her heart tightened.

"What is it?" asked Lord Montague.

The lady frowned. "I don't know."

The three of them fell silent, listening for sounds beyond the closed door. There were muffled voices and the heavy tread of feet coming their way. And then the door swung open.

Sir Francis Bryan stalked in, followed by armed guards. Lady Salisbury gasped and pressed a hand to her chest.

"Lady Salisbury," said Bryan, tipping his head. "Forgive this intrusion. But you and these members of your family are arrested by the king's order on suspicion of treason. You will all have to come straight with me."

Lady Salisbury rose in defense of her own. Her legs were weak, but her head was held high. "Not my grandson, surely?"

Bryan smiled a cold smile. Lord Montague glared at the man, clutching the back of his chair so hard his whole body shook. Lady Montague's grandson drew a sharp breath and dropped his spoon.

Then Bryan's smile fell away. "All of them!" he shouted, and he motioned for his guards to round the family up.

The guard stared at the child. What a pompous brat, pampered and spoiled! His round face favored that of his father and, worse, uncle. The boy had been silent for many hours now, playing with a few toys scattered on the cell floor and staring out the barred windows of his Tower cell. But the guard saw confusion and rage brewing in the boy's eyes.

At last he broke and spun toward the door with a raised fist. "I want to see my father! I have to see my father! Go get my father!"

The guard said nothing.

Suddenly the boy burst into tears and rushed at the guard, his teeth bared, his fists pounding the air and then the guard's chest. "I want to see my father! Now! You know who I am, don't you?"

The guard only laughed, shoved the boy back, and bowed mockingly. "Oh yes, I know who you are, Master Pole! They say someday you're going to be the king of England."

The boy made to come at him again, but then only turned toward the wall, fell to the floor, and wept.

* * * *

Henry stood gazing at his reflection in the tall mirror in his bedchamber as his grooms finished the laces and buttons of his doublet and trousers. He still chose to wear black, but his new wardrobe was elegant and regal, made of velvets and the softest brocades embroidered with silver and gold threads, set with diamonds, and trimmed with the fur of rare black wolves. The grooms smoothed the sleeves and straightened the hem, then one stepped forward to spray the king with rose water. Another stood upon a stool and secured a broad, flat silk hat dressed with a ruby on Henry's head. Then the king snapped his fingers, and the grooms bowed and left.

"The factions and fighting inside the court while I mourned were unacceptable," said Henry, turning to Charles Brandon, who had been waiting silently in the bedchamber during the morning's preparations. "I am appointing you president of the council and lord great master, so in my absence all would be answerable to you, and not Cromwell."

Brandon inclined his head. "Majesty."

"I am also appointing Edward Seymour to investigate the activities of the Poles." Henry put his fists against his hips, feeling hot fury rising up his neck. "Reginald Pole is the arch traitor whom God hates, nature refuses, and all men detest! Yes, and beasts would abhor, too, if they knew him!" He drew a sharp breath through his teeth. If he had the man in this room at this moment, he would tear him slowly apart and then feed him his own heart.

Henry removed the hat the grooms had given him and tossed it to the bed. He snatched up another from the dressing stand, and positioned it on his head. This one was even wider than the first and sported a peacock feather.

"How's your family?" he asked, studying his visage in the looking glass.

"They are well. Except my wife lost the child she was carrying."

"Then we both have lost something." Henry tested his weight on his leg. Spears of pain raced along the nerves, deep and agonizing. He could feel pus, thick and heavy, in the unhealed wound. "Sometimes I think I shall go mad, Charles. My leg is poisoned again, and it pains me. I am frightened that my son will catch the plague. And I have stopped sleeping well."

"Majesty," said Brandon, stepping forward until Henry could see his reflection over his right shoulder. "I know what it is we have both lost. What we have lost is our youth, and nothing in this world can ever return it to us."

The new ambassador from France, Louis Castillon, had a greater love for foods and wines than just about any man Henry had ever met. He was nearly as round as he was tall, with a head so round it appeared more a red bubble than flesh. His fingers were likewise pudgy and childlike, and it was with childlike abandon that the ambassador savored the great variety of foods placed on the king's dining table.

The evening was calm, with no winds or rains knocking on the windows, only the calls of nightbirds in the gardens and the distant howling of London dogs beyond the castle proper. The king's private outer chamber was calm as well, for Henry had commanded that he and the ambassador dine alone. There were personal matters to discuss.

First the king spoke of musical composition and dance, questioning the ambassador on his own preferences of instruments and steps. The ambassador ate and listened, replying with short answers that left Henry suspecting this man knew or cared little for the social graces of the English. Or perhaps he, like many French, felt himself superior to everyone else.

When Henry had had enough of the forced pleasantries, he took a loaf of crusty bread from a silver tray in the center of the table, tore off a large chunk, and said, "I wanted to talk to you in private, Monsieur L'Ambassadeur. I'm inclined toward a French bride, even though some of my advisers think I should rather seek an imperial match."

Castillon popped a boiled egg into his mouth and appeared to swallow it whole. "I admire Your Majesty's taste, and deplore that of your advisers. Perhaps they are not men of the world, as we are!" He smiled a smile that nearly sliced his face in half.

Henry took a sip of wine from his goblet, then held the cup in his hand, turning it slowly. "The lord privy seal spoke to me about two potential French brides. Maria, the king's daughter, and Marie de Guise, Madame de Longueville. I have heard further reports of Madame de Longueville, such that I cannot refrain from considering her as a wife."

Castillon lifted his own goblet, swirled the liquid and sniffed it. "A good nose. Peachy. Cat's piss. Not too sweet." He had a sip, and then a gulp. "What have you heard?"

"That Francis's daughter is too young for me, but that Madame de Longueville is much more suitable, being a widow who already produced two sons, as well as being, so they say, very voluptuous."

Castillon lifted his knife and slit open one of the plump pigeons on his platter. He licked his lips at the fragrant steam that rose from the pink flesh. "My master has told me he would think it a great honor if Your Majesty would take a French girl as your new wife. There is no lady who is not at his command." Castillon pulled a leg from the pigeon and held it up. "Except Madame de Longueville, whose marriage to the king of Scotland has already been arranged." He put the whole of the leg in his mouth, then withdrew only the bone. "Aaaaah!"

Henry frowned. "The arrangement could be broken. Tell your master I can do twice as much for him as my nephew, that beggarly and idiotic Scottish king!"

Wiping his mouth with his hand, Castillon looked up at the king in all seriousness. "Then, sir, in effect, you would be marrying another man's wife."

"I will marry whom I like! I am receiving offers from every quarter, Monsieur Castillon!"

Picking up an open oyster shell, Castillon held it close to his lips and smiled. "Forgive me. But His Majesty Francis proposes a double marriage. His nineteen-year-old son, Henri, to your daughter Mary, and one of Madame de Longueville's sisters to you. There are two of them, Louise and Renée. The former, remarkably for the French court, is still rumored to be a virgin!" Tipping the shell against his mouth, Castillon sucked down the fleshy oyster. "Take her. Take Louise. Since she is a maid. You will have the advantage of shaping the passage to your measure."

Henry burst out laughing at the ambassador's words. Then he lifted an oyster and slurped one down himself.

"I want to see my son. What have you done with my son? Where is my son?"

Edward Seymour stood with his arms behind him, watching Reginald Pole's brother Henry, the Lord Montague, pace back and forth in his filthy Tower cell.

"Your son is unharmed," said Edward. "He will remain unharmed until we are sure that you are not all traitors, like Cardinal Pole." The last two words were foul on his lips, and he gritted his teeth.

Lord Montague shook his head. Already the man was showing the strain of the Tower: the rumpled clothing, the large eyes, the rank stench of terror. "You know very well that my family has disowned Reginald. Neither my mother nor I condones or supports what he has done. We repudiate it and openly profess our allegiance to his gracious majesty."

Edward smiled. The other man's distress was pleasing. "All the same, it may be that you are hiding your true ambitions? You are the king's cousins and the last of the Plantagenets. The last of the White Rose. That makes you very famous, my lord, and very dangerous. Some say that you Poles are the true heirs, 'and will someday wear the garland and bring back happier days.' Don't they?"

Lord Montague stared at Edward, clearly shocked by the accusation, which made Edward smile all the more.

The king looked bored. Not a good thing, thought Cromwell as he and Charles Brandon were let into His Majesty's private outer chamber. Henry sat in one of his larger cushioned chairs, his bad leg over the arm, his fingers linked behind his head. On the table beside him were a violin, several books lying open, and papers half-written with great scratches of ink across some of the notations. It seemed as if his mind were scattered, and he wasn't able to focus on any particular pastime. As soon as the two men bowed, Henry said, "We must talk about marriage."

Cromwell was well aware of the distance Brandon had placed between them on the floor.

"The French, as usual, want to mess me around," said Henry. "Who does the emperor propose?"

"Your Majesty," said Cromwell, "the emperor has put forward his niece, Christina, Duchess of Milan."

"Tell me about her."

Brandon spoke up. "Originally from Denmark, she was married at thirteen to the Duke of Milan, Francesco Sforza, who died a year later. She is now sixteen, both a widow and, apparently, still a maid. And still living in Brussels with the regent, Mary of Hungary. She is reported to be a great beauty who likes nothing better than hunting and playing cards."

Henry smiled. "Hunting and playing cards? I like her already." He looked at Cromwell. "Ask our ambassador in the Netherlands to find out more about her."

"Majesty," said Cromwell. He bowed, and left the chamber. His secretary, Risley, was waiting in the corridor with another man, a fellow with slumped shoulders and an expression that Cromwell had once seen on a treed raccoon.

"My lord," said Risley, "our ambassador to the Netherlands, Sir John Hutton, is straight here."

Cromwell grabbed Hutton by the arm and steered him to a quiet place along the stone wall. "Sir John," he said, "I have some most urgent business for you to do."

"My lord," began Hutton, his brows jumping. "Mr. Risley warned me. I—"

"I want you to go out and draw up a list of potential candidates to share His Majesty's bed."

Hutton groaned. "My lord, I've not much experience among ladies, and therefore this commission to me is hard."

Cromwell tightened his grip on the man's arm, causing him to gasp. "You are to go to Brussels and make particular inquiries about Christina, Duchess of Milan."

Hutton winced and nodded.

"But while you are about it, go on to the Duchy of Cleves and make inquiries there about the duke's two sisters, Anne and Amelia. I am anxious they should enter the reckoning."

"Yes, my Lord Cromwell." At last Cromwell loosened his grip, and the ambassador hurried away.

"Your professions of loyalty were hollow, my Lord Montague."

Lord Montague sat upon the cot in his cell, staring at Edward Seymour. It had been several days since Seymour had seen the man, and even in that short a time, he was diminished all the more, with a terrible rash on his cheeks and his hair matted.

"So you said," replied Montague.

"No," said Seymour. "So *you* say." He took a letter from his jacket and began to read: "'I like well the proceeding of my brother, the cardinal. But I like not the doings in this realm and I trust to see a change of this world. I would wish that we were both over the sea. The world in England waxes all crooked. God's law is turned upside down, abbeys and churches overthrown . . .'" He glanced up at the prisoner.

"Who gave you that letter?"

"Do you deny writing it?"

Montague said nothing.

"Your letter has a postscript. 'The king is not dead but he will die one day suddenly. His leg will kill him, and we shall have jolly stirring.' Jolly stirring! Don't you mean laughter and dancing? You mean to have a party!" Edward uttered a single sour chuckle, and Montague turned to stare at the wet wall with dull eyes.

*   *   *   *

The chamber was filled with music, dancing, laughter, and conversation. Henry sat upon his throne beneath a gold canopy picking at the food on the table before him and watching the merrymaking halfheartedly. His leg throbbed mightily. Before attending the party, he had commanded one of his grooms to put fresh wrappings on it, but he scarcely dared to look at the injury as it was being done. It was all he could do to walk without the stick, but he did not want to unless absolutely necessary. He was a king, not a cripple.

"Sir Francis!" Henry gestured to Bryan, who stood a bit apart. Bryan quickly joined the king, and bowed.

"Majesty?"

Henry motioned for Bryan to sit just below him, then leaned forward to speak softly. "We have found evidence against Henry Pole, the Lord Montague. Now we need something against the lady. I ask you whether such dishonest, treacherous sons could ever have an honest mother?"

Bryan nodded, but before he could reply, Henry noticed a very pretty woman with wavy brown hair dancing among the others. "Who is that?"

Bryan followed the king's gaze. "She's the widow of the Earl of Egmond."

Henry smiled and touched his lip. "A widow?"

Bryan's eyes widened. "Wait! It's true she doesn't look it, but she's over forty!"

Henry squinted, surprised at the news, but still intrigued by the lady's looks.

"On the other hand," said Bryan, "there's a maid at court. She's only fourteen, but she already has a goodly stature. She's virtuous and sad and womanly."

Henry gave the man a warning glance. "Let the fruit ripen before you pluck it!" The grin on Bryan's face faded.

Cromwell entered the court at the far side, bearing a folded document. Henry raised his hand, and Cromwell moved through the crowds to the throne.

"Majesty," he said. "I have just received a letter from the ambassador in Brussels, Sir John Hutton, who has been gone these past weeks. He has made his inquiries on Your Majesty's behalf about the Duchess of Milan, the emperor's niece."

"What does he say?"

Cromwell opened the paper. "He writes, 'There is none in these parts for beauty of person and birth to compare with the duchess. She is not so pure white as the last queen, but when she smiles there appear two dimples in her cheeks and one in her chin, which become her very well.'"

"Does he mention any other ladies?"

"Only a sister of the Duke of Cleves. Anne. He says that—"

Henry shook his head dismissively. "I've heard about her. They say she is of no great praise either of her personage or her beauty."

"Forgive me, Majesty. But on the other hand, such a match could have its advantages. This realm has long been at the mercy of the machinations of the French or of the emperor. But Cleves is a member of the Protestant League, which daily grows in power across Europe, and could easily rival theirs. Thus could England at last make its own destiny."

Henry looked from Cromwell to Bryan to Charles Brandon, who stood near the wall drinking wine and watching from a distance. Then his gaze returned to the colorful, swirling motions of the dancers on the floor, and he thought of feminine pleasures. "Even so," he said, "I am anxious to see more of the Duchess of Milan. I want to be sure she is as beautiful as Hutton claims. Send Master Holbein to do a sketch of her by the next tide."

With undisguised pleasure, Sir Francis Bryan and several of his servants ransacked the private chambers of the now deserted Warblington Castle, home of Lady Salisbury and her family. They found nothing of value in the dining room, great hall, or parlors, save what the lady herself might have considered precious: crosses, crucifixes, statuettes of saints and martyrs. Paintings of the Christ in the throes of His Passion. But it all was worthless to Bryan. He knew what he sought and did not doubt he would discover it somewhere, in a trunk or beneath a mattress, in a bureau or tucked inside a pocket.

In the lady's bedchamber, as Bryan flung her dresses, one by one, from a clothing chest, a servant broke the lock on a blanket box at the foot of the bed. He pulled out several bolts of fabric and unrolled them on the floor.

"Sir Francis!"

Bryan turned from the lady's chest of gowns and walked over to the servant. He stared with ultimate and cold satisfaction at the discovery. There, among the cloths, were banners and flags bearing the emblems of the Pole family. The embroidery was exquisitely done, outlining lions and crowns in gold and silver threads.

"The royal arms of England," Bryan said. "My God. What expectation is there!"

He stared into the wooden box, then pulled out a tattered banner. "What's this?" He nodded for the servant to take one end, and together they unrolled it. It was quite large and heavy. Big enough to be seen from a distance. Big enough to rally men to a cause, even one so foul that it went against the supremacy of the king.

It was the banner of the Five Wounds of Christ.

Hans Holbein, master painter, sat at his easel in the parlor of the Lady Christina. She was posed near the window of her Milan manor house, her face tilted slightly, a delicate smile on her lips. She wore a gown of black velvet covered in a black coat trimmed in fox fur. Her hair was swept back beneath a peaked hood and her pale hands were folded and clutching a pair of satin gloves. At sixteen, she had in her eyes the gleam of someone much older and worldlier.

On a stool close to Holbein, looking from the painter's sketch to the lady herself, Sir John Hutton screwed up his courage and asked the question he'd been commanded to ask.

"With your permission, Madam," he said, pausing to clear his throat, "may I ask if you would consider marrying the king?"

Christina raised a brow but did not move her head. "You may ask, Sir. And as for my inclination, you know I am at the emperor's command."

Hutton almost clapped his hands at her response, but kept his hands still with effort. Dignity was of the utmost importance. "Oh, Madam!" he said. "How happy you shall be if it be your chance to be matched with my master!"

"Shall I? Why?"

Hutton shifted on his stool. "My royal master is the most gentle gentleman that lives. His nature is so benign and pleasant that I think till this day no man has heard many, if any, angry words pass his mouth."

There was slight movement at the easel. Hutton glanced over to see Holbein staring at him with a look of pure incredulity. Then he turned his attention back to the sketch.

"On the other hand," said Christina, who had not witnessed Holbein's expression, "is it not strange that the king's majesty was in so little space rid of his three queens! And they suspect that the first, my great aunt, was poisoned, the second innocently put to death, and the third lost for lack of care in her childbed."

Hutton blanched, and the lady continued her candid comments.

"Frankly, sir, if I had two heads, then one would be at His Majesty's service! Alas, I only have this one." Her faint smile disappeared, and her face clouded.

"M-madam," Hutton sputtered. "Let me plead my master's better qualities and appeal to your heart."

But Christina held up her hand. "No. You must not labor any further, for I shall not fix my heart that way. Unless, of course, the emperor commands me to!" With that, she regained her composure and did not move again, allowing Holbein to finish his sketches.

The Tower cell given to the Lady Salisbury was one of the smallest, coldest, and filthiest of them all, chosen specifically by Sir Edward Seymour to bring her down from her pious state to the knowledge that she was nothing more than a lowly subject of His Royal Majesty, and a deceitful subject at that. The floor was uneven and covered in mouse feces and old straw. The stones of the walls were jagged and wet, and the single window was too high for the lady to look out. Her bed was a cot with a thin mattress, and her toilet was a bucket in the corner. The strategy appeared to be working: her cheeks had grown sallow, her eyes suspicious, twitching at the slightest sound in the corridor beyond her cell, as if fearing the next moment might be her last.

As the lady sat shivering on her cot, Edward, with the help of his servants, held up two banners.

"Look," he commanded, "the royal banner and this, the most potent symbol of rebellion, discovered in your house!"

"Sir." The lady tried to keep her composure, but her body shook with cold and fear. "I am an old lady. I have done nothing wrong, or against the king's majesty."

Edward passed the banners to the servants and stepped closer to the woman. "You still communicate with your son Reginald. You write loving words, despite that he is a traitor. No doubt you plot new treacheries with him."

"No! How can you suppose that at my age I am capable of plotting anything? I wish only to live a quiet life, away from the world." She took a deep, tremulous breath. "Sir, my life has been filled with sorrow and suffering. My father and my brother were both executed, and now my oldest son and little grandson are here imprisoned. Oh sir! That the king in his mercy could have pity and forgive us!"

Edward rubbed his chin, then shook his head. "Madam, you are all attaindered for high treason against His Majesty. The evidence is great against you. For what you deserve you may well beg mercy. But who shall say if it be granted or not?"

The woman's resolve was shattered, and she put her hand to her mouth in horror and burst into tears.

*   *   *   *

"The Duchess of Milan is enchanting!" said Henry. He stood near the window of his outer chamber, letting the sunlight give him a clear look at the Holbein that had just arrived from Holland. He turned it back and forth, as if he could see more of her by doing so. "I am singularly pleased."

He handed the sketch off to Charles Brandon, who raised his brow and nodded admiringly. "The picture makes her look very pretty. Very full of life."

"Keep your hands off her!" Henry snatched the portrait away.

Brandon looked up sharply and chuckled uneasily.

Henry rubbed his chin. "After the wedding would follow our younger sons, ennobled with the ancient dukedoms of York, Gloucester, and Somerset. And Princess Mary could marry Don Luis." The king stepped close to Brandon, and his voice instantly went from lighthearted and pleasant to dark and ominous. Sweat had popped out on Henry's forehead and his cheeks were flushed. He glared at the duke.

"That's what you want, isn't it, Charles?" Henry continued. "You'd prefer an imperial wedding, just as Wolsey always wanted a French one. Everyone has an agenda, and what I want doesn't matter!"

Brandon's mouth opened, but he did not know what to say. His heart began to pound heavily in his chest and his arms flushed cold.

"The Poles have an agenda," Henry continued, leaning even closer to Brandon and sweating more profusely. His breath was hot and sour, and his words began to slur. "People talk about the poor little boy in the Tower, about poor old Lady Salisbury. But . . . but they have Plantagenet blood in their veins! My father told me if you leave even a sapling in the ground it can grow into a tree. And then that little boy . . . will have forty thousand troops flocking to his banners, and you will be a sucker!"

Then the king staggered, stumbled, and fell against Brandon with an agonized groan. Brandon caught him in his arms and cried out, "Majesty!"

Two of the king's grooms rushed to Brandon's side and carried Henry into his bedchamber, with the king screaming in pain.

"Fetch the king's physician!" Brandon shouted to a servant, who immediately dropped the linens he was carrying. "For God's sake, man, run!"

They laid Henry on the bed as the servant scurried from the room. Then Brandon slammed the door as the king drove his fists into the mattress and screamed again.

Chapter Nine

The king's private outer chamber was crowded with grooms, servants, and frantic nobles speaking in hushed tones, awaiting news of the king's condition. Several physicians stood by the window conferring softly and urgently. The closed door to the royal bedchamber was guarded by armed soldiers, who gazed at the hubbub with stern, unmoving faces.

As Brandon entered the outer chamber he noticed Edward Seymour among the courtiers. Seymour saw him as well and hurried over, looking worse for worry, his face pale and his eyes twitching.

"My lord," said Edward. "I must see the king!"

Brandon sneered. "Must? Just as I must see your nephew the prince sometimes, but you prevent it?"

"The king has lain ill for over a week. There has been no news of him. So there are rumors! Some say the king is dead."

"That would suit you, wouldn't it? Since your nephew would then be king."

"He is a child a few months old. That would be to no one's use. Not to mine, not to yours. And not to England's." He glanced at the guarded door and slowed his words. "With your permission, Your Grace, I would like an opportunity to disprove the rumors."

Brandon studied the man for a moment. His first thought was to toss him out, but then he decided such rumors needed dispelling. Even if the only person who believed the rumors was Edward himself. "Very well," he said.

The guards opened the bedchamber doors for the two men and then closed them again. The room was dark, with few candles burning at the bedside and the drapes pulled tight across the windows. Dr. Butts, the royal surgeon, stood by the fireplace with several other physicians, as helpless as any other man.

Edward stared at the king, who was motionless upon his pillows, his eyes closed, his body slick with sweat, the rising and falling of his chest almost indiscernible. Brandon could see the horror in Edward's face as he moved closer to the bed; the same horror Brandon had experienced when the king had collapsed in his arms. Henry's wounded leg, stretched out on a folded blanket, was exposed to the air, and the stench from the blackened flesh was so foul that Edward gagged and put his hand across his mouth and nose.

"What in the name of God?"

"This time the ulcer on his leg has failed to burst, as it has always done before," said Brandon.

Edward stared first at Brandon and then at the surgeon. "Then it must be lanced!"

The surgeon shook his head. "That might kill him."

Edward threw out his hands and stormed from the chamber.

Day melted into evening. Brandon remained with the king, moving in and out within the private chamber, standing at his bedside, conferring with the physicians—watching, hoping, praying. At some point in the night Sir Francis Bryan joined him and stood near the comatose king, keeping vigil, not knowing what else to do.

Brandon was silent for a long while, and then said, "Sir Francis, take a detachment of the guard and go to Hunsdon, so you and they may keep watch over Princess Mary with your lives. For if the king dies, some will be for the boy, yet others for her. So let it be."

Bryan nodded, his mouth set in a grim line, and walked out.

Kneeling beside the king's bed, Brandon folded his hands, squeezing them so tightly that his knuckles went white. "O Lord," he begged. "Lord, what shall I do?" He stayed there upon his knees, his heart trying to pray but his mind racing and unable to focus. And the night dragged on.

Near morning, Cromwell entered the chamber. Brandon heard him and rose. His body was numbed.

The lord privy seal gazed at the dying king, at the skeletal form that had not long ago been vital and energetic, issuing commands from his throne and riding the countryside, creating a new church and pondering the choice of a new queen. His breathing was more labored now, and even in his sleeplike state his body had begun to struggle, to kick and claw, as a man would do when drowning.

"Mr. Cromwell," said Brandon, "I bid you call for the surgeon barbers. I will answer for it."

Cromwell didn't hesitate. "Yes, Your Grace."

Within the half hour the surgeon barbers had gathered in the king's dark bedchamber. They hastily laid their array of vicious-looking knives upon a table clothed in white. A surgeon selected a particularly pointed instrument and, holding it with iron tongs, heated it over the coals in the fireplace.

Cromwell, Edward Seymour, and Bishop Gardiner had joined Brandon at Henry's bedside, to wait for whatever it was God had in mind for this, the king of England, to spare him or to take him to his eternal rest.

The surgeon moved close to the bed, studying the festering, swollen wound in the thigh and the blackened leg beneath it. He swallowed, and the click in his throat was audible.

"Your Majesty," he said, almost a prayer, "forgive me."

With that, he pressed the blade down into the putrefying flesh.

A small crowd had gathered in the courtyard at Hampton, beneath a window with parted curtains. Nobles and gentlemen, ladies and wives, wrapped in warm cloaks and capes, gazed up with anxious, hopeful faces.

And then, moments later, the king appeared at the window holding his infant prince in his arms and smiling down at his subjects. They burst into cheers and applause.

"Long live Your Majesty!" cried the crowd below. "God save Your Grace! God save the king!"

Henry turned slowly to allow his subjects a better glimpse of their royal prince, and then drew back from the window. He walked, with only the slightest limp, to one of Lady Bryan's many solemnly attired ladies and passed the infant over to her. "Soft, now," he said.

The lady held the child firmly and tenderly, lowering her eyes. "Yes, Your Majesty. Always."

Then Henry turned to Lady Bryan, who appeared more than joyous at the king's recovery from near-death. Even through her restrained and proper countenance, he detected a smile.

"How is the child?" he asked.

"He is the sweetest, prettiest boy that ever lived."

"Keep him safe. Remember, I will have no boys or dogs in these chambers, since boys are always careless and clumsy."

"Majesty."

"My Lord Cromwell."

Cromwell, who had held position beside the door, bowed, and allowed the king to exit the chamber before him.

Henry found the ride back to London even more invigorating than the ride from London to Hampton. He had seen his son, and his son was thriving: pink and fat and full of the bubbling, noisy energy with which God had seemed fit to bless healthy infants. Though his leg was still sore and stiff, the lancing had released the poison, and it was once again healing. He was alive; he was king.

The air on Henry's face was brisk and smelled of all the richness of the earth, of the abundance that was life. Henry urged his mount into a gallop, leaning forward to grip both reins and mane, lifting his head to the wind and savoring the cold. Behind him, he heard Cromwell grudgingly cluck to his own horse to catch up with the king, and behind him, the yeomen of the guard. After a long stretch at this pace, Henry drew the horse down to a walk. His and his horse's breaths matched each other, both hard and fast.

"Lord Cromwell," said Henry.

Cromwell rode up beside the king. His face was flushed with the ride. "Majesty?"

"Have you spoken to Castillon recently? What did he say about Madame de Longueville?"

"She has already gotten married to the king of Scotland."

Henry thought about this for a moment, and then dismissed it. "She'll regret it when she discovers what the weather is like up there!"

Cromwell nodded. "The ambassador mentioned that two other cousins of King Francis were potentially available to Your Majesty: Marie de Vendome and Anne of Lorraine. Apparently Marie de Vendome has already announced her intention to become a nun, but Castillon thought this not necessarily an obstacle."

Henry laughed. "How very French! So we have the two sisters of Marie de Guise, Louise and Renée, the latter still a virgin. And now these other two, one of whom wants to be a nun." He looked out at the rolling countryside, at a distant herd of cattle, and a brace of grouse fluttering from the tall grasses of the field. "I want pictures of them. I want to see them. I need to see and know the woman who is to be my companion for life."

"Majesty."

Henry turned slightly in his saddle. "What of the negotiations with the Duchess of Milan?"

"Your Majesty, in that regard there is a significant obstacle."

"What obstacle?"

Cromwell swatted a horsefly from his face. "There is the problem of affinity. As niece to the emperor, the duchess is therefore the great niece of Katherine of Aragon."

Henry waved his hand and grunted petulantly.

"In the past," said Cromwell, "such obstacles might have been over-come by papal dispensation."

"But," Henry added angrily, "there is no question of that now! Perhaps, as head of the Church of England, I shall be allowed by the emperor to make such a dispensation."

"Yes, Your Majesty. Naturally."

Henry looked ahead at the road, which dipped and then curved out of sight beyond the trees. It was still a long way to Whitehall, and he was suddenly weary.

"It will take a good sport to make me amorous again," he said, more to himself than to his secretary.

"Our Father, who art in heaven, hallowed be Thy name. Thy kingdom come, Thy will be done on Earth as it is in Heaven."

Kneeling, Lord Montague shifted his weight on his knees, trying to escape the searing pain brought on by the boils there and upon his shins and ankles. But it made no difference. To kneel and pray was agony; to humble himself before God in supplication and petition was misery. His hands, raw with the damp, were clasped and raised up toward the ceiling. A rat sniffed one knee and moved on.

He closed his eyes momentarily at the sound of the cell door open-ing. He knew who was entering. *God help me.* He turned to face his doom.

"My Lord Montague," said Bishop Gardiner as he followed Edward Seymour into the cell. "I am come to help you to a better place."

Montague struggled to his feet and clenched his fists at his sides. He stared at Seymour. "You know I am not guilty, you bastard. Only my brother is guilty, but you can't touch him, can you? So you have to kill the innocent."

Edward raised a pompous brow, sending a shiver of hatred down Montague's spine. "Your guilt has been established beyond question."

"No, it hasn't. There used to be procedures here, proper, legal proce-dures in this country, to establish who was guilty and who was not. But that's gone now. You don't even have to have a trial. So since there is no judiciary, what's left is only tyranny."

"You see," said Edward. "You condemn yourself from your own mouth."

Montague stepped threateningly close to Edward. "I tell you this, Lord Seymour. The king will be out of his wits one day!" Then he looked at Gardiner. "Where is my mother?"

"Lady Salisbury is here," the bishop replied. "Within this Tower."

"Please have a care for her, my lord bishop. Whatever she has done, be it so offensive as it may, she is an old and true woman who has always lived by God's precepts and done harm to no one."

"I will have a tender care for her, body and soul, my lord. Trust me."

Montague studied the cleric's face for a moment to see if he might be telling the truth. He chose to believe him.

Turning, Montague snatched up a wrinkled piece of paper from the small splintered desk. "I have written a few words to my boy. You may read them. They are only innocuous words of love. Please give this to him."

Gardiner nodded and accepted the paper.

"We have to go," said Edward. "The time is set."

Montague walked toward the door, then paused. "You know, my lord. Here is the truth. The king never made a man but he destroyed him again. So have a care, my lord."

He walked out into the dank torchlit corridor, followed by Seymour and Gardiner and two armed guards. He sensed the men slowing down behind him, and as he glanced back he saw Gardiner appear to hand something to Seymour. The note to his son? Certainly not. Surely the bishop, a man of God, would not betray such a simple promise at the moment his father was to die.

Surely, Heavenly Father. Gardiner will not deny me this one last thing! But though his heart wished it, his mind knew the truth.

Anne Stanhope giggled and playfully slapped at Sir Francis Bryan as he drew her hair back from her bare breasts and licked her nipple. They lay in Anne's bedchamber, alone except for a fly on the bedcovers and the morning sunlight strobing the floor as tree branches beyond the window swayed in the breeze.

"I thought your husband warned you to stay away from me," said Bryan, shifting up onto his elbow and running his finger along her lower lip.

"He did," said Anne. "But now he doesn't care. He said he couldn't be bothered to kill you."

Bryan laughed. "The less I know about your husband, the more he fascinates me. I know, more or less, where most people stand. Suffolk, Cromwell, I know their true beliefs, even if they try to hide them. But Edward. Who knows what *he* truly believes?"

"Would you like me to tell you?"

"For services rendered?"

Anne huffed cheerfully, then touched the corner of Bryan's eye patch. "You're not quite as good as you think you are."

"That's still pretty good. Now tell me."

Anne studied her lover, and then looked at the ceiling. "He believes in himself. In his destiny. Prince Edward is the key to his destiny. Nothing will stand in his way."

"He's a reformer?"

Anne gave him a sharp look.

"No," said Bryan, "you can answer. I am, too. I swear. Everyone knows. I hate popery with a passion. That's why sometimes they call me the Black Pope."

Anne burst out laughing, so loud the mouse scurried away into a crack in the wall. "Hello!" she said. "I've just been fucked by the Pope!"

Bryan made the sign of the cross over Anne's pubic mound. *"E nomine patri, et filii et spiritus sancti."* Then he lay back. "How does he think about Cromwell?"

"That I don't know." They remained silent for a moment, then Anne said, "But did anyone ever discover who shot Robert Packington?"

Bryan just looked at her.

*   *   *   *

"Of these French girls," said Henry, "I like the look of some more than others, but can the likeness be trusted? May the artist not be using some license, to flatter the lady or to please me? Even Master Holbein?"

Spread out upon the large table in the king's outer chamber were numerous sketches of young French ladies, all poised with slight smiles on their faces. He lifted one and then another, gazing at them and then putting them down again. Cromwell stood across the table watching silently.

"I can't help thinking of that phrase *caveat emptor*," said Henry, "let the buyer beware. How am I supposed to choose without seeing them in the flesh? Talk to Castillon."

Cromwell bowed, hands folded, his black robe rustling softly. "If Your Majesty might still choose to consider the simple and profound charms of Anne of Cleves or her sister, and the benefits to you and to this realm of a new alignment with the Protestant League?"

Henry did not reply, but picked up another portrait and dropped it down again.

The chamberlain at the door announced, "His Grace, the Bishop of Winchester."

Bishop Gardiner entered and bowed to the king. Then he exchanged an icy look with Cromwell as the man left the chamber.

"My Lord Bishop," said Henry, lifting up yet another sketch, frowning, and placing it back with the others.

"Majesty, forgive me," said Gardiner, moving close to the table. "But it has come to my attention that certain evangelicals are still preaching against the six articles of faith and Your Majesty's religious settlement."

Henry crossed his arms, listening.

"Mr. John Lambert is one such, who preaches weekly in London to large audiences. Mr. Lambert denies the real presence of God in the sacrament of Communion, saying rather that it is merely a symbolic commemoration of Christ's Passion."

Henry slammed his hand on the table and the sketches fluttered.

"Then Mr. Lambert is condemned by Christ's own words, who said, '*This* is my body!' If he does not recant, then he must be burned. I will not be a patron to heretics!"

Gardiner nodded, but Henry sensed a hesitation in his manner. "Is there more?"

"Perhaps this is none of my business, Your Majesty, but I am told that Mr. Lambert is well known to my Lord Cromwell. It appears they were educated together at Cambridge and that when, six months ago, Lambert was apprehended on suspicion of promoting heresy, Lord Cromwell had the charges dismissed."

Henry leaned back, his mind gone now from the potential brides and considering what Gardiner had said as carefully as he had considered the sketches.

Lady Salisbury could no longer stomach most of the poor meals brought to her by the Tower guard—slimy, stinking slop, often filled with tiny beetles—and she found herself throwing up nearly everything she was able to get down. The gown in which she'd been brought to the cell so long ago was now a sack upon her emaciated frame. Her bones ached, and she shivered constantly in the cold and the wet. She now stood in the tiny slice of daylight that filtered through the window and onto the floor.

"Will you tell me the truth?" she asked, turning toward Edward Seymour, who had entered her cell and stood staring at her as if she were not even human, but a rat or fly, or mere shadow on the wall. "What has happened to my son? My son, is he dead?"

Edward nodded. "He deserved his death."

Lady Salisbury fell to her knees and rent the bodice of her gown. She looked up at the man, who remained unmoved. "And my poor grandson, who has now lost his father? Where is he?"

"He is alive."

"Is that all you can say?"

Edward tipped up his chin in victory.

"Oh!" wailed the lady. "God forgive you!"

* * * *

The chamberlain's staff pounded the tile floor at the door to the king's Presence Chamber. "His Excellency, the French ambassador!"

Henry leaned forward in his throne as Ambassador Castillon, followed by several servants, entered the room. He was dressed in a cape of deep red, a doublet with wide, slashed sleeves, black shoes, and a jeweled cap. He removed his cap, swept his arm out, and bowed low.

On the dais step to the left of the king stood Cromwell, hands behind his back, jaw tight. Dull gray afternoon light from the windows leached the bright colors from the tapestries and the gold seals upon the walls.

"Monsieur Castillon!" said the king.

"Majesty."

"We have been considering all these candidates for our hand. They are . . . so many!" He laughed, but Castillon offered only a half-smile in response. "But the fact is, because so many of them appear attractive, I do not see how I could approach each individually. So, is it possible that King Francis would agree to assemble seven or eight of them at Calais, so that I could go there and make their acquaintances all at the same time?"

Castillon glanced from the king to Cromwell, then back again. Cromwell could see the pompous French indignation on his face. "No," said Castillon. "It is not the custom in France to send ladies of that rank, and of such noble and princely families, to be passed in review as if they were prize horses. Perhaps if Your Majesty desired one of these ladies, you could send an envoy to report on her manner and appearance? In the traditional way."

Henry shook his head. "By God, I trust no one but myself! The thing touches me too near. I wish to see them and know them sometime before deciding."

Castillon's brow furrowed, but then he chuckled. It was a strained and humorless sound. "Maybe Your Majesty would like to mount them one after another, and keep the one you find to be the best broken in?" Then his smile fell away and he stepped forward, his voice low and full of disgust. "Is *that* the way the knights of your Round Table treated women in your country in past times?"

Henry stood and pointed his finger threateningly. "You have ten seconds to leave this room," he said, "or I will beat you like the dog you are!"

Fear flickered across Castillon's face, and he bowed quickly, then turned about and left the chamber, his servants trotting after him. Henry dropped back into his seat and let out an angry breath.

"Mr. Cromwell!" He turned to his secretary. "An incorrigible heretic called John Lambert is now imprisoned in the Tower and likely soon to be burned." Cromwell knew Henry was watching for a reaction, but he did not give him one. "I believe you know Mr. Lambert?"

"I knew him many years ago at Cambridge."

"But not since?"

"Not to my knowledge, Your Majesty."

Henry rubbed his chin. "I suppose when you were at Cambridge you might have shared his opinions? Tell me, Mr. Cromwell, what do you believe now?"

Cromwell's mouth opened slightly, closed, and then opened again. "As the world stands, Your Majesty, I believe what *you* believe."

"Then," Henry turned more in his seat to face Cromwell straight on, "you think it right he should die?"

"Yes, Majesty. Unless he recants. Yes."

Henry sat back and waved a hand to dismiss Cromwell. But when the man was halfway across the room, Henry said, "I forgot. Tell me their names again."

Cromwell looked back. "Majesty?"

"The sisters of the Duke of Cleves. You mentioned them once."

"Anne and Amelia." Then he took a deep yet silent breath. It was time to tread cautiously, like a man crossing a frozen river. A Lutheran queen would safeguard the Reformation and help ensure his own continued power at court. He had to encourage the king in this direction, carefully but firmly. "I believe one would be an excellent choice."

Henry scratched his beard. "Send someone to look at them. We'll have a second opinion."

Mary smiled and held out her hand for Ambassador Chapuys as he entered her parlor. She had been anticipating his visit ever since word arrived that he would come to Hunsdon House. She'd not had news in quite a while, and was anxious to know how the marriage plans for the king, and for herself, were progressing. Yet she could immediately see from the expression on his handsome face that things had not gone as planned.

Chapuys bowed and kissed the lady's hand. Mary motioned for him to sit in one of the cushioned chairs by the open window.

"What news of the king's marriage to the Duchess of Milan?" she asked as she took her own seat and tucked her feet primly beneath her skirts.

"Alas, Princess, I think it is not to happen." Chapuys shook his head. "The duchess is the great-niece of your mother, so the affinity is too touching. Also, I think the lady does not want to marry the king. She has heard some reports about him which rather alarmed her."

This wasn't surprising, but was greatly disappointing. Then she asked another question, for which she knew the answer. "Then, I shall not marry Don Luis?"

Chapuys nodded. "They say that the king might now marry a French lady, and you one of King Francis's sons."

"Surely that would not please you?"

"Anything would please me, my lady, which made you happy."

Mary smiled ruefully, and placed her hand atop his. "I am afraid," she said, "I was not born for happiness, Excellency." He said nothing, and in his silence she heard his agreement. It hurt her heart, but was no surprise. After a moment she stood and wandered to a small table on which stood a small crucifix surrounded by candles in silver bases. The flames illuminated the sad but ethereal countenance of Christ. "I hear Lady Salisbury is kept in the Tower, and her son gone?"

"It is sadly so. Her grandson, too, is kept a prisoner."

Mary turned toward Chapuys. "That poor boy! I shall write to the king and plead for their lives. For what are they but an old woman and an innocent child? How should they threaten the throne?" Then she shook her head. Disgust edged her voice. "I am sure all of it is Cromwell's doing. I should not say this to many people, Excellency, but I say it to you, that I agree with those who say he is Satan's messenger. I swear he has poisoned the king's mind. If I could, I would strip him from the king's side and burn him!"

Swan Castle, the vast home of the Duke of Cleves, was sprawled upon a steep hill overlooking the Rhine. Impressive in its size, it boasted a 180-foot-tall tower topped by a stone swan, visible from quite a distance. It was the first thing that revealed itself in the heavy morning fog as Sir John Hutton and a second English envoy, Sir Beard, emerged from the forest beside the river. Hutton squinted and wiped sweat and damp air from his brow. His nerves and stomach had been tormenting him these last miles. If there were any other duty to perform he would choose it over inspecting ladies for the king. But thus was his destiny, and thus he was here, cramped gut and all. He spurred his horse off the main road and onto the winding path leading up the hillside. Beard clucked to his own mount and followed close behind.

Proper papers presented to the guards gained the men access, and a servant ushered them through the great hall and into a smaller, yet elegant presence chamber.

"Your Highness," announced the servant as Hutton and Beard stepped through the door. "The English envoys."

"Gentlemen." Duke William inclined his head and pursed his lips. He was a large man with a high forehead and facial hair that seemed more boyish than manly. His long, shapeless robes accentuated his bulk. Standing quietly about the chamber were a number of councilors, who studied the Englishmen with solemn curiosity.

Hutton and Beard bowed.

"Your Highness," said Hutton.

William stepped forward, chin up, hands on his hips. "Let us, from the beginning, be frank with one another. I hate the way the Italians, the French, and others always manage to speak so beautifully—about nothing at all."

The three men laughed.

"So," continued William, "His Majesty King Henry needs a wife, and he is interested in my sisters."

Hutton nodded. "His Majesty has been persuaded of their amiability and their suitability as royal consorts."

"Especially Anne, the eldest," said Beard, "who has been much praised in the king's hearing."

William cocked his head dismissively. "I am not surprised."

Hutton felt the tightness in his stomach intensify. "His Majesty would also propose a marriage of his daughter Mary to your eldest son. A liaison with the Protestant League and the recruitment of a hundred seasoned cannoneers for his army."

William nodded, and what may have been a smile settled on his thick lips. "Well, then. There is much to discuss."

Beard held up a hand. "But first we should like your permission to meet your sisters."

William's smile vanished. "Why?"

Hutton's arms flushed cold, but he kept his voice steady. "The king would expect us to report back to him on what we have seen. To say we have not seen the ladies would not exactly please him."

"He has also asked for a portrait of Anne to be sent back to him," said Beard.

William crossed his arms. "Unfortunately my court painter, Mr. Cranach, is ill and indisposed."

"In that case," said Beard, "we can send over Mr. Holbein, who is an admirable artist."

"Perhaps," said William. "But you are going too quickly. What do you think my country is, a meat market?" He snorted silently. "I will arrange with my chancellor for negotiations to commence, including the question of a suitable dowry. And you may have the opportunity, at some stage, of being presented to my sisters." Then he flicked his hand. The interview was over.

Beard blinked and took a step forward. "But Your Highness, we—"

"Will meet again," said William. "Good day, gentlemen."

Reluctantly, the Englishmen bowed and retired from the chamber to await William's next decision.

Cromwell nodded for the guard to leave him alone in the cell. Once the door was closed, he turned to gaze upon his old friend John Lambert. The man stood at the barred window, almost unrecognizable from his ill treatment in the Tower. Few people in this world could touch Cromwell's heart, for the world was cold and hard, and to survive, a man had likewise to be cold and hard. But Lambert was a companion from many years back, a good and kind man who had always treated Cromwell like a brother. Who had never spoken a false word against him, or asked of him any favors.

"John," said Cromwell.

"Thomas!" Lambert's filthy, bruised face lit up. "How good to see you again. And how excellently you have done in the world."

"I could wish our reunion were in some better place."

Lambert came close and embraced his friend. "Oh, I shall be quit of this room soon enough, and on my way to a far better place."

Cromwell set his teeth against each other. "John," he said quietly. "You do not have to die. All you need to say to satisfy the king is that after consecration, the wafer and wine are truly the body and blood of Christ."

"But you and I know they are not."

"You are only asked to say it, not believe it."

Lambert studied his friend's face. "Ah, Thomas, I see now what it takes for a man to prosper. He must make a practice of hypocrisy."

"There is no harm in discretion. And believe me, I want to spare you the awful pains which are prepared for you."

"Did not Christ Himself suffer awful pains, Thomas?"

Cromwell grabbed Lambert's arm, hard enough to startle him. "We don't need martyrs! We need living men who will go on quietly about the business of spreading our Reformation."

"But who will now believe a word I say if I alter my opinion on such a fundamental thing?"

Cromwell let go of the man. "I say to you again, John. Will you live or die? You still have a free choice!"

"My Lord Cromwell," said Lambert, his voice soft now, and sad, though not for himself. "I see that all this while we have not been talking about me at all, but about you. Nor about my poor conscience, but about yours. I see that you are afraid of guilt by association, and would rather I perjured my own soul."

Cromwell shook his head even as he knew the man was telling a dreadful truth.

"Alas," said Lambert. "It is the only thing I have left in the world."

"I am sorry you choose not to save yourself."

"Please," said Lambert, kindly now. "As an old friend, I beg you. Don't let it trouble your conscience any further."

Cromwell chose to watch the execution from a window in the Tower. The distance was preferable to standing among the crowd, who would no doubt murmur protests at the burning of the gentle man who had ministered to them. And the dank Tower air was preferable to smelling his friend's broiling flesh.

As the king had ordered in his six articles of faith, the penalty for denying Lambert's heresy would be death by burning. There was no mercy or recourse to be found.

Two guards led Lambert to the stake, which had been secured in the ground and surrounded with bundles of sticks. Lambert wore only a tattered, dirty gown. His head and feet were bare, and his arms were tied behind his back. Yet his face was peaceful and unmoved. Several women in the crowd raised their hands toward him as if asking for a blessing.

The executioner, wearing a black leather mask, bowed to Lambert. "Forgive me, Mr. Lambert."

Lambert nodded. "With this body of mine, deal with as you wish."

The executioner's assistants immediately pushed Lambert up against the stake and lashed him securely across the neck, chest, and hips. Lambert fixed his calm and steady gaze upon the torch that had just been passed to the executioner. The man raised the flame for the crowd to see, then held it down to the bundled sticks.

"It is a slow flame, Mr. Lambert," said the executioner as the sticks smoldered then caught fire.

Lambert smiled, a bizarre, ecstatic smile. "But it will still take me to Paradise!"

The fire spread out and around the stake, orange and red flames leaping and bobbing, and then they moved inward to engulf the timbers at Lambert's feet. Lambert drew his legs up with the first, scorching caress, but then he threw back his head and shouted, "All for Christ!" and forced them down again into the blaze. Cromwell clenched his fists against the windowsill as his friend's gown caught fire and the flames shot up around the priest's body, enshrouding his arms and head, setting his hair alight in a dreadful golden halo.

"All for my Christ!" Lambert cried again.

And the conflagration engulfed him completely.

When the body stopped twitching, Cromwell left the Tower for Whitehall Palace, where he was announced at the king's private outer chamber. He stood silently as the king, seated at a table, elbows planted firmly to either side of a silver plate, shucked and sucked down boiled oysters. A low fire burned in the grate upon the hearth. Cromwell kept his face turned away from it.

At last Henry looked up from his meal and nodded for Cromwell to speak.

"Mr. Lambert has gone to his execution."

Henry grinned sourly. "And to hell!" He tossed an empty shell onto the floor and picked up another glistening oyster. Then he frowned at his secretary. "And what more, Cromwell?"

Cromwell drew a letter from his robe and placed it on the table in front of the king. "Princess Mary begs Your Majesty to spare the life of Lady Salisbury, who was like a mother to her."

"Alas," said Henry, "she was also a mother to that monster Reginald Pole, who even Heaven cannot forgive." He slurped the meat from the shell and ran his fingers around his lips. He raised his brow again, waiting for Cromwell's next message.

"Duke William says his painter is ill. He cannot furnish images of his sister Anne."

The king flicked the shell away, lifted another, and held it poised at his mouth. "Send Holbein," he said. "I must see her image."

Hutton and Beard were called on in their chambers in Swan Castle to follow a servant down to the chamber in which they'd met Duke William. Hutton's nerves were jangling again. There had been no explanation as to the summons, and he was more accustomed to things going ill than their going well. He wished he were more like Beard, calm in all matters.

The servant opened the chamber door and ushered the Englishmen inside. But there was no one waiting for them. Hutton and Beard glanced around, confused.

But then a far door opened and William entered, followed by two women dressed in voluminous robes and tall caps from which hung thick veils. It was impossible to determine the women's figures or see their faces.

Hutton gave Beard a frantic glance. The usually collected Beard returned the same glance.

"Gentlemen," said William, stepping aside and holding out a hand. "You have my permission to look upon my sisters."

"Your Highness," began Hutton, "we cannot even tell which is Anne!"

One of the cloaked ladies said, "Sirs, I am Anne."

Both Hutton and Beard bobbed their heads, trying to see through the woman's veil.

"And I am Amelia, Your Honors," said the second lady.

Beard turned to William. "Highness, for our purposes, this is no good!"

William's mouth dropped open and his face twisted in anger. "No good?" he bellowed. "What? Would you see them naked?"

Hutton lowered his face, abashed but not surprised. He was used to such troubles. He was used to things going wrong.

The Lady Salisbury sat on her cot combing her greasy hair for lice, her hand shaking with age, cold, and terror. Her bare feet were braced weakly on the cold stone floor, and were covered in bites from mice and fleas.

Sir Edward Seymour looked at her for a moment, wondering if he might find something there to pity, but there was not a thing. In spite of the outrage he'd heard here and about—that it was a sin to treat an old woman so—he cared nothing for that. She was a traitor. Her entire family was traitorous. She would suffer for her haughty selfishness.

"Have you not been praying, lady?" Edward said, savoring the words as a yeoman of the guard stood beside him, staring icily at the woman. "Your head is going to be cut off now."

Lady Salisbury dropped her comb and stared. "No. No!"

"You should have made your peace with God. And with His Majesty."

"Leave me alone! Go away!"

Edward signaled the guard, who advanced on Lady Salisbury. But she screamed and leapt up, nearly knocking over the cot.

"For God's sake!" said Edward. "Have some dignity! Come with us."

Lady Salisbury threw her arms out wildly, stumbling back and forth in an attempt to keep away from the guard, and then she slumped in a corner, her hands tearing chunks of hair from her head. The guard grabbed her by the arm, and she screamed again.

Edward turned from the unseemly sight, and left the cell. He heard the guard dragging Lady Salisbury behind him.

Von Waldburg heard Cardinal Pole's piteous weeping before he even opened the door to the small seminary chamber. He found Pole on the bare stone floor, bent over, his hands clasped in desperate prayer.

"Eminence!" cried Pole when he saw the older man.

"My child," said Von Waldburg.

Pole reached up and grabbed Von Waldburg's hand. "He killed them! My brother! My poor mother! Oh, Gesù! Gesù!" Then he broke down again, covering his face with both hands, and wailing in distress.

Von Waldburg gave him a moment for his grief, but that was enough. There were critical things to accomplish that could not be done under the weight of tears or angst. He said, "The king of England is the most cruel and abominable tyrant. There is no doubt now that he must be overthrown by force. Better that he should die than risk the eternal damnation of all his subjects."

Pole's hands remained over his face. "But we can't do anything!"

"We can. His Holiness is ready to promulgate the bull of excommunication. The emperor and the French have made their peace and both are willing to point their swords at England. They will withdraw their ambassadors and prepare a fleet for invitation. The Holy Father expects you to return to the Netherlands and France to assist their preparations."

Pole looked at Von Waldburg. "Please! Not again! Let me help in other ways!"

"What?" Von Waldburg had no patience for this. "Tell me! Are you frightened?"

"Eminence, I—"

"You should thank God that He has called your family to Heaven!" Von Waldburg's voice rose. "You should not weep! What is belief if not belief in the will of God? You think the Holy Father wants you to go to the Netherlands for his own sake? Or do you think he has asked God for guidance?"

Pole opened his mouth then closed it. He appeared stunned, and immediately rubbed his face with the palm of his hand, driving away the tears. "Forgive me."

Von Waldburg nodded solemnly. "When I was a young priest in Germany, my family's house was occupied by Lutheran mercenaries. I had a beautiful sister whom I loved more than anything in the world, perhaps even more than God. They raped her, cut off her breasts, and threw bits of her to their dogs, right in front of my eyes."

Pole went pale.

"All of us," said Von Waldburg, "have burdens to carry, Cardinal Pole." Then he nodded and withdrew, leaving the other man to his prayers.

The boy no longer cried out for his father or grandmother. Lack of proper food, isolation, and utter despair had reduced him to a weak, grubby creature who seemed unable to tell friend from foe anymore, day from night, nobleman from peasant.

Edward entered the dismal Tower cell and beckoned the child to come to him. The boy struggled up from the straw- and feces-covered floor where he'd been sitting, knees drawn to his chin, and walked slowly over. His eyes were hollow, sunken, as were his cheeks.

Holding out his hand, Edward smiled. "Come along now, Master Pole." The boy took the hand and looked up at Edward with an expression of fragile hope, not knowing why they were leaving the cell or to what fate the leaving would take him.

Edward nodded to the guard, who moved aside to let them pass.

Henry stared out his private chamber window at the distant gray waters of the Thames and the tall, ominous walls of the Tower beside it. He smiled a cold smile. "There you are, Cardinal Pole," he said. "Now eat your heart."

Chapter Ten

The War Council was gathered in the Great Hall, the wealthiest nobles of the land, captains of the king's army, and naval officers, the most important of them seated at a long, gold cloth–covered table, the others crowded against one another, standing as close as possible to hear the proceedings. Many were already dressed as if for battle, helmets and swords at the ready. The air in the vast chamber was tense, filled with the sour scents of sweat and outrage. Armed guards stood inside and outside the hall doors, their spears and pikes crossing the entrances.

King Henry was seated at the head of the table. To his right were the Lord Suffolk Charles Brandon, Sir Thomas Seymour, and the earls of Shrewsbury, Derby, and Arundel. To the king's left were Sir Edward Seymour, Bishop Gardiner, Richard Rich, and Sir Francis Bryan. The empty chair belonged to Thomas Cromwell, who had stood to present the report he had received the previous afternoon.

"My lords," Cromwell said, glancing first at the king and then at the others, "since the signing of the Treaty of Toledo between the emperor and the king of France, there are vital and unavoidable signs of their mutual preparations for war against this realm."

Men exchanged looks of fury and fierce determination. Bryan, his elbow on the table, his hand stroking his chin, studied the others with his good eye.

"We know how much in these matters they have been urged on by the Vicar of Rome. And now we hear competent reports of fleets gathering at Antwerp and Boulogne, and an army in the Netherlands. Furthermore, the French and imperial ambassadors have been recalled by their masters."

"My lords," said Brandon. "We ourselves have not been idle under such provocations. Defense forces have been mustered and beacons set up along the coast for warning. Work has begun on ancillary forts that face the English Channel. In the north, our borders have been strengthened against the Scots. His Majesty's fleet of warships has been provisioned. And foreign vessels have been forbidden to leave these shores without royal permission, on pain of death."

"My lords!" declared the king. "How can anyone doubt that the Pope, that pestilent idol, that enemy of all truth and usurper of all princes, is now conspiring to corrupt England's religion and strip her of all her wealth. At such a time it is important for me to be among my people. I shall visit all the places where we are building forts and barricades to defend this realm, for the encouragement of my subjects and to the terror of my enemies. Gentlemen."

Henry shoved back from the table and stalked from the room. Those seated rose quickly to bow in his wake, and the others stepped back to give him room. Cromwell collected his papers and followed after the king.

As the others pulled into small groups to discuss the turmoil, Tom Seymour moved to Bryan, who remained seated, watching the activity around him.

"It seems we are threatened from everywhere, Sir Francis," said Tom, his eyes darting back and forth as if fearing a Frenchman might be among them, ready to kill him with a dagger. "Scotland, Spain, the Low Countries! We are like a morsel among these choppers."

Bryan chuckled. "And I'll tell you something else, Tom. According to Cromwell's agents, just two weeks ago Cardinal Pole left Rome on a secret mission."

Tom's brows went up. "Shall we be after him again?"

"As soon as we have more news of his whereabouts, we shall." He sat back in his chair. "Sharpen your knives."

The day had gone long, and Cromwell's head pounded as if assaulted by the king's cannons. He entered his office, where his scribes and servants were busily copying letters, drawing up papers, and bringing in and dispatching reports and messages. But as he approached his desk he noticed another man standing quietly by, waiting to be recognized.

"Ah, Master Holbein."

The artist bowed. "My lord."

Cromwell dropped into his chair, pressed the heel of his hand to his temple, and said, "I've another commission for you. The Duke of Cleves has given permission for you to paint his daughter Anne. You should leave at once."

Holbein tilted his head and gestured out at all the activity in the office. "Your Honor has so many pressing things, and yet you have time to talk about a painting?"

Cromwell lowered his voice. "This is no ordinary painting, Mr. Holbein. A great many things hang upon it." His voice went even lower, and Holbein had to step closer to the desk to hear him. "To that effect, however you find the lady, whatever her actual appearance, I pray you, use your art and give her at least a pleasing countenance."

Holbein stared. "Even if she is as ugly as sin?"

"I am fairly certain she is not so."

"But, still. You wish me, if necessary, to lie?"

Cromwell managed a smile. "Surely all art is a lie, Mr. Holbein?"

The journey from England, by ship and by carriage, had been nerve-racking. Holbein, though merely an artist and of no interest to any army or kingdom, felt the tension of the world around him, hot and oppressive like a heavy woolen coat. It was with no small relief when he crossed into the Duchy of Cleves—a friendly Lutheran land—and spied the imposing Swan Castle upon a cliff.

After being greeted by anxious Sirs Hutton and Beard, and then waiting alone in the parlor for more than an hour, setting up his easel and arranging his charcoal, a silverpoint stylus, brushes, paints, and boards upon a small table, then pacing back and forth from window to window, hands deep in the pockets of his cloak, tapping his teeth together, trying not to let impatience get the better of him—he met the lady at long last. A servant opened the door, and Anne and an elderly female servant entered the chamber a few steps behind Anne's brother, Duke William, who greeted the painter and then left him to his work.

Anne was a plain yet pleasant-appearing young woman, with a square jaw, small eyes, and shoulders a bit too broad for a lady. Her high-necked gown was burgundy trimmed in gold braiding, but bearing few jewels or other adornments. It was impossible to tell the color of her hair, which was swept back severely beneath an odd lace headpiece shaped like a bird trying to take wing. She curtsied and then stood where Holbein bid her stand, gazing emotionlessly in his direction, her hands clasped at her waist.

The portrait was to be done quickly, and therefore its size would be limited. Holbein selected a small piece of smooth wood, set it upon his easel, and began to sketch the outline of the lady with the stylus. Anne's lady pulled up a chair and sat close by, alert and ready to protect her mistress from the slightest hint of trouble.

After a while, the silence grew to be too much. Holbein, peering back and forth from his painting to his subject, said, "My lady, would you mind if I asked you a question?"

Anne glanced from her servant back to the artist. Her brows drew together.

"Forgive me," said Holbein.

"No," Anne said then. Her German accent was quite heavy. "Please. My English is not perfect, but I am learning from an English tutor."

Holbein nodded, and put his brush to the wood, fashioning a small smile where there was none. "Where did you grow up? Here in Cleves?"

Anne nodded. "With my mother, mainly. She was a good mother but—how to say?—a little strict. My sister, Amelia, and I . . . we were kept away from the world. She was careful after us. We could not see many people."

"So, tell me. What do you like doing?"

"Doing? Yes, doing. I like very much to sew. I am sewing every day."

Holbein softened her square jaw. "What else?"

"Else?"

"Do you like to dance? Do you play music?"

"No. I cannot sing or play music. Of course not."

Holbein paused and glanced up. "Why do you say 'of course not'?"

"In my country, women are considered very light, and not . . . not nice, if they are learned at school. Or have any knowledge of music. Is it not the same in England?"

Holbein let out a long, silent breath, and continued to paint.

"She is pleasing," said Henry, holding the miniature portrait that had just arrived from Cleves. "Has our ambassador also been able to see her properly?"

Cromwell, who had brought the portrait to the king in his private outer chamber, nodded and smiled. "Yes, Your Majesty. Sir John Hutton has written me in great praise of the princess's person." The secretary opened the letter that had accompanied the portait. "He writes, 'that as well for the face as for the whole body she is incomparable and excels the Duchess of Milan as the golden sun excels the silver moon.'"

As Henry studied the portrait, Cromwell studied the face of the king. He could see that the king was still uncertain. But he had to make sure Anne of Cleves became the next queen. He could think of no other way to secure the Reformation and his own personal security.

As Henry put the portrait down on the table, Cromwell took a small step forward. "Your Majesty, if I may?"

Henry nodded absently.

"The Duchess of Milan is no longer an option. Nor, since the emperor and the French are now in league against us, are any of the French women. Your Majesty is beset by enemies. Marriage to Anne of Cleves would bring with it the military and financial support of the Protestant League, and with such a bride, Your Majesty can look forward to the production of a duke of York, and many other sons."

The king looked down at the portrait, then back up at Cromwell. It was uncomfortably clear he had still not made up his mind.

"Your Honor," said Hutton as he and Beard bowed before Duke William in the duke's sunny presence chamber. Though the duke and his counselors were sour as usual, Hutton was light of heart. The letter he'd just received from England had been the news he'd been hoping for. The king was pleased with what he'd seen. Hutton had succeeded in making the match. "His Majesty was much taken by the portrait of your sister Anne. He encourages you to send your ambassadors to England to conclude negotiations of a suitable dowry, and so on."

Duke William looked at his counselors, then back at the English envoy. "His Majesty is once again premature."

Hutton's brow rose in confusion. *Dear God, now what?*

Beard said, "But surely . . . ?"

The duke shook his head. "I think the king should come to me publicly and on bended knee beg for my sister's hand. And for the protection of the Protestant League!"

Hutton's heart sank. He glanced at Beard, who was clearly in the same state of shock.

"In any case," said Duke William. "Anne is already promised, formally, to the Duke of Lorraine's son, and I do not see how I can break that promise and keep my honor."

It was a long moment before Hutton found his voice. "Your Honor," he said, "if true, this is most unexpected and unwelcome news."

The duke sniffed. "That is because you expected from the start to have your way with Cleves, and my sister. But my country is not a brothel, and my sister is not a whore. If your master truly desires an alliance, then he must demonstrate his respect for my country and put a better price on my sister's virginity."

Hutton felt his stomach cramp, but he gritted his teeth and stood still so it would not be as obvious to the others.

Outlook posts lined the crest of the imposing White Cliffs of Dover, with massive warning pyres stacked high and ready to be set should an enemy vessel approach on the Channel. Watchmen took turns studying the waters below, night and day, alert for any sign of unfriendly activity.

The early morning had brought a thick fog upon the land and sea, a gray, misty coat that clung to the skin and made it difficult to see very far. Two watchmen stood at their assigned places at the edge of the cliff, taking turns with a spyglass. They had to constantly wipe the condensation from the lens to keep the vision clear.

As one took a piss into the grass, the other trained the spyglass slowly back and forth. Then he gasped and cried out.

"What is it?" said the other, quickly closing the flap on his trousers.

Emerging through the fog was a wooden monster, its massive sails unfurled, its fluttering banners showing a black flying bird.

"Enemy ship! Flying the black eagle!"

"Let me look!" The second watchman grabbed the spyglass. He trained it on the huge warship and stared as more ships emerged from the fog, pitching in the swell of the waves behind the first ship. All flew the flag of the black eagle.

"Imperial ships!" he cried to the men who had gathered behind them. "Light the beacon! For Christ's sake, light the beacon!"

Grabbing burning torches from their smaller campfires, the men scrambled to the tall beacon and jabbed the torches into the kindling at its base. It went up with a roar, casting its orange glow across the terrified faces of the soldiers who fell in line to hear the orders of their superiors and to face the sea-borne enemy.

By the time the messenger reached the guarded gates of Whitehall Palace, his horse was run out, foaming at the flanks and panting hard. The young man paused as a guard looked at his documents and then waved him in, shouting for others in the courtyard to make way. Spurring his horse on across the yard, the messenger galloped to the front door, drew up his animal, and jumped from his saddle, A red-haired page snatched the reins and stared after the man.

Into the front hall and along the wide corridors he hurried, bearing news for the king. He was sweating and exhausted, but he forced his legs to carry him as fast as they could to the Presence Chamber.

The chancellor announced him and let him pass, and he stumbled in. The king and his councilors were gathered about awaiting the news, all staring at him as if they would devour him if they did not like what they heard.

The messenger bowed deeply, his chest heaving. "Majesty."

Henry stared at him. "You have a message from Warden Cheyney?"

"Yes, Your Majesty."

The king waved a hand, indicating that the letter was to be given to Charles Brandon, the Lord Suffolk. The messenger presented the paper, and Brandon quickly cracked the wax seal that held it closed. He took a breath, then read, "'From Sir Thomas Cheyney, Warden, the Cinque Ports. Your Majesty, Lords of Council, this morning we counted sixty-eight imperial ships in the Channel. I sent out two ships, and afterward, my boatmen were taken aboard the imperial flagship and shown every courtesy by the admiral. He said his fleet was bound for Spain, not England . . .'"

The messenger could see the tension ease in the faces of the councilors, though the king's expression remained unchanged.

"'. . . and that he meant no harm whatever to us, or our coast. If they doubted his word they had only to see how poorly armed his ships were, equipped more like merchantmen, their holds bursting with provisions for the emperor's voyage to Constantinople.'" Brandon smiled. "'On boarding their boats again, my men were saluted by the admiral's guns.'"

The king, at last, nodded. "It is good and welcome news," he said. Then he looked directly at the messenger. "Give this man a large purse for his trouble." Without another word, the king left the chamber.

*   *   *   *

"The imperial ambassador," announced the king's groom, who then stepped aside to allow Chapuys to enter Henry's private outer chamber. The groom bowed and backed out, closing the door behind him and leaving the two men alone.

Henry stared at the ambassador for a while, watching to see if it made him uncomfortable, which it didn't. At last he said, "I thought you had been recalled."

Chapuys shook his head. "There was some talk, Your Majesty. But I had no desire to leave here, nor did I think there was any cause."

"No cause?" Henry crossed his arms. "But your master and the French had formed an alliance against me. There appeared to be preparations for an invasion, encouraged by the Vicar of Rome."

Chapuys smiled slightly and said, "Your Majesty, I have been in this job a long time. I know when to believe what I'm told and when not to, which is most of the time. Though the emperor publicly embraced the French king, and even gave him the Order of the Golden Fleece from around his own neck, he still continued to hate him. More than any other enemy, my master fears the Turks, and yet the French are in league with them! How is such behavior from another Christian monarch to be forgiven?"

"Then, they are no longer allies?"

"No. The accord is already broken. Which means the Duchess of Milan is once more available for Your Majesty's bed."

Henry shook his head angrily. "It's too late! Am I supposed to be relieved that I have once more been a pawn in the game between your master and the French? I've had enough of it, do you hear me? I've had enough!"

Chapuys's smile faded.

Hutton wiped the sweat from his brow with the back of his hand and then wiped that hand on the hem of his green silk doublet. He and Beard stood in the wide corridor outside Duke William's presence chamber, awaiting yet another audience with the persnickety noble. The Englishmen had been announced, but for some reason—mere entertainment, perhaps?—the duke had made them linger at the closed door. Hutton gritted his teeth. He hated this assignment. He wanted to go home to London and be given some other duty. Almost any other duty would suit.

The door opened at last and a servant motioned them in. Inside, Duke William stood with his colleagues, who turned with dismissive looks at the envoys' entrance.

"I am surprised to see you back so soon, Excellencies," said Duke William.

Beard jumped in: "We have good news, Your Honor." Of course, Hutton could not be sure the news would be considered good. The duke was a most stubborn and irritating man.

"How so?" asked Duke William.

"His Majesty is so desirous to marry your sister Anne," said Hutton, "that he is willing to forgo any need for a dowry."

For the first time since they had met the duke months earlier, the rotund man smiled a genuine, if not greedy, smile. "He wants nothing?"

"Only his new bride in as short a time as possible," said Beard. "His Majesty will also pay Your Honor a considerable stipend for introducing him to the league."

Duke William's lips moved about as if tasting the offer on his tongue. Hutton quickly added, "Unfortunately, we remember that your sister is already promised to the Duke of Lorraine's son."

"That was indeed a great obstacle," said Duke William. "But on closer consideration, we have discovered the contract was never ratified, and so is not binding in law or in any other way."

Hutton glanced at Beard, then back at Duke William. "So, your sister is free to marry the king?"

The duke nodded his round head and stroked his boyish beard. "I will send my ambassadors to England to conclude the negotiations. Thank you, gentlemen."

* * * *

Sir Francis Bryan spent days in his palace chamber in private, attempting to break the code used in the circumvented missive. He first applied codes he'd unraveled in previous situations. Finding those useless, he sought other letter patterns that would be the key to the actual message, tossing aside those that did not work and trying others. Then, at last, late on the fifth day, it was done. He could read the encrypted letter. At long last he had the information he needed.

Sitting away from his desk, he stretched his neck and back, which burned from such long concentration over such tedious work. Night had fallen and the heavy blue drapes had been drawn against the darkness and the chill outside. Candles cast pools of light on the original paper and the stacks containing Bryan's many initial, fruitless efforts.

There was a rap on the door, and Bryan called out, "Seymour?"

"Yes."

"Enter."

Tom came in quickly and closed the door. He was clearly curious as to why he had been summoned at such a late hour. He moved across the room to stand over Bryan's shoulder and squinted in confusion. "What's this?"

"Cromwell's agents finally intercepted a letter from Cardinal Pole. It was on its way to Rome. I have managed to decode it . . . not without some difficulty."

"May I see?"

Bryan handed Tom the translation, and Tom read aloud.

" 'To Cardinal Von Waldburg. Forgive me, Eminence. I am in despair. Supposed to travel to Paris to meet King Francis. Have already written telling him I found the emperor very sympathetic to my mission. But fear it is not so. The emperor fears the Turks more than King Henry, so believes he will not act against him. So have postponed journey.' "

Tom glanced at Bryan, who nodded for him to read the final lines.

" 'Will go instead to papal city of Carpentras. Await further instructions from His Holiness.' "

Tom handed the paper back, and Bryan noticed it shook slightly from Tom's sudden excitement.

"Have you ever been to Carpentras?" Bryan asked.

"No," said Tom, "but I'm dying to go!"

Lady Mary gazed at Chapuys for a long, painful moment, and then strolled a good distance down the garden pathway away from him, the hem of her black cape rustling against the frosty ground. Chapuys gave her that moment, letting her have her private anger and sorrow. He stood silently, his breath visible on the cold November air. The lady finally slowed, and bowed her head. Then at last, she turned to face him.

"So," she said, "he is marrying a Lutheran heretic?"

Chapuys nodded, and walked up the path to join her. There were no tears on her young, wind-chapped face, only resentment. "So it seems," he said.

"And I shall marry no one?"

There was no happy way to share the news. "My lady, I—"

"No!" she said, raising her hand to cut him off. "I prefer it, in truth! Do you suppose I would like to be married off to the duke's heretic brother? Or some heretic cousin of his? I would prefer to live in a nunnery!"

Mary drew her arms around her, seemingly aware at last of how cold the air was. She shivered. "I do not know what to think of the king. He burns one Lutheran and then marries another! Well, if God so wills it, she might drown at sea!" She pulled her hood up over her hair and turned away. Without another word Chapuys accompanied her up the narrow garden path and back to the warmth of Hunsdon House.

Edward Seymour stood quickly from his reading when his servant announced that he had a visitor, Charles Brandon. He put his book on the chair and moved defensively to the center of the room, on guard, uncertain what unpleasant business this visit might entail.

But Brandon did not storm into the chamber as Edward expected. Instead, he approached with a smile and extended his hand.

"Your Grace," Edward said, still cautious, accepting the handshake but watching the other man's eyes. "To what do I owe this honor?"

"I came to congratulate you," said Brandon. "I understand the king has made you Earl of Hertford."

Edward nodded.

"And I believe it is time to patch up our past quarrels and differences, my Lord Hertford. There are better quarrels to be had!"

Edward could tell from Brandon's tone of voice that he was talking about Cromwell. Now, there was a topic Edward could most cheerfully sink his teeth and anger into.

"I am happy to agree with Your Grace," he said. Edward poured two goblets of wine and handed one to his guest.

Brandon considered the drink and smiled sardonically. "To think, all this time we have been ruled by the son of a brewer!"

The men raised their glasses and toasted each other and their new alliance.

"I am commanded to meet the princess at Calais," said Brandon after several healthy gulps. "A great many things hang upon this marriage, do they not?"

"The king's happiness, for one," said Edward. "And my Lord Cromwell's reputation."

Brandon wiped the corner of his mouth. His eyes narrowed and he glanced over his shoulder to make sure no one, not even a servant, was within hearing. "What a pity," he said, "if all should go awry, for some reason."

"I would have pity for the king."

"But on the other hand . . . ?" Brandon held Edward's gaze. *"Salut."*

One side of Edward's mouth lifted in a conspiratorial sneer. *"Salut."*

Chequers was a seaport city in the region of Calais in English-occupied France, a crowded, bustling town that stank of saltwater, fish, and the sweat of industry. It sat at the narrowest point along the English Channel, overlooking the Strait of Dover. Blessed with warm, agreeable weather in the spring and summer, it often was host to severe storms in late autumn.

It was with feelings of frustration that the envoy from London, Charles Brandon, Lord Lisle, and numerous other dignitaries and courtiers selected by the king himself waited about in the great hall at the mansion of the Exchequer, to the east of the city, listening to the howling winds and the driving rain. They'd arrived two days prior, preparing to greet the entourage from Cleves, but no sooner had they docked in Chequers than the skies boiled up and blew a fierce and thunderous storm from the north. The men had entertained themselves with wine and music and games, keeping an ear out for word that Princess Anne and her party had arrived.

Then, late in the afternoon, a servant scurried into the hall, bowed, and told them that the guests had come.

The Englishmen put aside their cards and dice and stood to welcome the visitors. Brandon moved to the front of the gathering to be the first to greet the lady and her steward and chaperones. But the people who entered the great hall caught Brandon off guard, and with a quick glance about he saw that those with him were equally taken aback.

The two men who led the party wore unflattering skirted coats and wide hats cut about the brim so that they looked like large starfish. Their trousers were not fitted, but billowed and gathered at the knees.

Lisle pushed past Brandon to greet the strangers. "Gentlemen." He held out his hand. "We bid you welcome to Calais on this most auspicious occasion."

The elder of the two men took Lisle's hand and shook it. *"Danke,"* he said.

"Ah," said Lisle, hesitating. Brandon wondered if these people spoke only German. That would be a most difficult obstacle for all involved.

"May I present you to His Grace, the Duke of Suffolk," said Lisle.

The man bowed and said, "Your Grace. An honor. *Ich bin Herr Hoghesten, der Prinzessin ihe Begleiter und das ist Graf Olisleger, ihr Gesandter.*"

Brandon understood only enough to know that Hoghesten was the princess's steward, and the younger man, Count Olisleger, was her envoy. This meeting could be most awkward.

Olisleger bowed and smiled. "Hello," he said, his voice cheerful, guttural.

Several of the Englishmen chuckled softly, and Brandon hoped it came across as a friendly reaction, not one of dismissal. They crowded around one another, craning their necks to see the ladies, who had yet to make their appearance.

Hoghesten stepped back to the door and nodded. At this, several ladies entered, moving silently and obediently into the hall. Their dress was as odd as the men's, frumpy, with none of the accents that customarily set off an Englishwoman's charms. Lashed across their bodices were cords and their stiff, modest necklines rose high above their collarbones. They seemed washed out from the rainstorm—or, Brandon feared, could this be the way they always looked? The ladies curtsied to the gentlemen, then turned as one final lady entered the room.

She wore a gray gown, a wide hat, and a heavy gauze veil over her face. She moved as if she were made of wood, without a trace of the flirtatious lilt of a French noblewoman or the unconscious, coy stroll of a young English lady.

"Here she is," said Olisleger, "Her Highness, Princess Anne, after a long time. My God!" He laughed as if he had thought it quite funny that they had taken so long to arrive, and Brandon, not to offend, laughed along with him.

Anne stepped forward to Brandon, keeping a respectful distance.

"You Highness," said Brandon with a bow.

"Good day, Your Grace," said Anne.

Thank God she can at least speak English, thought Brandon. *But what of her face?* "I'm afraid that the bad weather will prevent our sailing for a few days," he said.

Anne nodded. "I understand. Perhaps Your Grace could . . . ah . . . help me to explain how the English are eating?"

"Of course."

"And . . . hmmm . . . show me something the king likes to do?"

This time Brandon did not laugh, though he had a sudden urge to do so.

Dinner was elegant and uncomfortable, though everyone played his or her part. Anne dined more delicately than Brandon would have expected, though she did not seem fond of the boiled and roasted English foods spread upon the table.

When dining was done, Brandon invited the lady to the parlor. She arrived, still heavily veiled, and he offered her a chair at a small table. Then he sat and took out a pack of cards. Olisleger, Hoghesten, and Anne's ladies stood on one side of the room watching intently. Lisle and several of the courtiers from Whitehall stood on the other side of the room, also watching. Rain continued to pound the windows, causing them to creak and groan.

"His Majesty likes to play cards and gamble," said Brandon. "Do you play?"

"Oh, no," said Anne. "I think only men play the cards in my country. Yes? And is it not bad to gamble?"

"Not if you can afford to lose." Brandon shuffled and dealt the cards. He felt Anne's intense gaze on him as his hands moved, and he suddenly realized that the veil and hat were not as odd as he'd first thought, but actually quite pretty. He glanced up several times, trying to catch a glimpse of her face through the veil as the candlelight caught it from the sides, but could not.

"We'll play picquet," he said, once the cards were down. "It's not hard to learn."

"That is good."

"There are four suits of cards: *comme ça*: spades, clubs, diamonds, and hearts."

"Hearts?" Anne's voice was light, almost teasing. This caught Brandon by surprise. "You play with hearts?"

"Sometimes," said Brandon. "And here are aces, kings, queens, and knaves."

"Then all the court is here, yes?"

Brandon smiled. He took a pouch of gold coins from his pocket and placed some of the coins on the table. He slid half across the table to Anne and kept the other half for himself.

"Thank you," said Anne. As she cupped her hands over the gold, she asked, "Does the king always win?"

Brandon chuckled. "His Majesty does not like losing." Then he lowered his voice so the others in the room could not hear him. "What have they told you about the king?"

Anne was silent for a moment, then she said, "Why? What is it I should know?"

The city of Carpentras wore night like a black shroud of death, its homes and shops and narrow streets bathed in a darkness that the fires from lamps and lanterns struggled to penetrate. Even the late-December moonlight seemed filtered through a dense fabric, offering the weakest of illumination, and forcing those out and about after sunset to mind their steps.

Tom Seymour and Sir Francis Bryan picked their way along a particularly narrow alley to a dead end, where a woman in a hooded cape waited for them outside a brothel door.

"*Buona sera*," she said, looking each up and down in turn.

"You can take us to the cardinal?" asked Bryan.

"*Sì*. Come. Quickly. He is with us!"

She led them into a stuffy, stinking front room where, just feet away, in small wall-side stalls lit by sputtering tallow candles, shadowy men and women writhed and grunted against and inside one another. The stone floor was tacky, and the air steamed with breath and sweat.

Tom turned to their guide, whom he could make out now that she had shed her cloak. She was quite young, barely a woman. She was wearing a bright red dress, and her lips were painted to match her gown. "Where is the bastard?" he asked.

The woman held a finger to her lips to quiet him, then led the men down a narrow corridor, past more cubicles, to the last one on the right. This one had a curtain drawn across it. *So he can fuck in private?* thought Tom sourly. *Such a pious hypocrite!*

Tom and Bryan drew their daggers, shoved back the curtain, and stepped inside.

A red cardinal's cloak and hat hung from a wall hook, and upon the bed a naked black-haired whore slid up and down her customer's cock. The moment Tom and Bryan entered, she let out a squeak and froze, drawing her arms up to cover her breasts as if to protect herself from whatever violence was brewing. The cardinal, a fat, hairy old man, took a shocked, raspy breath, and stared up at the bed from his back, his eyes wide, his sagging cheeks trembling.

Tom saw immediately that this was not Pole. He sheathed his dagger, and Bryan followed suit.

"Sorry, *Signore*," said Bryan.

The cardinal coughed to clear his throat. "*Prego*," he said. "God be with you, my sons."

Tom and Bryan moved back into the corridor, where their guide was standing, head tilted, waiting to see if she would have a dead holy man in her house.

"We'll never catch him," said Tom. "What a waste of time!"

Bryan nodded at the beautiful red-lipped guide. "Perhaps not?"

He bowed to the woman, patted the coin purse in his pocket, and then thrust his hips out and winked. She smiled, understanding the universal language.

Henry frowned, gazing first at the miniature portrait of Anne and then at Brandon, who had just arrived from Calais and had not even had the time to change from his riding garb and boots into his court clothes. He'd come immediately to the king's private chambers at the king's command. "You didn't even see her face?"

Brandon shook his head. "No, Your Majesty. But she plays cards as pleasantly and with as good a grace as I ever in my life saw any noblewoman."

Henry huffed, walked to the window, put his hand on the glass for a moment, then walked back to Brandon. "She's to come to Rochester. I'm due to meet her at Canterbury in three days' time."

Brandon was silent, having nothing more to offer.

Henry shook his head, paced to the table to put the portrait down, but then immediately picked it up again. "I am more than ever impatient to see her. I cannot abide this waiting." He looked at Brandon. "What, then, is the news of Sir Francis Bryan?"

This Brandon could answer. "He and Sir Thomas Seymour are arrived at Carpentras, where Cardinal Pole is supposed to be hiding, since it appears he has grown fearful of assassination."

Henry laughed darkly. "He should be flayed alive, and I would wear his skin as a shirt!" Again he looked at Anne's portrait in his hand. "I tell you again, I cannot abide this waiting. It's been a long time. I need to nourish love!"

"I can understand."

"Can you?" Henry looked up from the portrait and moved closer to Brandon. "Can you, truly? I want to possess her, and yet I haven't even seen her! She's a complete stranger. What if I can't . . . ?"

"What if you can't . . . what?"

Henry rubbed his forehead, and Brandon could see a sudden, surprising vulnerability in his eyes. The king leaned forward slightly as if to say something, but then his expression changed abruptly. He stood straight and shouted, "Groom!"

A groom by the door hurried over and bowed.

"Fetch the Master of Horse!" ordered the king. "I'm leaving for Rochester."

They galloped east to Rochester, Henry well ahead, on his sorrel stallion, the Master of the Horse, Sir Anthony Brown, following, and four gentlemen of the king's Privy Chamber several lengths behind. Henry would not take the road at an easy pace; his body and soul screamed to race, to tear up the ground beneath him. He felt that the faster he rode, the younger he might become, that when he arrived at the manor house by the sea, he would no longer have a damaged leg or a stiff back, but would be a youth again, able to sweep his new lady off her feet with his smile, his charm—and, if the moment presented itself, his arms. His horse seemed to understand the urgency, and matched Henry's furious energy with his own, never faltering, leaping fallen logs and digging its hooves into the ice-puddled roads.

Sooner than Henry would have expected, he saw the town of Rochester ahead, the peaked roofs of its houses at the bottom of a broad, grassy knoll and the stone bishop's palace standing tall and proud above them, smoke curling out and down from its many chimneys.

They dismounted in the palace courtyard, passing the reins to several young pages in heavy gray coats, who stooped awkwardly, shocked to see their king up close and without notice. Henry gestured to Brown. "Tell the lady a gentleman is come to see her, bearing a New Year's gift! Go!"

Brown bowed and scuttled inside as the armed guards, taken completely by surprise, stepped out of the way and then looked at the king as if for more orders.

Henry paced the cobblestones, staring alternately at the door and the sky. His councilors waited silently, one holding a richly garnished collar of sable skins in his arms, intended as a gift for Anne. Henry stopped and stared at the door, wondering what was the delay, then, unable to wait any longer, threw his hands up and shoved open the massive oaken door himself.

Startled servants directed the king to Anne's private chambers, along a wide corridor and up a set of marble stairs. He did not give the guards at the top of the staircase time to announce his arrival, but rather strode through the open doorway, his bootheels loud on the stone floor. Ladies-in-waiting turned, gasped, and fell into curtsies. Brown, who was standing in the middle of the room speaking quietly to a young woman, looked up quickly and stopped talking. He bowed and stepped aside.

Then Henry looked at Anne.

And his heart sank.

She was dressed in dowdy, unflattering clothing that gave her little shape. Her frock's neckline rose nearly to her chin, hiding any womanly charms she might have had. Her hair was soft and yellow, and framed a round face. Henry thought he might have found something about her appealing, but her small eyes were pinched in a mixture of confusion and displeasure, and her lips were pressed tightly together as if she'd just eaten something bitter. She looked more like a clumsy cow maid—unsure of herself and her surroundings—than the graceful, sensual virgin he had envisioned.

Brown gave Anne a directive look, and it was then she realized who her visitor was. Her hand flew to her mouth, and she dropped into a deep curtsy. Henry stood inside the doorway, his legs locked, unable to move forward, as his companions caught up with him there, one still holding the sable skins.

Henry did not reach for the fur collar. He had no desire to present this woman with anything. Yet he knew he could not just walk out. Taking a long silent breath, he advanced on the lady, trying to form something on his face that would resemble a smile.

"Madam," he said.

"Your Majesty," said Anne, not looking up.

Henry took her arm, raised her from her curtsy, and gave her a chaste kiss on the lips. Anne's mouth fumbled against his own, and it was all he could do to keep from spitting.

"I've come to welcome you to my realm," he said, stepping back. "I trust . . . you will be comfortable here, before . . . before your journey to London."

Anne looked at her ladies, at Brown, and then again at the king. "Thank you, Your Majesty."

Henry nodded, thinking what he should say next. But there wasn't anything. And so he offered, "I . . . I shall see you anon."

Anne bowed her head. Henry signaled to Brown and his companions to leave with him, that very moment.

In the courtyard, Henry grabbed his horse's reins from the page and swung into the saddle. The other men mounted, glancing at one another, obviously puzzled by the king's reaction to the princess.

But how can they be? Henry thought. *They saw her as well as I did!* He whirled his horse toward Brown and pointed his finger. "How like you this woman? Do you think her so fair and of such beauty as has been reported to me? Tell me the truth!"

Brown stuttered, "I . . . she was not quite as I had expected, Majesty. In fact, she . . . she had some freckles I had not expected!"

Henry had not seen freckles, but that didn't matter. "Alas!" he snarled. "Who should men trust? I promise I see nothing of the things that were shown to me! I am ashamed that men have praised her as they have done!" He leaned over and grabbed the fur stole from his companion's hands, then turned his horse toward the castle gate and dug his heels into the mount's side. "I like her not!"

He rode off, throwing the fur stole into the mud.

Cromwell and Hutton waited at the outer door to the king's Presence Chamber as sleep-hungry petitioners stood shuffling about in hopes of an audience, gazing at the nobles with anxious yet weary eyes. Cromwell had received word that the king had just arrived back from Rochester and wanted to speak to the two men. A good sign, Cromwell guessed, that all had gone well and His Majesty wanted to discuss the wedding preparations. His heart, tight for so long, loosened a bit. It was quite a pleasant sensation.

But the moment the king rounded the corner and strolled past them, almost shoving his way through the courtiers in the hallway, Cromwell felt his blood go cold. The king was in no way happy.

"I like her not!" Henry said, without looking back.

Glancing at Hutton to see his own concern reflected on the other man's face, Cromwell held his head up and followed the king into the chamber.

Before Henry would speak, he ordered that he be attended by Brandon, Edward Seymour, Bishop Gardiner, and his other councilors.

Cromwell and Hutton waited as the other men gathered in the chamber, glancing up every so often as the king stared furiously out the window, alternately digging his fingers into the arms of his throne and crossing and recrossing his legs.

When all were gathered before the dais, Henry turned his attention to them. "I am most sore! It seems that princes in marriage suffer more than poor men, since they must take what is brought to them, while poor men are at liberty to choose."

There was a shuffling in the room, though no one spoke. Henry trained his gaze on Cromwell. "I have been deceived about Anne of Cleves. She is nothing like you reported to me. Nothing! She is like a horse, a Flanders mare!"

Cromwell kept his voice steady. He would have to make his point quite clear. "Your Majesty, you will remember that it was Sir John Hutton who described her as being like—"

Hutton held up his hand. "I never saw her properly! This was not my fault. I carried out my commission as best I could. I told you I was not good with women!"

Henry continued to stare at Cromwell. "My Lord Cromwell, do you deny you spoke to me of her beauty and the desirability of my marriage to her?"

"No, Your Majesty. And if I have misled Your Majesty and his council by commendations—based on false reports—then I am truly sorry for it."

Henry scooted forward on his throne. "If I had known what I know now, she would not have come here. But what remedy now?"

Cromwell noticed the councilors watching him for his reply. It seemed, in particular, that Edward and Brandon were enjoying his discomfort. "Majesty, I have to say that in my opinion there is none."

Brandon uttered something under his breath, as did several other men, but Henry gestured for them to be silent. "Go on," said the king.

"Today," said Cromwell, "the emperor is the guest of the king of France in Paris. They have renewed their alliance. If we now reject our

German allies, England will stand alone and friendless, and at the mercy of king, emperor, and even Duke William himself, if he chooses to retaliate against us. Moreover, Your Majesty, the princess herself has done no wrong, and if she should be sent home from here in disgrace, no man would ever want her. I am sorry Your Majesty has no better content."

There was a long silence. Then Henry said, "Well, I have none!" Then he stood from his throne and walked out without another word. Several of the councilors also left, while others drew into small groups to talk among themselves. Cromwell saw Edward and Brandon staring at him as he turned to exit the chamber.

Edward watched as Cromwell and Hutton followed the king out of the Presence Chamber, then leaned into Brandon and said, "The brewer's son must drink his poison!"

Brandon smiled and cuffed the other on the arm.

Chapter Eleven

Within the week, the court was readied for the presentation of Anne to the king and the court of Whitehall. Banners bearing H&A were strung from the ceilings and tapestries bearing the same hung on the walls of the corridors and the largest public chambers. Nobles and courtiers and their wives crowded into the Great Hall, which was ablaze with candles on tall stands and decorated with garlands of ribbons and velvet bunting. Some people whispered among themselves, wondering about this new Anne. Was she anything like former Queen Anne, whose careless actions had brought her to the chopping block? Was this Anne another wanton woman desiring power and prestige above duty and obedience? Still others quietly said they'd heard that Anne of Cleves was quite retiring, and also quite homely, of great contrast to Anne Boleyn in her beauty and boisterousness. Speculation traveled quietly yet urgently about the room. Almost everyone had an opinion, but no one dared let the king hear it.

Henry sat on his throne dressed in his most resplendent clothing—a coat of purple and gold fastened with huge buttons of diamonds and rubies, shoes decorated with embroidery and emeralds, a collar of pearls and gemstones. The best musicians were assembled in the balcony above, and as the door opened for the princess and her entourage, the trumpets sounded the royal trill.

Hoghesten and Count Olisleger came through the doors first, slowly, regally, followed by Anne and her ladies and two footmen. All were dressed in the peculiar, ungainly fashion of the Germans of Cleves. Anne's gown was more appropriate than the one Henry had first seen her in, made of rich gold cloth, though the style was still most unflattering, with a skirt that suggested little shape at the waist and hips and a bodice that laced clear up to the nape of her neck. Her yellow hair was caught up in a pearl-trimmed bonnet.

The crowd had stepped back to make room for the newcomers' entrance, but all craned their necks to see this, the next queen of England. Brandon stood at the edge of the crowd, where he could easily watch the procession, and he was surprised seeing the young woman for the first time. She was not at all as he'd expected, but unlike the king, he found her quite pretty and sweet. She gave him a small smile, and he bowed as she passed.

As Anne reached the foot of the king's dais, he stood and stepped down. "My lady," he said. "I am here to welcome you to what is yours." With that he took her in an embrace that appeared to be warm and genuine. Brandon watched Cromwell, across the way, as his normally emotionless face registered a trace of hope and relief.

Anne curtsied. "Your Majesty is very . . . gracious," she said in her halting English. "I am very happy."

Henry turned and held out his hand. His two daughters, who had been waiting at the front of the throng, stepped forward.

"My daughters," he said. "Princess Mary?" He motioned for the eldest of his daughters to step forward.

Mary, dressed in a scarlet gown with trumpet sleeves and wearing a gold chain set in rubies, took a step closer, though it was clear she was not pleased to be meeting yet another queen. She curtsied stiffly. "Madam."

Anne smiled gently and nodded.

"And Princess Elizabeth," said Henry.

The little red-haired girl, dressed in white and deep blue, stepped up and handed Anne a bouquet of flowers, then curtsied. "For you," she said. "I think they're pretty."

Anne took the flowers and touched the child's hair. "Thank you, Princess. And I think you are pretty, too." Then Anne turned to Henry. "I shall love them both."

The day was ended, and still Henry fumed about in his private chambers. He ordered Brandon to eat with him that evening, and after the initial dishes were served, he leaned over the table and said, "I like her not!"

Brandon nodded sympathetically. "But it seems Your Majesty must marry her."

Henry banged his knife on the table. "Who says I must? Cromwell? I have my lawyers working on it now. The betrothal can be prevented on two grounds. Either the German envoys have failed to bring an official commission from the duke authorizing them to conclude the legalities of the marriage, or they can't provide written evidence that her previous betrothal was formally rebuked." He tossed down his knife and pulled a leg off the broiled duck before him. Grease ran down his arm. "Either way, I can get out of it."

"I wish with all my heart that Your Majesty is successful. It seems to me that my Lord Cromwell is too keen to stress the lack of any remedy."

Henry took a bite of the leg, then waved it at Brandon. "The marriage was his idea. There were other candidates. The Duchess of Milan is supposed to be the most desirable woman in the world!"

"Perhaps," said Brandon, "in this matter, my Lord Cromwell has overreached himself."

"Perhaps." Henry put his elbow on the table and his chin in his hand. "Oh God! If there is no remedy, then I must put my neck into the yoke!"

The young messenger tapped on the door of Cromwell's office, yet no one opened it for him. He put an ear to the wood and listened, but heard no sounds: no chattering scribes, no feet moving about. This was odd, for even though it was evening, Cromwell often had his servants and assistants working long into the night. Easing the door open, the messenger stepped inside.

The room was empty. Several candles burned on the mantel and one on the desk, but there was not a soul there. He placed on Cromwell's desk the papers he was carrying, then noticed the ripe apples in a silver bowl beside the candle. He glanced about, then reached for the apple on the top, to slip into his coat and eat later.

Then he saw Cromwell.

"My Lord!" he exclaimed, pulling his hand back from the bowl.

The lord privy was on the floor behind the desk, on his knees, his hands clasped tightly. His head was down. Was he searching for something he'd dropped? He looked so strange there—funny, even—and the messenger almost laughed. Such a great and powerful man on the floor.

Cromwell turned to look up at the messenger. Then he pulled himself to his feet and touched his forehead, as if coming out of a trance.

"I'm sorry, my Lord Cromwell," the messenger said. "I didn't see you. I—"

Cromwell took a deep, raspy breath. "I was talking to God."

"But"—the messenger frowned, confused—"surely, Sir, you have to go to church for that."

Cromwell leaned on the desk and stared at him. "Do you understand nothing? God is not just in church. He is everywhere. And He does not need priests to speak for us. We can speak to Him ourselves, plainly and honestly, and He will listen. There is no need for bells, books, and candles, for incense and copes and mitres. All you need is your soul." He tilted his head, his eyes filled with an odd mixture of awe and despair. "Now go away and think."

The messenger bowed and turned.

"Wait," said Cromwell.

The messenger looked back. Cromwell reached for the apple and handed it to the messenger, then nodded for him to leave. Deeply moved, he took the fruit and left.

* * * *

Henry stood before the mirror in his bedchamber, his arms out as his grooms slipped a coat of crimson satin over his gold-and-silver gown. His hair and beard had been meticulously groomed, and new shoes, fashioned for the occasion from lambskin and set with diamonds, were on his feet.

The occasion, Henry thought sourly. *My wedding.*

He watched mournfully as the grooms adjusted the coat's shoulders and full quilted sleeves. They stood back then, allowing for the king to acknowledge that he approved of what they'd done. Reluctantly, Henry nodded. One groom, a young redhead with a curly beard, took a crystal bottle from the dressing table and sprayed the king with lavender water. Henry closed his eyes until the spray had cleared the air. Then he looked at himself in the mirror again.

Today is the Feast of the Epiphany, he said to himself. *And my wedding day.* He glanced beyond his reflection to Cromwell, who stood waiting near the bed. "So, there was no legal remedy?"

Cromwell shook his head. "None that it was possible to discover, Your Majesty."

Henry felt his neck tighten, and the ache in his leg flared for a moment. "I am not well handled."

Cromwell said nothing, waiting for the king to join him so they could travel together to the Chapel Royal. But Henry stood before the mirror and did not move.

"I think when you know the lady better—" Cromwell began.

"I don't want to know the lady better, Mr. Cromwell." Henry turned to face his secretary. "The notion of it . . . revolts me!"

Cromwell said nothing. Henry forced himself away from the mirror and crossed the room to the door. Suddenly, he spun about and grabbed Cromwell by the neck and thrust him against the wall. He drew his lips close to the other man's ear.

"My lord," said Henry, "if it were not to satisfy the world, and my realm, I would not do what I must do this day for no earthly thing!"

He stared at Cromwell until he could see the fear in the other man's eyes clearly, and then he let him go.

Brandon, Edward Seymour, and Edward's wife, Anne, met Henry and his grooms at the open chapel door. Dressed in their most elegant clothes, they were for all appearances a noble and happy ensemble, there to accompany their king on this, his happy wedding day. As the white-robed choir sang in the loft, Henry steeled himself, lifting his chin and setting his gaze ahead to the altar, where Bishop Gardiner waited. To the bishop's right stood Anne's entourage—Hoghesten, Olisleger, and Anne's ladies—standing proud and still, wearing their formal yet frumpy gowns and cloaks.

Henry set his steps to the singing, trying not to think about what he was about to do, yet unable to keep his mind off it. He kept replaying the image of Cromwell's face against the wall, the terror and the despair there. That was how Henry felt, and he wanted Cromwell to have a taste of the bitter drink. If he could, he would have poured the whole of it down the man's throat and sewn his lips shut.

As Henry neared the altar, Anne's company parted to reveal her standing there. Her golden hair was down and brushed loosely about her shoulders. The coronet on her head was set with gems and pearls, and she wore a golden necklace and earrings. The gentle smile on her lips made her almost pretty, though her gown of silver cloth hung much like a sack on her frame. She curtsied three times before Henry, then stood straight, her hands folded at her waist.

He knew he was supposed to give her a smile. After all, it was her wedding day, and her first. Yet he could not. He merely motioned for her to join him before Bishop Gardiner, who made the sign of the cross several times above the couple.

At least, Henry thought as the bishop began to recite the marriage charge and declaration, *there is no one else save these few people to witness this travesty.* For indeed, no other nobles, courtiers, or statesmen had been invited to the ceremony, and with the exception of the small gathering in the front, the chapel was empty.

*   *   *   *

The wedding night candles had burned down low in the king's bed-chamber, but the bed itself remained untouched, the linens and bedspread as smooth as they were that afternoon, when the grooms prepared the bed for the king and his new bride. On the headboard were engraved a large *H* and *A,* and chubby, sensual cherubs had been painted around the initials.

Yet Henry and Anne sat at a table in the bedchamber playing cards, each dressed in a nightgown. Had this woman been any but the princess from Cleves, Henry knew he would long ago have tossed out the nobles and ladies who stood watching them along the shadowed walls and bedded the lady with gusto. But there she sat, timid, smiling, anything but lusty and desirable.

Henry took a sip of his wine and looked at the cards in his hand and the pile of gold coins in the middle of the table. Anne had at least mastered this one game, though it was quite clear she'd also been told to let him win. Of course, he would have expected that, but with her, he found it irritating. As he did her soft sighs and her mild manners.

At last he put down his cards and faced the inevitable. "Shall we to bed?" he asked.

Anne nodded. "Majesty."

Henry stood and made a dismissive gesture, sending everyone else out of the room. Then he shrugged out of his gown, letting it fall to the floor at his feet. Anne kept her eyes averted and carefully removed her own outer gown, leaving herself clothed in only a thin white nightdress. He motioned for her to get into the bed first, and she did, lying there stiff as a piece of wood and staring at the bed's canopy. Then he climbed in the other side and lay down next to her, listening to her shallow, frightened breaths. Her fear angered him, but he would not let it show.

Slowly, he reached over and untied the cords of her nightdress, loosening the bodice. Then he slipped his hand beneath the cloth and caught one of her breasts in his fingers. It was soft and small, with little there to light his passion. Even the nipple remained pliant, unaroused, at the touch of his royal hand.

He took his hand out and slid it down her waist and thigh, then gathered the skirt and pulled it up above her hips. She was blinking rapidly now, as if waiting for the executioner to swing his ax. Henry's fingers found her hairy mound, and the feminine slit there, but it was dry as dust. She gasped as he slipped his fingers into her private entrance and probed her core, trying his best to find something about this woman to get him hard. But there was nothing. He pulled his fingers out and turned onto his side, away from her. It was a long time before he was able to fall asleep.

Catherine Brandon woke in the middle of the night to soft voices down the hall. She pulled her dressing gown around her and left her bedchamber. Faint candlelight glowed from the open parlor door, and shadows moved along the corridor.

"Charles?"

She went to the parlor door and gazed in, seeing the silhouette of two men sitting close together near the dying fire in the hearth.

"Sweetheart," said one, turning in his chair toward her.

"Charles," said Catherine. "I couldn't sleep. Who is there with you?"

"No one," said Brandon. "Go back to bed."

Catherine tilted her head, but still couldn't make out the other man.

"Shall I come to you later?" asked Brandon.

Catherine sighed, her heart tight at the softness in his voice. "If you could still be my sweet Charles," she said. She turned away, but Brandon stood and went to her, taking her arm.

"I am as good as I may be," he whispered fiercely, his breath hot on her cheek. "And you must take me as I am."

Looking at him in the darkness, she saw a trace of the man she had loved and married. She nodded a little.

"I love you, Catherine," he said.

She left the room without another word.

*   *   *   *

Cromwell stepped into the king's private chamber and watched as Henry, hunched over his table, signed a stack of documents and handed them off to messengers. When the last of the papers bore Henry's signature and the messengers were on their way, Cromwell stepped forward with the documents he had brought the king.

Henry glanced up, a lack of sleep pinching his eyes. Cromwell knew the weariness: he himself had slept little the night before, agonizing over the royal match and praying to God that Henry would love his new wife. Or at least find her tolerable.

As Henry lifted the first document to read it over, Cromwell asked, "How does Your Majesty like the queen?"

Henry dipped his quill into the well and signed the paper. Then he said, "Not as well as I trusted to have done."

"Was there some . . . particular reason?"

Henry put the quill down and stared at Cromwell. "Surely, my lord, I didn't like her very well before, and now I like her much worse! She is nothing fair and she has evil smells about her!" He sat back in his chair. "And I know she's no maid because of the looseness of her breasts and . . . other tokens which, when I felt them, struck me to the heart. So I had neither the will nor the courage to prove the rest. I have no appetite for unpleasant airs."

Cromwell's chest tightened.

"I left her as good a maid as I found her," said Henry. "Now leave me, my lord, I am very busy."

Cromwell bowed and backed away, his heart even more troubled than before.

They lay in the queen's bed the night that followed, Anne again flat on her back and staring upward as Henry moved his hands over her body. He tried to imagine she was any other lady at court, hoping to bring himself to a peak of excitement that would allow him to consummate the marriage. But it was no good.

Rolling onto his side, away from the queen, he wet his fingers with his saliva, then grasped his organ and began to pump it fast, rhythmically. Perhaps, if he could get his manhood ready on his own, he could penetrate the woman and have it done with. But as he listened to her quick, anxious breaths and thought of her small, childlike breasts and dry hole, his organ remained soft and unmoved.

Henry let go and flopped onto his back. Out of the corner of his eye he glimpsed tears trickling down the queen's cheeks, but there was nothing he could do. For her sake or for his own.

His leg had begun to torment him again, and he called for his physician, Dr. Butts, to examine it in his bedchamber. Dr. Butts nicked the swollen red blisters and washed out the infection, noticing that the king was distracted and, unlike other times, seemed less aware of the discomfort of the ministrations.

"There," said Dr. Butts, as he wrapped a clean bandage about the leg. "I've drained the pus from Your Majesty's wound. Your Majesty should feel no more pain, thanks be to God."

Henry frowned thoughtfully, then looked at the physician with a peculiar expression.

"Forgive me," said Dr. Butts, "but is Your Majesty troubled by other things?"

Henry touched his leg, then lowered it to the floor and tested his weight upon it. "Yes," he said. "I have been unable to consummate my marriage to the Lady Anne. I find . . . I find her body so disordered and indisposed that it doesn't excite me, it doesn't provoke any lust in me."

Dr. Butts did not reply. This seemed to draw out suspicion in the king. "Have you heard rumors of it?"

"None at all, Your Majesty!" said the physician, hoping his exclamation would hide the fact that he had heard that very rumor.

"It is not anything to do with my own virility. Indeed, these last nights I have had *duas pollutiones nocturnas in somno*."

Dr. Butts nodded. "Two nocturnal emissions."

"You see!" exclaimed Henry. "I know myself perfectly able to do the act with others, just not with her. With her, I have no appetite to do what a man should do to his wife."

The physician nodded again, having no advice, and hoping the king would dismiss him soon, to go about his other business.

Lady Bryan stood behind Anne, carefully removing the queen's jeweled necklace and earrings and placing them on a silver tray. Then she began to groom Anne's hair with a diamond-encrusted boar-bristle brush. Anne, seated on a velvet-cushioned bench, stared into the mirror, though Lady Bryan could see she was not looking at herself, but at some distant spot beyond.

"Madam," Lady Bryan asked, "how do you find the king?"

"Why, he is most kind and solicitous, Lady Bryan. When he comes to bed he kisses me, yes, takes my hand and bids me 'good night, sweetheart.' And in the morning he kisses me again and says, 'farewell, darling.'"

This was not what she'd hoped to hear. "My lady," she pressed, "we all hope you will soon be with child."

"I . . . I know very well I am not."

Lady Bryan passed with the brush. "But how do you know you are not?"

Anne looked down at her hands. "I know it well I am not."

Lady Bryan touched Anne's shoulder. "I think Your Grace is a maid still."

Giggling nervously, Anne said, "How can I be a maid and sleep every night with the king?" She lowered her head even more.

Putting the brush down and moving around to kneel before the queen, Lady Bryan said softly, "He must put his member inside you, and stir it, or else we will not have a Duke of York, which all this realm desires."

This was too much for the queen, and she sat up straight, her eyes flashing. "I am contented, Lady Bryan! I receive as much of the king's attentions as I wish! I know no more!"

Lady Bryan nodded and stood and helped Anne to her feet. She untied and removed her overgown, then drew the covers back on the bed. When the queen was settled, Lady Bryan smoothed the linens around her. She curtsied, blew out the bedside candle, and turned to leave.

"Lady Bryan?" Anne called softly.

Lady Bryan looked back. "Yes, Your Majesty?"

The question was innocent enough, but it sent a chill through Lady Bryan's heart: "If I cannot please the king, will he kill me?"

It was Lady Bryan's great desire to help the new queen remain queen, and she devised many activities she believed would transform Anne into a cultured, confident, obedient, and desirable wife. Though skilled in sewing, Anne was not so in many other things. She knew little of poetry, dance, or music. And so, to begin, Lady Bryan found a lady who was a patient teacher of the harpsichord.

One day, the queen's outer private chamber was filled with the simple yet pleasant tunes Anne was making on the instrument. Her ladies sat about sewing and nodding in appreciation at the queen's musical progress. Even the lowlier servants, cleaning ash from the hearth, discreetly removing the contents from the bedchamber pots, bringing in fresh fruits, and scrubbing the floor, smiled as they went about their chores, their heads nodding in time to the music. But then Anne's fingers struck a sour chord and she lifted her hands, dismayed.

"Like this, Your Majesty," said the music teacher. She showed the correct chord, and smiled encouragingly.

Anne nodded. "*Danke.* Thank you."

Lady Rochford entered the chamber and curtsied. "Your Majesty, Princess Mary is here."

Anne motioned all the other ladies to leave. Lady Rochford ushered the princess into the room, then moved into the bedchamber, where she stood just inside the door to listen and watch.

Mary seemed uncomfortable in the queen's presence. She curtsied formally and waited to hear the reason Anne had summoned her.

"Princess," said Anne, gesturing toward chairs by the window. "If you please."

Mary sat down, her face expressionless.

Anne leaned forward as if to take the princess's hands in her own, but then just folded them in her own lap and said, "I have received a letter from a cousin of mine. He is Duke Philip of Bavaria. It is a beautiful country with . . . with many mountains, yes? And . . . Philip, as I know, is a young man who has just inherited the title."

Mary glanced at Anne as if she had no interest whatsoever in this information.

"Philip would like, with your permission and His Majesty's," Anne went on, "to come to England and pay court to you."

Mary's lips pursed. "Why?"

"He has heard many things about you, Princess Mary. Many good things."

"I suppose he is a Lutheran, like you?"

Anne only smiled. "He is charming and . . . very handsome. I think you might like him a little. What shall I tell him?"

Mary tossed her head. "Tell him, tell him that he may come, if he desires and the king allows. But he is not to expect anything."

Anne smiled and stood. Mary followed suit, her face still set and unmoved. She curtsied and exited the chamber.

As Anne returned to the harpsichord and began to run her fingers along the keys, trying the new melody she'd been learning, Lady Rochford left the doorway and moved closer.

Anne looked up. "Lady Rochford?"

"Madam," said Lady Rochford. "I . . . I cannot help asking, since you have slept with the king a whole month, if he . . . if the marriage is consummated?"

Anne continued to play, now with only one finger, tapping out a sad-sounding tune. "What business is that of yours, Lady Rochford?"

"Majesty." Lady Rochford lowered her voice. "If you are still a maid, then I could explain to you certain things, things about men, about ways you can—"

Anne lifted her finger from the instrument and stared at the lady. "Must it be *my* fault, Lady Rochford?"

It was nearing midnight when Henry relinquished and came to his wife's bedchamber yet again. He stripped from his gown and lay for several long minutes before rolling toward Anne and fondling her breasts and the coarse hair of her pubic mound. Again, she lay without moving, without responding. He used his hand to work himself into a half-arousal, and made to mount her, but then he pulled back in revulsion. Her whole body was unappealing to both the nose and the touch, and there was nothing he could do to make himself feel otherwise.

Anne's breathing eased, now that it was clear he would not try to penetrate her. "It does not matter," she said, in an obvious attempt to be kind. "Your Majesty must not be so . . . sad. It is no matter to me. I think it will be good, in good time."

Henry got up out of the bed and threw on his gown. He strode from the bedchamber, his leg aching again, and mightily. As he stalked down the private corridor to his own chamber, he could hear her muffled crying. But so be it. It was not his fault. He had done all he could. There was no more to be done.

London was cold and white with a February snow. But the mood in the Presence Chamber was stifling and dark. Again the king had called his councilors together to discuss his dissatisfaction with his bride, and again he sought a suitable, acceptable way to be rid of her.

Henry watched as the men gathered and then bowed, each in turn. He was seated on his throne, a gilded cane in his hand, a ruby ring on one thumb and an ermine-trimmed robe around his shoulders.

"My lords," he said, "I confess to you that though I have lain with the queen almost every night these past weeks, my conscience will not permit me to consummate this marriage, because I am sure there is some impediment to it. I have done as much to move the consent of my heart and mind as ever man did, but the obstacle will not be out of my mind."

He scanned the faces of the men to make sure they were hearing him and understanding him without exception. "Perhaps the truth is that there was a precontract between the princess and the Duke of Lorraine's son after all, and so I am really married to another man's wife." Then he stared down directly at Cromwell. Likewise, Brandon, Edward Seymour, and Bishop Gardiner looked at the lord privy seal. "My lords, I leave it to you to investigate whether or not my scruples are justified."

With a flick of his hand, Henry dismissed them all.

Richard Rich moved up beside Cromwell as the men left the chamber. He'd seen the glances given Cromwell by Brandon, Seymour, and that bloody bishop, and knew things were shaping up most desperately.

"My lord," he said, "you must find some way to relieve His Majesty's conscience!"

The look Cromwell gave him let him know that he was well aware of the danger, and desperately aware he needed a solution.

"I tell you, Charles," said Henry as he and Brandon retired to the king's private chambers, traveling slowly along the corridors and stairs, Henry aided by his walking stick, "in some ways I am very weary of this life."

Brandon nodded, understanding. They continued on to the king's apartments, where the guards bowed and opened the doors. The men went in; the doors were closed behind them. Grooms came forward to offer assistance, but Henry waved them off.

His leg aching him dreadfully, he limped to the closest chair and dropped into it. He laid his stick across his lap, nodded for Brandon to sit by him, and then spoke candidly. "I cannot overcome my aversion to the queen sufficiently to consider her as my wife. I am sure God will not send any more children if I continue with this marriage."

"Was she such a maid that she didn't know what to do?" asked Brandon. "Not telling a woman what must happen to her on her wedding night is like sending a sailor to sea with no biscuit!"

Henry almost smiled at the joke, but he was in too much pain, both of body and spirit. "No. I don't think she's a maid. When I felt how loose her breasts and *cul* were I was struck to the heart. It is no wonder I couldn't . . ." He took a breath, but didn't finish the sentence. "I shall force Cromwell to bring about a dissolution of the marriage. I only went ahead with it for the sake of the realm, and now even that reason is forgot. The emperor and the king of France are at each other's throats again, and both have come courting. Who needs Cleves?"

Brandon reached for the flagon of wine on a small table by his chair. He poured a goblet for himself and the king. Henry took it and downed half of it without taking a breath.

"My Lord Cromwell," said Brandon. "Was the match not all his idea?"

Fresh pain flared in Henry's leg and he winced. He ignored Brandon's question, took another drink, and pointed a finger at his friend. "Oh God, that we could joust again, and ride to hounds. Do you remember when I tried to leap that ditch and fell in?"

Brandon and the king exchanged a smile. Smiling felt odd to Henry, like an acquaintance he'd not seen in years and didn't quite recognize.

"Yes," said Brandon.

"Wolsey was alive then." Henry took the last drink from the goblet, then turned it around and around in his hands, staring at his reflection in the silver.

The arrival of Thomas Cromwell in the private outer chambers of the queen caused a great commotion. Shocked to see the king's secretary there, the ladies curtsied anxiously and glanced at each other as if to say, "What can this man want?" One hastened to retrieve Anne, as the man standing in the center of the room wished he could be anywhere but there in that moment.

Soon the queen appeared in the chamber, dressed modestly in the fashion of her people, looking no more alluring than when Cromwell had first seen her. A shame. "My Lord Cromwell?"

"Your Majesty." Cromwell bowed. "May we speak alone?"

"Alone?" She glanced around. "Oh, yes. Of course." She said something in German to her ladies, who curtsied and withdrew into other rooms. Then she looked back at Cromwell. "My lord?"

"Madam." Cromwell tried to pick his words carefully, though none would be soft on her ears, he knew that. "I have come on a delicate matter. Forgive me. I . . . I must warn you against antagonizing the king."

Anne drew up, clearly shocked by the comment.

"I must remind you of the expediency of doing your utmost to make yourself agreeable to him."

It took a moment for the queen to find her voice. "Sir. I am not sure how I have given His Majesty offense?"

"It is in your interest, and in mine, to make your marriage to the king a success. If you were to find yourself, for example, quick with child . . ."

Anne's cheeks flushed. She held up her hand and turned away, obviously both stunned and embarrassed by the conversation.

"I am very sorry to talk of intimate things," Cromwell continued. "But you are queen of England. You have nothing private anymore."

There was a long silence. Cromwell felt his discomfort and impatience growing. Surely the woman understood the importance of his words.

Anne turned back. Her composure regained, she spoke, her words slow and cold. "How am I to be quick with child when the king leaves me a maid? I am not the Virgin Mary." She stepped closer to Cromwell, her English breaking down in her passion to be heard. "And since you say . . . you say I am nothing private, then I say you it is not all pleasing. I will do anything the king wants. But sometimes the"—she pointed to her own thigh—"the sore on his leg is so bad. It oozes blood and pus! And it smells. It stinks. Yes? You understand?"

Cromwell did, but that could not matter.

"Now," said Anne, "I am sorry, my lord. Please be assured I will go on doing all I can to make myself agreeable to His Majesty, who is always gracious and kind to me." She smiled, but the tilt of her head said quite clearly that he was dismissed. She would hear no more from him on the matter.

"Majesty." He bowed and left the queen's chambers, his jaw tight and his mind racing circles like an animal in a cage.

Sir Francis Bryan accepted Brandon's invitation to play cards in one of the castle's smaller, more private chambers—a study lined with bookcases and shelves containing collections of brass instruments and tools of science. Brandon needed privacy, a difficult commodity at times in such a busy and bustling household.

Brandon dealt the cards. He lifted his hand to study what he'd been given, then looked up at Bryan, whose arched brows seemed to indicate that he knew this was more than a card game.

"I'm sorry you failed to capture that arch traitor Reginald Pole," said Brandon, moving his cards into an order. "The king detests him above all men."

Bryan nodded over his own hand.

"However," Brandon continued, "he has other matters on his mind now. When I last spoke to His Majesty, he confessed he was, in some ways, tired of his life."

Bryan snorted. "His life or his wife?"

Brandon laid down a card. "They are much the same thing."

"Can he not find . . . distraction, as he has always done before?"

"Easily. But he is more jaded than before. The usual remedies won't suit. Something more . . . extreme might tempt him."

Bryan pulled a card from his hand and held it over the table. "Extreme, Your Grace?"

"Surely you get jaded, too, Sir Francis, sometimes? In which case, where do you go?"

Bryan played his card. He smiled and rubbed his mouth. "In this matter at least, Your Grace, I shall not fail the king."

Brandon sighed silently. He knew he'd found the right man for the job. He looked at the table and saw that Bryan had played a better hand than he, but it was a small matter at that moment.

* * * *

Lady Mary made her way through the crowded corridors of the Whitehall Palace, heading to her chambers following a morning in prayer. Courtiers smiled and bowed as she passed, but she would not look at them. Her mind was on God and His goodness, mercy, and justice.

Then a young man in a blue embroidered cape and feathered cap stepped in front of her. He removed his cap and bowed deeply. Mary stopped short, surprised, and glanced back at her ladies as if they might know who he was. They all appeared as confused as she was.

"Sir?" Mary said, turning back to the man.

He stood straight, one hand to his heart, the other arm outstretched. He was very handsome, with curly light brown hair, dark brown eyes, broad shoulders, and a disarming smile. "Princess Mary," he said in an accent Mary couldn't quite recognize. "I hope you can forgive my impetuosity? I know we should have been formally introduced, but . . . I couldn't wait."

"You are Duke Philip?"

The young man nodded enthusiastically. "May I kiss your hand?"

Mary hesitated, flushing, not knowing what was proper yet feeling an instant attraction to the duke. She nodded and held out her hand.

Philip took it gently and kissed it. Mary pulled her hand back, perhaps too quickly, she feared. She hoped he didn't sense her nervousness.

"I hope I might see you again, my lady?" said Philip. "With my cousin the queen present, of course."

"I had thought to leave court tomorrow for the country," she said, but even as she did she knew she would rather see more of this young man. "But I may delay my leaving, if it pleases you, for a day or so."

He smiled broadly and bowed again. She could not return his smile; she could not let herself be so transparent or vulnerable. It was always best to keep one's emotions close to one's heart. But still, the thought of seeing him again made her heart pick up its beat, and it continued to beat rapidly as she and her ladies continued down the corridor.

* * * *

The country house had changed little since Sir Francis was there, more than two years ago. It sat north of London, on a rocky ridge off a small, winding road, once a grand manor but now worn down, untended, and in disrepair. Weeds wound up and around the gate and fence, and the grasses and hedges, once tended by gardeners, grew tall and wild.

The interior of the house was even less cared for, with broken floor tiles, cracked windows, and walls streaked in mold and mildew. The mistress of the house was the dowager Duchess of Norfolk, an aging, discarded aristocrat who made her living peddling the young flesh of unwanted children dumped on her doorstep.

Sir Francis Bryan sat at a wobbly table in the front room with the dowager duchess, sipping cheap liquor from dirty tankards and chatting of the past months.

"I've missed you, my sweet Francis," said the duchess. She'd combed her hair and painted her face for the occasion, but her breath was bad and her teeth chipped. She reached out for his hand, and he squeezed hers affectionately. "I haven't seen you for ages. What have you been doing?"

"Trying to kill someone," he said.

"Did you manage it?"

"Not yet."

"I suppose you've come to look over my little darlings?"

"Only after I've feasted my eyes on you, my dear lady." Bryan raised his cup. He ran a thumb over the woman's lower lip and winked an eye.

The duchess chuckled, then slammed down her tankard and stood. She brushed off her skirt and said, "Come along. We have some new ones. Pretty little things. I sometimes find it hard to believe that whoever bore them cannot be bothered or obliged to raise them."

"You told me most of them were bastards," said Bryan.

"But aristocratic bastards, my sweet boy."

Bryan followed the woman down a dingy hallway, to a door, which she shoved open to reveal a dark, stinking chamber. It took a moment for Bryan's eyes to adjust to the dim light. The chamber windows were caked with mud and filth, allowing very little daylight inside. Sagging beds stood at odd angles about the floor, and additional straw mattresses were laid out on the tiles. Upon the beds and mattresses, sitting, lying down, and staring blankly at the walls, were countless girls and young women. Some were no more than eight. Others looked to be in their late teens. A few were dressed in rumpled, fouled gowns, while the rest were clothed in plain linen shifts.

Bryan stood in the doorway studying his options. Most were too young for the king's taste; others seemed too dulled by their circumstances to be of any use. But several of the older girls, seeing him, ran their fingers through their sticky hair and struck sensual, flirtatious poses. Anything, he knew, to impress someone who might be able to take them out of there. Their desperation and raw earthiness was just what His Majesty needed to sate his sexual appetite.

Then he saw the one. She was slender and delicate, with soft brown hair, a full and sensuous mouth, and long, womanly legs.

His trip had been worth it. He'd found the king's new distraction.

Cromwell could not sleep. Such a state was not unknown to the man, but in the past months his insomnia had been as much from fear and worry as from the overburden of work. He sat alone in his office in the wee hours of the morning, leaning over his desk in the light of several sputtering candles and reading through a stack of letters, reports, and Parliamentary bills, making notes in the margins where wordings were not clear and jotting questions that would have to be answered by the various authors. His back ached, as did his head, but as there was no ability to rest, he knew he should use his time wisely.

He heard a soft shuffling before he heard the voice.

"Father?"

Cromwell looked up quickly to see his son near the desk, a smile on his lips even as his brow was drawn in concern.

"Gregory!"

Cromwell hurried around his desk and gathered his son in his arms. He'd spent so little time with his family in the past years. His son had grown up quickly, into a young man with a wife and a child on the way. His heart swelled with love in that moment, though he stepped back to let his son go, not wanting him to know his longing, his sadness.

"Why on earth are you here?" he said.

Gregory, dark-haired like his father, with brown eyes and a square jaw, pulled a small pouch from his cloak. "I noticed you had forgot your pills from the apothecary. I didn't want you to be in pain."

Cromwell took the pouch, then motioned for his son to take a seat near the fireplace. He poured two tankards of wine and handed one to Gregory, then sat down near him. Shaking a pill from the pouch, he threw it into his mouth and washed it down with some wine.

Gregory glanced at his father's desk. "What are you working on?"

"I'm preparing bills for Parliament about the medical profession. Land laws. Overseas trade. And I'm trying to persuade His Majesty to appoint councilors only on their merits and nothing else."

Gregory nodded and took a drink. "You look tired, Father."

Cromwell waved the comment off.

"How is His Majesty?"

"He's fine. But his leg is sore and it bothers him. He gets irritable."

"Is that why he strikes you on the head sometimes?"

Cromwell put his cup down on the chair-side table. Surely someone must have reported this to his son. He didn't want Gregory to see him as weak, or the source of the king's anger. And so, he merely waved a hand as if it were nothing. "I'm used to that. My father used to do it to me when he was drunk, which was a great deal."

Cromwell could feel his son studying his face. So he continued, "I resent the king nothing. But others seek to undermine me, since I was born so low and they so high. And for other reasons, too."

Gregory smiled, almost sadly.

"But think not of that," said Cromwell. "Look after your own dear wife and the child she has in her belly. Love them as you love God and His holy word, and all shall be well."

"Yes, Father."

"Shall we pray?"

Gregory nodded, and the men slipped from their chairs and to the floor, where they folded their hands and closed their eyes. Cromwell felt the heat radiating from the coals on the hearth and the warmth of love radiating from his son, so close now. Tears sprang to his eyes, and he was glad Gregory could not see them.

"We beseech Thee, Almighty God, look up on the hearty desires of Thy humble servants and stretch forth the right hand of Thy Majesty, to be our defense against all our enemies. Through Jesus Christ our Lord."

Together they said, "Amen."

He was deep in his study of the Book of Matthew when he heard the footsteps approaching in the narrow passageway. Cardinal Pole, seated outside the door to his cell, reading his Bible, looked up to see a priest escorting a man in a black cape. Pole's heart lurched, and he stood abruptly. He did not know the man, and had come to distrust strangers.

"Eminence," said the priest. "This is Mr. William Gray. He has only lately arrived in Rome, but was most anxious to meet you."

Anxious so he can get near me and thrust a dagger into my heart? Pole thought, his muscles tense.

It was obvious the priest could see Pole's fears. He quickly frisked the man, then said, "He has no weapon, Eminence."

Pole let out a breath, though he remained guarded. "Mr. Gray, what can I do for you?"

"Eminence, I hope you forgive me for seeking you out. The fact is, I was a servant of Thomas Cromwell for many years, but at last I listened to my conscience. I have left everything behind and come to Rome, the better to serve God and the true Church."

Pole studied the man's face. It was open and sincere. "You are most welcome. We English Catholics are a large and growing community here in Rome." Pole nodded for the priest to leave them, then said, "Tell me, how does Master Cromwell fare with *his* master? We hear some rumors that the king is losing faith in his minister."

"Your Eminence is well informed. Lord Cromwell is surrounded by many enemies who perpetually seek his downfall and ruin. His position is tottering."

Pole clasped his hands and raised them to the ceiling. "Thanks be to God! I look forward to the time when his many misdeeds will be punished. The day will come when the lord privy seal will feel the pains of all those he has sent to die. And on that day, Londoners will witness one of the most joyous entertainments ever offered them." And then, for the first time in months, Pole felt himself smile.

Chapter Twelve

Charles Brandon, Edward Seymour, and Edward's wife, Anne Stanhope, were gathered in the parlor of the Seymours' apartments in Whitehall Palace waiting for Sir Francis Bryan. He had sent word that he had something they needed to see, something that would be of great interest to them. Of course, this piqued their curiosity, so they sat waiting, eating pastries, and drinking some excellent wine that Brandon had brought with him. Many candles had been lit and the fire was stoked. They wanted to be able to see well, whatever it was that Bryan had to present to them.

At last a servant came into the parlor and announced Bryan's arrival. All three moved to the edges of their seats as Bryan stepped in, shedding his fur-trimmed cape and bowing.

"Well?" Brandon pressed.

Bryan handed the cape to the servant, strolled to the table, and poured himself a drink. "I've found someone to amuse the king."

Edward glanced at Brandon then back at Bryan. "Who is she?"

"Katherine Howard. She's a distant relation of the Duke of Norfolk, but her background is—how shall I say?—not entirely conventional."

Anne scoffed. "Where did you find her?"

Bryan smiled and took a sip from his goblet. "That would be telling, my lady."

"I assume she's young and pretty?" asked Brandon, standing from his seat.

"See for yourself, Your Grace."

Moving to the door, Bryan pulled it open himself, and a young woman stepped over the threshold. She was indeed young and pretty, with brown hair brushed up into a lace coif, with seductive tendrils hanging free and coiling about her bare shoulders. Her faded blue gown, though threadbare, fit her young figure well, revealing a tiny waist and ample breasts. She lowered her eyes demurely.

"Katherine," said Bryan. "Here are the excellent people I told you of. His Grace the Duke of Suffolk. The Earl and Countess of Hertford."

Katherine curtsied, her gaze remaining downcast. "Your Graces."

Anne and Edward stood and came close to the young woman.

"How old are you, Katherine?" asked Anne.

"Seventeen." Katherine looked up, and her expression was no longer submissive but challenging and alert.

Anne smiled. "I wonder who taught you to count?"

Katherine lifted her chin all the higher.

"Tell us something of yourself," said Edward, walking around the young woman, considering her assets from all angles. "Your parents. So on."

Katherine shrugged. "My mother died when I was little. My father remarried, but I didn't know his wife, really. I got sent to live in the household of the dowager duchess."

Edward glanced at Bryan. "That would be the Dowager Duchess of Norfolk? Widow of the second duke?"

"I suppose so," said Katherine. "I didn't see her much. There were other children there, from lots of marriages. We ran a little wild. There was some fun it in." She sighed. "Then the fun stopped."

Anne touched the girl's hair and stroked her cheek. She ran her hands down her arms and took her hands, turning them over to examine them closely. Then she said, "Well, my sweet child, I think the fun is just about to start again. What say you, Your Grace?"

Brandon crossed his arms and grinned. "I think she looks fit for a king."

* * * *

Queen Anne summoned Princess Mary to her chambers. Ladies served them tea and cakes, and they sat at the window discussing the early spring birds, the beauty of the delicate March flowers, and the melodies Anne was learning on the harpsichord. And then Anne put down her cup and smiled at the young lady.

"So," she said softly, "did you talk to him? To Philip?"

Mary glanced down at the cake in her hand. She didn't want to discuss this. "A little."

"I believe he is a very intelligent young man."

"I couldn't tell."

"And extremely good-looking. He likes you a great deal."

Mary shrugged. "He doesn't know me. We have nothing in common."

A lady entered the chamber and curtsied. "Madam, Duke Philip asks for an audience."

Mary's heart skipped a beat and her throat went dry. She nearly dropped her biscuit. "I don't want to see him!"

Anne looked around the room, then pointed to the drawn curtain that covered the door to the queen's bedchamber. "Then go in there!" she said. "Quickly!"

Mary put the biscuit beside her teacup on the table, scurried to the curtain, and slipped behind it.

Anne stood and nodded to the lady to let the duke enter her chamber. Peering through the curtain, Mary saw that he was as she remembered him. No, even more handsome. His smile was wide and true, and his face quite noble. He bowed deeply, and then stepped forward into Anne's embrace.

"Dear cousin!" said Anne.

"Majesty!"

Anne nodded for Philip to have a seat. He took the chair in which Mary had just sat moments before.

"How do you find this country?" asked Anne.

"I like it very much," said Philip. "I think the English are a bold, proud, authentic race. I could most happily live here."

"Have you met Princess Mary?"

Mary drew a sharp yet silent breath behind the curtain. What would he say?

"Just once," said Philip. He leaned forward in his chair, his hands folded. "It was only a moment, but I relive that moment over and over again in my mind. I was told before that she was charming, intelligent, well read, gracious, and true heir of Katherine of Aragon. A true princess. But nothing prepared me for her beauty. Not the false beauty of vain women who paint their faces to seduce fools, but a beauty that comes from inside. To me, she is the most beautiful creature on God's earth!"

A thrill rushed through Mary's body, causing her to tremble. The smile she'd been suppressing now broke out on her face.

Queen Anne did not attend the court dance that evening; Henry had told her she looked tired and that it would be best for her to remain in her own chambers to rest. Of course, the queen had obeyed him without complaint or question. This was an ideal situation for the Seymours, for they had a presentation to make.

The Great Hall was filled with courtiers and nobles, all dressed in their finest gowns and coats, stepping and whirling like colorful birds to the tunes played by the king's hand-selected ensemble in the balcony. They danced stately pavans and allemandes, and then the energetic galliard, as Henry sat on his throne beneath its gold canopy, eating a pear and watching the festivities.

Katherine Howard's body and hair had been groomed by Anne Stanhope's ladies, and she was dressed in one of Anne's loveliest deep green gowns. A simple necklace of diamonds was around her throat, and a single emerald was fastened in her hair above her right ear. When the music began, Tom and Edward Seymour took her onto the dance floor and made a point of keeping her close enough to the throne so the king could not help but see her.

It didn't take long.

As Katherine curtsied and turned a graceful circle, Edward leaned close to her and said, "The king has noticed you. He may ask to see you."

Katherine's eyes widened and she cut a quick glance toward the throne. "What shall I say to him? What shall I do?"

Edward spoke clearly and plainly. "I told you. Just be yourself."

Brandon stood beside Henry's throne giving the king the latest news. But he could tell Henry was only half-listening. His Majesty's attention was keenly focused on the dancers below him, not on his daughter Mary and the queen's young cousin, who seemed to have eyes only for each other, but on the lovely young woman in the green gown and diamond necklace.

"The council has acted upon Your Majesty's requests," Brandon said. "We demanded written evidence from the queen's envoys about the pre-marriage contract with the Duke of Lorraine's son. They provided some, but in fact, the papers seem to suggest that instead of the usual formula, *per verba de futuro,* the actual wording on the document reads that she is given in marriage to Lorraine's son *'per verba de presenti,'* which is a binding contract which renunciation cannot undo."

Henry took another bite of the pear he was eating and said nothing, his eyes locked on the woman in green. "However," said Brandon, "even if these matters can be passed over, the council is still of the opinion that Your Majesty's failure to consummate the marriage is itself sufficient grounds for divorce."

Henry nodded absently. Then he beckoned Brandon to lean closer. "Who is that girl?"

"Katherine Howard. A relation of the Duke of Norfolk. She is only just come to court."

Henry tossed the pear core onto the table in front of him and said, "Bring her to me!"

*   *   *   *

The king settled himself in a shadowy corner of his private outer chamber, instructing his servants to blow out all but a few candles before they left him alone. Then he waited.

Minutes later, the chamber door was opened and Brandon entered with the young woman beside him. Brandon bowed. "Majesty, Miss Katherine Howard."

Henry flicked a hand to send Brandon out. Then he stared at the young woman, who curtsied and then stood as if not knowing what to do next. She was even more beautiful this close, with a strange wildness about her that was deliciously enticing. Yes, she was young enough to be his daughter, but her buxom figure revealed that she was of age, and ripe and, he expected, ready.

"Katherine," he said.

"Your Majesty." She curtsied again, almost nervously, squinting into the shadows to better see the king. When he said nothing, she bit her lower lip and looked about the room, clearly fascinated with the royal furnishings and adornments. She swung her hips back and forth like an impatient youth, and Henry found her behavior at once endearing and flirtatious. He felt a stirring in his loins that he'd not experienced in many months.

"Do you know who I am?" he asked at last.

Katherine stared back in his direction and giggled. "Yes, Your Majesty."

"No, you don't. Nobody does."

She cocked her head, confused.

"Please, be seated." Henry touched the arm of the chair beside him, and Katherine scooted over and plopped herself down. She pursed her lips in a teasing smile.

"Are you married?"

Katherine snorted with laughter. "No, Your Majesty."

"Can you read?"

"Enough to read a letter."

"Who writes to you?"

"Nobody."

Henry found the comment moving, that this young woman would have no one to send her missives. "Have you many houses?"

Katherine's eyes went wide and then she laughed again, so spontaneously and loudly and with so much life that it flooded the king's heart with joy.

The dancing and revelry in the Great Hall continued on into the night, with wine and large silver trays laden with food carried in by servants for those who cared to sit, laugh, and eat with their friends while watching the others on the dance floor.

In all her time at court, Princess Mary had never enjoyed a dance. She had always attended on command, reluctant to mingle, uncomfortable to move about from partner to partner, ill at ease touching the hands of strange men and even those she knew in passing.

Tonight, however, the music was more beautiful than she'd ever heard it, and she found her head whirling with happiness. Philip was attending the dance, and even when he was across the room, bowing and stepping around another partner, his eyes were focused on her.

Around she spun, happily curtsying and holding the arm or hand of yet another man, knowing that soon she and Philip would be side by side. And then he was near again, trading off a lady, turning, stepping, and he was with her, so close she could hear his breathing.

Then Philip exclaimed, "Ouch!"

Mary gasped. "What is it?"

"You stepped on my foot." He turned away and limped off the dance floor, with Mary following closely, wringing her hands. He stepped around a corner, out of sight from the rest of the court. When Mary caught up with him, she was shocked to see him standing up straight and grinning.

"I thought . . . ?" she began.

Philip put a finger up. "You didn't step on my foot. How could you? Your feet don't even touch the ground."

Mary blinked.

"I wanted a moment alone with you," he said. Putting his arms around her waist he drew her close. Mary felt a moment's hesitation, but she smiled at him, her eyes pleading.

Please. Yes. Kiss me.

And he did. Mary's heart and soul swelled as his lips urgently, passionately, and tenderly probed her own. Then he pulled back slightly.

"You're crying," he said.

It was then that Mary noticed the tears on her cheeks. She let out a tremulous laugh. "Only because I'm happy."

"Would you like to kiss me again?"

But before she could answer, he folded her into his arms again.

The dancing ended after midnight, the guests reluctantly giving in to weariness and the lateness of the hour. The musicians in the balcony wrapped their drums and fiddles, flutes and lyres, as the ladies and nobles drifted from the Great Hall and went their separate ways. As Mary, followed by her ladies, turned to move in one direction down the corridor and Philip in the other, she looked back at him to see him looking back at her.

"Good night, Princess," he said.

"Good night, Your Grace. Philip," she said. With a final smile, she turned and continued on toward her apartments, feeling light-headed and rapturous, planning already when she might next see her love.

Katherine sat slumped in her chair, her shoes off and her bare toes wriggling in the warmth of the fire on the hearth. One arm dangled casually off the side of the chair, the other was drawn up and cocked over her head. Henry thought that were he an artist like Holbein, this sight would be one he would paint and cherish.

Then he noticed Katherine staring at the ruby ring on his thumb. He scooted his chair closer to hers so she could have a better look. "You know where this ruby comes from? It adorned the shrine of Thomas Becket at Canterbury. The whole shrine glittered with jewels, left by pilgrims and princes. But this ruby was the greatest, most valuable gift of all. A king of France gave it as an offering to save his soul."

Katherine pursed her lips. "May I touch it?"

Henry removed the ring and handed it to her. She studied it for a moment and a sly look came over her face. Hoisting her dress up to reveal her knees, she reached down between her legs and pushed the ruby up and out of sight. Her lips parted provocatively and her tongue made a brief, sparkling appearance at the front of her mouth. Then she drew the ruby back out and handed it to the king.

Henry's pulse pounded in his temples and sweat had broken out on his forehead. As Katherine smoothed her skirts back down, he took the ring and put it to his nose, drawing in the heady, musky scent of a woman hot with desire.

It was clear Henry's leg pained him mightily, from the swelling and the cold, and once again he had to rely on his walking stick to move about. Cromwell watched as His Majesty limped across the floor of his private outer chamber to the window, and he wondered what was on the king's mind, fearing what he might hear, yet determined to show nothing of that emotion. Henry stared out at the tender mint-green buds of the trees in the nearest garden, then glanced back at his secretary.

"How is work proceeding on my palace at Nonsuch?"

Cromwell bowed slightly. "I'm happy to report that it is almost complete, and will be ready for your inspection come July."

"Hmm." The king put his ruby ring to his nose and sniffed it. Cromwell found this odd but didn't let on.

"I want to give a gift of land to Mistress Katherine Howard," said Henry. "There is some we recently confiscated from a felon, as I remember you told me. With two large houses upon it." He looked at Cromwell. "I wish to grant the whole to Mistress Howard."

Cromwell's jaw tightened.

"I hear that the council has found a flaw in the queen's pre-marriage contract," the king continued.

"Majesty." He needed to pick his words carefully. "It was not such a flaw that it could not be overcome by the queen's personal repudiation."

Henry left the window, his hands behind his back, and gazed at the ceiling. "There must still be grounds. Before God, I think she is not my lawful wife."

Cromwell remained silent.

Henry stopped pacing and stepped close to the secretary. Cromwell braced for whatever this might bring: A loud chastisement? Another slap to the head? But the king smiled and put a hand on Cromwell's shoulder. "Whatever people may say, Mr. Cromwell, either to your face or behind your back, you are my first minister, whose love and loyalty I have neither cause nor reason to doubt. If anything important is to be done, I know who will best do it."

"Your Majesty," said Cromwell. He bowed, and the king dismissed him.

Risley, Cromwell's secretary, waited outside the door, and together they hurried down the stone stairs and along several hallways to the main corridor. Immediately, Cromwell was surrounded by petitioners pressing their papers desperately in his face.

"My lord, please, I beg you! Read my petition!"

"This is all my life, sir!"

"For the mercy of Christ, read my petition!"

Over the noise of the crowd, Cromwell motioned for Risley to collect the petitions. Then he glanced over to see Brandon moving in the direction of the king's chambers. He hoped Brandon saw that he was smiling.

Spring became summer, with no clear solution to the problem of the king's marriage. Brandon entered the king's private chambers to find Henry plucking a sad, sweet melody from a walnut lyre.

"How was your meeting with the French ambassador?" Henry asked, putting the instrument aside.

"It was . . . very interesting, Your Majesty."

Henry scratched his beard. "Go on."

"He told me that the king is not averse to opening secret negotiations with us, with a view to disengaging the French from their disagreeable alliance with the emperor."

"Good."

"It seems we have an ally at the French court in the shape of Francis's sister, Marguerite of Navarre."

"Oh, I remember her shape very well."

Brandon smiled and nodded. "The ambassador also suggested to me how much Anglo-French relations would be improved if Lord Cromwell no longer stood as an obstacle to them."

Henry looked at Brandon and then retrieved the lyre. His expression was impossible to read.

Little Princess Elizabeth at last was asleep, her hands clutching a red-haired satin doll Queen Anne had sewn for her. Mary put the child on the queen's bed, kissed the tiny forehead, smoothed the red curls, and tucked a blanket around her. Then she quietly left the bedchamber through the curtains.

Queen Anne waited for Mary in the outer chamber. She smiled gently, but Mary could see something troubling in her eyes, and immediately her body stiffened.

"Poor Princess Elizabeth," said Anne.

Mary frowned. "Why do you say so?"

"The king has reduced her household again. And now Lady Bryan looks after the prince." The queen sat down and motioned for Mary to sit beside her. The queen's ladies sat at a respectful distance, baskets at their feet, sewing in their laps. "I fear Elizabeth will be neglected, as I was."

"You were neglected?"

"Of course. I was only a girl. What else to expect?"

Then suddenly the queen took Mary's hand. Something was certainly wrong, though Mary couldn't guess what it might be.

"I have some news," Anne said.

Mary nodded.

"Duke Philip has been sent back to Bavaria."

This was not what Mary had expected. Her heart lurched and her arms flushed cold. The memory of him kissing her and holding her rushed through her mind. His smile, his laughter, his tender bidding her farewell in the corridor. Was she never to see him again?

No!

"It was the king's decision," said Anne. "I cannot explain it."

And then the door to her heart slammed shut. She knew the betrayal her mother had faced, the loneliness and hardship, and knew there was no redress. Why had she dared think she might find love? That was careless and selfish. She should focus her thoughts on God, not man. What a fool she had been to let herself feel something for any man!

"You have no need to explain," Mary said, standing up and lifting her head. Though tears pressed at the corners of her eyes, she refused to let them fall. "It is of little matter. The duke was charming, but I would never have married him. He is a Lutheran, and I am a Catholic."

Without another word she left the chamber. Anne and the ladies stared after her with great sadness.

A small rowboat navigated the deep waters of the Thames, moving west against the current in the late hours of the night as the moon, bright as a gold coin, hung overhead in the black velvet sky. Manning the oars was Sir Francis Bryan, and seated in the back, his hooded passenger. The boat made its way past anchored merchant and trading ships, shallops and rafts, through floating garbage, and around swans and waterfowl that drifted, unconcerned, in their sleep.

Soon Bryan steered the craft ashore. He climbed out and tied the boat to a wooden stake in the riverbank. At the top of the rise was a small thatched cottage with a lantern glowing in one window. Bryan waited for his passenger to step from the boat, and the two trudged up through the wet weeds and clouds of gnats.

The cottage door was not locked. Bryan pushed through into the front room, where Katherine Howard stood waiting. Bryan had not told her why she should wait there in that shabby place, but she did not seem concerned. Certainly it was no worse than her previous home.

"Mistress Howard," said Bryan.

"Sir Francis," said Katherine, her head angled in curiosity.

"The king would like you to accept a gift." Bryan opened the leather pouch at his hip, removed a velvet cloth, and handed it to Katherine. She quickly untied and unrolled the cloth to reveal a diamond-and-pearl brooch that glittered regally even in the poor light of the window lantern and the sputtering tallow candles on the table.

"It's lovely," she said. "You must thank His Majesty."

"You can thank him yourself."

And then Bryan's passenger came through the door and pushed back his hood. Katherine smiled and curtsied. "Your Majesty."

Without another word, Bryan stepped outside into the swirling insects and the darkness.

Henry's heart was already beating faster from the sight of this girl in such a rough and earthy place, her eyes wide and knowing, her body lithe and ready. He lifted her to her feet. She grinned and kissed his ruby ring.

He glanced at the straw pallet in the corner of the room. She twirled away, reading his thoughts and desires. Smiling seductively, she unlaced her sleeves slowly and let them fall away from her slender arms. Next, she unfastened her gown and, giggling, wriggled out of it like a snake wriggling from its skin. Her linen undergown was last. Bending, she slowly, teasingly, lifted the hem up, past her knees, her hips, and the dark womanly path between her thighs. The smooth skin of her stomach was revealed and then her round, heavy breasts, the nipples already erect with excitement.

Unable to wait any longer, Henry blew out the candles and moved to the lady, where he tugged the undergown up and over her head, then threw her roughly onto the pallet. She laughed in his ear and he in hers. The straw crackled beneath them. He kicked her legs apart and had his way with her.

Bishop Gardiner knocked on the heavy front door of the Brandon house and waited in the late afternoon sun, shading his eyes and glancing over his shoulder to make sure no one had followed him. Moments later, Brandon opened the door and Gardiner stepped over the threshold. Waiting inside were Edward Seymour, Anne Stanhope, and Sir Francis Bryan. They had important matters to finalize. And their faces did not disguise the glee they felt at what they were doing.

Gregory Cromwell hurried through court and down the long corridor to his father's office in the palace. He found the man, yet again, seated at his desk leaning over a stack of petitions. One set of fingers was caught up in his hair. He looked to have aged twenty years in two, with his cheeks hollowed and eyes dark-rimmed.

"Father," Gregory said as Cromwell looked up from his work. "It's a boy. I have a son."

"Thanks be to God!" said Cromwell. Gregory came around the desk to his father and was caught up in a tight, almost desperate embrace.

Henry dropped to his knees on the freshly scrubbed floor and called to his little son, who toddled to him with a huge grin on his face and a curl of dark hair bobbing at his forehead. The child stumbled but then righted himself, and dove into his father's arms.

"My son!" said Henry. He held the boy tightly, almost as if he could take the boy into himself for safekeeping. Then he looked up at Lady Bryan and the other members of Prince Edward's household at Hampton Court and nodded his appreciation. The ladies bowed their heads and smiled.

A Privy Council meeting was called for mid-morning, and the men assembled in the Council Chamber. Most of the councilors had arrived by the time Cromwell, in his robe adorned with the garter, insignia, and decorations of his position, strode through the door, followed by an attendant carrying the great seal of Cromwell's office. Already seated around the long table were Edward and Thomas Seymour, Richard Rich, Bishop Gardiner, and other nobles. They sat talking among themselves about events in England, new horses, new wives, new babies, waiting for the meeting to be called to order. Charles Brandon came in directly behind Cromwell, but unlike the others, he remained standing near the door.

Cromwell went to the head of the table and sat. Then he said, "My lords, I ask this council meeting should come to order—"

But before he could finish his declaration, Brandon shouted, "Cromwell! Do not sit there! That is no place for you. Traitors do not sit among gentlemen!"

Stunned, Cromwell sat up straight and opened his mouth to chastise the Duke of Suffolk, but then the captain of the guards and several armed guards marched into the chamber and to the head of the table.

The captain declared to Cromwell, "I arrest you for treason!"

This was impossible! Cromwell's immediate fear turned to rage. He stood and threw his hat upon the table. "I am no traitor!" he cried. He looked at the councilors, trying to see their eyes, to see what lies had twisted and clouded their reasoning. "I ask you, on your consciences, am I a traitor?"

Several councilors pounded on the table and shouted back angrily, "Yes! Traitor! Traitor!"

The guards seized Cromwell's arms and hauled him from the table, his chair crashing to the floor.

"Stop, Captain," said Brandon, stepping up to the guards and staring coldly at Cromwell. "Traitors should not wear the garter." He grabbed the chain and seal and tore them from around Cromwell's neck.

Cromwell was left in a tattered, disheveled black robe. His body flushed cold with mortification and dread. He stared across the room, where his friend Richard Rich sat at the table, able only to watch helplessly, silently.

And then the guards dragged him out through the door as he continued to scream, "I am no traitor! I am no traitor!"

He knew the Tower well, and feared it as no man had ever feared it, because he had witnessed what went on in the cells, the chambers, and the dungeon. He knew the cold and the wet, the starvations and the isolation, the depravations, beatings, and horrific tortures. And now, surrounded by six guards with unsheathed swords, he was being dragged through its winding, torchlit corridors as if he were the most dangerous criminal alive. He stumbled along, his mind reeling, trying to think of an escape, trying to think of what he could say to persuade them to let him go. He was the lord privy seal, for Christ's sake! He was the king's own secretary! The Earl of Essex! The king had just affirmed his confidence in him! But his thoughts fell one upon the next, tangled like a stag in a snare, crashing about in his head until he thought he might faint.

Down another winding corridor and up a short set of steps. There, in the shadows, was a locked cell door with a small grille set in the wood. Two guards held his arms so tightly he thought they would be crushed. Another guard unlocked the latch and swung the door wide. It was a small and dirty cell stinking of filthy straw and human torment.

It was then Cromwell's tongue loosened. He twisted and lurched back against the grip of the guards. "No! No! I'm no traitor! I'm no traitor!"

Together the guards closed in on him and shoved him through the doorway. Cromwell spun about to try to get out again, but the door was immediately slammed shut and locked. Grabbing the bars of the grille, Cromwell pressed his face to the iron and stared out as the guards retreated, leaving him there with the rats and the darkness.

A mere three hours following Cromwell's arrest, Parliament met in the House of Lords to hear the Act of Attainder against Cromwell. Lords and bishops gathered in their black and red robes, stony-faced and silent upon their benches and in the balconies. Yeomen of the guard stood at the curtained doors, and the king was seated on his throne upon the dais beneath a red canopy and a gold crest of England. Enormous chandeliers hung from the high ceilings, blazing with countless white candles.

Bishop Gardiner took the floor to present the evidence.

"My lords," he said in a loud voice. "I am come here to introduce a bill of attainder against Thomas Cromwell on a charge of treason! The Earl of Essex, whom His Majesty has raised from a very base and low degree, and enriched with manifold gifts, is now proved a most false and corrupt traitor and deceiver . . ."

With this there erupted shouts of "Traitor! Traitor!" from various sides of the House. Henry stared out at it all, his hand resting atop his walking stick, his expression unmoved.

"Being a detestable heretic," Gardiner went on, "he has utterly disposed to set and sow common sedition among Your Majesty's true and loving subjects, has secretly set forth great numbers of false and erroneous books, tending to the discredit of the blessed sacrament of the altar. Being the vice regent for religion, supposed to reform errors, Cromwell has, without the king's knowledge, licensed and freed heretics to preach and teach!"

More lords bellowed, "Traitor!" Some stood to shake their fists in the air.

"My lords, we have evidence that on March thirty-first, in the parish of St. Peter the Poor, the Lord Cromwell did arrogantly defend these heretic preachers. He said that if the king would turn away from reform, yet he would not turn! And if the king did turn, and all his people, then he would fight in the field with his sword against him and all others. And he held up his dagger and said, 'Or let this dagger thrust me to the heart, if I wouldn't die for that quarrel. And if I live a year or two, it will not be in the king's power anymore to resist or hinder our great reformation.' And he swore an oath!"

Now the voice of anger and denouncement was as one. Bishops and lords leapt to their feet and began to chant, "Traitor! Traitor! Traitor!"

Edward Seymour stood among the crowd on the floor, watching in amazement. Next to him was Richard Rich, looking pale and discomfited.

Edward leaned into the man and said quietly, "Is it true that you loved this man, Sir Richard?"

Rich drew a deep breath. The cords in his neck stood out. "As a friend. But I chiefly loved him for the love I thought I saw him bear toward the king above all others. But now, if he be a traitor, I am sorry that I ever loved him or trusted him. I am very glad his treason is discovered in time."

Edward smiled and put his hand on Rich's shoulder.

The royal dinner table was set for the king and queen, laden with platters of venison, duck, goose, and coveys, silver bowls generously filled with fruits and breads, soups and puddings, and flagons of wine. Select courtiers stood in silent attendance against the walls, observing the formal occasion.

For the first time since her arrival in England six months prior, Queen Anne was dressed in an English fashion—a tightly fitting kirtle of blue with a low and squared neckline, revealing the slight rise of her breasts. Her skirt was wide and layered, and strands of her blond hair were combed out from beneath her crown to curl seductively at her shoulders. She looked uncomfortable in the gown, and Henry knew immediately that she had dressed herself this way in some desperate attempt to please him.

But it did not.

Anne smiled each time the king glanced her way, but it was clear she was extremely nervous. Her spoon trembled in her hand, and she did not attempt to make conversation.

At last Henry said, "I trust, Madam, you are happy and well treated?"

"I have no complaints whatsoever, Your Majesty. Everywhere I go, I am treated with great respect and kindness by everyone."

"I'm glad." Henry took a bite of venison, and as he chewed it he lifted the ruby ring and touched it to his lips.

Anne put her spoon into her soup, stirred it, then put the spoon down. Henry looked at her and saw her staring anxiously at the courtiers in the chamber. They were all men. Then Henry realized her worry. She knew the fates of his other wives, wives who for one reason or other had to be gotten rid of. Anne was more than nervous; she was terrified.

"You are not eating?" he said.

"I'm . . . I'm not hungry. Forgive me." She picked up a piece of bread and broke it, but then put it into her bowl. "Your Majesty, I . . . I wondered . . ." She lowered her eyes, unable to say more.

Henry put down his knife and sat back in his chair. "I am sending you away for a while, to my palace at Richmond, for your health, open air, and pleasure."

"Thank you," said Anne. Her voice was barely above a whisper.

Edward Seymour appeared at the door and nodded at the king. Henry rose and bowed slightly to his wife. "I have urgent business. Madam."

He joined Edward in a corner of the dining chamber, beyond the hearing of the courtiers, who continued to watch as the queen picked at her food.

"The council urges Your Majesty to consider the validity of your marriage, for the sake of Your Majesty's health and the safety of this realm," said Edward. "The council considers it sufficient that, as Head of the Church, you can have your bishops annul the union. But it would be more diplomatic if proof were found that the marriage was never consummated and that Your Majesty never willingly consented to it."

Henry rubbed his chin, thinking. Then he nodded. "You will send a deputation to see Mr. Cromwell. You will demand his written evidence in support of the case for annulment. Doubtless he remembers how often I said that my nature abhors that woman!"

Both men glanced at the table as Anne took a sip from her goblet, put it down, and stared at the food in her bowl.

The cell door squealed open and Cromwell, standing at the tiny barred window overlooking London and the Thames, turned to see Charles Brandon and the constable step inside. The weeks had been hard on Cromwell: he was unshaven, with filthy hair and a body that smelled of the foul peasants he had so often hurried past on the streets. Yet he stood erect, his head up, holding on to his dignity, the only thing he had left.

"Mr. Cromwell," said Brandon.

Cromwell bowed. "Your Grace."

The constable stayed at the door as Brandon strode across the cell, looking at the sagging cot, the small desk with its single candlestick, papers, and inkwell, the bedpan in the straw in the corner. "The king orders that you write him a letter describing how he found Anne of Cleves, what passed between you on that subject, and whether he told you he had consummated his so-called marriage, or not." He turned to Cromwell. "He also orders you to describe the impediments to the marriage and whether knowing them, you still arranged it."

Cromwell nodded. Brandon walked to the window and looked out. "His Majesty charges that as you will answer to God at the dreadful Day of Judgment, and also upon the extreme danger and damnation of your soul and conscience, to write down exactly what you know."

"I will most gladly do as His Majesty commands, I trust to his pleasure and satisfaction. I desire more than anything else the king's comfort and would willingly die for it."

Brandon sniffed. "I wondered if you could see your house from this window. The fact is, Mr. Cromwell, that only two hours after your arrest the king dispatched his treasurer there to take away your goods. There was so much stuff it took five cartloads to move it." He looked at Cromwell, clearly savoring the news. "The rabble came out to cheer them on. It was a pretty sight, I hear."

Cromwell's heart clenched, but he did not reply.

He drew the candle closer, dipped his quill into the ink, and stared at the missive he had begun. Alone, with Brandon gone, he had this one chance to obey the king and try to save himself. His lips were dry and his hands clammy. Stiflingly hot and humid air blew in through the window and caressed his face, and the rats came out of the straw to sniff about his feet.

"Finding Your Majesty not as pleased as I trusted to have done," he wrote, "I was so bold to ask you how you liked the queen. Your Majesty soberly answered, 'As you know, I liked her not well before, but now I like her much worse. I have felt her belly and breasts and thereby, as I can judge, she should be no maid. I left her as good a maid as I found her.'"

He paused, rubbed his aching neck. He'd included in the missive everything Brandon said the king required. He'd been working on it for well over an hour, wording it carefully to please His Majesty, if he was still able to be pleased in regards to this matter.

He dipped the pen again. "I beseech Your Majesty most humbly to pardon my rude writing and to consider that I, a most woeful prisoner, am ready to take the death, when it shall please God and Your Majesty." He paused, his chest tight, his breaths shallow and painful. "Yet the frail flesh incites me continually to call to Your Majesty for mercy and grace for my offenses, and thus Christ save, preserve, and keep you. Written at the Tower this Wednesday, the last of June, with the heavy heart and trembling hand of your Highness's most heavy and miserable prisoner and poor slave."

He wiped the sweat and tears that had formed on his cheeks, then penned his final plea at the very bottom of the paper. "Most gracious prince, I cry for mercy, mercy, mercy . . ."

Late at night, in the small house downriver from Whitehall Palace, Henry and Katherine lay next to each other on the straw pallet, spent from frantic sex. The lantern burned in the window, shedding the only light in the room. On the floor beside the pallet was a pitcher of wine, and both had finished off several tall tankardsful.

Katherine was reading aloud the letter Cromwell had written to Henry. Henry had not opened it before this time, and had brought it here for the lady to read aloud to him. She did so, giggling at intervals, brushing her hair back as it fell across the pages.

But Henry did not laugh. He listened silently, hearing the passion in the words, fighting the tears that welled unexpectedly in his eyes.

Suddenly he snatched the letter from Katherine and read the final words at the bottom of the page: "I cry for mercy, mercy, mercy."

He rolled away from Katherine so she could not see the agony on his face.

The queen was practicing the harpsichord with her ladies in attendance when Edward Seymour and two other privy councilors entered her private outer chamber, with Lady Rochford hurrying behind them in an attempt to make a formal announcement. "Madam," she said hurriedly, "their lordships are come."

Anne stood from her chair and turned toward the men, her sheet music fluttering to the floor. The councilors were dressed in their cloaks and caps of office; their expressions were most serious. *Perhaps,* Anne thought, *they have come for my arrest.* It was how the king managed those he did not care for, those who were in his way. But Anne stood straight, her head high.

"My lords," she said.

Edward bowed. "Madam, it is my duty to inform you that Parliament, the convocations of Canterbury and York, have found your marriage to the king to be invalid, on the grounds of your pre-contract with Lorraine, His Majesty's lack of consent to the marriage, and its nonconsummation."

Anne took a step backward, her hand to her heart.

"The marriage is thus declared null and void." Edward went on: "And from henceforth it is the king's pleasure that you call yourself his sister."

Anne's brows drew together as she tried to come to terms with what Edward had said. She looked at her ladies, who appeared as shocked as she was. Then she took a breath, closed her eyes for the barest moment, and nodded.

"In which case," said Edward, "I can tell you that the king has settled upon you a handsome annuity of four thousand pounds per annum, as well as the manors of Bletchingly and Richmond, and Hever Castle, so long as you remain in England. And since His Majesty confirms you are still a maid, you are free to marry whom you choose."

Anne nodded again, feeling light-headed. The men turned to go, but she called out, "Wait!" They looked back. "Please tell the king that though this decision must be hard and sorrowful for me, I accept and approve it, whereby I neither will nor can call myself the king's wife, considering this sentence, and His Majesty's clean living with me." She could hear the soft weeping of her ladies. "I hope I will sometimes have the pleasure of his most noble presence, and beseech the Almighty to send him long life and good health. And please, give him this." She took her wedding ring from her finger and held it out. Edward stepped forward and took it with a nod. "Tell him to break it into pieces, as a thing of no value."

The men bowed and withdrew. When they were gone, Anne fell into Lady Rochford's arms.

A dinner party was held in Charles Brandon's Whitehall Palace apartments, and all of Cromwell's enemies at court were invited. The crowd was lively, celebratory. Brandon, Edward, and Anne Stanhope sat at a table with Bishop Gardiner, Tom Seymour, and Sir Francis Bryan, having finished a rousing game of cards and deep into a fresh flagon of wine brought up by servants from the casks in the palace cellar. Catherine Brandon was the only soul present who seemed unhappy to be there, but, Bryan noticed, she kept her mouth closed, as well she should.

Scattered about the chamber were other lords, also playing at cards and dice, and some young, pink-cheeked noblewomen Bryan had his eye upon. He thought that tomorrow evening, when the traitor was done away with for good, he might arrange a private party of his own with one or two of them. Later tonight, however, he and Tom had other plans.

Brandon pointed a finger at Gardiner. "Will Your Grace be on Tower Hill tomorrow?"

Gardiner smiled. "Try to keep me away."

"I can vouchsafe to Your Grace that his final end will be the most ignominious ever!"

"So I have heard, Your Grace," said Gardiner. "So I have heard."

Anne put down her goblet and grabbed Bryan's arm. "What is Charles talking about? Tell me!"

Bryan smiled. "Cromwell is set to appear on the same scaffold as Lord Hungerford, otherwise known as Mad Walter!" Everyone at the table burst into laughter. "Who has been sentenced to death for various offenses, including sodomy, raping his daughter, and paying magicians to predict the date of the king's death."

"At least he doesn't have to pay them to predict the date of his own," said Edward.

"Cromwell will be humiliated!" said Gardiner. "The false churl who was so ambitious of others' blood."

Bryan leaned over the table and spoke quietly. "Ah, and that is not our only device. Tom and I have conceived some more sport at his lordship's expense." He winked at Tom Seymour, who nodded.

Then Bryan noted the grief-stricken look Catherine gave her husband from across the table. She shook her head, then fled from the room. Brandon looked down and away, his happy mood dampened.

Bryan scowled. Women had one purpose and one only. It was not their place to upset their husbands. He shook his head, then nodded at one of the fine ladies, who nodded and smiled back at him.

The Bit and Stirrup Tavern sat at a slight tilt on a muddy alley not far from the Tower. It was open into the wee hours of the morning, serving beer and ale to laborers and merchants, sailors and doctors. Buxom maids scooted in and out among the tables, holding pitchers aloft, trying not to spill anything as the men grabbed at their asses.

At a wall-side table, Bryan and Edward Seymour were entertaining a most unattractive, sloppy young man with greasy hair and a potbelly. Well after midnight, Bryan and Tom were light-headed with drink, but were nowhere near as drunk as the ugly young man at their table. He belched then swayed, grabbing the sides of the table to keep centered on his stool.

"Let's have another beer," said Tom, waving over a serving wench. "Sorry, there, what's your name, fellow? I forgot it already!"

The man tried to wave a fly from his face, but he couldn't get his hand to move in the right direction. "Gurrea, sir," he said in a slur.

"Gurrea," said Bryan. "D'you have the pox, or is it 'gone 'urrea'?"

Gurrea frowned then caught the joke, and they all laughed.

When their mugs were full again, Tom pushed one up to Gurrea's lips. "Drink up! Big day tomorrow."

Gurrea took a noisy gulp, then another, until his mug was empty. He wiped his mouth, and stammered, "I . . . oughta be in . . . bed."

But Bryan shook his head. "A last pint, man! I'm paying! And then let's drink to old friends!"

Gurrea blinked his red-rimmed eyes, stuck out his tongue, then downed yet another mugful. Bryan nodded at Tom. The plan was playing out nicely.

Tower Hill was situated outside the massive walls of the Tower on a windblown riverside knoll. The wooden scaffold had been there for many years, having served as the place of execution for countless aristocratic criminals and traitors. Unlike executions within the confines of the Tower, those on Tower Hill were open to the citizenry of London, and were attended with all the enthusiasm and relish of a county fair. Families brought baskets of food and blankets. Today, many had arrived before dawn so they could claim a good place near the scaffold. Latecomers pushed their way into the crowd in hopes of having a better view. The traitor Cromwell was to meet his Maker that morning, and it was well worth the effort to find the right spot to witness the beheading.

A cheer arose when the halberdiers, in their armor and helmets, took their place around the base of the scaffold, securing it from any possible attempt at rescue or disruption of the proceedings. They cheered again as the condemned men were at last seen climbing the hill, led by the sheriff of London and flanked by guards. The mob pushed as close as they could get, and were threatened back with the blades of swords.

Mad Walter came first, muttering and gibbering in distress, his eyes registering a dullness that suggested he had no clear idea what was to happen, but that he knew it would be bad. He stumbled ahead, those along the line laughing and throwing rotten fruit at his head. Cromwell followed behind several paces, staring ahead, trying not to listen to the taunts of the men, women, and children.

Reaching the base of the scaffold, Mad Walter stared up at the headsman, the block, and the newly scattered straw. He began to pick at his face nervously. Cromwell leaned to his ear and spoke softly: "Don't be dismayed, Lord Hungerford. Though the breakfast we are going to will be sharp, yet, trusting in the mercy of the Lord, we shall have a joyful dinner."

The crowd began to surge and shout impatiently. The sheriff nudged Cromwell up the steps first. As he glanced down, he saw Gregory standing tight against two halberdiers, distraught and weeping. His son reached up toward him. Cromwell leaned out and caught his hand for a brief moment, squeezing it affectionately. Then the sheriff pushed him hard, and he climbed the remaining steps, where the captain of the guard directed him to the front of the scaffold.

From this high point, Cromwell could see the full extent of the crowd, the exuberance and excitement on their faces, could hear the anger and bloodlust in their voices. Most he did not know: people who hated him but had never met him. And there at the front were Brandon, Tom and Edward Seymour, Bishop Gardiner, and Cromwell's old friend Sir Francis Bryan.

Soon it would be done. He felt his legs go weak, but prayed for strength that he would not fall.

Bryan moved over to the corner of the scaffold. He gestured toward the headsman, waiting on the platform to do his duty. Seeing the gesture, the headsman bent over to listen. His whole body seemed to wobble a little.

"Master Gurrea," Bryan whispered. "I trust you have a clear head this morning."

Gurrea grinned. Through the slit in the black mask, the man's eyes, raw and red, squinted and drooped.

Henry reached for Katherine's hand as their horses slowed to a walk up the steep Surrey hillside. Behind the couple rode several guards and nobles, accompanying His Majesty on this glorious morning adventure. The sunlight was brilliant, bathing the grasses and flowers with a golden, ethereal summer glow.

As they crested the hill, Henry drew up his horse and sat in awed silence. Katherine reined in her own horse, and gasped. In the green valley before them sat a brand-new palace, vast and tall, with blindingly white towers and cupolas, minarets reaching for the heavens, and great glass windows catching the blue of the sky. The roofs were peaked and set with shining tiles, and carved gargoyles and angels clung to the walls below the eaves. To the east of the castle were gardens filled with fruit trees, flowering shrubs, ponds, and marble statuary. To the west was a park filled with grazing deer.

"Look at that!" said Henry. "Nonsuch Palace! And my fool told me it didn't exist!" He tipped back his head and shouted joyfully, and his voice echoed down the hill and across the valley.

Cromwell spoke out. "Good people, I am come here to die and not to purge myself, as some may think I should. I am by law condemned to die and thank my Lord God that has appointed me this death for my offense. For since I came of age I have lived as a sinner and offended my Lord God, for which I ask Him heartily for forgiveness."

Mad Walter, standing at the top of the scaffold steps, bellowed, "Get it over with! For Christ's sake, get it over with!" Laughter rippled throughout the crowd.

Cromwell flinched, but held his composure. "I have also offended my prince, for which I also ask him for hearty amnesty."

"For Jesu's sake!" cried Mad Walter. "Cut his head off! Get it over with!"

"I heartily desire you to pray for the king's grace," said Cromwell, "that he may long live with you in health and prosperity and after him that his son, Prince Edward, that goodly imp, may long reign over you."

Someone in the crowd snorted loudly, and several others echoed the sentiment.

Cromwell took a deep breath; his throat ached. "Gentlemen, you should all take warning from me, who was, as you know, from a poor man made by the king into a great gentleman and I, not contented with that, not with having the kingdom at my orders, presumed to a still higher state. My pride has brought its punishment."

The captain of the guard jerked his head, indicating that it was time. Cromwell knelt in the straw before the block. He clasped his hands and closed his eyes, trying to imagine the face of God, trying to sense the blessed arms reaching for him. "O Lord, grant me that when these eyes lose their use, that the eyes of my soul may see Thee. O Lord and Father, when this mouth shall lose his use, that my heart may say, Father, into Your hands I commend my spirit!" He opened his eyes and shouted, "Pray for the prince and for all the lords of the council and for the clergy and for the people! Now I beg you again that you will pray for me." His gaze met Gregory's and he felt the sting of tears. Then he looked at the headsman, who seemed a bit unsteady on his feet. "Pray, if possible, cut off the head with one blow, so that I may not suffer much." The headsman nodded.

Cromwell laid his head upon the block and stretched out his arms. He stared down at the straw beneath his face and watched a little ant scurrying across and down into the dry tangles. It was the last thing he saw. He closed his eyes and offered his soul once more to his Creator.

Bryan crossed his arms and grinned as Gurrea, the headsman, staggered toward the block to do his job. It was immediately clear, the moment he swung the ax up and over, that he had little control over it.

The ax whistled and came down, not across Cromwell's neck but deep into the man's shoulder. Cromwell grunted like a bull and began to shake violently, his hands involuntarily drawing back toward him. Mad Walter grimaced, and the crowd groaned in disgust. Guerra pulled the ax out and swung it up and over again. The blade bit into Cromwell's neck, but not deep enough to sever the head. Blood spouted, spraying the base of the headsman's robe. Cursing under his breath, Gurrea pulled the ax out again and brought it down again and again, chopping the back of Cromwell's head and then missing the mark entirely, the blade biting into his back. Women screamed and turned away, and men stared in transfixed horror.

The captain of the guard seized the bloody ax from the drunken Gurrea and shoved him out of the way. He raised the ax and brought it down with all his might, hitting the mark perfectly.

Bryan nodded to himself. Job well done.

King Henry lay on the straw pallet in the little house on the bank of the Thames, bare-chested in only his linen braes, listening to the sound of the crickets and nightbirds outside the window. His gaze moved back and forth, back and forth, slowly, almost hypnotically. He was watching the open doorway, where he had hung a rope swing. Katherine sat upon it, swinging to and fro, her long hair streaming around her shoulders, the moonlight caressing her naked body. In the window, a lantern's flame flickered and moths beat themselves to death upon the globe.

Henry was the king of England. There was no more powerful, elegant, or revered king than he. God had seen that his enemies should fall—the rebels, the heretics, and the greedy. And perhaps a new love of his life waited before him. Time would tell, and in that moment, time held still for His Royal Majesty.

He beckoned to Katherine. She smiled willingly, and stepped down off the swing.

About the Author

Elizabeth Massie is an award-winning author of horror/suspense novels, historical novels, short fiction, and media tie-ins, as well as features for American history textbooks. She lives in the beautiful Shenandoah Valley of Virginia with illustrator Cortney Skinner, and is mother to Erin and Brian and grandmother to Anya and Elliot.

She believes every family has its history, from kings to peasants, and that it is the noble struggles that make our stories fascinating.

Her website is www.elizabethmassie.com.